DRAGON'S DARE

HIGHLAND FANTASY ROMANCE

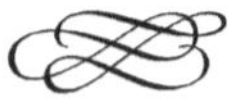

ANN GIMPEL

CONTENTS

Dragon's Dare   v
Copyright Page   vii
Author's Note   ix
Book Description, Dragon's Dare   xi
Reader praise for Earlier Books in This Series   xiii

Chapter 1   1
Chapter 2   13
Chapter 3   25
Chapter 4   37
Chapter 5   49
Chapter 6   61
Chapter 7   73
Chapter 8   85
Chapter 9   97
Chapter 10   109
Chapter 11   121
Chapter 12   133
Chapter 13   145
Chapter 14   159
Chapter 15   171
Chapter 16   183
Chapter 17   193
Chapter 18   205
Chapter 19   217
Chapter 20   229
Chapter 21   241
Chapter 22   253
Chapter 23   265
Chapter 24   279
Epilogue   289
About the Author   295

Book Description: Earth's Requiem, Earth Reclaimed, Book One 297
Earth's Requiem, First Prologue 299
Earth's Requiem, Second Prologue 303
Earth's Requiem, Chapter One 311

DRAGON'S DARE

DRAGON LORE BOOK FOUR, HIGHLAND
FANTASY ROMANCE

Ann Gimpel

**Tumble off reality's edge into myth, magic, and Celtic dragon
shifters.**

AUTHOR'S NOTE

Most of my books, even those from a series, work well as standalone reads. *Dragon's Dare* is one exception. While you don't need to read the entire series, one or more of the earlier books—particularly *Highland Secrets* and *Dragon Maid*—will greatly add to your reading enjoyment of this last book in the Dragon Lore series. Thanks for following along on my writer's journey. I'm deeply appreciative of each and every reader who've loved my books enough to keep coming back for more.

BOOK DESCRIPTION, DRAGON'S DARE

Bloated on chaos, the Morrigan gathers power. A trip through Hell yields quite the assortment of allies. Fell creatures straight out of myth and nightmare that haven't darkened Earth's boundaries for centuries heed her call.

Heartily sick of the Morrigan's maneuvering, the dragons are close to shutting their world off from everywhere, Earth included. If they do, every dragon shifter bond will be broken. Horrified, Lachlan and Britta launch a desperate campaign to hang onto their dragons.

Magic may bite back, but if the dragons take their magic ball and go home, Earth will fade, along with all other worlds. That suits the Morrigan fine. War and anarchy are her favorite companions, and she collects misery like children gather beloved toys.

In a stunning conclusion to the Dragon Lore series, Arianrhod goes back in time hunting Angus, Jonathan's father. Forty years apart was a steep price to pay, but the world needs Angus's magic, and she's done hiding her love for him.

Books in the Dragon Lore Series:

Highland Secrets, Book One
To Love a Highland Dragon, Book Two
Dragon Maid, Book Three,
Dragon's Dare, Book Four

Awesome story! Ann Gimpel is truly one of a kind when it comes to fantasy.

Yet again, this talented author has written a book that's a delight to read. The writing flows so easily that it would be a crying shame to miss it. Definitely recommended.

In particular, I loved the hero, Lachlan, and his dragon-dually, Kheladin. His voice was really well done, especially his accent, which I heard as I read. It takes an impressive amount of skill to write a dialect so well.

Humorous and original with steamy characters. The writing was wonderfully done. Small bits of quirk and humor were slipped in as Lachlan learned our world and it was entertaining. The plot moved forward at a nice pace, and the connections made in the story were believable and easy to immerse into the world created. -- Book Bliss Blog

A great paranormal romance. I really loved this book. The story line was great and easy to follow with a couple of nice twists and turns to keep you on your toes.

Highland Magic. This is the first book of Ann Gimpel's that I've read and I've not been disappointed. The characters are very vivid and endearing. I'm usually one who can see what's coming next, however Ann has really surprised me with her twists and turns. This book was pure heaven to read, had me hooked from the start.

To Love a Highland Dragon was a mix of two of my favorite fiction elements—hunky Highlanders and shapeshifters, specifically dragon shifters. I absolutely adored Lachlan, Maggie, and the dragon, Kheladin.

I'm not big on time-travel books, but this one I loved. It was awesome to read about the different levels of love between the characters.

I've never read a dragon shifter book before, and didn't know if I would like it, but this is one of those stories that carries you on a wave so wonderful you just don't want to get off.

Reader praise for Dragon Maid, Book Three of Dragon Lore:

Dragon Maid is book number three in the Dragon Lore series. It started right where book two left off. Dragon Maid is full of love, lust, action and adventure. I loved falling into the world of dragons and combined world of ancients and modern day time. The characters in this book are packed full of pride, love and determination.

The author does a phenomenal job of world building, delivering an intricate mythology, interesting characters and detailed setting all wrapped up in a neat bow. There are many secondary characters but I had no trouble keeping track of the cast, something I can't always say with other series. I may have said this once before, but the regional accents are absolutely amazing.

Book 1 was so strong and book 2 filled the series nicely. Everything that was strong from the first novel was still there— fantastic world building, strong and unique characters, hard-hitting action and steamy romance. I loved getting to see another perspective besides human and dragon in this book and learn more about the witches in this all-out war and the part they play in the battle and the universe that has been created.

Dragon Maid is the third book in the Dragon Lore series. I loved books 1 and 2 and was looking forward to reading this one. Ann Gimpel is an amazing author who manages to captivate her readers with her stories. This book picked up right where we left of in book one. Lachlan, Kheladin and Maggie are still fighting to destroy the Morrigan.

This book picks up right where the previous installment left off and hurls readers into a world of magic, action-packed scenes, a captivating romance, and a race to save the world with the help of a dragon and Mage from the past. From the first page to the last this is a read that draws you in, even if the mythos is confusing at times, and leaves you anticipating the next installment after the revelations revealed here.

Dragon Maid was such a captivating continuation of the *Dragon Lore* series. Gimpel weaves a story full of all the things I love most: passion, adventure, intrigue, and smexy times with a most delicious alpha male. -- The Book Chick

I really like these books and am constantly surprised by the detail that goes into this series. The world building is excellent and the storyline is an incredible one that just keeps building. Strong characters make this book truly stand out and the level of emotion portrayed is never sickly sweet but feels so realistic.

CHAPTER 1

Jonathan Shea cradled Britta in his arms. She was asleep, the rhythm and cadence of her breathing revealed her exhaustion. He still couldn't believe he'd found a mate, and a woman linked to a dragon at that. Britta KilKerran was actually the Countess of Cumbria, or she had been a few hundred years back. He wasn't certain such a title still existed.

It didn't matter. He'd offer up his life to protect the woman slumbering against his chest. He loved her dragon too, but Tarika scarcely needed his protection. When he thought of the scarlet-scaled dragon, one of the First Born, the place on his neck where she'd marked him with a mating bite tingled. It was her contribution to his bond with Britta.

She stirred in his arms. He stroked strands of long, red-gold hair away from her face and spun a small spell to keep her asleep. They'd just come from a major battle to free Tarika and Kheladin, another dragon, from the Morrigan's clutches. Both of them needed rest, but his heart and mind were too full to let go quite yet.

After years of never believing the rumor about his mother being a Celtic deity, he'd finally met her. He brought it on himself by calling for her when they desperately needed help, but he never believed she'd actually show up. Regardless, he couldn't deny her existence anymore—no matter how much he might want to. Arianrhod had abandoned him when he was so young he had no memories of her, and when he cut to the bone of things, he resented the crap out of her neglect.

Jonathan shut his eyes for a moment and summoned an image of his father. Tall and rangy with shaggy, rich brown hair and amber eyes, Angus had been a dreamer. He did his best for Jonathan, but often as not, he'd been caught up in some trance state or another. Though Angus hadn't said so, Jonathan understood his father was relieved when he grew old enough to be on his own. Once Jonathan left Ireland, Angus vanished. Their modest cabin near Inishowen remained, but Jonathan knew better than to waste time hunting for a man who didn't wish to be found.

Had Arianrhod seen Angus all these years he'd been missing? Jonathan could ask her, but she might just stare him down with those inscrutable eyes—one gold, the other silver—and not bother to answer.

He tightened his hold on Britta, and she nestled closer. She was more comfortable about Arianrhod being his mother than he was, but then she was far more comfortable with magic in general. He blew out a breath, recognizing his life would never be the same.

Not that he wanted it to be, but he would've preferred finding the love of his life without having to deal with a long-lost parent. Particularly one who stirred up a welter of prickly feelings. Now if Angus were to show back up, it would be a different story…

Britta wriggled against him, and her golden eyes flickered open. She regarded him sleepily through thick red lashes. "Ye canna rest, my love?"

Jonathan shrugged and offered a sheepish smile. "Lots to think about."

She cupped the side of his face in one hand. "Do ye wish to talk about anything?"

He shrugged again, feeling uncomfortable. What was there to

say, really? He was a little old to be struggling with parent issues. Besides he'd long since come to terms with his father's magic being too pervasive for him to spend much time around normal humans. Jonathan dealt with some level of that as well, but his job as a software engineer who designed games let him keep to himself.

Britta brushed her hand across his lips. "Whenever ye wish, I'll be here. Tarika too. She's verra old and much wiser than either of us. If ye canna get the information elsewhere, mayhap we can figure out what sort of hold the Celtic gods had on your da."

"Thank you. I'll keep it in mind." Jonathan reached around her and snagged a bottle of Irish whiskey off the nightstand. "Would you like some? I can get us glasses."

"Och, and I can drink from the bottle. No need to get fancy."

She smiled, and it transformed her into something so striking he couldn't look away. A high forehead gave way to sculpted cheekbones and a defined chin. One of his old T-shirts covered her from chest to knees, but the outline of her breasts was clearly visible through the well-aged beige fabric.

His cock stirred, and he rolled his eyes. "We made love twice after we got here. I don't understand why I can't get enough of you."

"Are ye complaining?" She quirked an arched red brow.

He shook his head and drew both of them to a half sitting position against the carved oak headboard. He uncorked the bottle and handed it to her. She drank deep before handing it back.

Britta narrowed her eyes and watched him drink. "We're far from home free," she blurted without preamble.

"Which problem are you referring to?" He placed the bottle on a side table not bothering to cork it. He wasn't done yet, and likely neither was Britta.

She moved away and sat cross-legged facing him, her lovely face creased with concern. "We may have permanently removed Connor and Rhukon and their dragons from the action, but there have to be other corrupt dragon shifters. We must seek them out and destroy them too."

Jonathan shook his head. "It won't matter unless we get to the heart of things."

"Aye, ye're correct. We must find a way to corral the Morrigan, or she'll just entice more mages and dragons with promises of limitless power." Britta caught her lower lip between her teeth. "Tarika plans to warn the dragons. She believes the dark mages want to drain their dragon bondmates' power."

Jonathan straightened and recaptured the whiskey bottle, taking another swallow. "I thought mages became dragon shifters because they loved dragons and wished to share their lives with them."

"Aye and that would be true—for most of us. Power lures dark mages, though. Far more power than can be had through the normal dragon shifter bond."

"How do you know?"

"I saw it in Connor and Rhukon's minds afore we thrashed them."

"You didn't say anything." He handed her the bottle. Maybe they should eat something, if they were going to drink much more.

"I would have. Eventually. Tarika and I needed to determine just what it meant. And if 'tis really true, or just conjecture on our part."

He kissed her forehead before swinging his legs over the side of the bed. "I'm going to cut up a bit of cheese for us and get some crackers." He pulled on a pair of black sweat pants, securing the waist string to keep them from falling down, and got to his feet.

"Excellent." She grinned. "Plotting revenge is hungry business, but ye dinna have to cover that amazing cock."

He bit back a laugh, enjoying the compliment, and made his way to the kitchen. His apartment was small enough to keep talking. "Did you discuss this with Lachlan?" he asked as he chopped cheese off a block and opened a box of biscuits.

"Nay, but Tarika and Kheladin figured out what was going on while they were held prisoner."

Jonathan returned to the bedroom and plopped the snacks on the bed next to Britta. "How does this bondmate thing work? Would

Lachlan be privy to the dark mage problem, if it's in his dragon's mind?"

"Not necessarily." She put cheese on a cracker and munched it down. "Not that Lachlan couldna force truth from his dragon, but if he saw no reason to be heavy handed, Kheladin could maintain independent thoughts, particularly now that we can remain in our own skins."

Jonathan looked at the crackers, but took another slug of whiskey instead. "What do you think about being able to be separate from your dragon? Before Kheladin uncovered the ancient magic that altered your bond, your shared consciousness was linked to one form or the other."

"Eat something." She handed him a cracker piled with cheese and waited until he put it into his mouth. "I liked the new system well enough—until the Morrigan shanghaied my dragon. Then I dinna like it at all." Britta tossed her hands in front of her. "Overall, I suppose 'tis an improvement since we can leverage both our strengths at the same time."

He settled himself carefully on the bed and ate another cracker before leaning against the headboard. He really was hungry, and the whiskey buzzed through his head, adding an eldritch glow to things. "We should target the Morrigan first and then hunt for other corrupt mage-dragon duos."

Britta frowned. "And here I was thinking 'twould be simpler to identify the dark mages first."

"Simpler, yes, but not smart. Once you begin that process, it'll tip our hand—and spur the Morrigan to further evil."

The line between Britta's eyebrows deepened. "Aye, ye're likely right. Must be those cunning, wee games ye design."

"*Cunning wee games* is it?" Jonathan aped her brogue and laughed. "Aye, lassie. If it's one thing designing computer games taught me, it's strategy."

"Ye'll need all that talent because the Morrigan is immortal."

"Yeah, just like my mother." Jonathan winced. Where the fuck had that come from?

"Mayhap your da too." Britta's voice was gentle. "From the feel of your energy, I'd bet on it." She paused a beat. "Was Arianrhod one of the reasons ye couldna sleep?"

He nodded reluctantly. "Who has a Celtic goddess for a mother?" When Britta opened her mouth, he hurried on. "Nah, don't answer that. I suppose I always knew the rumors were true, but she wasn't around, so I could ignore them."

"Dinna your da ever speak of her?"

"No. If I asked, he pulled magic that muddled my mind—made me forget what it was I wanted to know. After a time, I stopped asking. When I got older, witches in our coven looked askance at me, but Mauvreen kept them at bay."

Britta grinned. "I like her, and Maggie's grandmother, Mary Elma, too. Nothing quite like a strong witch to keep me on my toes."

Jonathan snorted. "Lachlan certainly treats Mary Elma with kid gloves, and if I'm any judge, that's far from normal for him."

Britta's grin widened. "Maggie's his mate. Of course he'd be respectful of her grandmother, but beyond that Lachlan's a different man than the one I knew in the sixteen hundreds and earlier. Less brash and headstrong. Losing over three hundred years to being ensorcelled would change anyone, though."

"No kidding. I meant to ask him about that experience, but there's never been time. Back to Mauvreen, she was like a mom to me, always around, making certain I had what I needed."

"Did she never have children of her own?"

"No. No men that I could see, either. Magic runs strong in her, and she devoted her life to honing her craft alongside Maggie's grandmother. Speaking of which, Mary Elma was going to rally the covens to help with whatever plan we hatch up."

Britta waggled a finger in front of his face. "Och, and ye'll not sidestep things so easily."

"Sidestep what?" He handed her the whiskey, knowing full well what she meant.

"Arianrhod takes some getting used to."

Defensiveness prickled at the back of his neck. "Any parent who abandoned you would."

"Och aye, but she isna just *any parent*. She's the virgin huntress, and having a child in tow would've been a wee bit challenging to explain."

"She should've thought of that before she—" He bit off the rest of his sentence. It sounded whiny and sanctimonious.

Britta moved the cracker plate to a side table and straddled his lap. Her golden gaze bored into him and she pried the whiskey bottle out of his hand, laying it aside, but not letting go of his hand. She pressed a breast into it, and he felt her nipple stiffen at the contact.

"What were ye thinking about when first we touched?" Her gaze never left his. "When first we kissed?"

His cock roared to life from the heat of her body sitting across his lap. Breath hitched in his throat, and he rubbed her nipple through the thin fabric separating his hand from her breast. "Not a fair question," he mumbled.

"Och, and why not?" She pressed into his hand and moved her fingers between them to curve around his rigid flesh. "Do ye believe we're the first to ever be so hungry for one another 'tis all we can think about?"

"You're talking about sex, but babies are different..." He sputtered and tried again. "There are things to prevent—"

She laid her other hand, the one not curled around his cock, across his mouth. "Ye doona know. Ye werena there, so ye canna judge."

Truth in her words shamed him, but his uneasiness faded fast as desire flashed through him, turning his nerves to molten heat. He fumbled with the string at his waist, eager to get to his cock. She was naked beneath his T-shirt, so he could slip inside her, feel the enchanted heat of her surround him.

She added her fingers to the task of untying his drawstring, and their hands bumped against one another. The sound of their breathing pounded against his ears.

"Gods, but I love you." He gave up on his pants long enough to trace her full lower lip with his thumb.

"Aye, laddie, I love you too." She squirmed, and warmth from her core seared him. Britta bent forward and closed her mouth over his. Her breath was sweet from the whiskey they'd shared, and her tongue snaked inside his mouth, dancing with his. He clasped her hips between his hands and dry thrust against her body, so impatient to penetrate her, blood thundered through his veins.

An alien sound intruded, but he couldn't make sense of it. Until he heard it again and froze.

Britta tore her mouth from his and straightened. Color rose from her neck to the top of her head, and she swiveled her body to face Arianrhod. "Ye dinna knock. Ye should've."

"Aye, but I did knock. And so many times one of the neighbors came out to see what the ruckus was." Arianrhod's unusual eyes— one gold, one silver—twinkled with amusement. She shrugged. "I knew you were here, so I waited until the neighbor thought I left, and then let myself in."

Jonathan got his breathing under control. His cock would take longer, but Britta still straddled him, so she hid the worst of things.

"I apologize for what appears to be poor timing." Arianrhod turned away to offer them privacy. "I'll wait in the front room, but you must dress, and we must talk."

"Are we going somewhere?" Britta asked.

"Aye, traveling clothes would be appropriate. I should've been more specific." Arianrhod walked through the door leading to the small combination livingroom and kitchen, clad in battle leathers that fit her tall, lithe form like a second skin. Her silver hair was braided in many small sections, but it still hung to her knees.

"How'd you find us?" With a last, lingering caress, Jonathan moved Britta off him and got off the bed to hunt down something to wear.

"Ask something important."

Arianrhod's voice floated back to him, and he felt like an idiot. Of course, the moon mother goddess, who controlled the tides and was also the virgin huntress, could manage something as simple as locating one with her own blood. For Christ's sake, even he could've accomplished something like that.

"'Tis on account of most of his blood not being in his brain at the moment," Britta trilled, followed by a burst of laughter.

Arianrhod joined in, adding peals of mirth to Britta's.

"If the two of you plan on male bashing, forget it." He swatted Britta's ass, as she bent to work her legs into leather breeches not unlike Arianrhod's.

Jonathan donned dark wool trousers and a black turtleneck. He tossed a plaid lumberman's jacket over one arm and made his way toward the living room. As an afterthought, he doubled back for the whiskey.

Arianrhod hunkered before one of the many bookshelves lining the room, looking through its contents. She straightened and turned to face him. "Eclectic," she murmured.

"Glad you approve," he said stiffly.

"Och, and ye're not happy with me sifting through your things."

She hadn't posed it as a question, so he said, "That's right. Tell me what was so important you had to break into my home."

She drew her silver brows together. "A wee bit harsh, but true enough. Will ye sit?"

"No, I'd rather stand."

Britta walked in from the bedroom, brush in hand, and perched on the edge of an easy chair. Once there, she worked on her long hair, untangling and braiding it out of the way. "Doona mind me." She sent half a smile skittering across the room, aimed for Arianrhod.

The goddess twisted his straight-backed computer chair so it faced the center of the room and sat. "Ye are both in danger," she said without preamble. "The Celts dinna censure the Morrigan—"

"What?" Britta screeched. "Why ever not? Surely they recognized her culpability."

Arianrhod rolled her eyes. "Aye, of course they did. They are far from stupid, but flawed as the Battle Crow is, she's one of them."

"I doona understand." Britta's voice returned to its usual, musical cadence. "Dragons punish their own, why not Celts?"

"We never have."

"If that's true," Jonathan broke in, "why did you expect they'd react differently this time? It took a lot of effort to drag that bitch in front of the Celtic Council."

"Because the Morrigan broke the compact between us and dragons by kidnapping them. That she plotted to siphon dragon magic through the corrupt dragon shifter bond was an additional offense."

"How do ye know that last?" Britta demanded. "'Tis what I suspect, yet we never talked of it, and neither Tarika nor I know for sure."

"Same way ye do, Missy." Arianrhod's voice cracked from weariness, or emotion, Jonathan couldn't tell. "I read it from the minds of the dragon shifters we killed."

"Did ye mention that to the other gods?" Britta asked.

"I dinna get a chance."

Britta tossed a cloak across her shoulders and linked an arm through Jonathan's. "We must leave. Now. The Celtic Council will answer to me for their disgraceful inattention to duty."

Arianrhod shot to her feet. "Not yet." Power spilled from her in waves, and it was all Jonathan could do not to step back a few paces. "I told you we must talk, and talk we shall. Corrupt dragon shifter mages are far from new. That's who ensorcelled Lachlan and Kheladin hundreds of years back. Multiple tasks lay afore us, and we must sort how to attack them."

The goddess's power snaked around Jonathan, and she walked until she was nose to nose with him. "Unfinished business simmers between us. I would deal with it afore aught else."

Jonathan squared his shoulders. "It's not necessary—"

"Aye, but 'tis." She spoke over him. "Sit or stand. I doona care, but what ye will do is listen."

"Would ye like me to shield myself so I canna hear?" Britta asked.

Arianrhod sent an appraising glance her way. "Nay. Ye're his mate. Ye need to hear this too. While ye're at it, invite your dragon to listen through the bond ye share."

CHAPTER 2

Arianrhod tossed her head in irritation—or maybe foreboding about what had to come next—and stared at her son, standing with his arms crossed over his chest. Straight, dark hair spilled past broad shoulders. From the glimpse she'd caught when she interrupted him making love, he was built much like Angus, with a leanly muscled torso and long legs. His face was all sharp angles with a square jaw, high forehead, and angled cheekbones. Dark stubble dotted his cheeks and chin, and he had the same whiskey-colored eyes as his da.

How the hell could she have produced such a stubborn offspring?

Och aye, 'tisn't such a mystery after all. He's much like me.

She swallowed a smile and used power to force him to meet her gaze. It wasn't as easy as she assumed it would be.

"Fine," he growled. "I'll look at you. Do you make a habit of forcing men to do your bidding? Is that how you finagled Angus into your bed?"

"I'm going to ignore that, but I've killed men for less. If ye canna keep a decent tongue in your head, hold silence."

"Got it," he said tightly, "but don't expect me to jump when you snap your fingers."

"From what just occurred at the Celtic Council—and here in this room—it appears no one does my bidding, yet 'tisn't important." She made certain her gaze never wavered. "Ye resent me for leaving you."

Jonathan narrowed his eyes. "What child wouldn't?"

"I dinna have a choice—"

"Of course you had a choice," he shouted. His voice sounded cold, but the words hit her like hot, angry bullets. "You picked your mockery of a role as the virgin huntress over mothering your child."

Arianrhod waited, but he didn't say anything further. "Are ye quite done?"

He nodded curtly. "Nothing you can say or do will change what happened almost forty years ago."

"Mayhap not, yet ye will hear me out. Angus is descended from Cathbad and Nessa, daughter to Eochaid Sálbuide, king of Ulster. Your da is one of their grandsons."

"Cathbad the Druidic seer?" Britta asked. Her golden eyes shone with interest.

"Aye, the same." Arianrhod nodded.

A muscle danced in Jonathan's cheek. "That explains Angus's trance states, but not why you left."

Arianrhod squared her shoulders as she faced her son. No place here for anything other than unvarnished truth, no matter how it sat with him.

"I dinna plan to conceive a child. Once I found I was pregnant, my first thought was to quietly do away with you and not bother Angus with it. We were beset with dark mage dragon shifter problems then as well. Before I'd fully charted a course of action, Cathbad came to me in a vision. He told me I must bear you because ye had a critical role to play in future events."

Jonathan clamped his jaw tight. Britta, who'd finished with her hair, walked to his side and wove an arm around his waist, but he didn't hug her back. "So I'm what?" He sneered. "The second coming of Christ?"

Anger flared, but Arianrhod kept it in check. "Doona jest. I asked for specifics, but Cathbad dinna give me details. 'Twas then I shared the news with Angus, and we planned carefully. I told the other Celts I was going to Caer Sidi, my special world, to tend to the tides. The lie offered me space to spend my pregnancy and nursing with the Selkies. Angus slipped away when he could and visited us in the Irish Sea."

"That's why the sea folk knew you," Britta burst out and leaned closer to Jonathan.

"Apparently so, but why can't I remember any of that?" he asked. At least the cold, dead tone had left his voice.

"Angus and I altered your memories when I left you with him. It would've been inconvenient for ye to hold images of living with the Selkies. And of me. Though I imagine a few slipped in from time to time." Arianrhod swallowed hard. She hated emotion, but it thickened her throat. "'Twas the hardest thing I've ever done, erasing all memory of me from your young mind."

Tears formed behind her lids; she blinked them back. "I loved you. And I loved your da. Cutting myself off from the two of you was only possible because I believed we'd find one another once ye were grown."

"How old was I?" Jonathan asked in a strangled tone.

"Two-and-a-half. I put it off as long as I could. Ceridwen called me back. The others were at one another's throats, and she needed my calming influence."

"What about me?" Jonathan moved so fast his hand was a blur, and he gripped her arm hard enough to hurt, dragging Britta after him. "I needed you. I was your child."

Arianrhod yanked his hand from her arm, but held tight to it. "What? Ye think I dinna know that? Ye think I dinna think of both of you every single day since and mourn my decision? I approached

Angus after I'd been gone six months, but he told me I couldna return."

"Da would never have said that." Jonathan's face could've been carved from stone, and he extricated himself from her grip.

"Aye, but he did. He and Cathbad were in close and constant communication. The Druid made it clear my place was with the Celts, though not forever." She took a ragged breath and blew it out. Then she did it again to steady herself. "I traveled back in time to meet with him, since I couldna raise him any other way. He said when ye called for me, I was to come, and provide whatever help ye required." She swallowed bitterness. "He also told me not to seek him out again."

Jonathan twisted his hands together in front of him until the knuckles whitened. "Have you seen Angus? He vanished after I left Ireland."

"Nay. My first guess is he's with Cathbad, which would explain why ye havena heard from him."

"A fair assumption, to be sure," Britta cut in. "Since Cathbad lived over a thousand years ago." She hurried on. "How did Angus come to leave his own time? Or has he lived these many years first in the Old Country and now here?"

A lie sprang to Arianrhod's lips. Protecting her kin was so deeply ingrained, it was second nature, but she shook her head and opted for truth. "Och, and I'm not proud of this. My brother and Arawn snatched Angus from the time travel tunnels when he wasn't much more than a lad. They altered his memories, so he wouldna be able to return."

"Why?" Britta chewed her lower lip and kept hold of Jonathan, almost as if she expected him to haul off and launch himself at Arianrhod.

"I'd like to know that too," Jonathan muttered. "I had a bellyful of your brother, Gwydion. Da was a gentle soul, no match for the bully that dragged information out of me."

"Ye only saw one aspect of your da," Arianrhod said gently. "He had strength—and courage to burn—but he was focused on two things: raising you and avoiding excess contact with my kin, so they wouldna figure out who ye were and use you like they'd used him."

"Ye dinna answer why the Celts wanted Angus in the first place." Britta said.

"He was a multi-faceted Seer, who could dream both the truth and the future. He could also slip between worlds without leaving a trace and do a lot of the Celts' dirty work. Things they dinna want associated with them. Once Cathbad figured out who had his grandson, he agreed they could keep him—but not forever."

"Let me guess." Britta inhaled sharply, her nostrils flaring. "Ye told Angus who he was, helped him recapture his memories."

Arianrhod nodded. "That I did, and I have yet to forgive Gwydion for his deception."

Jonathan narrowed his eyes. "Back to you and me. Let me make certain I have this right. You left me because of something a long dead seer said? Doesn't being a goddess trump being a seer?"

The tears she'd blinked away welled. "Scrying the future was never one of my gifts. Surely ye understand I couldna ask Bran, Celtic god of prophecy, about my son—the son forbidden to me under Celtic law." Arianrhod forced more words before her courage failed her. "I doona expect ye to forgive me. I told you so ye'd hold knowledge of your beginnings. Every man deserves as much."

Jonathan just looked at her. Pain darkened his amber eyes, but he held himself proudly, his spine arrow straight, and shoved his hair behind his shoulders. Clearly her actions had cut deep, but he'd found a way past her desertion long ago. And why wouldn't he have? Though young by Celtic standards, he was well into adulthood, judged by human criteria.

"Tarika took you up on your offer to listen in, and she finds this fascinating." Britta's voice chopped into Arianrhod's bleak thoughts. "She knew Cathbad and Nessa, and many of their offspring, including Conchobar."

"What else did your dragon say?" Arianrhod asked, relieved to have something to focus on beyond her maternal failings.

"That we must find Angus."

"Aye, I'd already determined as much. I nearly went in search of him, but wanted to make certain you and the witches knew to beware of the Morrigan."

"I'm coming with you," Jonathan said.

Arianrhod felt her eyes widen in surprise. She hadn't expected him to volunteer to do anything with her. Anger still flickered around him, turning the air a reddish hue, and his posture remained stiff, unyielding.

"Tarika says we should come too, but her first duty is traveling to Fire Mountain. Once she's there, she'll ensure every single dragon shifter mage is subjected to full and complete testing. We must make certain their dragons aren't at risk."

"It's fine if you want to go with her—" Jonathan began.

"Nay. I'm coming with you." Britta spoke over him, repeating what he'd just told Arianrhod. "I suspect 'tis why we donned traveling clothes."

Arianrhod's heart warmed. She liked the dragon shifter maid who stood before her, courageous and self-confident in her own skin. "Ye'll be most welcome. Regardless whether Jonathan forgives me, I welcome you as my daughter."

"Thank you." Britta cracked a smile. "I'll take that as a compliment."

Arianrhod smiled back. "'Tis. I rarely solicit anyone's company."

"Let's go." Britta snugged her cloak around her with her free hand. "We'll locate a time travel portal and be on our way."

"I must warn the witches first," Arianrhod said. "'Twas my other reason for not leaving."

"Tarika already informed them." Britta hesitated, likely listening to the dragon speaking into her mind. "The covens are gathering. They'll move their timetable up."

Jonathan unwound Britta's arm from around his body and

shrugged into his wool jacket before stuffing his feet into a pair of boots sitting in front of the sofa. After bending to lace them, he muttered, "Let's get this show on the road."

"Aye, we can leave." Arianrhod eyed her son. "Ye dinna ask me aught about what I told you."

"Maybe it's because I got used to you being gone a long time ago. I appreciate knowing more, but it doesn't change anything."

She cocked her head to one side but remained silent. She'd said enough, and it was a wise woman who knew when to shut up.

He sent an appraising glance her way. It wasn't easy, but she held herself open to him and felt him sift through her mind, hunting for truth. After a pause so long it set her teeth on edge, he withdrew from her thoughts.

"I'll meet the two of you at a portal," he said. "I need to lock up and move my car behind the building if we'll be gone for a while."

"Meet us here." Arianrhod sent an image into his mind. Once he nodded, she pushed the door open with magic and walked through, gesturing for Britta to follow her.

JONATHAN TRAILED his mother and Britta out the door of his flat, listening as they chatted about how neither of them had the slightest interest in automobiles. Britta hadn't lived in modern time long enough to learn to drive. Arianrhod had, but her awareness of twenty-first century trappings started and stopped with computers. Even there, she was a reluctant recruit…

Britta and Arianrhod cleared the stairwell, chatting as if they'd known one another for years. Jonathan refocused his attention. He would've needed to employ magic to continue to track their conversation.

Though he maintained a staunch exterior, he was sure both women were well aware of his inner turmoil. They'd almost have to be with their magical ability. He locked the door and set a hasty ward. It wouldn't keep the Morrigan out, but it would tell him if she came looking for him.

An unpleasant thought surfaced. If he was an integral part of some sort of long-lost prophecy, a lynchpin as it were, surely Cathbad wasn't the only one who knew about it. The Morrigan ferreted out that he was Arianrhod's half-human son. Now she'd had time to process that prime piece of data, was she hot on his trail because of it?

As Jonathan considered the possibility, he remembered how Gwydion, Arianrhod's brother and warrior magician for the Celts, had grilled him—after he determined Jonathan was Arianrhod's son. It seemed unlikely the Celts held much back from one another, so it was only a matter of time before all of them became aware of his parentage. Of course, his bloodlines didn't necessarily lead to Cathbad's prophecy, but still...

His muscles tightened into rocks. He'd done battle with the Morrigan the day he met Britta. Jonathan fingered a scar running from below one eye to his jaw. The Battle Crow had flayed him open with her beak, but that was before she had any idea who he was.

Not much I can do about any of this.

He still stood before his door, rooted in place. Giving himself a firm mental shake, he pelted down the stairs, intent on stashing his car out of harm's way. Streets were narrow in Inverness, and he risked getting sideswiped if he left his vehicle where it was.

The clicker chirped when he activated it, and he slipped behind the wheel of his Volkswagen Passat. It was one of the few luxuries he allowed himself, but he loved driving. Before meeting Britta, he spent the time he wasn't designing computer games piloting the car along lonely routes through the Scottish Highlands. The craggy peaks and pristine, roaring brooks soothed his soul.

"At least now I know why," he murmured and tapped the ignition, guiding the sleek car around to the rear of his building.

Celtic magic ran deep in both Ireland and Scotland. No wonder normal humans annoyed him most of the time.

Jonathan killed the engine and sat drumming his fingers on the leather-clad steering wheel. It wouldn't take but a moment to summon power and travel to where he was meeting the women. He didn't know if he'd ever develop any level of comfort around his mother, but he did give her points for courage. She'd spoken what was in her heart, and she could've covered it with a web of deception. At least she was trying, even if it was more than a few years tardy.

He made a sound midway between a grunt and a snort.

His mother and Britta looked like long lost friends. Maybe women were like that: able to develop an easy camaraderie. He didn't know. Hadn't spent enough time around them to figure out the mystery of what it meant to be female. Many witches made it clear enough they'd love to warm his bed, and he'd taken a few up on it, but they never touched his heart. It hadn't felt fair to keep on fucking them since he couldn't share much more than his body.

Britta was something new entirely. He'd known from the moment she materialized in Kheladin's cave how special she was. Tarika took form first, but when she ceded their shared consciousness to Britta—a buck naked Britta—he'd been smitten, first by her body, but later by the totality of her. Mind, soul, spirit.

Daylight darkened beyond his windshield. He glanced up, fully expecting storm clouds presaging a thunderstorm, but a huge winged form blotted out the sky.

Fuck!

No time to pull magic and vanish. He bolted from the car and drew himself tall. The Morrigan took her time floating to the ground a few feet from him. Once there, she fluffed her wings and eyed him intently as if he were a choice morsel.

He blew out an annoyed breath. She might enjoy cat-and-mouse games, but he didn't. "What do you want?" he snapped. "Be quick about it. I'm late for an appointment."

The air around the crow glistened wetly. When sheaves of iridescence cleared, a tall woman dressed in an expensive-looking charcoal wool business suit emerged. A green silk blouse was unbuttoned far enough to display the upper curves of her breasts. Blonde hair cascaded down her shoulders, and she tapped one high-heeled black pump on the cobblestoned street.

"Do ye like me better now?" She batted sea blue eyes his way.

"Not particularly. Why are you here?"

"Is that any way to treat an old friend?" She licked full red lips suggestively.

"Friends don't scar one another." He pointed to the side of his face. "I'm leaving." He reached deep and stirred the magic living within him, intent on going anywhere but here. He wouldn't go to the meeting point, but nor would he remain where he was. If he had to fight, he'd have a better chance outside the city. Plus he was concerned about collateral damage if an unsuspecting human wandered by.

"Stop that!" She wove her hands in an intricate pattern. It damped his magic, but only a little.

"You'll have to do better than that," he snarled.

"I had no idea ye were one of us, or I'd never have marked you, but now I've tasted your blood, ye're mine. Ye know about blood magic. 'Tis the oldest power there is." She moved her hands faster.

Anger kindled in his belly, and he sent a bolt of power arcing her way. "Stop it. I don't want to talk with you. Make nice with you. Hear your apologies, or anything else. I'm leaving. I can't stop you from following me, but I suggest you don't." He blew out a harsh breath. "My Celtic blood gives me a place among you. I'm sure Ceridwen would love to hear you accosted me."

He kept careful eyes on the Morrigan. He wasn't certain about what he just said, but the crow hadn't told him he was full of shit, so maybe he was onto something.

She dropped her hands before extending them, palms upward.

"What would ye tell her? No sin in paying a visit to one of my kinsmen."

"That kinsman would rather you left." Jonathan narrowed his eyes. "Now."

"Och, but we could have a bit of entertainment, ye and me." She covered the distance between them so fast he didn't see her body move. Breasts pressed into him, and she wrapped her arms around him, grinding her hips against his pelvis. "Britta need never find out," she whispered into his ear. "I wanted your da, but ye're even more attractive than he was."

Lust flared, heating his loins. The bitch had to be using magic—blood magic—but if he didn't do something—and pretty fucking fast—she'd ensorcel him into making love with her. His cock swelled, achingly hard. Images flooded his mind of backing her against the stones of the building, hiking up her skirt, and…

"No!" he roared and pushed her away so hard she stumbled backward. In the moment when her spell wavered, he slammed up wards to keep her out.

The seduction flowing from her in luminous waves shifted to anger that pounded against his shielding. Her sea blue eyes changed to black, and the Crow took shape where the woman had stood.

Jonathan didn't wait around. He had magic aplenty sizzling and ready. Making certain to keep his wards in place, he visualized a deserted loch a few miles north of Inverness. The world tilted, dissolving around him as his traveling spell took over.

Maybe she'd follow him. He'd find out soon enough. One thing was certain. Talking with her was a waste of breath. And goddamned dangerous. She was much stronger than him magically, and he'd be a fool to forget it.

CHAPTER 3

 ritta paced from one side of the grove of hawthorn trees to the other and back again. They were only a few miles north of Inverness, and the Scottish Highlands rose around them, craggy with snow-capped peaks. Jonathan should've caught up by now, yet a good half hour had ticked by. She came to a decision and summoned power.

"What are ye about?" Arianrhod, who'd been off to one side apparently lost in thought, snapped to attention.

"I'm going back. 'Tisn't like Jonathan to be late."

The goddess frowned, then shook her head once. "Give the lad a spot of time. His head must be full of what he heard. Mayhap he's sorting—"

Britta let her spell fritter away in a brisk, north wind and turned to face Arianrhod. "The *lad* is actually a full-grown man. Nay, something's amiss. I feel it in my bones. He may be ambivalent about you, yet he adores his da and wouldna forego an opportunity to be reunited with him."

"I still say we should wait at least another few minutes. If ye leave, he'll likely show up, and then we'll just be calling you back."

"Bonded one!" rang in Britta's head.

25

Arianrhod's mouth twisted into half a smile. "Aye, and 'twould be Tarika, if I were to guess. Not that I was listening in, but 'twas impossible not to hear."

"My dragon is like that." Britta smothered a laugh. "If ye asked her, she'd tell you she rules this world and all the other ones as well. But ye'd know as much. Ye met her when we rescued her and Kheladin."

Arianrhod nodded her head. "Aye, but I dinna get much of a chance to speak with her. I surmise that will change verra soon."

Britta stepped beyond the shadows of the treed enclosure that hid one of many entrances to the time travel portal. No room for Tarika in the small circle with a standing stone at its center.

She shaded her eyes from the wind in time to see her dragon emerge from the ether, her red-scaled body glistening as if she'd flown through a rainstorm. Golden eyes the same shade as Britta's twinkled as the dragon skidded to a halt with microns to spare between them.

"Aye, and 'tis glad I am to see you." Britta flung herself at Tarika and wound her arms around her bondmate's neck. She didn't even clear a quarter of the span, but the dragon's inner heat seared her, reminding her of why she'd joined her life to the ancient creature standing by her side. She loved Tarika with everything in her heart, soul, and mind.

Until she met Jonathan, Tarika was all she needed. No man had gotten close enough to do more than doff his hat and say, "Good morning, my lady." Linking their lives with Jonathan had been a joint decision. She and Tarika did everything that way, though. They'd been inseparable for hundreds of years.

The dragon bathed her with steam before taking a step away and turning her whirling golden gaze on the goddess. "Arianrhod. 'Tis good to see you again." Tarika's earthy voice rumbled against the silence of the hawthorn grove.

To Britta's surprise, the goddess bowed low, her silver hair sweeping the ground before she straightened. "Aye. The pleasure is mine, First Born."

Tarika puffed smoke, tinged with flame, and Britta knew she was pleased by Arianrhod's respect. Scales clanked as she glanced about. "Where's Jonathan? Is he not going with you to retrieve Angus?"

"In the first place." Arianrhod stepped forward before Britta could open her mouth. "I'm not at all certain Angus is retrievable. If he doesna wish to return to this time, we canna force him."

The dragon narrowed her golden eyes with more scale clanking. "Aye, I ken that, but it doesna explain where Jonathan is."

"He was supposed to be right behind us." Worry surged, souring Britta's stomach. "I was about to retreat to his home to see what happened."

"I'll accompany you," the dragon announced. "If there's trouble, better the two of us together—"

Familiar energy leapt behind her, and Britta spun to see Jonathan striding from the sacred grove she'd just left.

"No need for any of that," he said jauntily. "I'm here now. We can go—unless Tarika has need of us." He turned to the dragon, who sent steam spewing toward him until he was lost in clouds of it.

"What happened?" Britta pressed.

"The Morrigan happened, but we can discuss it later." Jonathan's head emerged from dragon steam, and he rolled his eyes. "What a crafty, conniving bitch she is."

"Och, and ye're only now figuring that out?" Arianrhod crossed her arms beneath her breasts.

"Apparently she had the hots for da and thought I'd make a fine substitute—"

Britta closed the distance between them in a flash and grabbed his arm. "She dinna—force you."

Jonathan wove his arms around her, and she hugged him back. "Not for lack of trying, but no. I'm goddamned lucky I escaped with my balls intact. If I'd known how feral she was, I'd have done a better job warding myself. I was expecting another attack like when she flayed my face open with her beak. When she shape-shifted into a hot babe, I should've known what she had in mind."

Tarika stomped closer. "After I'm done at Fire Mountain, I shall make a point of letting the Celtic Council know."

"Mayhap if 'tis you, they'll pay better heed than they do with me," Arianrhod muttered.

"I'll make them *pay heed.*" Tarika tossed her head, and a tongue of flame shot from her mouth. It made the greenery smoke, but the trees and bushes were much too wet to burn. The gray cloud cover sank even lower, and rain pelted down.

Britta let go of Jonathan and turned to face her dragon. "Ye stopped afore leaving for Fire Mountain for a reason."

"Aye, that I did." The dragon nodded, double rows of teeth gleaming in her half-open mouth. "I would speak with you privately." She glanced meaningfully at the spot on her back where Britta rode.

Britta wanted to ask why the dragon didn't just use their special, shielded mind speech, but was certain Tarika had her reasons. Perhaps the Celt had the skill to listen in. She ran lightly to Jonathan and kissed him. After raising a hand at Arianrhod, she said, "Back verra soon," before vaulting to the dragon's back.

Tarika spread her wings almost before Britta was settled, and they left the ground behind in large, arcing circles.

"*Listen carefully,*" the dragon instructed. "*I fear the corrupt dark mage problem has escalated to the point where we may end in a full-scale war against the Celts. If that happens, I shall be forced to remain in Fire Mountain to support my kin.*"

Britta read additional meaning in Tarika's carefully crafted message. "*Ye're afraid the Dragon Council will cast all dragon shifter pairings asunder.*"

"*Aye, 'tis exactly what I suspect will happen. And that is best case scenario. From there, 'tisn't a leap to confronting the Celts about their refusal to corral the Battle Crow once they knew she plotted with dark mages to drain dragon magic.*"

"Well, they certainly dinna do aught when Arianrhod dragged the Morrigan in front of their council. Of course, she dinna get an opportunity to tell them that part, but the information about the Crow kidnapping dragonkind should've been enough."

"What it may come down to," Tarika went on, ignoring Britta's last statements, *"is our bond might be broken, whether we wish it or no."* The dragon hesitated. *"I came today to tell you goodbye if I dinna get another opportunity."*

"Nay! I refuse to accept that—" Pain lanced through Britta's chest at the thought of being separated from the other half of her life.

"Ye may not have a choice." Tarika gentled her mind voice. *"I will do everything in my power to maintain the pairings where the mage is beyond suspicion or reproach, but dragons tend to overreact, and I may not prevail."*

A sob tore from Britta, followed by another. Her throat narrowed with grief, and she understood why she was flying atop the dragon's back and not standing where Arianrhod could watch them. Even if the goddess had the grace not to listen, Britta's distress would've been impossible to hide. She clutched Tarika's familiar scaled hide so hard her hands bled.

"Does Kheladin know?" Britta choked out, not bothering with telepathic speech.

"Aye. He and Lachlan had this same conversation, and Kheladin is already on his way to Fire Mountain."

"What about the dragon shifter mages who still share a form with their dragons?" Britta demanded.

"They'll engage in the same ritual as we did to break the bond. Only difference is they may not be offered an opportunity to form a new one."

Rumors she'd heard battered her consciousness. Her next words tumbled from her. She had to know if the stories were true. *"Will your magic dim if the bond is broken? Will I lose my mind?"*

The dragon hesitated so long, Britta feared she might not answer. *"Twas rumors promulgated by mages to maintain the bond—and hold reluctant dragons by their sides. I doona believe any of it was ever true."*

Britta thought she should feel relieved, but an aching sadness filled her. Life without Tarika was untenable, unthinkable. *"Surely we can find a way through this."* Her voice was hesitant, not sounding anything like the imperious Countess of Kilkerran usually did.

"That will depend entirely on what the Celts are willing to do about the Morrigan. When they come to us asking if we can imprison her in Fire Mountain, we'll know they're serious about fixing the problem. If that doesna occur..."

"What can I do?" Britta lifted her face into the wind to dry her damp cheeks.

"Bury all evidence of this conversation where Arianrhod canna ferret it out. Ye must compose yourself afore we land."

"But she's Jonathan's mother," Britta protested.

"Aye, and she's also a Celt. Up until a verra few days back, it appeared the Celt part came first. We doona know to what extent that's changed."

Cold, wet air cooled her as she breathed it in, and Britta steadied herself. *"How will I know what the Dragon Council decides?"*

"I will come for you, or ye'll be summoned to Fire Mountain. If our bond is to be broken, we must come together one last time."

The finality in Tarika's words made it hard to breathe. Britta focused on making her lungs inflate once, and then again, to combat steel bands wrapping around her chest. She wanted to hug the dragon close and never let her go, but Tarika would expect her to be strong. Hell, she expected it of herself. She hadn't been a simpering ninny when she'd gone to Fire Mountain in search of a dragon, and she'd be damned if she'd dissolve into one now.

"That's better." Tarika's spoken voice mirrored the same pain and resignation gnawing a hole in Britta's soul.

"This isn't goodbye," Britta said. "I won't let it be."

"Like I said earlier, ye may not be offered that choice. Tell me when ye're ready, and I'll—"

"I'll leverage my own power. If I have to hold a memory of you, I want it to be in the air with your wings spread and the wind rushing past us." Strangling on grief that burned from the inside out, Britta drew magic and made her way to the grove where Arianrhod and Jonathan waited.

Jonathan.

How could she remain with him? What would she have to offer now that she felt like a scarred, empty shell?

Stop it! I canna give up. I must believe Tarika will talk sense into the others. Beyond that, I must keep going. Jonathan loves me. I canna let him down because I feel sorry for myself.

She straightened her spine and walked back inside the twisted branches that formed the grove. Hawthorns were hardy trees; their branches grew in patterns that looked like faces or animals. Today the configurations all held sorrow, but that was her doing, not theirs.

"I'm ready," she said. "Sorry for holding you up."

Arianrhod peered closely at her. "Can ye speak of whatever upset you?"

"Nay. Let's go. 'Tis a lengthy journey, and we've wasted enough time."

Jonathan drew his dark brows together into a thick, worried line, but mercifully didn't ask her anything. He threaded an arm around her waist and chanted to open a gateway to allow them to twist the threads of time.

JONATHAN WANTED to go after Tarika and shake the truth out of her. She was bonded to him too through the bite she'd insisted on when he and Britta first made love. Clearly, the dragon hadn't wanted to include him or Arianrhod in whatever had shaken Britta so profoundly. Traces of tears remained on her cheeks, and her normally rosy complexion was the tone of old ivory.

Protectiveness raged through him. No one would ever hurt his beloved. Not on his watch. Not even if it was her bondmate. He itched to burrow into her mind, drag the truth from her so he could fix what caused her so much pain, but he respected her too much to plow past her barriers.

The time travel portal ripped a hole in the ether before them. Jonathan gestured Arianrhod and Britta through, before stepping into the pulsating gray-pink tube that would take them wherever they wanted to go—more or less. Though the time tunnel was marked by nodes that flashed past when the thing was in motion, figuring out how to read them with precision was an art he'd yet to master.

Arianrhod perched on her haunches, keeping clear of the walls. He did the same and motioned for Britta to settle between his spread knees. He wrapped his arms around her and drew her against his chest. He might not be much use making certain they didn't overshoot Cathbad's time, but he could comfort the woman he loved.

The doorway closed seamlessly, and the tunnel lurched into a familiar rocking motion that meant they were underway. An hour slipped by, and then another. As he understood things, they were going back toward the beginnings of time. "What year are we aiming for?" he asked.

"Seven hundred, give or take a few years," Arianrhod replied. "Doona fash. I'm keeping a close eye on the nodes. 'Tisn't much farther now."

"We should be fairly close to Fire Mountain, shouldn't we?" he murmured, half-thinking he still wanted to track Tarika down. "Isn't it just past Earth's beginnings?"

"Aye and nay," Arianrhod replied. "Fire Mountain was the first world and dragons the first living creatures, formed of fire afore Earth was even born. Though we reach it through this time passageway, Fire Mountain exists in a place of its own, beyond thought and time as ye recognize it."

"We're not going there." Britta spoke for the first time since they'd left the hawthorn grove.

"Why not?" Arianrhod quirked a curious brow.

A closed-off look crossed Britta's face. "I doona wish to speak of it. We shall see if Angus wishes to return—and mayhap discover what Cathbad knows of Jonathan's role in the many problems we face."

He tightened his arms more firmly around her, and she leaned against him. "Ye canna fix this," she murmured. "Doona try."

"Of course I can't fix whatever's wrong since I have no idea what it is." His voice was sharper than he meant it to be, and he quickly added, "Sorry. I don't want to make it worse."

"Nor do I," Arianrhod broke in. "We'll be stopping verra soon. Brace yourselves. This has been a much easier trip than the first one I escorted you on, but sometimes the transition isna gentle."

Gray-pink walls vibrated around them as the passageway shuddered to a halt. Arianrhod barked a few words and the skin—or whatever the material was that surrounded them—split open.

Britta pushed to her feet, and he followed her. A whooshing from behind them told him the portal was gone—drawn in upon itself to wherever it went when it wasn't in use. His legs were stiff from squatting for so long, and his feet tingled as circulation came back into them.

They walked into a starless, moonless night. Jonathan started to zip his jacket, then glanced at Britta in leathers and a cloak. "Do you want my coat?"

She glanced at him. The drawn look hadn't left her face. "Nay. I'm fine." Britta addressed her next words to Arianrhod. "Which way to Ulster or wherever we can find Cathbad?"

"He'll find us."

"How do ye know that?" Britta asked and summoned a mage light. It cast a soft violet light in the inky darkness.

Arianrhod gifted her with a crooked smile. "'Tis how it's worked the last two times I came here. I believe he dreams our arrival. Failing that, if Angus is truly here, he'll sense both me and his son."

"And if he's not?" Jonathan asked.

"Cathbad may well know his whereabouts." Arianrhod rotated her shoulder blades, clearly as uncomfortable from their protracted time in the tunnel as Jonathan felt. "I'm going to walk a bit, try to get the kinks out of my muscles."

"Do ye wish to do the same?" Britta eyed him.

"Sure." He kindled his own light—blue where hers was violet—and draped an arm around her shoulders. A million questions burned in his mind, but he didn't ask any of them. When she was ready, she'd tell him about Tarika.

They set off at a brisk pace, scribing a circle around the large clearing they'd come out in. The air was clean, much purer than what they'd left in the twenty-first century. It tasted sweet on his tongue and soothed his pollution-scarred lungs.

"Thank you," she said so softly, he wasn't certain she'd spoken.

"For what?"

"Not trying to drum information out of me."

He stopped and turned her till she faced him. "It's not easy. I want to slay whoever—or whatever—caused you such pain."

She laid her head in the crook between his neck and shoulder. "Knowing ye love me with such ferocity is a great boon."

He stroked her hair and felt her body melt into his. The night was still very dark, but they stood in a circle illuminated by their mage lights. Britta tilted her head and gazed at him.

"Are ye excited to see your da?"

He turned the question over in his mind. "Not so much excited as needing to reassure myself he's fine. From the time I was maybe ten or twelve, it's hard to say who took care of whom. His visions came more and more frequently, and I'd stand guard over him. He was helpless then and for a little while after."

"Aye. The soul leaves the body in true vision states and flies free."

"Is that it?" He smiled softly. "I never knew exactly, other than I sensed he needed me to keep watch. Mauvreen and some of the other witches helped. One or another was always there while I was in school, and they made certain there was food in the house, and I had what I needed."

"There's more," she prodded.

He nodded. "When I was finally done with high school and leaving for college, he tried to apologize to me, but I wouldn't let him. He taught me so much that most fathers wouldn't have. About kindness and compassion, and believing in myself and my own power." Jonathan hesitated, searching for words. "Still, I had a hard time wrapping my mind around him really and truly being gone. Mauvreen told me not to hunt for him, that it'd be a waste of time."

"Ye dinna believe her."

"No. I didn't. I searched for years. Certain if I hit the right deserted castle or falling-down manor house, there he'd be."

"Och, son." Angus's unmistakable rich voice drifted out of the darkness.

Strong arms surrounded Jonathan and Britta from behind. He let go of her and turned to hug his father. Words felt inadequate, so he hung on tight to the rough weave of the woolen jacket Angus wore. Christ, he'd missed the man in his arms. He tried to infuse everything he couldn't say into his touch and hoped Angus understood.

Long moments passed. When he finally let go and stepped away, Jonathan said, "You could've told me goodbye."

"Nay. I couldn't. It would've made it impossible to leave." Whiskey-colored eyes glistened with unshed tears in the glow of the mage lights. Despite the years, Angus's hair was still the same rich mahogany, and his face was unlined. He held himself tall, with the same easy grace Jonathan remembered.

Jonathan drew Britta to his side. "I'd like to introduce the woman I plan to marry."

Angus bowed, a courtly, old world gesture, and raised Britta's hand to his lips. "My lady. It appears my son chose wisely."

"We chose each other," she retorted from beneath furled brows. "It makes my heart content to meet you, though."

"I'm glad to lay eyes on my son once again—and to meet you as well. Yet I'm apprehensive too. That you've sought me out tells me we've come to a critical juncture, one from which the Earth may not recover. I've dreamed so many possibilities, it's not possible to determine which will prevail."

Arianrhod slipped from the shadows. "Angus. 'Tis a blessing to see you once again—even if it comes on the heels of grim tidings"

Angus shifted his attention to the goddess. Love and longing spilled from him in bright, shining waves. He held out a hand. She ignored it and dove into his arms, pulling him close.

Jonathan tried not to listen, to give them the illusion of privacy as years of longing gave way to kisses and tears and soft words of love.

Britta grasped his hand and led him several yards away. "They'll be fine now," she murmured.

"How can you know?" Jonathan asked.

"The Celts found out about you."

"No more need for secrets, huh?" He pulled her into his arms.

"None at all. Arianrhod's kin may not approve of the choices she made, yet they canna change them anymore than they can alter the tides she controls."

"All four of you lovebirds get over here," another male voice boomed from the darkness. "We have far more important business than that of the heart to dispatch."

"Cathbad?" Jonathan murmured softly next to Britta's ear.

"That'd be my guess," she replied. "Whoever it is wears the mantle of command like a second skin."

CHAPTER 4

rianrhod cloaked herself in invisibility, as Angus embraced Jonathan. She didn't want to intrude on their heartfelt reunion. She also wasn't certain he'd be glad to see her, and she took those few minutes to steel herself for the worst. Gods, he looked amazing, as if no time at all had passed since their last meeting. The time he'd tightened his jaw and told her they couldn't continue to meet surreptitiously, that it wouldn't be good for their son. He'd offered her the same choice he extended before: to stand by his side openly—or not at all.

She hadn't been totally honest with Jonathan about that, and he'd called her on it, his face like a mask as he snapped, "Da never would have said that."

What if she'd followed her heart and not her Celtic duty? She inhaled sharply. No point in conjecture. What was done was done, and she couldn't go back. A glance told her Angus and Jonathan had moved beyond hugging to talk, and she listened while Angus described the critical juncture that might well push them toward a *Gotterdammerung*. Dusk of the Gods. She chewed her lower lip. The Germans always had a knack for drama, yet the term was apt.

She dropped the illusion surrounding her and strode forward, parting shadows as she went. "Angus. 'Tis a blessing to see you once again—even if it comes on the heels of grim tidings"

After the briefest of hesitations, he held out a hand. Banked desire blazed to life in the depths of his whiskey-colored eyes. She ignored his hand, pushing it aside as she wound her arms around him and immersed herself in his clean evergreen scent with overtones of the sea.

He closed his arms around her and held tight, murmuring endearments in Gaelic. Something tightly coiled within her relaxed just a little, and she dared to hope a life lived openly with the only man she'd ever loved might, just might, be possible.

"I've missed you so, my love," he said. "Many a time I wanted to leave here and seek you out, but when I dreamed the outcome, it was never what I hoped."

Arianrhod threaded her fingers beneath his hair and angled his head so she looked into his eyes. "Ye'd have been correct. My duties at the Celtic Council expanded these last twenty years. Ceridwen's called on me more and more often."

A corner of his mouth twisted downward into a sardonic smile. "Is that brother of yours still an asshole? And his sidekick, the god of the dead?"

She bit back a laugh. "Och, but they wouldna describe themselves so. They did grumble—and more than a little—after ye disappeared."

"I just bet they did. I don't suppose they came up with a replacement."

She moved a hand to the side of his face and stroked the dark stubble growing on it. "How could they? Ye're one of a kind."

"Nice to be appreciated. Most have to wait until they're dead for that honor."

She moved her fingers to cover his mouth. "Doona speak of such things. It tempts fate—and not in good ways."

He shut his eyes for a moment and brushed his thumb over her lower lip. "Ye've met our son. Did I keep my end of things raising him?"

"More than your end, my love. He's an amazing man. Strong. Sure of himself. Courageous. Compassionate." She hesitated. "A lot like you."

"Arianrhod. My love. My heart—"

"We can be all those things to one another now."

He drew his brows together. "What changed?"

"Two things. The Celts know about our son, but even if that hadna happened accidentally, I was on the brink of telling them myself and hunting you down."

"What would you have told me?" His deep voice rumbled near her ear, and he smoothed hair away from her face.

"That I loved you and was ready to face whatever consequences ensued once I stopped hiding what we were to one another." Her next words came hard, but she had to know. "Do ye still want me?"

"How can you even ask?" He wrapped a hand around the back of her neck and closed his mouth over hers. She remembered the touch of his lips and lost herself in kissing him back. The desperation of lost years added fervor to their embrace, and she drank in the wonder of the man in her arms.

She'd been a fool to believe her Celtic kin were more important.

"It doesn't matter," Angus spoke into her mind. *"We're together now, and together we shall remain from now until forever."*

"Did ye dream this?"

"Aye, I did, but only last night."

She broke their kiss. "If ye dreamed it, why did ye look surprised to see me?"

His lips curved into a soft smile. "I wasn't surprised, not exactly." He paused for a beat. "Not all my dreams come to pass. I wanted this one so badly, I didn't let myself hope it might."

"But surely, when ye saw Jonathan—"

"All four of you lovebirds get over here," a male voice boomed from the darkness. "We have far more important business than that of the heart to dispatch."

Arianrhod gave Angus a quick kiss then said, "We'll talk more of this later."

She moved out of the circle of his arms and strode toward Cathbad. He had a deep voice with a unique cadence she'd recognize anywhere. Sudden light blazed, illuminating him in the middle of a circle. He looked exactly as she remembered him.

Long dark hair framed his sharp-boned face, hanging loose in front, but the back portion was braided close against his skull. Dozens of braids trailed down his back. He was taller than Angus and broad-shouldered. Leather garments embellished with red and blue dye clung to his frame, and boots laced to just below his knees. A war axe swung from a sheath by his side, and a broadsword was attached to his back by a scabbard with thongs that wrapped around his body. Still more weapons draped from cunningly crafted bits of rawhide. His face held the same ageless quality that marked the Celtic gods.

Arianrhod squared her shoulders. "When last I came here, ye told me not to return."

"Aye." His amber eyes gleamed with keen intelligence. "Ye remember, do ye?"

"Are ye still of like mind?" she persisted, not wanting to pick scabs off old wounds, but needing to know if she'd have a fight on her hands if Angus left with her.

He drew himself tall. "If I were, ye'd not be here speaking with me now. I have ways of shielding my corner of the world. Angus was needed here after his long absence at the hands of your kin. I dinna wish ye to disturb his concentration."

Angus trotted to his grandfather's side. "You might have offered me a choice. Christ! You're as bad as the Celts."

Cathbad made a sigil against evil with his right hand.

Angus made a snorting noise. "Maybe not quite as bad."

"Blood comes first." Cathbad skewered him with a sharp look.

"Ye'd do well to keep it in mind. 'Tis why Arianrhod chose the Celts over you."

She winced at the unvarnished truth in his words and opened her mouth to reply, but Jonathan and Britta saved her the trouble.

Jonathan extended a hand toward Cathbad. "Nice to meet you, sir."

Cathbad furled his brows. "Sir, is it?"

"I'm Britta KilKerran," Britta announced and tilted her chin at a proud angle. "Countess of Cumbria."

"My lady." Cathbad inclined his head. "Cumbria doesna exist as such—yet. Where is your dragon? I sense the bond."

"In Fire Mountain, working to talk sense into the Dragon Council."

"'Tis a good lead-in to what we must discuss." Cathbad pressed his lips into a stern line before continuing. "What I am about to tell you must remain among us. Angus knows some of it, but far from all." He swept his gaze from one to the other of them.

Arianrhod held herself open to his scrutiny. She knew without being told that if she kept him out of her inner places, he'd banish her from what came next.

Finally seeming satisfied, Cathbad clasped his hands behind his back and began to talk. "Some of what I will say is known to you. Some may feel incorrect, yet hold your questions until I'm done. Dragons were the first creatures, and Fire Mountain the first world. Long ago, it took immeasurably strong magic to travel from there to Earth, or any of the borderworlds.

"Since leaving Fire Mountain felt impossible, Dragons kept to themselves for eons, but as frequently happens, a few wanted to venture forth, explore beyond the barriers of their world. Two of the First Born, Xenan and Taera, combined their power and blasted a path to Earth."

"When was that?" Arianrhod asked and then shook her head, remembering Cathbad's request for silence. "Never mind."

His amber gaze, twin to Angus's, bored into her. "Turns out my next words will answer your question. The dragons showed up just before the fall of the Roman Empire. Because they dinna bother to hide themselves—being dragons, they assumed no one would be so foolish as to wish them harm—the predictable occurred. People deified them, built shrines to them, and worshipped them. The Church saw them as a threat and launched efforts to kill them, which were laughable. No mere human could do away with a dragon.

"Xenan fell in love with a mortal woman. With Taera's help, they created the magic to form the dragon shifter bond—the original one that allowed mage and dragon to maintain their individual bodies and still be bonded. The dragons and Xenan's bondmate, Katherine, returned to Fire Mountain. 'Twas the first time a human had laid eyes on the dragons' home world."

Cathbad drew a flask from within his leather shirt and drank deep. The pungent scent of mead filled the clearing, and he offered the flagon to Angus, who stood next to him.

"The other dragons were furious. Dragon mated with dragon, and that was the beginning and end of it, so far as they were concerned. When Xenan protested, said he loved Katherine but chose to demonstrate that love by bonding with her, not lying with her, no one listened to him. A dragon made off with Katherine, intent on tossing her into a crater. Other dragons made certain Xenan couldna follow.

"Taera took to the skies, begging for Katherine's life. She offered to take over the bond in Xenan's stead. I have no idea how she prevailed, but she did. When they returned to the Dragon Council, Taera was Katherine's bondmate, and the basis for today's dragon shifter bond was formed. Xenan was so relieved Katherine was still alive, he accepted the new arrangement with nary a word of protest."

Cathbad took the flask from Angus. He tipped it back and swallowed a time or two, swiping the back of his hand across his mouth when he was done. Arianrhod extended her hand, and he gave the flask to her.

Cathbad inhaled deeply and blew out the breath. "Likely you're wondering what this has to do with anything, yet history creates a foundation for understanding the present. Through the intervening seventeen hundred years, many dragon shifter pairs emerged. Most were strong mages, and the bond benefitted both them and their dragons.

"A few dark mages poisoned the well. The first ones I knew of were Rhukon and Connor, yet there may have been others afore them. These dark mages, who embraced the dragon shifter bond to drain their dragons of power, dinna come up with the idea on their own. Nay, the Morrigan is behind their hideous plotting—"

"I'm not disagreeing," Arianrhod broke in. "And I know ye said not to ask questions, yet I must know if ye believe the Battle Crow is acting alone. Not that I'm defending her, but I've known her a verra long time. She always was a troublemaker, but nothing like this."

Cathbad cast an appraising glance her way from beneath lowered brows. "Perceptive of you. The Morrigan tossed her lot in with the Furies. She ran into them on one of her forays into the past, and they struck up a partnership."

"But they're fair," Jonathan protested. "They mete out punishment to those who've broken mortal law."

"Apparently they corrupted each other," Angus said. "The Morrigan would be drawn to the *mete out punishment* part, never mind if the recipient deserved it."

"Silence!" Cathbad bellowed. "There's little enough left to tell, then this can turn into a roundtable as we decide what to do."

He snatched the flask back from Arianrhod, but didn't drink. "The Furies were imprisoned in Hades. The Morrigan freed them, and in their gratitude, they offered up ideas for the Battle Crow to sow further hatred and discontent. Since the Crow was spurned by a dragon she wished to take for a lover, she designed a cunning payback, knowing it would take centuries to fully play itself out.

"We've come to the endgame. Dragons are on the edge of sealing their world off from Earth. If they do that, they'll take Earth magic with them, and all of us who have power will eventually die out. Mankind may not hold power, yet their existence depends on magical vibrations holding evil at bay."

He turned to face Jonathan, Britta, and Arianrhod. "You saw one of many versions of the future when you rescued the dragons the Morrigan kidnapped. It wasna pretty. People lived in caves and were slowly starving to death—if disease didn't kill them off first."

"So there are worse things afoot than losing my dragon," Britta murmured.

"Aye, far worse," Cathbad confirmed.

"What do you mean losing Tarika?" Jonathan broke in, sounding nonplussed. "Was that what upset you so badly before we left?"

"Stop!" Cathbad held up a hand. "I've laid out the bones of this thing. Now we must determine a way to ensure it doesna come to pass. Time is fluid. Many possible futures exist. 'Tis our task to keep Earth from entering a downward spiral with only one predictable end."

"Seems to me if we get rid of the Morrigan, we'll be home free," Jonathan muttered.

"And how will ye go about that?" Arianrhod demanded. "When I dragged her afore the Celtic Council, they told her she'd been a bad girl and let her go."

"It's a wee bit inconvenient she's immortal," Angus muttered.

"Surely if the Celts understand how close dragons are to instituting an irreversible action, they'll act," Britta cut in.

Arianrhod rolled it around in her head, not liking the answer she came up with. "Not necessarily."

"Why not?" Britta demanded. "Their magic is at risk too."

Arianrhod screwed her face into a grimace. "They willna see it that way. They willna believe the Morrigan would fuck them over to quite that extent."

"Do they realize she dallied with the Furies?" Angus asked. "Parleyed with those outside her own Pantheon?"

"I dinna know, so mayhap most of the others dinna, either. Yet Ceridwen sees everything. Her cauldron serves the same purpose as Cathbad's visions, though she rarely shares what she sees." Arianrhod took a measured breath. "Now I think on it, likely she knew about me, yet never said aught about it."

Cathbad drew his brows together and creased his forehead in thought. "There's little love lost betwixt Ceridwen and dragons. She wasna in favor of them breaching Earth's boundaries as I recall."

"So maybe she's playing it close to the bone," Jonathan said.

"What do ye mean?" Arianrhod asked. "Speak more plainly."

"Just that perhaps she sees this as an opportunity to barricade the dragons back in Fire Mountain." He shrugged. "She might have some eleventh hour plan to keep them from stripping the earth of magic."

Arianrhod shook her head. "If 'tis true, she's been quite close-mouthed about it."

"Ceridwen doesn't share much," Angus said, repeating Arianrhod's earlier statement.

"I've dreamed many possible scenarios." Cathbad spoke over them. "I believe our strongest hope lies in talking the dragons into helping us kidnap the Morrigan and sequestering her in Fire Mountain."

"They'll never agree," Britta said flatly.

"Why not?" Jonathan quirked a curious brow. "They recognize how toxic she is."

"They see it as the Celts' job," Britta said. "Tarika told me as much."

"Dragons haven't stepped in many times when their assistance would've been invaluable," Angus said. He grinned wryly. "Now that

I've spent so much more time in trance states, I assumed they had some sort of non-interference policy."

"They do," Britta confirmed. "If something doesna relate directly to dragons, they willna lift a claw."

"But this has everything to do with dragons," Arianrhod broke in. "Rogue dragon shifters draining dragon magic is dragon-linked if anything ever was."

"Have you been back to Fire Mountain since you and I were there?" Angus asked her.

Arianrhod shook her head. Visiting places she'd been with Angus made her feel his loss even more keenly, so she avoided them. "I havena seen Eletea, either, the dragon we rescued after she killed one of the dark mages."

"Maybe that would be as good a place to begin as any," Angus said. "She did offer us a permanent welcome in Fire Mountain, but it may be null and void now."

"Ye'll find her in the Highlands, not Fire Mountain," Cathbad said. "I agree, 'tis as good a place to begin as any."

"Arianrhod and I will try to find her," Angus offered.

His easy inclusion of her in his plans warmed Arianrhod's heart, and she leaned closer to him.

Britta straightened her spine. "Jonathan and I will hunt down Lachlan and Maggie. We'll let the witches know what's happening, and then we'll go to Fire Mountain—if the dragons let us in." She eyed Cathbad. "Which of us will ye travel with?"

"I canna leave here just now." Cathbad narrowed his eyes. "No need for any of you to return. I'll dream your progress."

Angus tightened his jaw. "If we're not successful, I'll return here to wait out what happens next."

Arianrhod gripped his hand. "Not without me, ye willna."

"If it comes to it, would Tarika be welcome here?" Britta asked, her golden gaze fixed on Cathbad.

His nostrils flared. "If your dragon chooses to defy her kin and leave Fire Mountain, knowing it will be impenetrable to her afterward, aye she'd be most welcome here." He softened his voice. "Doona hope for that. While it may happen, I havena seen it in my visions."

Sudden knowledge flashed through Arianrhod, and she let go of Angus to face Cathbad head on. "This place…" She waved her arms expansively. "'Tis set aside from the flow of time, somehow. That's why ye never age, and why time doesna move forward here."

He nodded. "At first, 'twas protection against Mongol hordes sweeping through the British Isles, but I discovered the magic I weave holds this tiny part of Ireland apart from the texture of time. I saw no reason to alter it."

"Your magic will dissolve too if the dragons leave, won't it?" Arianrhod asked.

Cathbad tucked the flask away and spread his hands in front of him. "I doona know. 'Tisn't something I can dream an answer for."

CHAPTER 5

*A*ngus latched a hand around Arianrhod's arm. "We should leave."

She turned to him. "Did ye know about this place existing outside of time?"

"Aye. We can talk more of it as we travel. It's the last bastion if things truly blow up in our faces."

Jonathan strode to Angus's side with his hand extended, but Angus swept him into a heartfelt embrace. "Travel safely, son. If things go well, we'll meet in Fire Mountain."

"And if they doona?" Britta made her way to where they stood.

"Good point." Angus let go of Jonathan. "If any of you run into something insurmountable, return here."

Arianrhod frowned. "It may not be possible."

"Nothing is certain," Cathbad agreed.

"Since we're heading for the Highlands anyway, I'm going to take one more shot at the Celtic Council," Arianrhod said. "They need to know the truth, even if it doesna alter their actions."

"I'll wait for you outside Inverlochy Castle," Angus muttered, not particularly wanting to renew his acquaintance with Gwydion, Arawn, or the others.

Arianrhod looked askance at him. "Like hell ye will."

"We're out of here," Jonathan said. "Let's be proactive about this and believe we can defeat the Morrigan once and for all."

Cathbad held up a hand. "She holds strong magic. If ye remove her from the equation, other things will shift. Doona ask, because I doona know quite what. Yet trust that a world without her in it may hold changes ye doona care for."

Arianrhod blew out a tightly held breath. "Damned if we do, eh? And damned if we doona. Not much of a choice, really."

"Nay, there isna." Sorrow twisted Cathbad's mouth into a hard, flat line. "I can reach Angus through shared visions. Mayhap Jonathan too, yet I'm not certain of that."

"Guess we'll find out." Jonathan joined Britta, who'd already summoned a portal for them to leave.

Conflicting emotions battered Angus, as he watched his son step through the gateway. Pride. Sorrow he hadn't been more present while Jonathan grew up. Relief his son had become the man he was meant to be, one who could play his role as lynchpin in the upcoming conflict.

"How do ye suppose I feel?" Arianrhod asked softly. "I wasna there at all."

Angus gazed at her. "You were inside my head."

"Aye. Best get used to it. We should go too."

Angus fought back a laugh. "Same old, imperious virgin huntress I fell in love with."

"I told you your time would come," Cathbad said, a soft smile on his face.

"I didn't believe you. Not until I dreamed it last night," Angus said. "Thank you, Cathbad, for making me whole, teaching me what I'm capable of."

"Ye figured out most of it on your own."

"Aye, but I still appreciate the time I've spent by your side, learning from you. The Celts never taught me a thing that didn't benefit them."

"We could debate Celtic failings for many hours. Go." Cathbad made shooing motions with both hands. "Ye have much to do, and time grows short."

"Thank you." Arianrhod angled her glance at Cathbad.

"For what?"

"Taking care of the man I love when I was too lost in my own mythos to see truth."

"Even if ye'd seen it sooner, 'twasn't your time—until now." He hesitated. "We shall meet at least one more time. Beyond that, I doona know."

"I'll look forward to it." Arianrhod turned away.

Angus felt the air hum with power, as she summoned magic to call the time travel tunnel for them.

Standing by her side felt right. He added power to hers and watched the air around them shade from pearl to a warm violet. She leaned against him, and he wound an arm around her shoulders. He tried out words in his mind, but none came close to expressing the deep emotion churning through him. Instead, he let his touch convey joy, gratitude, and relief, mingled with desire so sharp he wondered if the time travel tunnel would eject them for making love.

A gateway split the air before them. Arianrhod turned her multi-hued eyes his way and beckoned. "Our chariot has arrived."

He grinned and followed her into the shaft that would lead them back to the present. "I wish it were really a chariot—or a car."

"Why's that?" She settled herself on the floor in the center of the narrow, oblong cylinder with pulsating gray-pink walls.

"Cars and chariots have seats where we could stretch out." He let himself down behind her and wrapped her in his arms so her back was crushed against his chest. The portal whooshed shut, and the shaft began its characteristic rocking motion.

Arianrhod reached behind her and draped her hands over his shoulders. "Why would we want to stretch out?" she repeated, a coquettish note in her voice.

The undulating motion of the time shaft pressed her body against his. Caught between them, his cock zapped to attention, and he thrust against the curves of her ass. "That's why. It's been a long time, Ari."

A low moan escaped her, and she twisted in his arms until she faced him. "I thought about you every single day. Hell, not an hour passed when I dinna see your face and long for you in my arms."

He tightened his hold on her, cradling her against his body. "The time tunnel kicked us out when I got angry. Wonder what it'll do if we make love?"

"Can we take the chance?" Desire spilled from her in iridescent waves that made multicolored motes dance around them. "Cathbad said time grew short."

Angus reined in lust so pervasive it came close to choking him. He'd dreamed her so often, made love to her in his dreams in every conceivable position. His favorite memory was from a small shepherd's cottage in front of a fire he'd used to call a trance state. Once he came back to himself, she'd melted into his arms…

"Och, your thoughts are on fire. If we doona trust the time portal not to spit us out, mayhap we should take a wee break from it." She threaded her arms around him and pressed her fingers beneath his hair, holding his head while she licked the seam between his lips.

He opened his mouth to hers and kissed her, remembering her scent as it rose around them, jasmine, cinnamon, and something intensely female and unique to her. He cupped a breast in his hand, rubbing the peaked nipple between his fingers. The leather between his hand and her flesh heated from his touch.

She wriggled in his arms, and the friction against his cock as she moved was almost unbearable. He reached between her legs with his other hand, not bothering to undo the lacings of her breeches. It was too complicated, and he wanted her so much he could barely think.

Their kiss deepened, developed independent life as their tongues sparred, withdrew, and pressed forward again. He felt the ridge of her nubbin through her pants and rubbed in hard little circles, beyond caring what the time tunnel would do to them. If it wanted to reject them, surely it would've done so by now. Her hips bucked beneath his touch, and her breathing quickened. She placed a hand over his and showed him what she needed. Her body shuddered, and he knew she was coming. Both of them were ripe for this, needed each other the same way they needed air to breathe.

A foreign hum tickled the edges of his hearing, the sound was seductive, inspiring. It took a moment before he understood the sentient being that formed the time shaft not only approved, it was encouraging them. He understood songs and loving. The Selkies taught him that.

Apparently Arianrhod came to the same conclusion. Never breaking their kiss, she shoved a hand between them and grappled with the lacings holding his trousers in place. His cock sprang free, and she ran eager fingers up and down his ridged flesh. Climax rode close to the surface, but he forced it back. He wanted to be inside her, feel the heat of her around him for the first time in almost forty years.

He ripped his mouth from hers. "Slide your breeches down and straddle me."

"'Tisn't so easy as all that," she panted. Her lovely golden skin was highlighted by a rosy tint from her orgasm.

"I'll get your boots. One of them at least." He fumbled with the laces holding her knee high hunting boots around her lower leg and jockeyed one off. She made short work of the waistband of her breeches and slid one leg free of them, followed by ivory, silken smallclothes.

He spanned her waist with his hands and turned her so she straddled him, with one knee on either side. She grasped his cock and positioned him at the opening to her body. Angus wanted to wait, to take things slow, but he sank inside her in one powerful thrust.

"Jesus. God, but you feel amazing," he gasped. "I'm so close. Let me move you, or this'll be over before we've even begun."

She crooned to him in Gaelic, told him she loved him with her body, heart, soul, and mind, while she tightened herself around him in small, rhythmic contractions.

He stilled, willing himself to breathe. Just breathe. Finally, it felt like he could move and not explode immediately. He drew her hips upward, then back down as he thrust inside her. She found his mouth with hers and kissed him long and deep, sinking her tongue inside his mouth.

Control eluded him, like chasing after dust in a stiff breeze, and he drove into her, hungry for her, desperate for the woman in his arms. The scent of their lust stoked his need, and the time tunnel's song intensified, kindling unbearable eroticism that drove him beyond reason. Semen ripped out of him in sheets of blazing ecstasy. The rhythmic contractions of her body around him told him she'd reached a second peak.

He held her as close as he could while their bodies shuddered together. She raked her nails down his back, leaving trails of white heat in their wake. Another climax crowded close on the heels of his first, leaving him wrung out and shaken, and wanting more of the same.

She reared her head back, breaking their kiss. "I love you. Gods, I love you."

"You're the most amazing woman, Arianrhod. I fell in love with you years ago and never stopped." He smiled, and twin joy materialized on her lovely, ageless face.

"Och! I hope we dinna overshoot things." She twisted out of his arms and peered at a node as it flashed by.

"Well?" He was still grinning. He couldn't help himself. Delight coursed through him, spilling out in torrents.

"We're good. Two hundred years to go yet, but we should set ourselves to rights." She lifted herself off his still-erect cock and drew her clothing back into place.

"Here." He handed her a square of soft leather from one of his pockets, and her boot.

She blotted herself before doing up her trousers and stuffed the rag into her clothing. While she got her boot on, he forced himself back into his pants and worked the laces around his erection.

"We didn't get much of a chance to talk," he murmured.

"Nay, but we caught up in more important ways." She checked another node, and the air crackled with magic as the time shaft slowed. "We discovered something."

"What, besides each other? I didn't think it was possible, but I want you more now than I did the first day I laid eyes on you."

"We found a way to placate the time tunnel guardian." She tossed an impish grin his way. "If I'd known 'twas this simple, mayhap we could've averted the time it dumped us a hundred years from home."

He made a sound between a snort and a laugh. "Maybe not. As I recall, it happened pretty damned fast. One minute we were inside, and the next we were rolling onto wet, rocky ground."

He stood and drew her to her feet. "Ready?"

She met his gaze with her multi-hued eyes. "Never been readier. Let's go face my kin."

He followed her out into a fading day. For once it wasn't raining in Scotland. "Not sure I like the 'let's' part of that sentence. I could go my entire life without laying eyes on your brother and Arawn again."

The time shaft was still singing as it whooshed shut and disappeared. Arianrhod spun to face him. "Ye are my mate. Ye canna hide from my kin forever."

"Forever might not be all that long."

She narrowed her eyes. "No matter how ye add it up, the only way to face bullies is to stand proud. Ye were too young to stand up for yourself when my brother and Arawn kidnapped you, but ye're a man now." Arianrhod hesitated, as if deciding what to say next. "I'm still sorting out your magic. In many ways, what ye command is more powerful than at least some of my brother's ability."

"You didn't mention Arawn."

A corner of her mouth turned down. "Nay. I dinna. The god of the dead is a major force to be reckoned with. The dead dance to his tune, and no one in their right mind wants to face down an army of shades."

Angus looked around to get his bearings. They were north of Inverness, not far from Inverlochy Castle. To human eyes, it lay in ruins, but the Celts had resurrected it with magic, and it served as their meeting hall. "Do you suppose anyone would be there if we dropped in now?" he asked.

"Aye. Someone is always there. Shall we?" She set off at a brisk trot, and he paced her.

A colorful sunset flared to the west in shades of red and gold. Maybe things with his old adversaries wouldn't go as badly as he feared. It wasn't that they'd treated him appallingly—once they moved past their original sin of abducting him. They'd housed him, fed him, made sure he had clothing, even looked to his education. The latter was accomplished through telepathic force-feeding, but it didn't take as long as attending school would have.

What they'd done that still rankled was wiping his memory, so he had no idea where he came from. No notion which way home lay. It kept him under their thumb and working for them until one assignment threw him and Arianrhod together...

"We're here."

Her voice broke into his musings, and he followed her up the steps of Inverlochy Castle. What began as crumbling marble gave way to fully formed steps as illusion fell away. They followed magnificent staircases up two floors. Any furnishings had long since been removed, but the occasional bronze or marble statue graced long, empty hallways.

Arianrhod stopped at the end of the third floor hall and pushed open a door, stepping inside with Angus right behind her. He scanned the opulent room and the twelve-foot high oaken doors carved with runic symbols that they'd just come through. He recognized many of the symbols; they chronicled stories of the Celtic gods.

Crystals and natural stone in every hue of the rainbow made a prism of fading daylight as it flared through leaded glass panes. Rich carpets covered the stone floors, thick wool woven with depictions of Celtic glory. A fire burned in an enormous hearth situated directly across from the entry doors.

Ceridwen sat before the blaze stirring her cauldron. When she glanced at them and cleared her throat in a muttery growl, a handful of Celts looked up from where they'd scattered themselves about the room, no one too close to anyone else. Ceridwen flowed to her feet in a graceful motion. "What have we here?" Her voice was low, musical, yet it held a hint of threat—at least to Angus's ears.

"I have news." Arianrhod didn't make any effort to walk closer to Ceridwen or her cauldron.

Gwydion bounced upright from where he'd been seated on the far side of the room and loped toward them, stopping when he was nose-to-nose with Angus. He wore white robes, sashed in green, and his ever-present staff was clutched in one hand. Blond braids flowed behind him. He skewered Angus with sharp blue eyes.

"Ye're back, and with my sister in tow." A sneer carved his handsome face into something menacing. "No need to stay away now we know about your bastard son."

Angus didn't think. He let the power within him surge to the surface and drew his hand back, slapping Gwydion across the face so hard the sound was like a gunshot. "No one says anything derogatory about Jonathan. No one," he growled. "Do you understand me?"

Gwydion raised his staff. The carved, polished wood took on an angry red glow. "Ye forget yourself—human," he snarled.

"I'm no more human than you are." Angus lifted clenched fists.

"You want to fight? Toss that staff in the dirt, and do it like a man, not a coward who kidnaps helpless youths."

"Watch who ye call coward." Gwydion shook his staff.

A woman dressed in battle leathers surged forward. Long, blonde curls bounced around her muscled frame, and her aquamarine eyes glowed with anticipation. "Och aye, by all means, let's have a fight. 'Tis been deadly dull around here for far too long."

Angus didn't take his gaze from Gwydion. "Who are you?" he asked the woman.

"Andraste, goddess of victory," Arianrhod snapped. "She's nearly as bloodthirsty as the Morrigan."

"Aye, sister, and I'll take that as a rare compliment," Andraste purred.

"For the love of the goddess, will the lot of you stand down?" Ceridwen materialized between Angus and Gwydion, though he had no idea how she'd gotten there. She was so tall, he looked across at the back of her head. She splayed a hand on Gwydion's chest and gave him a shove that sent him back a few feet. "We have bigger problems than your ego…brother."

He shot an aggrieved look her way, but retreated to the back of the room, grumbling, "Ye havena heard the end of this, Angus."

"Aye, but he has, and ye'd do well to remember it." Ceridwen made a chopping motion with one hand in Gwydion's direction before turning her attention to Angus and Arianrhod. "You came here for a reason. I doona approve of your coupling, yet 'tis like pitching a fit over forty-year old gossip. What's done is done." She stopped to take a slow breath. "Cathbad never would've allowed you to be together if—"

"Ye found your way back to Cathbad?" Gwydion bellowed, still on his feet. "How the hell did that happen, *Arianrhod*?" His sarcasm as he pronounced his sister's name was so palpable, Angus wanted to rush across the room and bash his face in.

"Ye knew as much. We've had this conversation, and once was too many times by my way of thinking," Arianrhod retorted, aiming her comment at Gwydion. "What ye did was wrong. Once Cathbad found Angus through a vision state, I made certain he knew of his grandson's whereabouts. Both the Druid seer and his blood kin deserved that much. Ye likely doona agree, but Angus's place was by Cathbad's side. 'Tis where he's been since our son grew up. Besides…" She narrowed her eyes. "Cathbad never agreed to loan you his grandson permanently. Ye tricked them both—"

"Enough!"

Power boiled around Ceridwen so hot and vicious, Angus expected his clothing to catch fire. The goddess of the world raised her voice until it hurt Angus's ears to listen, yet he had no choice.

"No one speaks unless I give them leave. Not another word. Is that understood?"

She glared at a silent room out of dark, thickly-lashed eyes. Floor-length dark hair shot with silver swirled around her. She wore battle leathers, similar to Andraste and Arianrhod, yet a paler color. "Better," she grunted. "Arianrhod. Say what ye came to say."

"Then what?" Arianrhod eyed her coolly.

"Then I decide what happens next."

CHAPTER 6

Arianrhod swallowed around a painfully dry throat. She'd been talking for the better part of an hour, but at least Ceridwen hadn't told her to shut up. The goddess of the world had a notoriously short attention span when she had no intention of doing anything to alter the status quo.

"To sum things up, the dragons will close Fire Mountain off from all other worlds and take Earth magic with them. They'll also sunder every single dragon shifter bond. Earth will enter a downward spiral and will eventually end up a dead world, incapable of supporting life."

"Ye're repeating yourself." Ceridwen screwed her face into a disapproving scowl. "How do ye know the Morrigan and Furies are in league with one another?"

Angus straightened his back. He'd been silent—until now. "My grandfather saw it in a vision."

"I dinna ask you." Annoyance sharpened Ceridwen's words.

"Nay, but he was there watching over things to allow Cathbad to delve more deeply into the problem," Arianrhod said.

"Much as I doona relish the task, we must summon the

Morrigan here and ask her if 'tis true." Ceridwen's normally upright posture slumped. "I'll do that right—"

"Hold! She's lied every single time ye've asked her aught," Arianrhod countered. "This time willna be any different." She sucked in a ragged breath. "The question isna if she's guilty, but what we," she waved her arms expansively to include the large room, "are willing to do about it."

"I never thought dragons belonged here." Starkness encircled Ceridwen's words, lending emphasis.

"Why not?" Andraste, who'd never returned to her seat, edged forward. "They're the epitome of courage, indomitable warriors."

Ceridwen twisted to face her. "Aye, and they're also arrogant, entitled, and notoriously indifferent to anything not directly dragon-linked."

Arianrhod clamped her teeth together with an audible *clank* and studied the floor.

"What?" Ceridwen looked even more annoyed.

Should I?

Arianrhod shrugged. What the hell? "If ye substitute Celt for dragon in your last sentence, ye'd be describing us as well."

Ceridwen bared her teeth in a snarl. "How dare you?"

"She's right," Andraste piped up. "We are arrogant and entitled, and many a time we should've intervened in human affairs but chose not to. As I recall, we could've ended a war or two—or made certain they never began in the first place."

"This? From you?" Ceridwen shook her head. "Ye live for battle."

"Mayhap I've become tired. Regardless, I doona wish the dragons to take their toys and go home if it means our magic fades along with all the rest."

Arianrhod cast her gaze around the room. Twenty or so Celts sat scattered about, but none met her eyes. "Well," she demanded. "Speak up. What will you? Is protecting the Morrigan from long overdue justice worth what we give up if she runs free?"

"'Twas my question to ask," Ceridwen growled.

"Then ask it," Andraste shot back.

Gwydion, Arawn, Bran, and several others gathered in small groups, muttering among themselves. Arianrhod reached for Angus's hand, gripping it tightly. The next few moments would decide all their futures, and whether she and Angus would wait out what remained of eternity in the bastion Cathbad had built to hold evil at bay.

Gwydion glanced up from his huddle. "The Morrigan admitted guilt in kidnapping two dragons, clearly breaking the compact between Celts and dragonkind."

"We allowed her to leave," Ceridwen reminded him. "Accepted her excuses."

"'Twas a mistake," another Celt called from the back of the room. "I thought so at the time, and I still do. And then we dinna know of her plotting to drain dragon magic through the dark mages."

The muttering grew in cadence and volume until Ceridwen shouted, "Silence. I would have your votes on this. White or black marbles in my cauldron. Now."

The group shuffled to bins against the back wall that held voting marbles. Arianrhod joined them. She had no idea if the count would be close, but she wasn't taking any chances. The cauldron flashed so brightly when she cast her black marble into it, she shut her eyes against the glare.

Angus waited for her where they'd been standing, and she rejoined him. "At least Cerwiden called for a vote," she whispered into his ear.

"Aye. That seemed like a good thing to me too. What happens if—?"

"Ssht. It willna be long now."

The last Celt cast her marble into the cauldron. Its contents created a small whirlwind that rose above the edge of the huge, black pot and slopped over its edge. The maelstrom surrounded Ceridwen, who'd made her way next to her cauldron. For long moments, both were enveloped in a fiery nimbus.

Arianrhod was fairly certain the vote had gone her way. The only other times she'd taken part in this ritual, the pot's reaction was much more subdued—and the Celt in question found innocent.

Smoke, fire, and steam cleared. Arianrhod smothered a smile. Ceridwen's cauldron reminded her of a rampaging dragon. The goddess of the world, looking none the worse for having walked through fire, raised her arms in front of her. When she spoke, her voice was weary, resigned, but it didn't waver.

"Find the Morrigan. Corral her. Take her to Fire Mountain and turn her over to the dragons to imprison."

"What if they doona admit us?" Gwydion asked.

"Figure it out," Ceridwen shouted. "Now leave. All of you."

Arianrhod grabbed Angus's arm and yanked hard. "Ye heard her. Let's go."

He raced along by her side, as they headed for the huge doors at the end of the hall. "Where are we going? After Eletea or the Morrigan. And in which order?"

"We'll work that out once we're outside. I know that tone. She doesna like to lose, and she lost on two fronts just now. Dragons remaining on Earth being the first—unless they decide to leave anyway."

She and Angus burst through the doors and pelted down two flights of stairs to the main level where they let themselves out the front door and through the illusory curtain that kept Inverlochy Castle invisible to human eyes.

"What's the second war she lost?" Angus demanded, breathing hard.

"Siccing us against one another." Arianrhod slowed from a dead run to a sedate trot. "Insofar as I know, 'tis never happened afore."

"I have to admit I'm surprised. I never actually expected the Celts to lift a finger if it didn't benefit them directly." He grimaced. "Ouch. Didn't mean for that to sound quite so blunt."

"Och aye. Well, 'tis the truth, and nothing I dinna know about us."

He drew to a halt, forcing her to stop too since she still had hold of his arm. "If we seek Eletea, we should head north, deeper into the Highlands. We've been moving due east since we left Inverlochy."

She felt mildly embarrassed. She'd been heading toward her home, intent on private time with Angus, yet they had higher responsibilities. There'd be plenty of time for lovemaking—if they managed to stem the tide of destruction threatening the world.

He quirked a roguish brow and drew her hard against him, running his lips through her hair. Cradling the back of her neck in one hand, he rubbed tense muscles. "I thought it was something like that, and aye, I helped myself to your thoughts. I'd love to step outside all this. Gather you close and run away somewhere—but there's nowhere to go. Soon there may be nowhere safe at all if we can't track down the Morrigan."

"Mayhap not even then." She cupped the side of his face in one hand and traced the lines of his cheekbone and jaw. "None of us knows what the dragons are really thinking. There may be many who welcome an opportunity to withdraw from contact with men."

"Don't borrow trouble." His crooked half-smile warmed her.

"Aye, we have a passel of them without my conjecture, eh?" She stood on tiptoe and brushed her lips across his.

He tightened his hold on her and kissed her hard, sparring with her tongue until their teeth clattered together. She felt him stiffen against her belly, and it took all her self-control not to drag him into the narrow space between two old stone buildings and take him into her mouth. Or maybe she could slide her pants down and bend over something handy. It was dark enough, no one would see them...

Angus ripped his mouth from hers, his breath unsteady. "Enough. Not that I don't appreciate the images rioting through your head, but if I keep kissing you, I refuse to take responsibility for what happens next." The air rippled around them as he summoned magic, presumably to move them deeper into the

Highlands. The spell intensified his scent, smelling of freshly-turned earth and the sea.

She mingled her power with his and waited for the weightless sensation as the spell took hold. This was one of the reasons she'd never bothered to learn to drive. What use was it when she could go anywhere she wanted by leveraging magic? Mist surrounded them, full of the rich feel of the Highlands, one of the last truly untamed places on Earth where magic roamed free. The hills and barrows still housed the *Dreaming*, a place immortals went when their long lives dragged at them.

The spell spit them out, and she looked through her third eye. Jagged, snow-capped peaks rose around her, as the haze cleared. "We're in the right place," she murmured and called a mage light into being. It glowed a soft violet near her shoulder.

"Aye, I recognize it from when I saw it in trance. Now all we have to do is find Eletea."

Arianrhod shut her eyes and sent power spiraling around her, searching for life forms. Information pinged back from insects, birds—and dragons. More than one it appeared. "Someone's here," she said.

"Aye, and they're headed our way." He pointed skyward.

Angus watched two dragons winging toward them. The night was dark enough, it wasn't possible to make out their color, but one looked about the right size for Eletea. She was one of the smallest adult dragons he'd ever met. Who was the other one? Surely not Cavet, her erstwhile mate who'd plotted behind her back to see her imprisoned, so he could bond with a dark mage.

Danne, Eletea's egg-mate, was in on the scheme, but he was dead. Arianrhod killed him in a battle beneath Rhukon's manor house.

"We'll know soon enough who they are," Arianrhod said, having divined his thoughts.

He felt her deploy power, holding it in abeyance. Because it made sense, he did the same. Eletea was gutsy and principled, and he hoped one of the dragons heading their way was her. He'd grown fond of the young dragon in the time they spent together. She'd been unfairly targeted both by the Celts—for killing one of the Morrigan's distant relations—and by the Dragon Council that had jumped in with gusto and forced her to justify her actions.

One of the dragons bugled a greeting, and he let go of the defensive magic he'd gathered, recognizing Eletea's voice. Arianrhod followed suit; the air glittered as their energy dissipated. The dragon pair circled lower and lower, before landing a few feet away.

Angus sprinted for Eletea. "It's good to see you again. We have much to catch up on."

"The pleasure is mine, Angus." Eletea turned dark eyes with golden centers on him. They glowed warmly.

He stared at the other dragon. Not Cavet. He'd been red, and this one was copper, the same color as Eletea, but in slightly darker shading.

"It doesn't matter who I am." The other dragon stretched its neck tall. "I've come to make certain Eletea returns to Fire Mountain. We're calling all the dragons home."

Damn! It's happening sooner than we feared.

Angus had a lot of questions, but picked what seemed most relevant. He extended his hands in front of him, palms up in a gesture of supplication. "Are dragons truly planning to shut the gateway to Fire Mountain?"

"That's for us to know." The dragon snapped its jaws together. "No matter what we decide, we must be prepared."

Eletea lowered her snout until it rested on Angus's shoulder. "These are good humans. You shouldn't speak so harshly to them."

"Pfft." The other dragon blew smoke-tinged flames fifty feet into the air. "The woman is a Celt. They're who refused to censure their own. The Morrigan is at the bottom of our current problems. Dragons won't be safe until we're on the far side of a barrier betwixt her and us."

Arianrhod nodded to Eletea. "Nice to see you again." She gazed at the other dragon. "We were recently at the Celtic Council where we voted. The vote went against the Morrigan, and my kin are hunting her."

"For what? To tell her she was a bad girl." The dragon sneered and blew more smoke that hovered above its head. Whirling golden eyes reflected Arianrhod's mage light.

The air around Arianrhod flickered as she battled a sharp retort. Angus saw it in her mind, so presumably the dragons did as well. She tossed her hair over her shoulders. "Aye, I'm angry—I'm not trying to hide it—but as much at my blood kin for stalling so long, as I am at the Morrigan. They're hunting her to haul her to Fire Mountain. Presumably, ye have ways to imprison her where she canna escape."

Before Angus could say anything, Arianrhod hurried on. "Please doona seal off your world afore we have a chance to set things right. If we canna get to Fire Mountain, we'll be stuck with the Morrigan for whatever time Earth has left."

The other dragon, larger than Eletea by a third, threw its head back and snorted steam. Angus assumed it was laughing. When it got hold of itself, it said, "And a just punishment that would be." It slapped Eletea with its foreleg. "No point in hanging about to listen to them whine. We're leaving."

"You may be," Eletea retorted, "but Angus is my friend. He and Arianrhod saved my life when Rhukon and Connor kidnapped me. I would speak with them."

"I told you, we're leaving."

Eletea drew herself to her full height and faced off against the other dragon. "And I told you I'm not. You can't order me to do anything. You're not on the council, and I don't answer to you."

"Cheeky. If Cavet were still around, I'd encourage him to ride harder on you, correct your manners."

Angus rolled his eyes. At least he knew what sex the other dragon was. Male. None of the females had ever approved of Cavet's heavy-handed tactics. Even if he hadn't aligned himself with evil, he was still the dragon equivalent of a male chauvinist pig. Angus was glad Eletea dumped him. He hoped she'd done a whole lot more—like incapacitating the bastard forever.

"Ye could help us locate the Morrigan," Arianrhod suggested, her tone silky smooth.

Angus picked up the slightest hint of a compulsion spell woven into her words.

"Why would I want to do that?" The dragon tossed his head. "She's your problem and your job. I hope you never find her. I want to keep our world for us. Dragons. The way things stand now, no one can ever predict who's going to show up, and most of you are nothing but trouble."

Arianrhod opened her mouth, but Angus caught her gaze and shook his head. He wanted the full story, so he knew exactly what they were up against.

Oblivious, the dragon plowed on. "Not just you pesky Celts. The Greeks show up. And the Romans, but the Norse gods are the absolute worst. They're almost always drunk, and the men have an unnatural curiosity about sex with our women." The dragon trained its whirling gaze on Arianrhod. "You're scarcely innocent. You bedded Keene, and more than once. You thought we'd never tell your Celtic kin you fell off the virgin princess pedestal. You were right, we didn't, but we threatened Keene with banishment if he ever touched you again."

Angus stared at her, caught between bewilderment and anger. Not that he owned her or had any say in who she had sex with, but a dragon?

"Are ye quite done?" Arianrhod crossed her arms beneath her breasts and faced off against the other dragon. Her cheeks blazed with color. Without waiting for him to answer, she continued. "Not that it's any of your affair, but Keene courted me well over a hundred years ago—afore I met Angus. He made his way to my home in the Highlands and plied me with flattery and fire. I'll not apologize—for either of us. At least now I understand why I never saw him after my second *invited* visit to Fire Mountain."

Angus blew out a harsh breath. Before him. The dragon happened before him. In that moment, he understood that he saw Arianrhod as his woman and made his way to her side, wrapping an arm around her waist. Protectiveness surged. No one would ever have her but him. He'd see to it.

She turned her attention his way. "Aye, and I love you too. No man came near me once we made love. Look into my heart and find truth in my words."

"I don't have to. I believe in you—and in us."

"This is so tender, I may choke on my own fire." The other dragon shot a torrent of flame skyward.

"You're being insufferably rude." Eletea directed her words at the other dragon. "This is my home. Under our law, I can order you to leave, and I am."

"You must come with me," the dragon insisted. Taking on a wheedling tone, he said, "You were my assignment. The council will have my neck if I return without you."

Scales clanked as Eletea shrugged. "Not my problem. I'll come when I'm ready, or maybe not at all." She paused for effect. "Maybe I'll stay and help my friends, Angus and Arianrhod."

"You'd pick humans over your own blood kin?" Outrage rippled through his words, and a gout of fire burst from his mouth.

"In this instance, yes." She folded her forelegs across her scaled chest.

The larger dragon spread his wings. He took a running leap and clawed his way into the air, still breathing fire.

"I hope ye doona regret that, lass." Arianrhod tilted her head, presumably watching the other dragon. "There he goes. Through the barrier and back to Fire Mountain."

Angus saw the flash of light too. Dragons had their own methods of traveling to their home world that didn't involve the time shaft. He wasn't totally clear on the mechanism they employed, but it was some sort of dimensional shift that rearranged the warp and weft of time.

"It's good he left," Eletea said without preamble. "We have much to talk about. The Morrigan was here just before Jaek showed up. She offered me a dragon shifter bondmate, with rosy promises of vast increases in my power."

"What'd you say?" Angus ground his teeth together, worried for his friend.

"I mostly listened and told her I'd think about it. She said she'd return tomorrow or the day after to hear my decision."

"Do ye suppose she's making the same offer to every dragon not in Fire Mountain?" Arianrhod asked.

"It's a good guess," Angus replied. "She's not stupid and may have figured out the other Celts are finally done with her maneuverings."

"Either that or someone who cast a white marble to save her ass ran and warned her," Arianrhod muttered fiercely.

"What do you mean white marble?" Eletea asked and crinkled her scaled brow in confusion.

"'Tis a long story," Arianrhod said. "Do ye have a place we could sit and talk? And is there aught to eat here?"

"Yes to both." The dragon made a face. "I hate offering because I abhor anyone on my back, but get on, both of you. I'll fly us to my cave. I killed three sheep yesterday. One remains. You're welcome to it, but you're on your own preparing it since I eat them raw."

"We'd be most appreciative." Angus smiled. "What happened to Cavet?"

The dragon's eyes whirled faster. "Simple, really. I told him I knew all about his chicanery—and his plans to bond with evil. I promised I'd keep my mouth shut, but only if he went back to Fire Mountain and made me a blood vow to never bond to a dark mage."

"What happened?" Arianrhod leaned forward.

"Cavet always was a coward. He kept his end of the bargain, so far as I know. Hop up. If the Morrigan really returns tomorrow, we need a plan."

Angus drew magic and landed gently astride the dragon. Arianrhod joined him, settling between his legs. "We're all set," she called cheerily.

Eletea spread her leathery, copper-colored wings and beat the air with them to gain elevation, but not much. Apparently, they weren't going far.

"Whatever happened with alerting the Dragon Council to the corrupt dark mage problem?" Angus asked as they flew.

"I did. They listened—and apparently did nothing, until now." Eletea banked lower circling to land. The second her feet touched the ground, she barked, "Off me. Now."

"Thank you for the ride." Angus jumped down, then reached up to help Arianrhod. Not that she needed his assistance, but he liked the feel of her in his arms.

"This way." Eletea pointed with a wingtip and lumbered toward an opening in a rocky cliff.

Arianrhod walked to Angus' side. "'Tis been forty years since she told the Dragon Council about the dark mages. I wonder why they're just now getting around to doing something about the problem."

It was an excellent question since it made the dragons as culpable as the Celts for their current spate of difficulties. Angus rolled it around in his head as he followed the dragon into her cave.

ritta walked out of the time shaft into the velvety darkness of a moonless night, still struggling with the empty place inside her. She was still bonded to Tarika, but the specter of losing her dragon weighed heavy. Jonathan tried to engage her in conversation through the long journey from Cathbad's lands, but she hadn't had anything to say. In the end, he just held her, which was probably a good thing. It kept her from tearing at her hair and screaming her pain to the skies. If she'd done that, the time shaft's guardian would've ejected her summarily. It hated negative emotions.

"We're headed to Mauvreen's, right?" Jonathan asked.

Britta nodded, not knowing if she was eager to see Lachlan, or if he'd make things worse. Surely he was just as bereft by the possibility of losing his bond to Kheladin as she was about Tarika. "Aye. Like Angus said, 'tis as good a place as any to begin. I have no idea who'll be there, though."

He glanced around, presumably getting his bearings. He was much more familiar with Fort William in its modern configuration than she was. It wasn't that she couldn't find Mauvreen's since she'd been there before, but it would take him much less effort.

"We could walk," he suggested. "It's not far."

"As opposed to?"

"Using magic."

She raised her arms above her head and twisted her torso from side to side, stretching out muscles stiff from their journey in the time tunnel. "Walking is fine."

He captured her hand in one of his and turned her to the north, guiding her down the side of a narrow street a few yards from where they'd emerged. "Excellent. It's my first choice too. How are you doing?"

"About as ye'd expect."

He hesitated, maybe collecting his thoughts before he spoke. "I feel presumptuous saying this since I've only known Tarika a short time, but I love her too. I won't feel her loss as keenly as you, but I'll miss her if—"

Britta stopped walking and rounded on him. She jabbed his chest with a forefinger. "Doona talk like that. Doona think like that. We. Will. Not. Lose. Tarika. Any other thoughts tempt fate—and not in a good way."

A man walking toward them started at the sharp tone of her voice and crossed the roadway. Britta shook her head and lowered her voice. "We shouldna draw undue attention to ourselves. The Crow likely has spies everywhere."

Jonathan took her hand again, and they resumed walking. "Do you really think so?"

"Aye, and why not. She's a canny one, and spies are the life's blood of those like her. Why?"

"She apparently has me in her gun sights." Breath hissed from between his clenched teeth. "I deluded myself she'd have difficulty locating me if I dropped off the radar for a while."

"What's radar?"

"What you're really asking is what my expression means. Radar is an electronic means of locating something."

"Got it."

"If we end up with Cathbad, none of this modern mumbo jumbo will matter a twit."

Something about his tone snagged her out of the pit her thoughts had devolved into. "Ye'll miss it, won't you? Not the jargon so much as the only time ye've ever known."

"Of course." His words were simple, but emotion ran beneath them. "Until the Morrigan nabbed us after we had dinner the first night I met you, I'd never used my power much. Never believed Arianrhod was my mother." He paused a beat. "The truth of things is, I was ambivalent as hell about my magic. Part of me still is, but that part's growing smaller."

"I would think so." She smiled in spite of herself. "Wielding power is far more than convenient. 'Tis a gift, and not just one ye call on to defend yourself."

"I'm discovering that." His upper arm stiffened where it pressed against hers and he stopped, scanning the darkness.

"What?" She braided her magic with his and looked too. When she finally located what alerted him, she silently offered him points for sensitivity. The disturbance was so subtle, she wouldn't have given it a second thought.

"That." He directed a beam of their shared power.

"Aye, I already found it. Hold a moment. I'm not certain quite what we face."

"Whatever it is, it's right next to Mauvreen's, maybe even around her house. I can't tell from here."

"We're perhaps a quarter league from there." she murmured.

"Maybe a little less. My guess would be half a mile."

"Math." She rolled her eyes. "Never my favorite. How many miles in a league?"

"Three."

Britta probed the wrong-feeling place from every angle she could, but they weren't close enough. "We have to be nearer. 'Tis a good thing we dinna employ magic to get there. If we had, and there's truly a snare laid round the house—"

"We'd have fallen right into it," he cut in. "I get the picture. This way." He pointed down a side street. "We'll take alleyways until we're a couple blocks away."

It didn't take that long for Britta to understand what they were up against. She jerked on Jonathan's arm. "We stop here."

"Why? What'd you sense?" He drew to a halt and wound an arm around her.

She leaned into him for a moment, reveling in his warmth and solidness. Other than Tarika, she'd spent her life alone. "Dragon magic, no doubt summoned by one of the dark mages, surrounds Mauvreen's—"

"But she had her own warding system around that house," he cut in. "There's no way anything could've broken through it."

"Ye dinna let me finish," she said softly. "I sense her warding, and the other power sitting atop it. They're likely at a stalemate. Dark magic canna penetrate, yet whoever is inside canna leave, either."

"Crap!" He curled his free hand into a fist. "If one of those bastards hurts Mauvreen…"

"She's likely added to her warding. See if ye canna break through and talk with her." Britta waited, feeling power surge around Jonathan. The air simmered with an electrical charge, smelling of ozone mingled with the sea. He truly didn't appreciate how strong he was magically, but now wasn't the time to bring that up. It was unbelievable that even after all they'd gone through, he was still of two minds about his ability.

The glow around him dissipated, and he turned to her with his brows drawn into a thick, worried line. "Mauvreen's there. So are Lachlan and Maggie. Mary Elma went back to the States a few days ago to raise the covens on that side of the Atlantic."

"Keep talking. Between the three of them, they should've been able to find a way through." Britta chewed her lower lip, sure she wasn't going to like what came next.

"Lachlan's worse than useless. Maggie's been trying to get through to him, but he barricaded himself in the basement. Because she's distracted, and new to her power as well, she hasn't been much help to Mauvreen."

"Did she say how long since the dark barrier went up?"

"This morning. Why's that important?"

"It might not be, but I don't have much to work with, and I'll take all the information I can get." Britta bit harder on her lip, until she tasted blood.

"We have to do something," Jonathan blurted. "Mauvreen practically raised me."

"Aye, and I've known Lachlan for hundreds of years. I'll be damned if I can figure out why he's acting like a ninny with a broomstick up his ass."

Hands landed on her shoulders, and Jonathan shook her, but not hard. "You know exactly why. I felt your despair while I held you during our journey back from Cathbad's. You're strong, Britta. You had to be to defy convention and choose something other than a husband and marriage."

"Lachlan's strong too," she protested.

"Maybe in a different way. It sometimes takes men a while to decide they're going to stand and fight when they run into something that threatens them." He frowned. "If Lachlan is as welded to Kheladin as you are to Tarika, my guess is he's wondering if he'll be able to find a way to do anything without his dragon. You heard him describe how it felt when he ended up back in his own time, dragonless. He suffered terribly for the few hours before Kheladin showed up to resurrect their bond."

"Och aye, now ye mention that, I do recall it." She straightened her shoulders beneath Jonathan's hands. "Yet sinking into self-pity is a luxury he canna afford just now, not with two women depending on him."

Jonathan grinned, and then began to laugh.

"I fail to see what's so funny."

"The two women in question are kickass bitches. They're just as capable of taking care of Lachlan, which they're doing by the way, as he is of tending to them."

A snort made its way past her lips, followed by another, but she bit back laughter that wanted to follow. "Aye, I see your point. Meantime, what may fix this mess—and give us access to Lachlan so I can pound sense into his thick head—is if we attack the barrier from our side at the same time as Maggie and Mauvreen tackle it from within."

"What should I tell her? Mauvreen's waiting to hear back from me."

"We need to move a shred closer. Tell her to draw earth and fire five minutes from now and focus it on the portion of the barrier facing due south. We'll do the same from our side. That should be enough to blast a hole in it. Once we've established a weak point, ye and I can leverage it and blow the whole mess up."

He was silent as he communicated with the witch. Britta pictured Mauvreen with her corkscrew red curls and eyes the color of aged spirits. She liked the woman, respected her grit.

"Good to go." Jonathan lifted his hands from her shoulders. "Let's get into position."

Britta led them close enough to get a clear view of their target. The air surrounding the house pulsed with an unnatural brightness, but it must not be visible to mortal eyes or whatever passed for law enforcement would've shown up long since. Mauvreen lived in a stately three-story stone manse with ivy crawling up its sides. The witch's illusion made certain that passersby saw a whitewashed cottage at the end of a brick walkway, with wild roses growing rampant.

Innocuous enough, no one would look twice.

The combination of dual magics made the manse appear one moment, the cottage the next. Britta blinked to clear her earth eyes and dialed in her third eye so the manse stopped wavering in and out of view.

"On my count of three," she said.

Jonathan stood shoulder to shoulder with her, and his magic pulsed with hers. She counted down the last few seconds and loosed their combined energy, hoping it would be enough. The southern edge of the dark spell flashed so brightly, she hooded her eyes, grateful she had inner eyelids, just like her dragon.

"We did it!" Jonathan bellowed and heaved his magic into the fracture they'd created.

Marveling at power that could lay waste to the world, Britta shaped the flow blasting from him, focusing it until a muted explosion told her they'd accomplished their goal. "'Tis gone. At least for now."

"Wait."

"Why? We can go inside."

"I'm shoring up Mauvreen's casting so those bastards can't just roll on back through here and do the same thing again. If you help me, it'll go faster."

Britta reined in her anxiety to kick Lachlan's sorry ass from here to Ireland and bent to the task. It was actually a sound idea since it might keep them from being trapped once they set foot inside—if the rogue dragon shifter returned. She'd sensed that particular magic in the barrier as they dismantled it, but couldn't identify which dragon it belonged to. Tarika would've known, but she wasn't here.

Jonathan cut the flow of his power and dropped his hands to his sides. "Okay. That should hold them off—at least for a little while."

"It may not have been a *them*. I sensed a single rogue dragon shifter's hand behind this, none other."

"Fine. It'll stymie him for a while. Or her." Jonathan shot a mischievous grin her way. "I built a few booby traps into my working. They'll bite back if anyone fucks with them."

"A little trick ye learned from computer game design?" She quirked an impish brow.

"You might say that."

~

Jonathan curled a hand around her arm. "Let's go. I want to make certain everyone's all right." He vaulted for the house with Britta right next to him. At least the battle had shaken her out of her earlier funk. He'd felt helpless, cradling her against him in the time tunnel. Hadn't known what to say to comfort her. If Lachlan was sunk deeper than that, he worried the other dragon shifter might not be reachable.

Then he thought about Maggie. Granddaughter of the most powerful witch alive, she'd been worse than ambivalent about her power. Magic killed her parents; it was why she ended up being raised by her grandmother. Maggie made it clear from a very early age she wanted nothing to do with witchcraft or magic. She'd gone to medical school and was a practicing psychiatrist when Lachlan crossed her path.

Jonathan smiled to himself. Maggie's road to owning her magic was nearly as rocky as his. She caved after Rhukon dragged Lachlan back to the Middle Ages, and magic was the only way to get him back.

"Goddamned, fucking son of a bitch, but I'm glad to see you." Mauvreen flew down the stone steps leading to her front door and threw herself at Jonathan. Her wild red hair fell to her waist in a fiery tumble.

He closed his arms around her, grateful beyond words she was her normal, irascible self.

"We're glad to see you too," Britta said.

"Come on. Let's go inside." Mauvreen stepped back from Jonathan. "Christ, I'm glad you got over your hesitation over using your ability."

"Me too." Jonathan started after the woman he'd always considered his mother.

"Hold a moment," Britta said from the bottom of the steps.

"What?" Mauvreen twisted to face her, balanced between an

upper and a lower step. "We need to get Lachlan and Maggie and clear out of here before whoever trapped us does it again."

"Ye have time. Jonathan did something to your ward to strengthen it."

Mauvreen furled her brows his way. "You'll have to tell me about it, but not just now." She turned back to Britta. "Why'd you tell us to wait?"

"I need to know about Lachlan. As Jonathan would say, hit the high points so I understand how to approach him."

Mauvreen pressed her lips together. Her amber eyes glittered with concern. "I felt bad for him, but there wasn't a thing I could do. He and that dragon of his had a shouting match—bellowing match more like—in the side yard. Kheladin was crying; there's a pile of gems I could retire on laying in the grass if I can find time to collect them. Lachlan was crying too." She shook her head, and red curls flew every which way. "Damn if I know what it is about men and tears. Anyway, the dragon left. Lachlan stumbled back inside. Maggie tried to talk with him, but he shoved past her. It didn't take him long to find the way to the basement, and he barricaded himself in. That happened hours ago. Before whoever came and cast that hideous net over my house."

Mauvreen paused to take a breath. "I'll be goddamned if I've ever sensed quite that level of malevolence before. I did my best to counteract it. Maggie tried, but her heart wasn't in it since she's so worried about Lachlan—"

"'Tis enough." Britta nodded sharply. "I know what I need to do."

"Ye needn't do a thing," Lachlan's voice rumbled from the doorway. "I've come to my senses and am shamed I did nothing to help when Mauvreen and my mate faced a rogue dragon shifter. Kheladin would disown me if he knew."

"Thank God for small favors." Mauvreen blew out a frustrated-sounding breath before she made her way past him into her house.

Jonathan took the remaining steps two at a time. He extended his hand to Lachlan. After a lengthy pause, the dragon shifter took it. His green eyes held sadness, resignation. Tawny hair fell to his shoulders, and an old-fashioned tartan wound around his torso before it formed a kilt. Knee-high lace-up boots graced his feet.

Lachlan let go of his hand. "Come inside. If Maggie's not furious with me, we can leave."

"Maybe we could get some food while we're here?" Jonathan pushed the hopeful note out of his voice. Hours had passed since they last ate.

"We can do that," Mauvreen said from somewhere in front of him.

Jonathan followed Lachlan into the front room. Maggie stood before an enormous stone fireplace looking like one of the Valkyries. Her long, blonde hair was braided close to her head, and icy anger blasted from her blue eyes. Tall and lanky, she wore black trousers and a close-fitting navy blue shirt.

Mauvreen crossed the large room. Her low-heeled shoes clacked over hardwood floors, and beige skirts swirled around her full-figured frame. She laid a hand on Maggie's arm. "You inherited Mary Elma's temper."

Maggie doubled up her fist but stopped short of jamming it into either Mauvreen or the stones lining the fireplace. She jabbed her fist in Lachlan's direction. "He was about to walk away from everything we are to each other. From the prophecy that says if we're not together, Earth is doomed."

"I wasna. Not really. Ye overreacted. I've apologized." Lachlan inclined his head. "And more than once. I willna grovel."

"I did not *overreact*—" Fury streamed from Maggie in waves.

"We doona have time for this." Britta stepped between them and faced Lachlan. "I want my dragon back too, but we havena lost them yet. I went through the same despair and desolation ye feel. The only difference is I dinna have a place to run to. We came from Cathbad's, and we hatched the beginnings of a plan. Our task—Jonathan and I—was to collect you and go to Fire Mountain. We must talk the dragons out of their ill-conceived plan to shut their world off from all others."

Lachlan's green eyes lit with what looked like hope. "What are we waiting for? Ye can fill in details on the way."

"Hold up there. We need to wait for a few things to happen," Mauvreen said. "I assume we'll be embroiled in a full on battle before too long the way things are headed, and the witches' role needs fleshing out. If we leave, I have to let Mary Elma know. When she shows up here, she'll sense the debris from that shit-storm of magic and worry herself sick."

"Secondly," Jonathan broke in, "Lachlan and Maggie have to find a way through their pain. If they can't, the time shaft won't take them—maybe not the rest of us, either, if we're with them."

"Maggie, lass—" Lachlan began.

"Don't *lass* me," she snapped.

Mauvreen rolled her eyes and grabbed Maggie's arm. "I don't care how you figure this out, but you have ten minutes tops. We'll be outside."

She gestured to the others and headed for the curved front door.

"I'll meet you in front of the house," Jonathan said. "After I make a small detour through the kitchen."

"I'll help you." Britta followed him. "I'm fair starved myself."

"Fine." Mauvreen called after their backs. "I'll settle on the front stoop by myself. While I'm there, I'll come up with a few possibilities for how the witches can help—and maybe collect a few of Kheladin's gemstone tears."

"Thanks, Mauvreen." Jonathan pushed through the swinging door into the kitchen. High-ceilinged, it held a bank of leaded panes on one side that looked out on nearby mountain peaks. Oak cabinets, a center island, and stainless steel appliances spoke to a total remodel several years back.

"I like her," Britta said.

"She's pretty amazing," Jonathan agreed as he scooped food from cupboards and the refrigerator and dropped items into paper sacks.

They could eat on the front lawn while they strategized. "She'd come to Ireland and stay for weeks on end while Da was off in his own world. Closest thing to a mother I had, but I play that card close to the vest when Arianrhod's around."

"Wise of you. Guilt and jealousy are not good bedfellows." Britta crinkled her nose with knowing amusement. She reached into a cupboard before he could close it and grabbed another box of crackers. "Arianrhod means well, but in her mind, ye're still the lad in nappies she left with Angus."

His upbeat mood sobered. He grabbed the bags he'd filled and ushered Britta out the back door. "Arianrhod will get past that soon enough. It's impossible to fight next to someone and still see them as a helpless toddler." He gestured with his chin since his hands were full. "We can walk around the house. That way, we won't disturb Lachlan and Maggie."

"At least they're not screaming at one another." Britta followed his lead out the door.

Jonathan turned to smile at her. "Yeah, let's hope it's because they're kissing and making up."

$\mathcal{A}$rianrhod trod gently, winding her way among the stacks of gold and jewels that comprised Eletea's hoard. The dragon led them ever deeper into an undulating cave system, and Arianrhod dialed a few more lumens into her mage light after she tripped over a pile of gold coins from a much earlier time. The dragon glowed, but she was far enough ahead, it didn't help.

Angus walked behind her. "I've been in dragon caves before," he said softly, "but never one where they actually lived."

"So ye've not seen a hoard afore?"

"Nay. Pretty impressive."

Arianrhod laughed. "What's truly impressive is watching what happens if ye disturb so much as a single minor gemstone. It may not appear there's any order to these items, but Eletea knows exactly where each belongs."

"Indeed I do, goddess," rang from ahead of them.

"How do you keep track of everything?" Angus asked.

"It's a dragon thing. When I add something to my treasure, it registers in my mind. If the thing moves, I know it—and act accordingly."

"Do you ever tire of things and get rid of them?" Angus almost ran up against Arianrhod's back since she'd stopped in a smallish cave where Eletea spun to face them. The sheep she'd told them about lay off to one side, a pile of picked-clean bones on the other. Unlike the tunnels leading to the cave, this one didn't contain treasure.

"Dragons never downsize," Eletea declared. "Do you want to work on the sheep while we talk? If you don't have a use for the guts, toss them my way."

Angus walked to the carcass. He drew a knife from a sheath hanging from his waist and went to work.

Arianrhod settled on a large, flat boulder that was a convenient height. "Did ye tell the other dragon, Jaek I believe ye called him, about the Morrigan's visit?"

"Of course not," Eletea replied. "If I had, he'd have dragged me away from here bodily, no matter what I wanted, and sorted out the pieces later."

"Tell me everything the Morrigan said." Arianrhod crossed her arms beneath her breasts and glanced at Angus. "Do ye need help?"

He looked up from stripping skin and thick, matted fur off the sheep. "Nay. Eventually, I'll need fire, but not for a while."

"I can supply that." Eletea sent flames shooting upward, followed by steam. Both disappeared far above them, lost in the cave's high ceiling. "Now I've thought about it," the dragon went on. "The Morrigan must be building an army of dragon shifters. She told me my power would increase a hundredfold if I bonded with a human mage."

"Did she say aught of the dragons planning to close Fire Mountain?" Arianrhod narrowed her eyes.

"She did, but she inferred I'd be a fool to throw my lot in with them because I'd be stuck there forever." Eletea shifted position to the accompaniment of clanking scales. "She guessed correctly that I'm not fond of Fire Mountain. Many of my kin don't care for it, either. Too confining. Nothing to do. A landscape that never changes."

Arianrhod worked to smother a grin, but it found its way out anyway. She uncrossed her arms and placed them behind her, leaning on them, palms on the earthen wall. "Ye sound like youth everywhere."

"I'm not that young," the dragon protested.

"Doesna matter. Go on."

"Not much more to tell." Eletea twisted her head to glance at Angus holding a stack of meat. "Put it on those stones just there."

"Thanks." He laid several pieces of mutton where she'd indicated and straightened. "I'll be right back. I'm going outside to rinse my hands in the creek." The clack of boot soles on stone faded as he retraced their steps from earlier.

The dragon focused fire at the stones until they heated and the meat began to sizzle. "If there's a way to trap the Battle Crow and deliver her to Fire Mountain, I'm not seeing it."

"Agreed. There aren't enough of us." Arianrhod creased her forehead in thought. "How do ye feel about pretending to go along with her plan?"

The dragon's eyes whirled faster. "You mean be a spy?"

"'Tis exactly what I mean." She leaned toward the dragon, then changed her mind and got to her feet so she could walk next to her. "'Tis dangerous, yet 'twould give us important information."

"Like how many dark mages have formed a bond with dragons."

"Aye, and how the Morrigan plans to leverage them." Arianrhod sketched out Cathbad's prediction about dragons taking Earth's magic when they shuttered themselves in Fire Mountain. "My guess —and 'tis just that, a guess—is the Battle Crow figured something out to countermand the gradual draining of at least her magic and those linked to her."

"How could she do that?" Eletea blasted the cooking stones with more fire.

Arianrhod walked to where the meat crackled and smoked, and bent to turn the pieces. "I have no fucking idea, which is why having you inveigle your way into her inner circle would be verra helpful."

"I heard the last of that." Angus trotted briskly into the inner cave. "I don't agree with using Eletea in that way."

"But I want to help," the dragon protested.

"Surely there are ways that don't involve putting yourself right in the line of fire," he countered and sent a reproachful glance skittering Arianrhod's way.

"Be reasonable." She spread her hands in front of her. "If ye see a better way, I'm open to it."

"Do you think the Morrigan will allow Eletea free rein to come and go once she's been indoctrinated into whatever the Crow's inner circle knows?" He forged ahead without waiting for her to answer. "For all we know, the invitation was a trap. She won't have forgotten we rescued Eletea from Rhukon and Connor. I'm certain they shared that information with the Morrigan long before they died. Come to think of it, they wouldn't have had to say a word. The Morrigan showed up while you fought—and killed—them and their dragons."

"Mmph. Aye, 'twas when I hauled her back to face the Celts—and they let her go. I hadna considered that angle, though I should've." Arianrhod made her way to the meat. She poked it and moved it to cooler stones off to one side. "'Tis done enough."

"I still think it's a good idea," Eletea said.

"Not if it means your death, it's not," Angus retorted. He picked up a piece of meat and bit off a morsel, blowing on his fingers to cool them.

"I'm sure I could wriggle my way out."

Arianrhod shook her head. "Nay. Angus is right. If ye were surrounded by dark mages and their dragons and the Crow, ye'd have Hell's own trouble extricating yourself." She stuck her knife blade into a chunk of mutton, chewing and swallowing as she considered an alternate plan.

"The safest route is for all of us to be gone before the Morrigan returns." Angus picked up another piece of meat.

"I'm not going to run," Eletea announced.

"Battles are built on strategy," Arianrhod told her. "Betimes the best strategy isn't direct confrontation—particularly not against that one."

Angus handed sheep bones and guts to the dragon, who crunched them down. "We really only have two choices. Try to get reinforcements before the Crow drops in or leave."

"Guess again," a cheery falsetto trilled from the front end of the cave system.

"Goddammit!" Arianrhod dropped the uneaten part of her meat next to her and turned to face the Morrigan.

The crow shimmered into one of her human guises—a medieval noblewoman with long black hair and a low cut gown—at the entrance to Eletea's living quarters. "Dinner? How lovely. Surely ye doona mind if I help myself." She brushed past Arianrhod and grabbed a piece of mutton that she shoved into her mouth.

"Ye brought your crow manners, I see," Arianrhod muttered.

"Och, and what does it matter?" The Morrigan snapped up another piece of meat.

"This is a dragon's home." Eletea drew herself tall. "I didn't invite you in, and you're not welcome here."

"Nice try." The Morrigan didn't even look up from shoveling the remaining mutton into her mouth.

Eletea shot flames between the Morrigan's hands and the pile of meat.

"Why you sorry excuse for a reptile." The Morrigan pulled her hands back, rubbing reddened places on them. "And here I tried to do you a favor."

"For the love of the goddess, spare us your lies." Arianrhod exhaled a weary breath. Dealing with the Battle Crow was tiring on a good day, and impossibly draining when she wasn't prepared for it. "Ye set a trap for Eletea. Ye never had any intention of helping her. Plus, the shifter bond with a dark mage siphons power from the dragon, weakening it over time. Eletea knows that, as does the Dragon Council."

"Funny they dinna do aught about it." The Morrigan smirked. "They were told close to forty years back according to my informants."

Another gout of flame landed close enough to the Morrigan her skirts caught fire. Rather than batting them out, the Crow took her native form with an ominous snap of her beak. "Fire canna hurt me," she informed the dragon. "Save your ammunition."

The dragon's eyes whirled so fast they became a hypnotic blur. Arianrhod forced her gaze away, but was slow on the uptake. By the time she figured out the dragon had skidded past a boiling point, she'd launched herself at the Morrigan with fire, scales, and claws.

The Crow spread her wings, screeching. She flew at the dragon, attacking with her razor-sharp beak, but didn't make any progress against Eletea's scales. The cave filled with smoke, steam, and fire until Arianrhod's eyes stung, and it burned to breathe. Between the shrieking crow and the bugling dragon, her ears ached until she drew magic to protect them. While she was at it, she erected a protective bubble around herself and Angus to clear the air.

"Shit!" Angus exuded pure fury. Rage crackled from his eyes in hot jets of menace. "We have to help her."

"Aye, and our best bet is magic. We're going to cast a sleeping spell."

"But that'll knock them both out."

Arianrhod dragged Angus closer to the wall to avoid being crushed by Crow and dragon as they hurtled across the room, glued together in mortal combat. "Do ye have a better idea?" she growled. "We canna separate them. At least then, we can move Eletea out of here."

"She wouldn't want to leave her hoard with the Morrigan."

"If the Crow is stupid enough to help herself, she deserves whatever happens to her. I canna do this alone." She pressed her mouth into a worried line. "Hell, I'm not certain I can do it joined to you, yet 'tis the only alternative I see."

"At least this gets us out of Eletea's misguided desire to masquerade as a dragon in search of a mage."

"There is that," she agreed and gathered power. "I'm sorry I suggested she put herself at such grave risk. Ye control earth, let me take care of fire."

"If you want them unconscious, I'll draw on water more than earth."

"Whatever ye need. Watch the barrier around us, since this willna do any good if we turn into Sleeping Beauty too. On my count of three…"

Arianrhod added a tracking element to their spell since it had to catch the battling pair before it could incapacitate them. The elemental mixture flew across the room, and a muted boom rocked the cave until dirt and stones fell about her. To be on the safe side, she called a second casting to make certain the structure didn't collapse—at least not until after they were out of it. Too bad if Eletea lost her treasure, but a serious cave-in would stop the Morrigan for a goodly amount of time.

After she woke up.

The sounds of battle ceased abruptly, but the cave was still so full of smoke, it was hard to see. Arianrhod didn't wait around. She withdrew her magic, refocusing and shaping it to a different purpose. Without instruction, Angus sensed what she needed and added strength to her mix. Damn, he was talented at shaping earth and water, particularly water. Maybe it was his Druidic bloodline.

"Found her," Angus called from somewhere inside the smoky murk the cave had become.

"Excellent. I'm ready and linked with you. Keep your hand on her as an anchor, and I'll get us out of here."

The cave walls shimmered, replaced by clean air outside. She sucked it in hungrily, willing it to soothe her smoke-scoured lungs. Angus and the dragon plopped down by her side.

"How long will she be out?" Angus gestured toward the dragon.

"Only until I spin a counter spell." Arianrhod scooted next to the dragon. She laid a hand on her head, chanting softly, and reached inside the creature's mind, careful not to get snared by the complexity of Eletea's memories.

"Come back," she urged. "Now. We doona have much time."

The dragon bucked beneath her touch. Scaled lids snapped open, and she rocked upright woozily. "Where are we? What happened? Where's the Crow?" She spun about wildly, her gaze raking the Scottish moorlands.

"I'll answer all your questions." Arianrhod tossed compulsion into her words, too tired to be subtle about it. "For now, trust me enough to believe me when I tell you we must leave."

"I'm not leaving that bitch in my cave with my hoard."

"Aye." Angus strode to her side. "You must. There's no other choice. Not really. The Crow's not stupid enough to take anything from a dragon. That would earn her the enmity of every single dragon on earth."

The frantic set of Eletea's shoulders softened. "You're right. I'm not thinking. Other dragons would know. They'd see it in her mind. It pains me to say it, but it'd help our cause if she did take something." More smoke, steam, fire. "Fine. Take me wherever, and we can sort it out from there."

Arianrhod thought fast. They needed food, rest. "We'll go to my home. 'Tisn't far from here, and it's shrouded in so many layers of illusion, no one will be able to penetrate them. Not even the Crow. Join your magic to mine, both of you. Otherwise, you'll never make it past my wards."

"How long do you think that one," Angus jerked his chin toward Eletea's cave, "will remain dead to the world?"

"Hard to say." Arianrhod grinned. "Let's not stick around to find out." She inhaled deeply, still working to cleanse her lungs of the taint from the cave. Though she felt drained, tapped out, still she couldn't let her guard down. Not yet. Chanting determinedly, she forced power to her bidding, grateful beyond words when dragon magic roared into her, followed by Angus's unique energy signature.

Full to bursting with fresh magic, she loosed her spell and breathed easier when the white-washed walls of her castle rose around them. Before she relaxed entirely, she sent power spinning in a wide arc to make certain they were alone.

Good.

No one had breached her home's defenses since she left. "Be it ever so humble..." She mock bowed and led the way up a dozen broad steps into the sixteenth century castle.

She stared around the great room, appreciating its simplicity. She'd never gone for the opulent wall hangings or rich carpets the other Celts preferred. Her home boasted gray flagstone floors with the occasional throw rug to give chilled toes a break. Fireplaces graced every room, and she used them for heat, rather than installing more modern central heating, because she preferred the crackle of wood to the *whoosh* of a forced air fan. Her manor house could've housed a hundred. There were rooms she hadn't laid eyes on in centuries. Mostly, she shuttled between the great room, the kitchens, her bedroom, and the room where she kept her bows and knifes. Guns had come into fashion, but she didn't care for them. Too noisy and bulky for her taste.

"Fascinating." Eletea craned her long neck as she took in the castle's interior. "I always wondered what these old rock piles looked like from the inside."

"It's amazing," Angus said and strode to Arianrhod's side where he drew her into a quick hug. "I can't wait to see the rest. This place looks enormous."

She snorted. "It is. I'm afraid the grand tour will have to wait. Follow me to the kitchens. We'll eat and map out what to do next." Arianrhod narrowed her eyes, gauging the dragon's height. "Ye'll have to bend a bit to get through yon archway at the end of this room. Other than that, ye should fit handily."

"I'm not worried. I don't suppose you have anything raw where we're going. All that magic I expended made me hungry."

"I'm sure I can find something if ye doona mind it being frozen."

"Blech." Eletea twisted her face into a grimace that showed her double rows of teeth. "Waste of good meat, but I can thaw it quick enough."

"Come on then." Arianrhod trotted the length of the great room. She moved beneath the arch at its end and down a long hall leading to half a flight of stairs that would spit them out in the kitchens, though she'd only used the primary room for many years.

"I understand why we're eating." Angus caught up with her. "But we should go straight to Fire Mountain after that."

"We may. But the Morrigan is here. If I can alert Ceridwen and the others in time, mayhap they can capture her from Eletea's cave."

Angus pushed the door open for her, and then continued to hold it for the dragon. Arianrhod turned to make certain she didn't need to help, but one advantage of Eletea's relatively small size was she was lithe. Convinced the dragon would be fine, Arianrhod ran lightly ahead to lay out something to eat so all of them could replenish their strength.

"Did you try to reach Ceridwen?" Angus strode into the kitchen's main room.

Arianrhod was gathering cheese, crackers, and wine from various places and piling them on a long counter. "Nay. My magic is depleted, but 'tis my first task once I have enough ability to do more than cast a mage light."

"Where's this frozen meat place?" the dragon stood dead in the center of the kitchen gazing about.

Arianrhod stifled a grin. "I'll grab you something. Do ye have a preference between beef, chicken, or pork?"

A faraway look flickered behind the dragon's eyes. "Beef, please. The farmers get so riled up whenever I kill cows that I stopped eating them."

"Bet they blame the local wolves." Angus quirked a brow.

Eletea's shoulder's sagged. "Indeed they do. I couldn't live with myself if they murdered another one because of something I'd done."

"Here." Arianrhod tossed several packages wrapped in butcher paper on the table. "Have at it. There's more where that came from."

Eletea closed on the meat as if it were a holy object, cracking through the paper with a sharp talon. "Thank you."

"Doona mention it."

"Do we get anything more substantial than cheese and crackers?" Angus came around to swap her rump.

"We could." She eyed him. "If ye wouldna treat me like a common tavern wench."

"Let me help you make us something." He buried his face in her neck and kissed her.

"Food," she clarified, moving away from his touch. His lips thrilled her, but if she gave in to the desire heating her blood, they'd never eat, and she wouldn't get around to raising Ceridwen until it was too late—

"Of course I meant food. You have a dirty mind."

"'Tis one of the reasons ye fell in love with me."

"I won't argue with that. Now how about some of that beef Eletea's swooning over sliced up with whatever you have for vegetables in a stir-fry?"

She munched down a cracker with cheese on it. "Sure. Pour some wine for us, then ye can teach me what a stir-fry is. I've never heard of such a thing."

"Is it quick?" The dragon looked up from a piece of bloody, dripping beef.

"Aye, quickest meal I know," Angus replied. "Don't worry. I want the Morrigan's head as much as you do."

The dragon smiled showing bloodied teeth. Arianrhod stared hard, hoping the grisly chunks of raw beef weren't a harbinger of what would happen next.

CHAPTER 9

Mauvreen was walking in small circles talking on her cell phone when Jonathan came around the corner of the stone manse, with Britta just behind him. It was still night, and he called a muted mage light to illuminate their path. Telepathy wasn't terribly effective over long distances, so he assumed Mary Elma or one of the other highly placed witches in the U.S. was on the other end of the line.

Mauvreen pursed her lips into a scowl. "Not particularly welcome news. I'll be in touch." She tapped her phone's display and slipped it into one of many pockets in her voluminous skirts.

"Nothing good, I gather." Jonathan settled on the lowest of the front steps and dug into the grocery bags for cheese and an apple.

Britta settled next to him. Pulling a knife from a waist-sheath, she carved cheese off the hunk in his hand and proceeded to munch on it. Once she'd swallowed, she glanced Mauvreen's way. "Are ye going to tell us what new thing's gone awry?"

"I may as well eat too. God knows when I'll get another chance." Mauvreen scooted closer and peered into both shopping bags, extracting a bag of dried figs and some almonds. "Apparently rogue dragon shifters have been living in the States too."

"Impossible." Britta spoke around a mouthful of crackers.

"If it's impossible, why'd Mary Elma end up in a flame war with half a dozen of them?" Mauvreen cocked her head to one side.

"Was anyone hurt?" Jonathan asked.

"Of course." Mauvreen bit off the words. "Those fuckers are immortal. We lost four witches." She shook her head. "Things haven't truly even begun yet, and already we've sustained losses. It doesn't bode well."

"Nay. It doesna." Britta chewed thoughtfully. "Betwixt Tarika and me, I thought we were aware of most dragon shifter pairs. Certainly the Dragon Council knows all of them."

"Are you sure about that?" Mauvreen narrowed her eyes. "They may be aware of all the sanctioned pairings, but how about the other ones?"

"If ye mean like Rhukon and Connor, they at least pretended to be working the right side of the street."

"Maybe there's a bunch that didn't bother." Mauvreen dropped the figs back into one of the food sacks. "Christ, but I wish to hell we knew more. It would help direct our next moves. Right now, we're flying blind."

Fury roiled through Jonathan, curdling the food in his gut. He wanted all the grim details of what happened to Mary Elma's witches, but that would burn up time. Time they might not have. Maybe he could collect information the same way Angus did—via dreams. Glean something to make the big picture clearer.

He looked from Mauvreen to Britta. "I'm not certain I can communicate with Da or Cathbad through trance states, but maybe I should try. Cathbad knows things. It's possible something new cropped up that might help us."

"Do ye have any idea how to go about that?" Britta asked.

Well, do I?

"I do." Mauvreen's voice held harsh overtones. "Fire and blood. If Jonathan inherited Angus's gift, the rest will happen naturally."

"You have to say more." Jonathan leaned forward, hands clasped in front of him.

"Build a fire with magic, and then open both arms to allow your blood to mingle with the flames. I watched Angus do it enough times. The slits are here." She mimicked horizontal cuts across her inner arm. "And here." She made two more slice marks about two inches lower, just above her wrists.

"Are ye certain about it?" Britta cast a suspicious glance Mauvreen's way.

"Sure as I can be about anything." A corner of her mouth twisted into a wry grin. "Look here, Missy. I loved him long before you came into his life. I'm not likely to suggest anything that might harm him."

"Wonder how Lachlan and Maggie are doing?" Jonathan craned his head around to look at the house. "I may not know much about wielding power, but I at least want to make certain negative energy isn't floating about to muck things up."

"I'll go look." Britta got to her feet. "'Twill give me a chance to speak with Lachlan, and make certain his sorrow over the specter of losing Kheladin isna still clouding his judgment."

Jonathan looked up at her. "How are you doing with the same problem?"

She shrugged, looking uncomfortable. "'Tisn't easy. The pain comes and goes. When fear that I'll lose my bond threatens to blind me, I remind myself she and I are still linked. I canna believe the Dragon Council will truly force every dragon to renounce their mages. Most dragons that are well-bonded will fight such a move."

"Hope you're right about that," Mauvreen muttered.

Britta didn't answer, just turned and trudged up the stairs. The door snicked open and then latched shut behind her.

Jonathan laid a hand on Mauvreen's arm. "It's bad isn't it? I haven't done much with the covens here or with my magic, but this seems cataclysmic."

She nodded slowly. "You never asked, so I never told you, but

I've been around since the early seventeen hundreds. Witches have faced many trials—burning, hanging, ostracism—but those were at the hands of humans. We've never dealt with other magical beings out for our blood."

"Did Mary Elma say why they attacked? Presumably, the dark mages have been there all along, even if we didn't know about them. What changed?"

"If I had to guess, it's Maggie's link to that fucking prophecy. Someone—likely the Morrigan—made certain every single dark mage knows that so long as Maggie and Lachlan are linked, they'll never prevail."

"What? So they're picking off people Maggie loves to make her angry, draw her out?"

"Best explanation I can come up with. Thank Christ, Mary Elma's still very much alive." She paused, and then lowered her voice. "I wasn't kidding when I told Maggie she inherited Mary Elma's temper. She lost her parents in a magical war. If anything happens to her grandmother, I can see her tearing the world apart to extract revenge. Lachlan would do his damnedest to protect her, but if you keep taking chances—"

"—eventually you get burned," he finished for her. "What do you think we should do?"

"The covens in the States have their hands full. I need to round up the ones here and across the North Sea in Europe. Best we can do against something immortal is defensive magic. So maybe hunkering down and conserving our power until they attack us may be wisest." She paused for a beat, clearly thinking. "I like your idea about mining the dream world for data."

"I'll give it a try once Britta's back. In the meantime, I haven't ever told you how much you always being there meant to me when I was growing up. Thank you."

Her amber eyes sheened with tears, but Mauvreen was tough and none of them spilled over. "The best way to thank me is by staying alive."

"That's pretty high on my list too." He twisted toward the house at the sound of the front door opening.

BRITTA TRAIPSED out of the house behind Lachlan and Maggie.

They'd indeed made up and seemed none the worse for Lachlan's meltdown. He managed to pull himself together and told her with conviction he'd never be parted from Kheladin, if he had to dismantle Fire Mountain stone by stone. She didn't voice her thoughts, which were that he underestimated the Dragon Council's ability to shape reality to their liking. Dragons were a force best not taken lightly.

Lachlan made it to the bottom of the steps and bowed low in front of Mauvreen. "Again, I apologize. My behavior makes a mockery of your hospitality. I shall not cause you further problems."

"Me either." Maggie bent and kissed Mauvreen's cheek. "Did you talk to grandma?"

"Yeah. It's not good. Dragon shifters wiped out a few witches in the States. It might be a while before Mary Elma gets freed up enough to jump back across the pond."

"Dragon shifters in the United States?" Lachlan's nostrils flared in disbelief. "I dinna think such a thing was possible."

"Aye, and I said much the same," Britta chimed in.

"The energy is wrong," Lachlan said with conviction. "Too new, too brash. It wouldna support the right kind of magic for the dragon shifter bond to flourish—if ye could even find any mages who studied long enough for a dragon to accept them, which I doubt."

Britta nodded to herself. She'd known it wasn't possible, but hadn't been able to pinpoint why. "That explains one thing," she spoke up.

"What?" Jonathan and Mauvreen asked in unison. The impact of their combined gazes was mildly unsettling.

"The only kind of dragon shifter pairings in the States are dark mages, and I'll bet they lured the dragons there for just that purpose. Dragons avoid the newer parts of Earth. Ye'll find them here and in Europe and China and other places where complex civilizations date back thousands of years, but not elsewhere."

"Do you know why?" Jonathan frowned. Britta knew him well enough to understand he was trying to make sense of the information.

"Ask Tarika when we see her next. She'll know," Britta said with more conviction than she felt. If the goddess was very, very good to them, her bond with the dragon would emerge from chaos unscathed.

"I'll make a point of it." Jonathan got to his feet and trotted to Britta's side. "We will not lose her. You have to believe."

"Same thing I told him." Maggie thumped Lachlan's chest with her forefinger.

"Moving forward," Jonathan cut in. "I'm going to do what I can to communicate with Cathbad or my Da."

"How will ye do that?" Curiosity lined Lachlan's green eyes. "Are ye a dreaming seer like them?"

"Possibly."

"No time like the present to find out." Mauvreen stood and started up the stairs.

Britta hooked her arm through Jonathan's. "I want to watch and see how this works."

"We do too." Lachlan snapped up the food bags. "I'll watch over these."

"Hey!" Maggie elbowed him. "I'm hungry too. Yelling is hard work."

"I dinna say I wasna going to share," he protested.

Britta made shooing motions with the hand that wasn't attached to Jonathan. "Move. Sooner we toss this ball in the air, the sooner we'll discover if it buys us aught."

They made their way inside. Britta took an extra few moments to add an additional layer of shielding around the house. If she understood correctly, Jonathan would be helpless in trance—his soul walking free from his body—and she wanted to ensure they weren't disturbed.

Mauvreen waited for them near the massive stone fireplace in her living room. Large enough to accommodate half a steer, its soot-blackened stones rose to the twelve-foot ceiling. She looked askance at them. "You can all stay, but you must be absolutely silent —no matter what."

Murmurs of assent filled the air, and she beckoned Jonathan forward. "Take your shirt off. It makes things easier."

"You just want to see me naked."

"I said shirt, not the whole shebang." She sent an indulgent, maternal glance his way. "You are quite a striking specimen, though."

"He's mine!" Britta put out her hand and took the shirt Jonathan removed, laying it over the back of a chair.

"No one's challenging your right to him, particularly given that dragon bite on his neck." Mauvreen focused a variant of her maternal warmth Britta's way. It made her want to smile and hug the witch, but she stayed out of the way.

Mauvreen pointed to the cold hearth. "First, call on your power and get a fire going. It doesn't have to be very big because once we get your blood flowing, it'll maintain it."

"Will I need more tinder than is in there?" Jonathan asked.

"Probably not."

"Ye'll need that hair up and out of the way." Britta ran lightly to his side. She didn't want to take the time to braid his hair, so she smoothed it back, tying it in a queue at the base of his neck with a length of leather she fished out of a pocket.

Mauvreen smiled approvingly. "Good call. Hair burns, and sometimes this casting calls the flames higher than you expect. Think I'll get my own out of harm's way. She bunched her thick, unruly hair into a rough ponytail and wrapped something stretchy around it.

"What's that?" Britta asked, fingering the leather substitute.

"It's called a scrunchy. Jonathan, get that fire going."

He knelt in front of the cold hearth and chanted softly. Hesitant at first, a tongue of flame finally leapt upward, followed by another. The cold, gray light of dawn crept through the room's many windows, illuminating his bare torso.

Britta could've stared at him forever. Such a beautiful man with his coal black hair and broad, well-shaped shoulders. Muscle corded down his arms and flowed across his flat abdomen, disappearing into the waistband of his pants.

"What next, Mauvreen?" Jonathan asked, never taking his attention from the fire.

Britta felt the power he fed to the flames, urging them to bite into the wood.

"Take the dirk from your belt and make shallow cuts on the inside of your forearms exactly where I showed you."

He drew the knife firmly across his flesh. The blade was sharp because blood welled immediately. He stared at the red line, transfixed. Where it dripped into the flames, they shot upward, almost as if his blood summoned their compliance.

"Be quick about it," Mauvreen hissed. "You must make all four cuts before the trance takes you away from this room."

She had to say it again before Jonathan wielded the knife, deepening the original cut and following it with three more. A sweet smell filled the room. Britta sniffed, drawing it into her lungs as she worked to determine what it was. Familiar, yet not. The closest she could come was mead, spiced to the hilt with wildflowers, anise, mint, and cinnamon.

A breathy sigh, almost a moan, rose from Jonathan before he slumped forward, his arms still dripping blood into the willing flames. They danced, twirled, formed shapes and colors, as if his blood fed their essence.

Alarmed, Britta started forward, but Mauvreen was faster and closed an iron grip around her arm. "You can't disturb him. If you do, his soul could be trapped somewhere we couldn't retrieve it."

Britta shook herself, feeling like a stupid fool. She understood the dynamics of soul-walking. "Sorry," she muttered and pulled her arm from Mauvreen's grasp. "How long will he be like that?"

The other woman shrugged. "Hard to say. Angus had trance states that were over and done with in a quarter hour. Others lasted far longer."

"What can we do?" she asked.

"Nothing," Mauvreen replied. "We stand watch over his body and wait."

JONATHAN TUMBLED DOWN A LONG, dark well. Light waited at the bottom, but it took all his self-control not to grapple for the slick sides of the circular structure to slow his trajectory.

It's like a computer game. I have to believe the troll won't get me.

He grinned to himself and shot out the tunnel feet first into a cavern with smoky sconces lining the walls. True to his hopes, he slowed at the end and floated the last few feet. A turquoise pool lay in the center of the cave with steam rising from it, suggesting it was warm. Stone benches circled the pool and after he turned in a full circle, he spied Cathbad lounging on one.

He started toward the Druidic seer. "What is this place?"

"One of many dreamer's grottos. Most of the others aren't this commodious." Cathbad straightened from his slouch and extended a hand.

Jonathan gripped it. "I'll indulge myself in amazement that I can do this later. Tell me what changed since we left your world."

Cathbad shook his head. "That would take far too long. Ye canna remain for more than a few minutes, not your first time, not if ye wish to ensure your soul finds your body again. When ye've done this more, ye'll be able to stay longer."

Jonathan sat next to the seer. "Tell me what I need to know."

Cathbad bent toward him as if he feared prying ears might be close. "I doona know how the Morrigan accomplished this, nor does it matter. She made another trip through Hell and strengthened her alliance with the Furies. While there, she added other Infernals to the mix."

"Like who?" Jonathan racked his brain, trying to remember his mythology.

"Circe, Medea, Hecate, Tantalus, Ixion. The list is long. She'll have access to Gryphons and Harpies and other abominations too."

"Do you know why?" Jonathan bit hard on his lower lip to keep it from trembling. He was furious more than scared.

Yeah, just keep telling myself that. I'm in so far over my head, it's not even funny.

Cathbad sent a sharply appraising glance his way. "If ye werena frightened, ye'd be worse than a fool. The Morrigan gathers power like maidens collect suitors. She thrives on chaos and plans to take full advantage of the dragons' outrage to wrest control of Earth for herself and her cronies. 'Tis what she promised them for their complicity with her demands."

"Why aren't they smart enough to see through her? Christ! I see her for the power-mad bitch she is. Why can't they?"

"Because they're just as conniving as she is, and they thrive on power and control. Your time is nearly up."

"What can we do about it?"

Cathbad drew his brows together. "I've dreamed many possibilities. The only ones that end well include an alliance with the dragons. Ye must get them to throw their lot in with you."

Jonathan inhaled raggedly and then did it again. The task felt hopeless. From what little he'd seen, dragons couldn't give a rat's ass for anything that didn't directly benefit them.

"Exactly." Cathbad patted Jonathan's shoulder, having obviously been inside his head. "Your task is to make them understand it's not to their benefit to barricade themselves inside Fire Mountain until the world ends."

"Easier said than done."

"Nothing worthwhile ever came easy. Seek me out again when ye have need of me."

The smoky cavern dissolved into grimy motes of ash that choked him. He settled back into his body with an unsettling *thunk* that made nausea rise in his gorge. His head spun and he moaned as he gripped the fire-warmed stones of Mauvreen's hearth.

"Leave him be." Mauvreen's sharp voice, the one nobody argued with, shot into his head like a cannon blast. "He'll come around in a few minutes."

CHAPTER 10

$\mathcal{A}$ngus drained the last of the wine from his glass and set it down. A soft snore drew his attention to Eletea, who'd curled in a satisfied circle of scales after consuming what looked like a quarter of a cow.

Arianrhod placed a finger over her lips in the universal sign for silence and beckoned to him. He got up, careful to make as little noise as possible, and followed her out of the kitchen and up the stairs to the great room.

"Poor thing," Arianrhod murmured once he joined her. "She must be exhausted."

"We all are," he replied. "Yet, there's no rest in sight. None that I can see, anyway. Did you try to raise Ceridwen?"

"Not yet. It's only in the last verra few minutes I've had enough magic to try." Her lips curved into a wry grin. "'Tisn't like I'm a bonny lass of a hundred anymore. I burned through a lot of power, and it takes time to replenish."

He circled his arms around her and drew her against him. "You'll always be my *bonny lass*. Gods, I missed you." He kneaded the tense muscles in her neck and shoulders, feeling her melt into him.

"Aye, I missed you too." She wriggled out of his embrace. "Stop that. I need to concentrate."

"I could bend the dream world to reach her through that cauldron of hers."

"It may come to that." Arianrhod walked to the far end of the room and stopped, placing both hands on the black-veined marble lintel above the fireplace. "Give me a moment."

Angus gazed hungrily at her as she stood, head thrown back, eyes closed. Her silver hair, half in and half out of braids, brushed the floor in places. Her leather garments outlined her muscled frame. Broad shoulders led to full breasts, and her narrow waist set off flared hips to perfection. For once, she had neither quiver nor bow, and he wondered why she'd left her home without them. As he sifted through memories, he realized he'd never seen her without them—except when he visited her and Jonathan in the sea.

Her face took on a drawn look, and she opened her eyes as she turned to face him, hands clasped before her. "I found her. And told her."

"And?" Angus prodded. "Will we return to the cave to help corral the Morrigan?"

"I wish 'twere that simple. The Morrigan managed a distress call —even while unconscious—and some Celts responded. Once there, they instituted a counter spell and freed her."

The implications sank in, and Angus battled fury that turned his guts to a mass of writhing snakes. "Who?" he demanded. "Who'd be so irresponsible to—?"

Arianrhod made a chopping motion with one hand. "Either she doesna know, or she isna telling me."

"Likely the latter. Once you told me she knew everything." Angus crossed the space between them until he stood toe-to-toe with Arianrhod. The air surrounding her simmered with discontent. Restless displeasure shot from her, jabbing him with small darts as her temper kindled.

"I dinna forget. Apparently, she doesna want us to get in the way."

"Of what? Last I checked, we were on the same side." Angus ground his teeth together. This was getting worse and worse. He'd never cared for the Celts. How could he? They'd lied to him, used him, but this was ridiculous. Ceridwen needed all the help she could scare up. What the fuck was wrong with letting them in on whatever next steps she was planning?

"It doesna make me happy, either, yet she doesna see the world that way."

"What way?" He felt confused, and then he understood. "Fine. You were in my head."

Arianrhod narrowed her multi-hued eyes. "Have we backslid to where I need permission?"

"Never mind." His back felt like someone had inserted a steel rod from the middle of his shoulders to his ass, and he rotated his shoulder blades. "Do we have orders?"

"What do ye mean?"

"It's clear enough. Gwydion and the others gave me instructions. What did Ceridwen tell us to do?"

"Nothing. She said she'd be in touch." Arianrhod curled her lips into a scornful expression. "I doona *take orders* from anyone, not even her."

Standing still became impossible. Years of hatred for the ones who'd robbed him of not only his youth, but a chunk of his adult years roared to the fore. "I'll be outside," he gritted out and dashed for the front door, afraid what he'd say if he stayed put.

He kicked the door open, shattering the bolt, and pelted down the steps. With no clear destination in mind, he began to run, throwing his mind open to whatever might bubble to the fore. When he careened into Arianrhod's wards, he switched direction. He'd mobilized trance states before like this. The first time it happened was an accident, but once he understood fire wasn't the only gateway to the dream world, he'd utilized motion more than once.

Visions flooded him, and he trusted his feet to find the way without active assistance from his mind. An electric shock rocked him—more warding—and he turned back the way he'd come, still moving fast. The information bombarding him with image after image was so shocking and so infuriating, he wanted as much data as he could mine before the sending winked out.

Arianrhod caught up to him as he ran through a rose garden at full speed. Not just caught up, blocked his path. "Stop!" She thrust both hands flat against his chest. "Oberon's balls, just stop."

He ran up hard against her, surprised he didn't knock her over. Half in one world, half in the other, he inhaled short, panting gulps of air, leaning against her. Her magic augured into him, and he heard her murmur something he couldn't make out, maybe because it wasn't a language he'd ever known.

"Give me time," he choked out.

Instead of answering, she led him to a stone bench and patted it. He sat heavily and hunkered forward, head in his hands, as he summoned his soul back from where it ranged free in the dream world. Strong hands kneaded the length of his back and across his shoulders as he found wholeness again.

"Better?" she murmured.

"Much. You touching me helps draw me back."

"Idle flattery. More likely, ye doona want me to stop."

He straightened and turned to face her, where she sat next to him. "Aye, that too."

Arianrhod captured his gaze with hers. "Here I thought ye needed fire and blood to summon trance states."

"It's the first road, but there are others. Some I never mastered, and I stumbled on the one I just used quite by accident. When I asked Cathbad about it, he grinned and said maybe I had enough anger to carry it off."

"No point in being angry with Ceridwen. She is who she is." Arianrhod shrugged. "I gave up on that one long ago."

He bit down so hard, his jaws ached. "Aye, and no reason to be angry at any of the rest of them, either." His hands curled into fists of their own accord. "It's so hard loving you. You're one of them, yet you're not. Keeping the two separate challenges me."

She raised an arched brow. "Aye, I have much the same problem. I love you more than I value my place in the Pantheon. If I dinna, I'd never have come when Jonathan called, regardless of Cathbad's prophecies."

"He's not me."

"Nay, but opening the door to him opens another to you." She withdrew her hands from his back and squared her shoulders. "I made my choice. 'Tis you."

"Maybe you should wait until I tell you what I just saw before you make that decision." He forced himself to his feet, still disoriented from the dream world, but some things were crystal clear. Girding himself for the worst, he shoveled his hopes and dreams of sharing his life with Arianrhod into a tidy pile and buried them deep. He knew how to conceal his emotions because he'd done it all his life. He'd been by himself since he was fifteen years old.

She stood and gripped his arm, positioning herself so she faced him. "Doona do that."

"Don't do what?"

"Ye tossed up walls around your soul faster than even I could." She captured his face between her hands and angled it so he couldn't look away. "Nothing ye say will change my mind. Nothing. Even if ye walk out my gates, it willna stop me from loving you."

"You were quick enough to walk away from standing proud by my side when Jonathan was a baby."

Something flickered in the depths of her eyes. Shame. Resignation. Yet she didn't look away. "Aye, and I was wrong, but I canna rerun the clock." She took a deep breath. "Tell me what ye saw. Whatever this is, we'll face it together."

"Maybe not." His hands ached from the tightly balled fists, so he extended his fingers, flexing them. "The ones helping the Morrigan are Gwydion and Andraste."

She recoiled as if he'd slapped her, letting go of him.

"I told you it would make you reconsider." Angus layered a few more bricks onto the barrier between him and his heart. He'd come to reluctant terms with a life without Arianrhod the day she walked away from his cottage in Inishowen, a few months after she'd left Jonathan with him.

"Och aye, Gwydion's treachery doesna upset me. My brother's been a bastard since the day he was born, but Andraste was my friend."

"Maybe she still is." He paused, thinking. "Or maybe her first love is a good fight, and she'll sign on with whichever side promises the most conflict."

"Likely true enough." She send a meaningful glance scuttling across the air between them. "Angus."

"What? We should wake Eletea and get moving."

She pushed his arms out of the way and wrapped hers around his body, nestling her face into his neck. "I'm not reconsidering. Nothing ye've said makes me proud of my kin, or makes me want to disavow my love for you. Quite the opposite. I'm mortified Ceridwen's taken to making my decisions for me. She must've assumed the information would upset me, nor did she believe I'd take on my brother in battle."

Her words sank in, and he choked back disbelief. He'd been certain she'd walk away from him—because she'd done it before. Walk away from him to stand by Ceridwen's side sorting out Celtic political tangles. He threaded his arms around her and pulled her close, hands splayed across her back. Emotion thickened his throat as he hunted for words, not finding any that came close to expressing the relief turning his heartstrings to mush.

"Forty years without you is a big enough price to pay for my arrogance," she went on. "I'm not willing to sacrifice any more than that."

"If Earth flickers and fades, we may not have much time. I wasn't there when the rest of you visited the future to free the dragons, but I dreamed it, and it was ghastly. Those poor humans, fighting with everything they had to stay alive and failing." He stroked her hair where it fell down her back, threading his fingers into its silky silver strands.

"Aye then, we'll take whatever we can. When things get verra bad, we'll retreat to Cathbad's time capsule and tackle the problem from there. Who knows? Mayhap 'twill be more of us keeping your blood kin company than ye imagine."

Wrapping a hand around her neck, he slanted his head and kissed her, drinking in the sweet taste of her lips and tongue. Her nipples pebbled where her breasts were crushed against his chest, and he felt his own tighten in return. Desire pierced him like a live thing, and he brought his hands around to the laces of her breeches, scrabbling to untie them.

She tore her mouth from his. "I want to make love, but we should go."

Angus cupped her cheek in his palm. "Five minutes won't make much difference. It shouldn't take much more than that, as much as I've missed the feel of your body around me."

A languid smile emphasized sultry heat pouring from her eyes. "Aye, and I'm so close, ye could touch me and I'd spend."

He pulled the free end of her lacings to loosen her trousers and pushed her breeches and smallclothes partway down her legs. The heady scent of her drove him mad, and he reached between her legs to rub her nubbin. For a moment, she leaned into his touch with a breathy sigh, but then she twisted away and bent over the stone bench they'd sat on. The creamy globes of her ass outlined her sex, and breath clotted in his throat. He undid his own pants and drew out his painfully erect cock. Wrapping a hand around it, he positioned himself behind her and sank deep, groaning with delight as she tightened around him.

Reaching around her, he inscribed hard, little circles atop her clit and pushed himself the rest of the way in. She bucked back against him, encouraging him to start thrusting. When she dissolved around him in a climax, he let himself go and drove into her, never letting go of her center with his fingers as he urged her toward a second peak.

He rode a fine edge, bringing both of them higher as he thrust into her. His cock swelled, bigger, harder, hotter—until the whole world disintegrated around him. The rhythmic contractions of her muscles pulled him over the edge, and semen gushed from him in hot sheets of white ecstasy.

Panting and gasping to fill his lungs, he reluctantly pulled himself from the luxury of her body. "If I had my way," he managed between breaths, "I'd stay inside you forever."

"Aye, and I'd welcome you." Snatching a handful of some sort of shrub, she wiped herself with the leaves then tossed them aside. She pulled ivory silken smallclothes up her shapely legs, followed by her breeches, which she laced into place.

Angus watched her, mesmerized by her movements. His cock stood out from his body, hard as if he'd never come. He pushed himself back into his clothing with difficulty. "I never get enough of you."

"The only uninterrupted time we truly had was in the sea."

He nodded. "It was hell whenever I had to leave you. At least I was there for our son's birth. I wasn't at all certain I'd make it. Your brother had me sunk up to my ass spying for him twenty years in the future."

A soft smile made its way from her mouth to her eyes. "I knew ye'd be there. We waited for you."

"You didn't put our baby at risk, did you?"

"Of course not." She closed her arms around him. "Jonathan and I talked about it, and he knew we had to wait."

"You spoke with him, while he was inside you?"

"Surely. All mothers do."

He hugged her back. "Aye, but it's because they love their unborn children, not because they expect them to understand."

She shrugged in his embrace before wriggling out of it. "Magic makes a difference—for nearly everything. We must form a plan."

"I thought the original plan was for us to gather Eletea and meet the others at Fire Mountain."

"Aye, 'twas, but that was afore the Morrigan landed close enough to nab."

"She's free. How do you know she hasn't left for another time?"

"Instinct. She'll be hell-bent on revenge for what we did to her." A feral, bloodthirsty grin split Arianrhod's face, and for once she looked like the thousand-year-old deity she was.

"I assume we're not going to kick back in Fire Mountain and wait this one out?" Angus sent an inquiring glance her way.

"Oh hell no. Wouldn't miss it for the world. Lucky for us, she doesna know where I live. Even if she did, she couldna get through my warding, but she never was one to give up easily—or at all."

Angus considered her words. "If you're correct, we won't have to locate her. She'll find us."

"Strategically, if we ever needed dragons, 'tis now. They'd allow us the ability to meet her in aerial combat."

"In the end, it comes down to dragons on every front."

She caught her lower lip between her teeth. "Aye, whoever has the dragons on their side will win this fight."

"Maybe Eletea has some ideas. If anyone knows about other dragons in this area, it'd be her."

"I heard my name." The dragon lumbered down the central aisle of the rose garden, making her way toward them. "Sorry I passed out in the kitchen. Guess I was more tired than I thought. Besides," she sniffed the air delicately, "it appears you made good use of the time to yourselves."

Angus laughed. "When we weren't fighting, and I wasn't sunk deep in visions."

"Fighting, fucking, future-seeing…" Eletea stopped a few feet from them. "Not all that much difference. They all evoke strong emotion." She bent her head until it was level with theirs. "Do we have a plan?"

"Depends," Angus replied. "Are there dragons besides you in the Highlands?"

She puffed steam, bathing them with wet warmth. "Why?"

Arianrhod sketched out the information they had, ending with, "'Tis a prime time to face off against the Crow, but we'll do better if we have at least one other dragon."

Eletea's eyes whirled faster. "Most of us don't like bearing you on our backs. We're nothing like the myths make us out to be."

"Do ye hate the Morrigan enough to bend your principles?" Arianrhod asked.

Eletea pointed her snout skyward and blew flame-tinged smoke. "That's not the point. Something you said struck me as valid, though. You need buy-in from dragons as a whole, not just from me. While it may be satisfying to face the Crow, she has other Celts on her side, and you may not win because of that."

"The best method we have of securing the dragons' help is by delivering the Crow to them wrapped in chains," Angus pointed out.

"Fighting the Crow is a risk I'm willing to take." Arianrhod extended a hand toward the dragon. "If ye willna accept us on your backs, we'll fight side-by-side with you, and let ye deal with the Crow if she takes to the skies."

"Back to other dragons," Angus cut in. "Are there any?"

"There were," Eletea said. "I have no idea if Jaek lured them back to Fire Mountain after he left us."

"I'm thinking not," Angus said, recalling the conversation where Jaek said, *You were my assignment. The council will have my neck if I return without you.* "He made it sound like he was your personal escort."

"One way to find out." Eletea straightened. "I'll try to raise the other dragons, but I can't do it from within these wards. Too many and too thick."

"You'll be at risk outside them," Angus protested.

"I'll chance it." The dragon grinned, showing her double rows of teeth.

"We'll come with you." Angus glanced at Arianrhod, seeking confirmation.

"Indeed we will," she concurred. "Follow me closer to the edge of my protective illusion, and I'll carve a way through that doesna lead the Crow right to my holdings."

Angus thought about what else they could do to shore up their side of things. "So long as we're at it, I'll see if I can't raise Jonathan. If we're going to wage a war, we'll need all the help we can get."

"Can ye dream him?" Arianrhod glanced at Angus, curiosity stamped on her features.

"Probably, but it's much more straightforward to employ telepathy. It should work, so long as he and Britta haven't left this time."

She smiled and hooked an arm through his. "Aye. Start with the easy methods."

"If the two of you are done making moon eyes at one another—" The dragon blasted steam their way, and Angus swallowed a quick retort as he fell into step by Arianrhod's side.

She threaded her way out of the rose garden and into one beyond that held aromatic herbs. "No time like the present to line up our allies," she murmured and opened a stone gate with a short blast of power.

CHAPTER 11

*B*ritta fought against Mauvreen's iron grip around her upper arm, but the witch reinforced it with magic. "Let me go to him," Britta demanded. "Don't make me hurt you."

"That, Missy, would be a huge mistake. Leave him be. He'll come around in a few minutes." The witch screwed her face into a grimace. "You're nearly as much trouble as Maggie when she dropped onto my doorstep from out of nowhere."

"I resent that," Maggie muttered. "I was scared."

"You were a mewling ninny," Mauvreen retorted. "Good thing you got over it fast, or I'd have slapped you."

"Wise of ye to treat fairly with my mate," Lachlan spoke up.

"While I'm grateful the two of you made up, I've known her since she was in diapers," Mauvreen retorted. "Furthermore—"

"All of you be quiet." Britta eyed Jonathan, and worry roiled in her gut. He rocked from side to side, moaning as if he were in pain. "Did Angus look like that?" she asked Mauvreen, who still had hold of her.

"Exactly like that—until he got more comfortable with his magic." Mauvreen's steely gaze softened. "You may love him, but you can't protect him from his destiny."

"Do ye know what that is?" Britta locked gazes with the witch.

Mauvreen shook her head and loosened her hand. "There. He's whole again. You can go to him now."

"Let me know if you need me," Maggie broke in. "I am still a doctor, even if I haven't used my training recently."

"Thanks. Healers are always welcome." Britta hastened to Jonathan where she knelt next to him and wrapped her arms around him from the side, crooning in Gaelic. "Did ye find Cathbad? Ye were gone for longer than made me comfortable."

He straightened from his slumped position and moved from his knees to his butt as he turned to face her, disentangling her arms in the process. He shook himself and rubbed his forehead. "Got a hell of a headache, but yeah I found him. Didn't have to hunt, either. I fell down a long dark tunnel into a cavern straight out of Jung's collective unconscious, but Cathbad was waiting for me there." Frowning, he narrowed his eyes. "How long was I gone? Cathbad said I couldn't stay long—until I got more familiar with using that aspect of my power."

"Half an hour." Britta sat across from him so their knees touched, but she kept her hands folded in her lap, despite an overwhelming urge to wind her arms around him again and never let go.

The crooked smile she loved lit his austere features. "Not so long as all that."

"Aye but she," Britta jerked her chin at Mauvreen, "wouldna let me near you for a good ten minutes after ye returned to us."

"Never mind reliving the details." Maggie moved closer, followed by Lachlan. "What did you find out? Is there anything specific we need to do right now?" She bent and gripped Jonathan's wrist, obviously feeling for a pulse, and smiled before she let go. "Nice, strong heartbeat."

Jonathan tossed a long-suffering glance her way. "Nothing like having an M.D. verify I'm still alive. What I found out is that dragons hold the key—to everything. Cathbad said whoever has the dragons on their side will win."

"Seems simple enough," Britta muttered. "It also suggests they willna barricade themselves in Fire Mountain."

"I canna see where they'd cast their vote to support the Morrigan and her dark mages," Lachlan broke in, frowning. "But if they're cut off from all of us, well then they canna pick up either banner."

Jonathan frowned. "Somehow I didn't think dragons throwing their lot in with the dark mages was the problem. They hate the Morrigan. It's only if they tell all of us to go to hell, we'll be screwed."

"That'll happen if they follow through with their threat to cut Fire Mountain off from Earth," Maggie said. "Since Cathbad's visions intimate the dragons have a key role to play—"

A bell chimed nearby, and Britta started. "What in the goddess's name is that?"

"My cell phone." Mauvreen fished it from a pocket and glanced at the display. "It's Mary Elma. Give me a moment. If she's calling me back so soon, it's either very good news, or very bad." She walked a few feet toward the kitchen and held the thing to her ear before saying, "What's up?"

"Some parts of life in these times take getting used to." Britta snorted. "We've always had telepathy, but now humans have something that works almost as well."

"Indeed." Lachlan dropped to the carpet next to Britta and Jonathan. Maggie grabbed a cushion off a nearby chair before doing the same thing. "It's looking like a trip to Fire Mountain," she said. "We need dragons. Lots of them—"

"Shit!" Jonathan scrunched his eyes shut.

"What is it?" Britta's earlier panic flashed through her. She leaned forward and placed a hand on either side of Jonathan's head, ready for anything from healing magic to casting out fell forces.

"Stand down, Valkyrie!" Angus's amused mind voice echoed in her head.

Jonathan's eyes flew open just before he twisted his features into a sheepish grin. *"Don't mind me,"* he said to Angus. *"I was just surprised. Not sure why, but the last thing I expected was for you to raise me. Did something happen?"*

"*Afore ye answer,*" Britta cut in, "*do ye need me to leave the conversation?*"

"*Nay. We're north of you, deep in the Highlands, with Eletea. Battle is imminent. Join us. We're a wee bit shy of troops.*"

Jonathan pushed his shoulders upright. "*What about the Celts? I know you're not fond of them—and with good reason, but—*"

"*They're divided on the Morrigan. Get here as fast as you can, and I'll fill in the details then.*"

"*We can do that,*" Lachlan said, followed by, "*Sorry, I dinna ask afore I listened in.*"

"*Any chance either of you could get your dragons back to help?*" Angus asked.

Britta exchanged a glance with Lachlan. The other dragon shifter shrugged. "*I doona know, but we'll do our damnedest.*"

"*Can't ask for more than that.*"

"*Where exactly are you?*" Jonathan inquired. "*The others are better at using magic to track location than me. I prefer coordinates.*"

"*For now, you'll have to work with what I have,*" Angus replied.

Images flashed into Britta's head in rapid succession. Apparently Lachlan's too because he said, "Och, and I ken that place. If I hadna discovered it afore it sank into spells, I'd never have known it was there. I avoided it after that because I had enough problems with Rhukon to keep me occupied, and I feared 'twas a sorcerer's home."

"*Ye might say so.*" Arianrhod's dry humor reverberated through their shared mind link.

"*Dragons or no, guard your backs traveling to us,*" Angus said. "*We'll be watching for you, since you won't be able to contact us once we retreat within Arianrhod's warding.*"

Britta started to say she understood, but Angus severed the sending from his end of things. She glanced in Mauvreen's direction, but the witch had edged closer to the kitchen door and was still deep in discussion with Mary Elma.

"I'll try to reach Tarika," Britta said. "'Twill likely go better if I'm out of doors."

"I'll join you." Lachlan rose to his feet in a single, fluid motion. "Perhaps by now our dragons will have had a bellyful of listening to their kin trash dragon shifters."

"One can hope." Britta forced her mouth into a smile. What she wanted to do was drop everything so she could beat a path to Fire Mountain and pound sense into the reactionary dragons who thought closing the first world off from Earth would do anything but court disaster. She'd had time to think about their plan and felt certain a boomerang effect would haunt the dragons. The reverberations from a dying Earth would stretch across the veil separating it from Fire Mountain. Survival on that world was tenuous at best because they had so little water. Anything that upset the balance would mean the end of dragonkind too.

She got to her feet and bent to kiss the top of Jonathan's head before she walked toward the front door with Lachlan behind her.

Once they were outside, he asked, "What are ye hatching up?"

"Why do ye believe I'm *hatching up* anything?" She arched a brow as she glanced his way.

When he grinned, he looked like a roguish youth, and she understood why he'd swept Maggie off her feet. What was less clear was why the bevy of women who'd thrown themselves at him in the centuries prior to that hadn't had similar luck. He'd bedded dozens —likely hundreds—but none snagged his heart.

"I've known you a long time," he countered and followed her down the steps. "Let's catalog what we know. To the best I can see, there're at least two separate prophecies afoot."

Britta nodded. "Aye, the one about ye and Maggie, and the other about Jonathan—though none of us are clear just what that entails."

"Since the fates threw us together, my guess is they're entwined somehow. It makes sense. The energy Maggie and I generate willna do a twit of good if magic dies when the dragons shut Fire Mountain."

"Aye, but why bother with the one prophecy, if it was so dependent upon the other?" Annoyance mingled with a feeling she was being buried alive trickled through her. Solving puzzles never was her strong suit; she preferred her information clearly laid out. "'Twould help if we had a few more clues about Jonathan." She tried for neutral words, but detected a bitter undernote.

"I've heard of prophecies where one must happen afore the other can find its way. Never fear, we'll work it out, lass." Lachlan laid a quick hand on her shoulder. "I'll do what I can to raise Kheladin."

Britta took a deep breath, followed by another, as she watched Lachlan trot away from her. "Might go better if ye're outside the warding around this place," she called after him.

"Give me credit for a few brains." He didn't bother to turn around, but she heard him well enough.

Britta made her way past the edge of Mauvreen's illusion, wards furled in case whoever attacked the witch's home had returned. Sensing she was alone, she dismantled the protections around her to maximize her chances of reaching her dragon and inhaled deeply once again to steady herself. Anger wouldn't help her cause. She needed every scrap of magic available to her, and strong emotion might bleed off a critical fraction that would make all the difference.

When she was as calm as she was likely to get, she summoned an image of Tarika in all her immense red-scaled glory. Dragons kept growing until they died, and Tarika was old. As one of the First Born, she laid claim to being one of ten original dragons to be born in the flaming calderas of Fire Mountain. Her father had been a First Born too, back in the days when dragon clutches consisted of a single egg. Alleging kinship to Dewi, the Celtic dragon goddess and Nidhogg, the Norse dragon, the First Born were as close to royalty as dragons allowed themselves to come.

Britta had made her way to Fire Mountain as a very young woman, much younger than most mages who presumed to become dragon shifters. She'd run away from her overbearing father and scheming mother and their plans to marry her off to the Duke of

Something-or-Other, with warnings ringing in her head. She was too young. No dragon would take her. She remembered nail-biting terror during the last stretch in the time shaft, traveling on spells borrowed from another mage—one already bonded with a dragon. If she returned dragon-less, she'd be forever barred from Fire Mountain. If she really annoyed the dragons, they could go so far as to kill her. Mages only got one shot at luring a dragon to bond with them.

After the time tunnel ejected her at the edge of a volcanic gash in the red, dry world, she hunkered in shadows for hours before she forced herself to stand tall. No dragon would want a craven, a maid who crept into their world with her tail betwixt her legs. She reminded herself she was the Countess of Kilkerran. She may be young, green, untried, yet she had a good heart and would commit herself mind, body, and soul to her dragon—forever.

She didn't know how Tarika found her. Or maybe they found each other. Britta wandered in Fire Mountain for hours before she came over a rise and saw Tarika standing there. When she turned the full force of her whirling, golden gaze on Britta, it was akin to what she'd always imagined it would feel like to find the man of her dreams. A lurch in her chest. An undeniable draw.

Britta pulled her mind from the past and focused her magic outward, pushing toward the dragon she'd been inseparable from for hundreds of years.

"Tarika. Tarika. This isna right. We are bondmates. Ye belong by my side."

Britta held her breath and waited before calling again. Standing on a grassy swale at the edge of moorlands, she understood she'd been holding on by the thinnest of margins. No wonder Lachlan closeted himself in the basement. The dragon shifter bond had branded him—and her as well. Tarika was part of her heart. Her soul. The vows she'd taken to bond with the dragon cut deep. Far too deep to lay aside.

What if Tarika were truly lost to her forever? How could she go forward? What kind of partner would she make for Jonathan, or any other man if he got sick of her mooning over her lost dragon and moved on without her?

Enough! She gave herself a brisk mental shake. *This isna helpful. I must believe, or all truly will be lost.*

Because she didn't know what else to do, she called for Tarika again. And again. Minutes ticked by forming first a quarter hour, then a half. She was surprised the others didn't hunt her down. Britta scanned the empty skies one last time, and her shoulders slumped in defeat. Her magic hadn't been enough to bridge the kinetic gap between Earth and Fire Mountain. Clearly Lachlan hadn't had any better luck. She'd have felt any dragon coming through a breach in the ether, not just hers.

Britta willed a break in the endless blue-gray sky, but nothing happened. She felt the quick, hot bite of tears behind her lids and pounded a fist into a nearby tree. This started out as a longshot, and it hadn't worked.

Damn it to the nine Hells and back again.

The dragon's absence didn't excuse Britta from being strong, from keeping her emotions in check. The others needed her. From the sound of Angus's sending, they'd be in the thick of things, and very soon. Battle was a combination of luck, wits, and attention. If she allowed herself to sink into a pit of gloom over Tarika, she should do everyone a favor and not go back inside. Attitudes like hers sank ships—and battles.

Lachlan found a way through. I can too.

Britta pushed breath between her teeth and stood straight. She turned toward Mauvreen's and chanted softly to slip past the witch's spell that Jonathan had augmented with his own power. Lachlan plodded toward her from the opposite side of the front yard. Though he tried for a jaunty trot, it was obvious he was as devastated as she by their failure.

She raised a hand in his direction, and he nodded back before their paths crossed. "Och aye," he said. "'I was hopeful ye'd have better luck than me."

A high-pitched squeal battered her hearing, sounding like a million bolts of cloth ripping into shreds at the same time. "What the hell?" Britta spun in time to see the sky split asunder followed by a flurry of red and copper scales, as two dragons pelted through to the accompaniment of fire and bugling.

"Tarika!" She shrieked and barreled toward her dragon at full speed.

Lachlan bellowed, "Kheladin," at the same time, but Britta couldn't see him because her eyes flooded with tears, and she wound her arms around Tarika's scaled hide.

The dragon did something she'd only done once before in all their years together. She bent and lifted Britta between her forelegs and cradled her against the small, smooth scales of her chest. Britta clung to her talons, but only for a moment. She was a dragon shifter mage, goddammit, not some sniveling female.

"I've never been so glad to see anyone or anything," she admitted, looking into the dragon's whirling eyes. "But ye can put me down."

"What if I'm the one who wants to hang on a little longer?" Tarika laughed, showering Britta with steam.

"Who am I to argue with a dragon?"

"That was the right answer." After one more hug, Tarika set Britta on the ground.

"Does this mean the Dragon Council reconsidered?" Britta asked.

"Those stupid, arrogant pricks!" Flames shot from Tarika's mouth, traveling fifty feet into the air.

"Mmph. Guess that's a nay. Ye left anyway?"

"Aye, with Kheladin hard on my heels. We heard the two of you calling us and chose our side in the battle to come." Tarika clanked her jaws shut. "Doona mistake things. 'Twill get bad. Worse than your worst imaginings if the idiots we left in Fire Mountain shut the gateway."

Kheladin lumbered to where they stood with Lachlan astride him. When Britta glanced his way, she saw traces of tears on his cheeks and understood entirely. "We are exactly where we belong," Kheladin announced. "My wager is the other dragons bonded to mages see it the same way and will leave just like us."

Britta recalled what Jonathan had shared of Cathbad's message. "Dragons will determine the outcome of this war, according to Cathbad."

Kheladin shook himself. Copper scales flew everywhere, and his green eyes whirled faster. "'Tis nice to be appreciated for the powerful creatures we are—"

"—yet more than a little daunting to be cast into such a primary role," Tarika cut in dryly.

Mauvreen's front door slammed against its stops. "Damn my eyes," the witch cried. "Dragons! Things may be looking up after all."

Maggie and Jonathan flew down the stairs and made beelines toward their mates and dragons. Jonathan screeched to a halt a few inches from Tarika, grinning like a fool. "May I hug you?"

"Ye needn't ask." Tarika blew steam all over him, until he and Britta were encased in a warm, damp fog. "Ye carry my mating bite." The dragon bent until she could rest her forelegs on his shoulders. "What's this I hear about Cathbad and dragons?"

"He said whoever has the dragons on their side will win."

The dragon creased her scaled brow. "He dreams many possibilities. 'Tis how his gift works. Did he outline any of them specifically?"

Jonathan shook his head. "Sorry. I couldn't stay very long. Maybe I could go back. I'm recovered from—"

"I thought Angus needed us now," Britta cut in.

Jonathan squinched his face into a grimace. "You're right. There're so many balls in the air, they're hard to keep track of. And you haven't heard what Mary Elma tossed into the mix yet, but there's good news on that front too. Several covens are sending—"

"Give it to me in order," Tarika demanded and settled onto her belly on the lawn so they could sit around her. "Everybody front and center," she roared. "The sooner Kheladin and I know what there is to know, the sooner we can be on our way to meet Angus, who I presume is with Arianrhod."

"And Eletea." Jonathan smiled.

Tarika grunted, blowing smoke. "Another dragon who marches to her own tune and bows to no one. Good! We need all of them we can find."

$\mathcal{A}$rianrhod staggered slightly and withdrew the magic she'd focused to help Eletea and Angus. Reaching Jonathan was easy. The Highland dragons had proven more elusive, but Eletea finally mind-linked with a pair living not far from the Callanish Stones on the Isle of Lewis in the Outer Hebrides.

Arianrhod inhaled sharply and huffed out a breath. "Do ye think they'll show up?" she asked the dragon.

"Probably not." Eletea shook herself, making her scales rattle discordantly. "The only reason they're still here and not back at Fire Mountain is because they ignored the edict to return. If they're flouting orders from the Dragon Council, the likelihood of them coming to our aid is slim."

"Ye dinna go back with Jaek," Arianrhod pointed out.

Eletea grinned. "I probably would've if the two of you hadn't shown up."

"Were the ones in the Hebrides the only dragons in the Highlands—besides you, that is?" Angus asked. He sifted his hands through his unkempt hair and added, "Sorry I wasn't paying closer attention, but it took more effort than I expected to reach Jonathan and hold him long enough to talk. We're not used to communicating that way."

"There were others." Eletea focused her whirling gaze at the ground. "Maybe there still are, but they're handing me short shrift. Many took Cavet's side of things and blamed me when he left."

"No matter. We'll work with what we have." Angus drew his brows together into a thoughtful expression. "Something about all this doesn't quite ring true. I don't care for Gwydion, yet I can't see him helping the Morrigan. Whenever she came up, he made his distasteful feelings for her quite clear."

Arianrhod narrowed her eyes. Angus was correct. There'd never been any love lost between the Crow and either her brother or his close sidekick, Arawn, god of the dead. It was at least possible Gwydion and Andraste had launched a strategy to make the Crow believe they were on her side, but the harder Arianrhod thought about it, the more dead ends she ran up against.

"I canna see the point in pretending to be her ally," she said at length. "If they wish her ill, she'd see through any charade soon enough."

"Dragons! I feel dragons approaching." Eletea's head snapped up, and she spread her wings.

"Nay! Doona leave to greet them." Arianrhod held up a hand. "The Crow appeared to me once as a white dragon."

"I remember that," Angus cut in. "She turned into one of her human guises and tried to seduce me."

Eletea hissed steam. "Dragons are coming. Their energy plucks at me. I'd know if it was something else masquerading as one."

Tension tightened Arianrhod's muscles into knots. She felt power approaching too, and at a high rate of speed. "Could that pair from the Hebrides get here this fast?"

"Of course. They could've leveraged magic and been here moments after we spoke." Eletea screwed her face into an annoyed expression. "While I don't agree with cutting Fire Mountain off from Earth, on a philosophical level I understand why dragons might tire of dealing with ignorance—"

"Enough!" Angus shifted his stance until he faced the disturbance that alerted Eletea dragons would converge on them soon. His face was set in tense planes, and Arianrhod felt him draw power and ready it for use.

She did the same, feeling like an ass for not thinking of it first. Maybe they should retreat behind her wards, but a quick glance at the stone wall surrounding her castle told her they wouldn't make it. They'd just create a handy path through her protections for whatever was heading straight for them.

The air sizzled, making crackling noises, and a distinctive fiery smell unique to dragonkind assaulted her. It wouldn't be long now.

Power built, pressing against her from all sides. A gash tore the air from ground level to ten feet up, and Tarika's red scales surged through. Arianrhod released the breath she'd been holding, but didn't let go of her power. Who knew what might gallop through the breach on the dragon's coattails. Kheladin burst through the opening, followed in quick succession by Jonathan, Britta, Lachlan, Maggie, and Mauvreen.

Arianrhod was still peering through the hole in the sky when Tarika barked words to seal it. The air glistened wetly, shimmering in spirals before it reformed as if nothing had ever disturbed it.

"Come with me." Arianrhod crooked two fingers, releasing her stored power in a *whoosh*. "We're all accounted for, and we'll be safe behind my wards."

"Nice to see you too." Britta grinned.

"Save the greetings for after we're inside." Arianrhod rode herd on a smile that wanted out. Damn, it was good to see everyone. She'd been of two minds about their original plan to regroup in Fire Mountain, where dragons controlled who came—and who was allowed to leave. Their current arrangement suited her much better. Her house. Her rules.

Guess I'm as much of a control freak as the dragons.

"You're only just now figuring that out?" Angus slipped an arm through hers and bent his power to slicing through the illusion protecting her castle from discovery.

"Ye were inside my head."

"Aye, and has it come to me needing permission?" He repeated her question from earlier.

She elbowed him and chanted to expedite moving the group through her defenses. They pushed through the pathway she created, ending up in a stone courtyard outside steps leading to her front door. How quickly could they catch each other up, craft a battle plan, and be gone? She worried if they waited too long, the Morrigan's trail would grow cold.

"I have witches arriving," Mauvreen announced. "Maybe as many as a hundred."

Arianrhod flinched. She'd kept the location of her castle a secret for hundreds of years, and that isolation served her well. Once bunches of magic-wielders knew about it, the freedom she'd come to value would evaporate, but these were desperate times, and it couldn't be helped.

"What about the other Highland dragons?" Tarika addressed her question to Eletea. The smaller dragon inclined her head before spreading her forearms in front of her.

"I tried. Only ones I could reach were that pair on the Isle of Lewis."

"Are they on their way?" Tarika arched a scaled brow.

"Hard to say, but probably not." Eletea shrugged.

"I'm going back outside the wards," Tarika said. "If there are dragonkind here, they'll come to my call."

"You might have better luck than me," Eletea muttered. "Being a First Born and all."

Tarika shot flames her way, but they bounced off Eletea's copper scales. "Show some respect, youngster."

Eletea drew herself up tall but barely came to Tarika's forelegs. "I'd respect our council more if they'd done something about the dark mage problem forty years ago when they first found out, after I told them about it."

"Forty years?" Jonathan sounded outraged. "They've known dark mages drained dragon magic for plenty long enough to address the problem. How could they not have taken action?"

Tarika turned her red snout his way. "We live long lives, so we're rarely in a hurry. It saves mistakes."

"How could stamping out the Rhukons of the world ever be a *mistake*?" Jonathan glared at Tarika, and the dragon puffed smoke at him until he doubled over coughing.

"We can hash this out later." Britta patted Tarika's scaled hide. "We'll find out what one another knows. By the time ye return with news of whether we'll have more dragons or no, we should be damn near ready to leave."

Tarika rolled her eyes and dusted Eletea with more fire. Her body shimmered as she retraced her steps and left the castle courtyard.

Jonathan stared after her. "I still can't believe they could've fixed this and didn't."

"Believe it. Accept it. Ye canna do aught to change it, and chewing over dead bones only breeds maggots." Arianrhod clamped her jaws together before she said something she'd truly regret.

"You lost the right to chastise me when you left me with Angus." Jonathan stomped in front of his mother and crossed his arms over his chest.

"I wasna rebuking you, merely stating fact. If ye wish—"

Angus stepped between them. "This isn't productive. Let's trade information and move forward."

"Sorry," Jonathan muttered.

"Aye." Arianrhod sent a crooked grin at her son. "Ye come by your stubbornness honestly."

The corners of his mouth twitched before he grinned back. "Right on that count. Mom."

Arianrhod winced, not knowing if she liked hearing herself called that or not.

Britta sidled to Eletea. "Ye really should treat Tarika with a bit more deference. She is your elder and sister to your mother."

"All dragons are related if you scratch deep enough, but I get it. I'll keep my thoughts to myself."

"She likes you," Britta said.

"Pfft. You're just saying that." Eletea clanked her double rows of teeth together.

"Nay. Her last words afore we left Mauvreen's were 'Another dragon who marches to her own tune and bows to no one. Good! We need all of them we can find.'"

"Really?" Eletea preened. "She really said that about me?"

"Aye, lassie." Lachlan walked to the dragon. "That she did. When will these witches show up?" he asked Mauvreen.

"Within the hour. We'll have to be on the lookout for them, though. I gave them the general area from your memory of this place, but not specifics."

"What memory?" Arianrhod felt thunderstruck and whirled to face Lachlan. "Ye've never been here."

"Lass." He met her gaze, his green eyes somber. "Ye dinna always live here. Afore ye, a count or a duke—I canna recall just whom—owned these lands."

"'Twas a duke."

"What happened?" Maggie asked. "Did he die and you bought the place?"

Arianrhod swallowed a snort. "Ye're such a modern child. It doesna work that way here. If I hadna taken matters to hand, the duke's relations would've moved in after he suffered an unfortunate horseback accident and broke his neck."

Angus creased his forehead in thought. "Before anyone could stake a claim, you made it appear the place had vanished."

"And wiped it from a few memories. I couldna rid myself of a handful of servants who refused to leave. I dinna have the heart to kill them, so they served me until their deaths." She clapped her hands together. "How I came by my home isna important. The way I see things, we'll travel to Eletea's cave, which was where we left the Morrigan ensorcelled. She's free now, but picking up her trail will be easy enough."

"We may not have to. If it were me, I'd just wait for you," Kheladin said. "She's one to carry a grudge, and she'll guess ye'll return, if only to strengthen the spell keeping her asleep."

"Aye, she'll not know Ceridwen told me she's free."

"Who stands on her side beyond the dark mages and their dragons?" Maggie asked. Her blonde hair was escaping its braids, and her blue eyes snapped dangerously.

"Gwydion and Andraste—"

"'Tisn't possible!" Lachlan boomed. "I know them both. Hell would turn to ice chips afore they'd align themselves with such evil."

Angus sketched in what he'd seen in his vision while Lachlan's face grew darker and darker. "I doona believe it," he muttered after it was clear Angus was done speaking.

"The dream world doesn't lie." Angus's words were simple, as he faced off with Lachlan.

"I dinna say 'twas a lie. Mayhap ye misinterpreted. What exactly did ye see?"

Tension streamed from Angus. His muscles flexed as he stood by Arianrhod's side.

"Maybe 'tisn't a good idea—" She kept her voice level, placating. Their cause would be doomed before they began if they challenged one another, rather than seeking common ground to move forward.

"It's all right." Angus met Lachlan's gaze evenly. "I saw Andraste and Gwydion go into Eletea's cave. They summoned power to drill through the layers of debris and spells we buried the Morrigan with."

"Did ye see all of them walk out of the cave?" Lachlan persisted.

Angus nodded. "Aye, and chatting it up like magpies at a tea party."

"I still canna believe they dinna have ulterior motives. Some strategy that required her trust," Lachlan muttered under his breath.

"Maybe you don't know them as well as you think," Angus said before looking away. "You and that dragon of yours were asleep for a long time."

"That we were. Yet they helped Maggie and me after I awoke. We'll find out the truth of things soon enough."

Jonathan stepped closer. Muscles played across his jaw. "We have bigger problems than the Celts. The Morrigan aligned herself with the Furies, Tantalus, Circe, Medea, Hecate, Ixion, and maybe others as well."

"Where'd ye find that out?" Lachlan sputtered.

"Cathbad. I visited him in the dream world."

"Why dinna ye say aught about it after ye awoke?" Britta demanded. "'Tis major information ye omitted."

Jonathan shook his head. "I'm not sure. First, I was disoriented, then things happened fast. Mary Elma called Mauvreen, and you went hunting for Tarika."

"But when we were filling Tarika in afore we left, surely then…" Britta drew her forehead into a mass of creases as she frowned. "Mayhap fell power is afoot. Power that dinna wish ye to remember. Is there aught else?"

"Isna that enough?" Lachlan demanded.

"There was one more thing," Jonathan cut in. "Gryphons and Harpies are part of the mix."

Arianrhod swallowed back outrage—mixed with a healthy dollop of fear. Harpies. Soul stealers. She hadn't tangled with them for hundreds of years. The only plus in all the bad news was she didn't have to tell Lachlan and Angus to move past their differences. They had more than enough trouble to occupy them without creating more.

Everyone converged on Jonathan scrabbling for details—exact words—from Cathbad. Arianrhod listened with half an ear and redirected most of her attention to Mauvreen. "How do ye see the witches blending in with a battle plan?"

"Depends what we're fighting. We can herd and amplify your power, which may be helpful against immortals. Hecate was part of that list of the Morrigan's allies." Mauvreen bit her lower lip, leaving marks in it. "She protects witches. I can't believe she'd turn against us. Circe and Medea are her underlings, so I'd not be overworried about them, either."

"Hecate and her minions aside, have ye faced Harpies afore?"

Mauvreen scrunched her face into a harsh mask. "Of course. We know to keep out of their way. Those bitches suck your soul out through your mouth."

Good. One less thing to explain.

"Will ye have a leader?"

"Me." Mauvreen tapped her chest. "I led hundreds of witches against those idiots who were hell-bent on burning or hanging us. I've forged operations against immortal magic too." A savage smile etched into her face. "I prefer what I can kill, but I'm not picky."

Maggie left the group around Jonathan to join Mauvreen. "The hanging/burning crew didn't exactly give up after Salem." Her tone held bitterness and regret.

A quick peek into the other woman's head told Arianrhod that Maggie's parents had died in one particularly nasty conflagration. "Will ye be with Lachlan and his dragon, or with the witches?" she asked.

"Lachlan, if it comes down to a choice, but maybe it won't."

Tarika burst into the courtyard, showering everyone with scarlet scales. "No other dragons," she said without preamble. "We're better off without that pair, anyway." She shook her head looking troubled. "We doona have the time to investigate now, but 'tis possible they've bonded with dark mages. The feel of their magic is wrong, twisted."

"Do you think they'll show up and fight for the other side?" Angus asked.

Tarika bugled, but the normally merry sound held menace. "I

thought of that, so I made certain they wouldna leave the Isle of Lewis anytime soon."

"If they're bonded, could their mages undo your work?" Arianrhod asked, all too aware something similar had just happened with the Crow.

"Not for a verra long time. Are we ready?"

"Once my witches arrive, we will be." Mauvreen tossed spiky curls out of her face.

"Did ye hear about the Infernals targeting us?" Britta asked her dragon.

Tarika nodded solemnly. "I see and hear whatever ye do. 'Tisn't the best news, yet nothing I havena faced afore."

"My guess is the Crow will be waiting for us near Eletea's cave," Kheladin said.

"I agree." Tarika flexed her talons in front of her. "She's dangerous. Doona underestimate her. She's had years to plot and plan. When dragons failed to react once they knew about her complicity with the dark mage problem, it made her bold."

"How would you know that?" Jonathan spoke up. "You and Britta weren't anywhere near this time until you showed up in Kheladin's cave that night."

She lowered her head until she looked him right in the eye. "It doesna matter where we are. Dragons hold shared memories that funnel to every First Born. What they know, I know."

His eyes widened. "Like a huge motherboard with links for every dragon."

She blew steam his way. "Strange verbiage, but something like that. One variable we havena considered is the other Celts. Some may show up to fight on our side."

"If Gwydion and Andraste are there, should we share Angus's vision implicating them in freeing the Crow?" Arianrhod pushed her tongue against her teeth considering the wisdom of such a move.

"Nay." Lachlan's answer came quickly. "We can judge their intentions better if they doona feel defensive."

"I hope that doesn't come back to bite us in the ass," Angus said.

"I don't see how it can." Mauvreen, who'd been hovering a few feet away, moved closer. "If we engage in fighting, they'll be forced to make a quick choice which side to join."

"They're immortal, though," Maggie cut in thoughtfully. "They could pretend to help us and knife us in the back. Sabotage is actually easier when someone's standing next to you."

"Let me think this through." Jonathan made his way to an artfully arranged pile of multi-colored stones and scooped them into his hands. Kneeling on the grassy courtyard, he arranged the stones in patterns. Done, he eyed them and made a few adjustments.

"What's all this?" Britta knelt next to him.

"White is us." He pointed. "Grey is dragons. Dark grey is the enemy, and these greenish stones are witches. I need more colors for the Celts and more still for the Infernals and their abominable pets." He inhaled sharply, his nostrils flaring. "If I were building a computer simulation, the conclusion I'd come to is we need more of everything. More men, more magic, more tricks up our sleeve. Otherwise this will be a suicide mission—at least for everyone who can die."

Jonathan eyed his mother. "Is there any way to make the witches immortal, even for a short time?"

Arianrhod flinched. Not answering was high on her list until Angus grabbed her arm. *"I see it in your mind,"* he said in shielded speech, but the dragons likely heard him anyway. *"Say it."*

"But it's forbidden," she protested.

"What's the worst your kin could do to you?" he countered.

"Good point."

She licked dry lips and twisted to face her son.

CHAPTER 13

Jonathan battered back surprise. His question had been rhetorical, and he hadn't expected Arianrhod to do anything beyond shaking her head, yet here she was staring him down. Determination turned her eyes to molten metal.

Tarika lumbered forward. "If ye hold secrets to ensure our victory, I command—"

"Even ye doona hold dominion over aught but dragons." A flicker of Arianrhod's imperious nature resurfaced. "Aye, I can cast a working to keep the witches alive through the span of many hours, no matter what wounds befall them."

"What about me?" Jonathan asked. "Will it work for Da and me?"

"Ye already hold immortality since ye've spent time with Cathbad, and whomever he touches doesna die."

"Good to know," Angus muttered. "When I asked Cathbad the same question long ago in a vision, he said I'd live a long time, but didn't elaborate."

"What's the downside?" Mauvreen put her hands on her hips. "That kind of magic always carries a powerful punch. So potent, we may not want it."

"Aye, and ye may not."

"Don't stop there." Mauvreen crooked two fingers.

Arianrhod stiffened. A play of emotions rippled across her ageless features before she smoothed her face into its usual inscrutable mask. "The truth of it is I doona know. Not exactly. 'Tis been many centuries since any of us cast that spell. The long and short of it is, ye may not find your way back."

Mauvreen drew her brows into a thin, low line. "Back from where? Are you saying we'll go mad?"

"Nay. Not exactly. 'Twill be different for each of you the magic touches. Some of you will die. Not immediately, but ye willna live long after the spell plays itself out. Some will sink into madness, and others willna notice anything changed."

"I don't get it," Mauvreen said flatly. "What makes the difference?"

"None of us could ever figure it out," Arianrhod replied, "which is why Ceridwen forbade that particular working hundreds of years back. To the best of my knowledge, it hasna been cast since around fourteen hundred."

"It's scarcely an immortality spell if you die anyway," Mauvreen sputtered.

"Aye, but ye doona die during the battle," Arianrhod retorted. "That's the important part."

"What do you think?" Angus exchanged a pointed glance with Mauvreen.

She expelled air in a rush. "Who the hell knows? Death on the battlefield's not a great option, but it appears death is one of the possible outcomes from that magic too." She shrugged. "Dead's dead the way I see it. Going mad is worse than dead. I can't make this decision for anyone else, but I won't be first in line to sign up."

"Is that a nay?" Arianrhod narrowed her eyes.

"For me, it is." Mauvreen squared her shoulders. "I'll take my chances with power I'm familiar with."

Jonathan held back, sorry he'd even posed the question since it was such a can of worms. Rather like a wildcard that no one could predict until it was played—and that never did the same thing twice running. He made his way to Mauvreen's side and touched her arm. "It might be wise to not mention this at all. If I'd known all the ramifications, I'd never have brought it up."

"I'll think about it, but right now my bent is that it's a choice each witch needs to make for themselves."

"We doona have time for that," Arianrhod protested. "They're not even here yet, and we must be gone. As 'tis, we've tarried longer than I believe wise."

Energy shifted around Jonathan, familiar wisps of glittery power. "Witches!" He cast a wide net, seeking them, but was stymied by Arianrhod's warding. He gestured to Britta to help him and slipped out of sight of the others.

On the far side of his mother's enchantment, witches popped through gateways in twos, threes, and fours. He smiled at the sight of familiar faces and sent up a hasty prayer to Danu they'd come through unscathed.

"This way," Britta called, shooing them through the warding as they arrived. "Time for greetings later."

Jonathan waited until everyone had arrived, and then followed Britta back through the opening they'd carved in the wards. Mauvreen had already herded the witches into a rough group and was speaking hurriedly. He hoped to hell she wasn't outlining Arianrhod's doom-and-gloom immortality gambit. Nothing like quenching hope before they even started.

This isn't a computer-simulated action adventure game.

Maybe not, but the same principles apply.

Angus materialized from where he'd been huddled with Arianrhod and Lachlan and gestured toward the witches. "They were your family when I was lost in dreams, and I was grateful to them for watching over you." He spoke near Jonathan's ear. "When you were young, I never could explain how helpless I felt when the trance states swept me away. I tried, but I didn't have the right words."

"You don't need to explain it now, either." Jonathan turned to his father. "I knew you loved me. It's all any child needs."

Eyes the same shade as his bored into him. "You say that now, but you had some rough times. No one knows how today will end, so I wanted to make certain—"

"Let's just get through what's looming in front of us. Computer games are nothing like what we're heading into, and I don't feel very prepared. It's what I was thinking about before you started talking to me."

A corner of Angus' mouth turned downward. "I spent my life in dreams. How do you suppose I feel? We're both mated to warrior women, but I refuse to let Arianrhod take care of me."

"I heard my name." She threaded her way through the crowded courtyard. "We're ready to leave."

"I assume we're using magic to travel." Jonathan eyed his mother.

"Aye. 'Tis the only course that makes sense."

"There are a lot of us. Where will we come out?"

"Next to Eletea's cave, of course. Where else?"

Jonathan inhaled gingerly. How to make a suggestion his mother wouldn't reject out of hand? "Won't we create a huge disturbance in the kinetics? Or however you sense overlapping magical energy fields?"

"Aye, but it canna be helped. Unless we travel by foot or put some of us in cars and have the dragons fly." She clapped her hands smartly together. "Whatever it is, out with it."

"We could still use magic but come out a couple kilometers away."

"If anyone awaits us, they'd still feel a kinetic shift."

"Yes, but at least they won't be close enough to damage us."

"Mmph. 'Twould give us time to prepare if we're not drawn into an immediate skirmish. I like it. Soon as I tell the others, we're gone."

Her mind voice boomed in his head as she fed images and coordinates to everyone.

"We're flying," Britta announced as she ran to his side, light on her feet. "So are Lachlan and Kheladin. Eletea too, of course."

Jonathan turned to her. "Excellent idea. That way we can get a feel for how many we face."

"How many and what." Britta made a sour face. "'Tis the *what* that's troublesome. Come on." She headed toward Tarika, who hunkered next to the castle's outer wall system.

He loped after her. "I didn't realize you wanted me to fly with you."

"'Tis a little clumsier maneuvering with two atop Tarika, but we'll manage. She sent me to get you."

Even though they were probably flying into Hell, excitement quickened his pulse. He'd only ridden atop Tarika twice, but they'd been the most exhilarating experiences of his life. She and Britta shared a body the first time, so Britta was in the dragon's mind while they engaged the Morrigan in aerial combat.

Power simmered in the air all around him, making it glisten as everyone carved portals in the ether and left. Pride swelled through him. The witches could've said no. This wasn't their battle, not truly. Or they could've sat on the sidelines waiting to see if the Celts and dragons could work things out. Instead they were here, marshaling their ability, offering themselves freely.

He caught up to Britta when she reached the dragon. "Did Mauvreen tell the witches about Arianrhod's booby-trapped immortality offer?"

She shrugged and cast magic to move them both to Tarika's broad back. "I have no idea." She straddled the dragon, right at the base of its neck, and he sat behind her.

"She kept her mouth shut," Tarika said. "I listened in."

"Why?" Britta asked. "Whenever ye get that tone, there's a reason behind it."

"Ready?" Tarika ignored Britta's question. "Jonathan, reach around Britta and grab my lower horns just in front of you. That way, I can duck and weave, and neither of you should be in danger."

She extended red leathery wings, beating them hard. Once, twice, and they were airborne.

Jonathan watched as Arianrhod's castle disappeared into its layers of illusion. From fifty feet up, all he could see was a hazy whiteness that could've been anything. "Why were you worried about the immortality spell?" He repeated Britta's question.

"Too much magic mucks things up."

"I doona understand," Britta said. "If we face a handful of Infernals, plus a rogue dragon shifter or two, plus the Morrigan, 'twill keep us more than busy. How could more magic make things worse?"

Tarika blew fire in front of her, cutting off the flow when a small bush burst into flames. "There's also the question of Gwydion and Andraste, plus the Infernals' pets like Gryphons and Harpies. That's a lot of magic in one place. When many divergent types of power are expended in close proximity, strange things can happen."

"Like what?" Jonathan still held a mental image of his colored stones and stood ready to rearrange them, and his fledgling strategy.

"If I could predict such things, I wouldna be concerned." This time Tarika exhaled smoke. It burned his lungs and skin when they flew through it. "The addition of yet one more level of power might create a tipping point that will be our undoing."

"Define *undoing*." Britta tensed against his body, and her words held a curt note.

"The last time something like this happened, Europe sank into the Dark Ages. It took hundreds of years to recover."

Jonathan wanted to protest that the world had changed. They had technologies now to preserve them from the ignorance that had pushed people into small holdings, but he wasn't at all certain it would make much difference. In many ways, Earth stood at a far more precarious nexus now than it had seven hundred years before. A few more degrees of heat, a few more feet of oceanic rise, and they'd be in a world of hurt.

"Exactly," Tarika pronounced, having obviously helped herself to his thoughts.

Before Jonathan could say anything, Kheladin drew near with Lachlan and Maggie astride him. "Not much farther to go, and it's mighty quiet down there." The dragon dipped his long neck downward.

"Aye, too quiet," Lachlan said dourly. He glanced around. "Where's Eletea?"

"Good question." Tarika extended her mind voice, calling her.

"Don't get your scales ruffled." The small, copper dragon flew toward them at an angle from the east.

"What were you up to?" Tarika asked, once Eletea was close enough to hear without using telepathy.

"Trying to see if anyone sent a greeting party to warm themselves next to my cave. Don't worry, I made myself invisible."

"Another dragon could've sensed you," Kheladin growled.

"Well, they didn't. Anyway, I overflew my cave and didn't see a thing."

"Maybe we'll end up tracking the Crow after all," Britta muttered.

"We're landing. There." Tarika pointed with a wingtip just before she banked into a descending turn.

Britta straightened from where she'd been slumped against Jonathan. "Hold. Stay in the air. Something comes."

He pushed outward with his power, testing, tasting, sensing subtle disturbances in the weave of the air around him. At first nothing came to him, but then he felt it too. Delicate, elusive, just a hint of difference. He'd never have noticed if Britta hadn't spoken up. He nodded to himself. They were stronger as a pair. Some things alerted him that she missed, and the other way as well.

"To the north," Kheladin cried, rotating his wings like oars.

The smell hit him first. A cloying rottenness that reminded him of death, decay. Whatever it was knew they were here, so there was no reason to hold back. He pulled power, opening the reservoir deep within him where it dwelt. Britta did the same and threaded her magic with his into a potent brew.

"See what I mean about magic colliding?" Tarika bugled. "The mix from the two of you is almost enough to drive me from the skies."

"Do ye need us to temper it?" Britta asked, alarm lining her question.

"Nay, but imagine this amped a hundredfold. A thousand—"

"Harpies!" Lachlan bellowed. "I knew I recognized that stench from somewhere. "Doona let them touch you. Or breathe on you. They immobilize you with their breath, and then close in to steal your soul." He latched an arm around Maggie. Her blond hair was in tight braids against her skull, and her eyes were wide, terrified, but power shimmered around her.

Good. She's not too scared to defend herself.

He redirected his thoughts in a hurry, as a dozen bird women flew through a gash in the air, squealing, squawking. Long red hair swirled around their torsos, and silver eyes spun much like the dragons'. They were naked from the waist up, but their lower bodies were thickly feathered in colors from black to a soft gray. Wicked looking red-tipped talons grew from their fore- and hindlegs. Black wings erupted from between their shoulder blades.

Fire blazed from Eletea's mouth and enveloped one of the Harpies. Her hair caught fire, but nothing else burned. "What the hell?" Eletea screeched and flew closer.

"Nay!" Tarika shrieked. "Call earth magic. Mix it with fire. It's the only way to kill them."

Good to know. Jonathan adjusted the mix of magics flowing through him.

Eletea did a midair somersault, narrowly missing a Harpy heading right for her. Fire and smoke streamed from her. Tarika feinted left toward a trio grinning at them like a gang of teenaged gargoyles. The air around Eletea took on a bluish hue.

"Watch out!" Tarika screamed. "Or ye'll find yourself back in Fire Mountain."

"Thanks. Got it." The other dragon pin-wheeled her wings, and the feel of magic sheeting from her shifted to a higher frequency still.

Lachlan and Kheladin chivied two Harpies away from their fellows. So much power flowed from Lachlan, he glowed like a beacon as his dragon shot powerful darts into the Harpies' ivory-skinned breasts. Blood blossomed, gushing in black rivulets that grew into torrents. With hideous shrieks that threatened to rupture Jonathan's eardrums, the pair plummeted from the skies.

With Lachlan and his dragon diverted, another creature closed on their flank. Maggie saw her first and screamed a warning. Power pulsed from her—witch magic mingled with Lachlan's distinct signature—but the Harpy kept coming with her lips pulled back from her teeth in a silent snarl.

Lachlan shifted to face their newest assailant. Kheladin flew straight at the Harpy, shooting fire at her, along with magic so strong Jonathan wished for dark glasses. Light bloomed across his corneas, and he couldn't see much. A frantic cry from Lachlan cinched that they needed help.

Jonathan switched up his defensive strategy and let go of the dragon's horns. He needed his hands free to cast power more effectively. "Why are they leaving us alone?" he cried.

"'Tarika's a First Born. Even evil respects that," Britta said. "Can ye see what you're doing? That last strike nearly hit Maggie."

"No. I can't see. Not very well."

"Let me direct things."

"But you can't see any better than me."

"Aye, but I can. I have an inner eyelid. 'Tis part of the dragon shifter bond to protect me from fire."

Smoke thickened around them, and Jonathan pulled his shirt over his nose to cut down on the stinging when he inhaled. Through occasional breaks in the murk, he saw another Harpy—

was it the same one?—attach itself to Maggie's back and drag its talons through her flesh. Britta was deep in his head, in his heart, tapping shamelessly into his power as she flung handfuls at the Harpy, intent on saving Maggie.

No matter what they did, the Harpy hung on. Nothing stopped her. Maggie screamed, a piteous sound that ripped a hole in Jonathan's mind. Agony roiled through that sound—and hopelessness.

"Why isna the Harpy dying?" Britta shouted to Tarika. "I've hit her directly many times."

"Shielding. Something I havena come across afore. I'm landing. They're clumsy on land, and we need all the help we can get."

"Eletea! Kheladin!" Jonathan raised his mind voice. "Land. We'll regroup."

Between maintaining a defensive perimeter around himself and Britta—in case whatever kept the Harpies away from Tarika didn't extend to them—and constantly rebalancing so he didn't fall from Tarika's back, he lost sight of everyone else.

"Can you make us invisible?" he called to the dragon.

"Aye, but then I willna have as much power to defend us."

"Maybe just when we land then. Give us a few seconds to get our bearings, figure out where we can shoot without hurting our own."

"I'll do the best I can."

Britta leaned against Tarika's neck before focusing their combined power on a target he couldn't see.

"Is the Harpy still attached to Maggie?" Jonathan battled a sinking feeling. Out of all of them, she and Eletea were the weak links. Neither was immortal. The other witches weren't, either. Tarika landed with a thud.

"Och aye, 'tis worse than that." Britta chanted until the air immediately in front of them cleared.

The scene that slapped him hard was Lachlan holding tight to Maggie while the Harpy clung to her back with those wickedly sharp red talons. Blood spurted from multiple wounds in Maggie's back and sides. Lachlan and Kheladin were coated with it.

The expression on Lachlan's face was drawn, furious, terrible. Apparently giving up on magic, he drew a short dirk from somewhere and stabbed the Harpy in her neck, drawing the blade across it until black blood geysered, bubbling around them.

Kheladin settled heavily on the ground a few feet away, twisting his neck to spray the Harpy with fire.

Jonathan leapt from the dragon's back and pelted toward where Lachlan fought to wrest Maggie from the Harpy. Britta followed hard on his heels.

"Ye're not invisible," Tarika screeched. "Watch the skies."

A cursory glance told him no Harpies had followed them down besides the one carving holes in Maggie. "We need them off Kheladin," Jonathan yelled.

"We'll fight the battle we must, not the one we wish we had," Britta retorted. Light flashed around her as she vaulted to Kheladin's broad back, knife at the ready.

No more room on Kheladin, so Jonathan pushed as much lethal energy as he could muster at the Harpy from the ground while Lachlan and Britta stabbed her over and over. The smell of her blood made him long for unconsciousness. It stung his nostrils and made his stomach heave in rebellion, except there wasn't time to be sick. Images of wickedness so twisted and pervasive they defied words bombarded him.

Children flayed alive, flesh hanging from them in bloody strings.

Animals impaled with darts while they screamed and writhed in agony.

A woman who looked a lot like Britta tossed on a pyre and burned alive.

A dragon being dismembered, while its whirling eyes registered resignation—and horror.

"Doona look," Tarika said into his mind. "Harpies steal your hope. Once 'tis gone, they finish you off by taking your soul. Ye doona wish to be immortal without one. Trust me on that."

Christ! How do I not look at something blazoned across my brain?

He shook his head hard and held Britta in his mind's eye. Britta with her red-gold hair and imperious bearing. Britta telling him she loved him. Britta writhing beneath him as passion rocked her.

Britta.

Britta.

Britta.

The horrific imagery from the Harpy finally receded. It might've taken moments, but it felt like hours. He inhaled raggedly, and was instantly sorry. Harpy stench made him feel he'd never be clean again.

Kheladin directed more dragon's fire right at the Harpy. Maybe it was the combination of everything, but the fucking abomination finally let go of Maggie. Instead of falling to the ground, it folded in on itself and dissipated in a mass of smoking, stinking motes of slimy crud.

If Jonathan's stomach had been in an uproar before, it went into full rebellion, but he choked the sickness back. Even vomit tasted better than the reek of Harpies.

Lachlan landed lightly near him with Maggie cradled against his body. Jonathan opened his mouth to ask a question, but Lachlan's haunted eyes were all the answer he needed.

Britta jumped down from Kheladin, who'd begun to keen.

"Stop that!" Lachlan commanded. "She willna die. I'll see to it." The air around him burned bright red. Moments later, he was gone.

Kheladin dropped his head to his chest. Tears flooded gemstones around him.

Tarika closed from one side, Eletea from another. "We need you," Tarika said, her tone sharp. "Ye will fight by my side."

"Aye, First Born. I hear and obey," Kheladin said in a dry, dead tone.

"I got two more," Eletea said. "That's six down. Six to go."

"Ye're assuming no new ones show up," Kheladin countered.

"I didn't see any more," she said. "Trust your bondmate. He's taken Maggie somewhere safe."

"Either that or to bury her." Kheladin kicked his head back and spread his wings. "First Born. Fly with me. We'll kill those bitches." Without waiting for Tarika's reply, he beat the air with his wings and was gone.

With an irritated snort, Tarika followed, but not before she told Eletea, "Remain here. Kill any who escape us above."

Jonathan turned his eyes skyward. They still stung like hell from smoke and Harpy stench. Britta stood shoulder to shoulder with him. "What was Kheladin singing that upset Lachlan so?" he asked.

"The dragon dirge for the dead."

"It sounded different than what you sang for Malik and Preki."

"'Twas the same."

"I don't understand." He inhaled a weary breath. "Maggie wasn't dead. I'd have sensed it."

Britta turned sorrowful, golden eyes on him. "Ye're correct that Maggie yet lives, but she may as well be dead. The Harpy stole her soul afore we killed it."

CHAPTER 14

Tarika returned in a flurry of wings and settled back next to them. "Listen hard." Her eyes whirled faster than Jonathan had ever seen them. "I figured out your role in all this. Ye must follow Lachlan."

"Of course." Britta squared her shoulders. "We'll leave right away. Do ye know where he went?"

"Aye, I know, but ye're not going. Jonathan is. This is what he was born for. He must follow Lachlan and Maggie to Fire Mountain. Lachlan's gone there to plead for her life. The only way to save her is to bond her to her own dragon."

"Me?" Jonathan stammered. "But what can I do?"

"Your path will become clear once ye arrive." Tarika tossed her head. "'Tis far more than helping Lachlan, and ye must find your way without help from me."

"I still think I should go with him," Britta persisted. "He's never been to Fire Mountain. I can help. I'm sure of it."

"Nay, ye'll fight astride me. Your place is here." Tarika shot a meaningful glance at Britta just before she catapulted through the air and landed on the dragon's back.

"I could've done that myself." Britta nursed a sullen tone. "Ye dinna have to force me."

"Aye but I did. 'Tisn't the time for discussion."

"Assuming I can even find the place, what if the dragons won't let me in?" Jonathan demanded. Out of all the questions hammering him, it was the most worrisome of the lot.

Tarika bent low. Heat bloomed along both sides of his face as she dug a talon deep. He smelled the coppery scent of his own blood, felt it flow wetly down his cheeks.

"Ye've been marked by a First Born. They have no choice but to accept you, listen to you." Tarika blew steam on his stinging face. "Because ye carry my mark, ye can take the dragons' paths to our home. I'll blast a hole in the ether, but ye must go through it. Ye'll come out in Fire Mountain."

"Will Lachlan already be there?" Jonathan shook his head. The question sounded lame. If he had some key role to save Earth, he'd never put it together until he stepped back, absorbed the bigger picture.

Tarika snorted smoke. "Of course not. The time shaft is much slower."

"What should I look for once I get there? Is there a particular dragon who could help me?"

Tarika showered him with more steam. "Quiet. Seek faith in yourself. When ye cut to the bone, 'tis all any of us ever have. Quiet that river of doubt drowning you and ready yourself to leave."

"I love you," Britta shouted. "For the love of the gods, be careful."

"Ye doona caution heroes." Tarika puffed enough smoke the outline of her and Britta dimmed. "Ye trust they'll figure things out."

The air directly in front of him split, making a rending, ripping noise that he felt all the way to his toes. Before he could dissect the wisdom of trusting Tarika's instructions, he forced himself to leap through. He twisted to tell Britta he loved her too, but the world he knew was gone.

Darkness threatened to crush him, to steal his breath. Surely the dragon wouldn't have sent him to his death. Trust. Faith. Hope. He clung to all three, as his lungs exploded with the need to breathe. He'd never been to Fire Mountain. What if dragons processed oxygen differently? What if he wouldn't be able to breath there, either?

Got to get hold of myself. Now.

Britta went there and lived through it.

He pushed panic to a rear corner of his mind. He wasn't dead. Not yet. He tucked his face into his stretchy top, inhaling molecules of air trapped in the fabric. The absolute black surrounding him grayed around the edges, or maybe it was his consciousness ebbing. He cupped his hands in front of his face to capture whatever air might be there, and took a tentative breath.

Yes!

Oxygen. Not much, but more than there'd been moments before. He chided himself for being a fool. If there was some task he'd been born for, surely the gods—or the Fates, or whoever—wouldn't kill him off before he had a chance to tackle whatever it was.

The gray continued to lighten. Wind whistled around him, pushing from behind. He planted his feet as best he could on a shifting surface. At least his lungs had quit seizing, and he inhaled like a starving man. The pressure behind him grew until he feared it would squash him against whatever held him captive. This wasn't anything like the time shaft, with its friendly gray-pink walls and space to both sit and stand.

He summoned power to avoid being crushed, jockeying it to hold onto the slender slice of space he occupied. It helped a little. Before he could think up his next move, the thing he was in ripped open and ejected him onto red sand. He landed on his belly and somersaulted upright to look back at whatever he'd been in, but it was gone. The air shimmered in heated waves, and he looked out on a dry, dead world. Distant volcanoes belched sulfur fumes.

He tested the air with a series of shallow breaths that singed his mouth and nose and made his eyes tear with pain. Once he got past the shock of the hot, scorched air, it didn't hurt anymore.

Thank fucking Christ. A breathable atmosphere.

He ran a tentative finger down both sides of his face where Tarika had marked him. The gouges weren't bleeding—if they'd still been open when he arrived, the parched climate sealed them—but they ran deep. One was likely right on top of the healing scar from the Morrigan.

He struggled to his feet, dusting sand off his pants and gasping like a landed fish as he adapted to the heat. It was well over a hundred degrees, maybe as much as a hundred-twenty. He gazed around him, turning slowly in a full circle. Nothing green met his search. How the hell did anything live here? Let alone something as big as a dragon.

Jonathan felt as unprepared as he'd ever been. His hedge against his father's protracted absences was knowing where everything was and having plans piled over the top of backup plans. Even as a child, predictability and organization were his comfort zone.

"Gotta get over that," he muttered. Nothing stirred around him, and he sifted through ideas. What should he do? Which direction might yield dragons? Where would Lachlan and Maggie drop into this world? When they did, how could he help them? Hell, how would he find them?

Beyond that, he was here to do far more than play backup to Lachlan. Tarika's parting words cinched it. Not that doing what he could to help save Maggie's life wasn't important, but someone had gone to a lot of trouble to ensure Angus and Arianrhod produced him. If he had some critical role to play, he wished to hell they'd filled him in. Given him a few clues or maybe props.

Sweat beaded his forehead and ran down his sides. He considered taking off his shirt, but one glance at the pitiless suns blazing overhead convinced him it was a bad idea. He rolled his eyes at the incongruity of things. Two suns made their way across the sky—if they traveled east to west, it was closing on late afternoon, but maybe another sun occupied a different transit point. He swiped the back of one hand across his forehead. This world definitely didn't need another sun.

He was stalling, but for the best of reasons. For once in his life, he had no plan. No idea which way to go. Another scan of shimmering heat waves rising from red sand revealed a dragon winging its way toward him. This one was black and appeared to be in a hurry, its wings beating furiously.

Moments later, it dropped to the dry, baked surface close enough to touch him. "What are ye doing here?" it screeched. "Our world will soon be closed to those like you. Leave." It made flapping motions with both wings and forelegs. "Leave now, or your life is forfeit."

Jonathan pushed his shoulders back and faced the dragon, staring up at it, but avoiding looking right into its hypnotic blue-green eyes. "I carry the mark from a First Born. My understanding is you cannot cast me out."

"What?" The dragon sputtered cinders that set Jonathan's pants on fire in a few places. He batted at the smoking fabric.

The dragon bent until its head was on a level with Jonathan's and peered at his face, skinning scaled lips back from double rows of teeth. "Ye spoke true. What do ye want? State your business. Right now."

Good question. Hard to comply since I'm not certain myself.

"Well?" The dragon straightened and folded its stubby forelegs over its shiny black-scaled chest. "I doona have all day."

Best to start with the easy stuff.

"Lachlan, a dragon shifter mage—"

"I ken who he is well enough." The dragon spoke over him. "What about him? What does he have to do with ye being here?"

"He'll be here soon with his mate. She's wounded—"

"Too bad for her." The dragon interrupted again and rolled its whirling eyes. "I still doona understand what this has to do with you. Or why Lachlan would bother bringing her here."

Jonathan clamped his jaws in a tight line. "If you'd let me get more than three words in a row out, maybe then you'd understand."

"Fine. I'm waiting."

Jonathan sketched out Maggie's predicament as he understood it and her need to bond with a dragon of her own.

"It'll never happen." The dragon said flatly. "We're done with your kind. And the Celts. And the Norse gods, and the Greeks. All of you. Done." He dusted his forelegs together.

Jonathan opened his mouth to argue that it was a bad idea, that closing Fire Mountain would have consequences that might backfire and sabotage the dragons, but he lacked hard evidence, so he waited. The dragon was chatty. Maybe he'd let something slip that Jonathan could use.

"Nothing ye've said explains why ye're here. I understand why Lachlan will show up, but what's your connection? Surely ye dinna travel all this way to help him." The dragon puffed smoke and changed topics. "How is it ye carry a mark from Tarika, one of our First Born?"

"My mate is bonded to her."

Surprise flexed through the dragon's scaled face. "Ye're Britta's mate?"

"Yes."

The dragon tossed its head back and roared with laughter, spraying everything in a twenty foot radius with cinder-laced spittle. "She picked a human. What a waste."

Anger kindled before Jonathan could tamp it down. "Look closer," he growled.

"Ye invited me." The dragon smirked before it bent and gripped Jonathan's chin between two six-inch talons as shiny and black as the rest of it. In true dragon form, once it immobilized its prey, it forged a path into his mind.

The heat he'd felt before was nothing compared to what rumbled through him. Jonathan's brains were baking from the inside out when the dragon let go in a hurry and backed up a step of two. "Arianrhod," it sputtered. "And Cathbad, but not quite so directly. Why didn't ye say so?"

"Would it have made any difference?" Jonathan wanted to rub his aching temples and jaw, but kept his hands by his sides. Any show of weakness might encourage the dragon to further bully-boy tactics, and for the moment, Jonathan seemed to have gained the upper hand.

"Maybe. Probably not. We're done with all of you."

"Has your council fully decided that?"

The dragon looked away, but Jonathan surged forward with a truth casting. "Answer me."

"Nay. Not yet."

Riding on instinct, a relatively new experience, Jonathan pushed into what looked like a breach. "Tell me where I can find them. I would speak with your council."

"Our Seers said today would bring…surprises." The dragon's imperious tone faded.

"Maybe I'm one of them. Where can I find your council?" Jonathan repeated.

"Over there." The dragon extended a black wingtip. "It's a long way."

"I'll figure it out. My magic works here. Can you tell me how far, or send an image into my mind, so I know what I'm looking for?"

"I may pay for this, but I'll take you." Steam hissed from between its double rows of teeth. "If it comes down to it, tell them ye commanded my compliance through your link with Tarika."

Jonathan bit back a grin. So Tarika's name carried weight here. Good piece of intel. Maybe he could pick the dragon's brain a bit as they traveled. "I'd be most grateful for your assistance." He inclined his head. "I'm Jonathan Shea. What's your name?"

The dragon hesitated, looking away. Moments slid past before he raised his head. "I am Keene."

A familiar chord thrummed inside him. Where the hell had he heard that particular dragon name before?

"I'll save you the trouble of searching your memory. I once loved your mother, but we shall not speak of her. 'Tis one condition of my help. Get on my back."

Jonathan inhaled so sharply, he almost choked on saliva. Mother's dragon lover? Out of all the dragons in Fire Mountain, what were the odds for him to draw this one as his guide? Was it an indication things were coming full circle? If so, what things?

If it's an omen, it's pretty fucking murky.

Christ, there was a lot he didn't know. He wished for Tarika—and Britta—but thinking of them reminded him of the battle, and urgency pounded into him. Whatever his business here, he had to get it wrapped up and get back. Tarika and Britta couldn't die, but all those witches who'd pitched in to help raise him sure could.

He kept his face as clear of emotion as he could, as he cast a spell that dropped him onto Keene's back. "Nice to meet you." He aimed for a neutral tone. "Ready when you are."

Keene spread huge wings and beat the air with them. Jonathan grabbed the dragon's horns and hung on. He wanted to ask so many things, but Keene had been quite clear they wouldn't talk about Arianrhod. After his initial chattiness, the dragon didn't seem inclined to talk at all.

The best way to get others to open up was to offer something new, so Jonathan went on a data gathering expedition. "We're under attack. It's one of the reasons Tarika marked me and opened the kinetics to get me here fast."

"From whom?" Keene didn't sound very interested. Maybe he was relieved Jonathan wasn't going to bring Arianrhod up, or maybe it never occurred to him Jonathan wouldn't follow his instructions to the letter.

"The Morrigan and a bunch of her allies. I fought off Harpies before I came here."

Keene swiveled his head to glance at Jonathan. "Serves those bloody Celts right for not taking the hard road and shipping the

Crow to us centuries ago. She's been major trouble since she was hatched."

"Haven't Celts and dragons had something like a non-interference policy?"

"Never heard the term, but I can guess well enough what it means. The answer is aye. They stayed away from our politics, and we from theirs."

Jonathan hesitated, unsure where to pound the spike into the can of worms he was about to open. Should he aim for the ends in an attempt at subtlety? Or should he blast the middle, knowing retreat wouldn't be possible. Blowing out a tense breath, he picked option B.

"Tarika said the mix of too many kinds of magic in a single place can spell disaster. Do you know why?"

"Of course. Every type of magic disturbs the kinetics holding worlds in place. If ye move too many elements at the same time, the world's roots erode, and the whole thing becomes unstable and may fail."

"Give me an example."

"If the Celts and Norsemen and Greeks all showed up here at the same time and blasted away with their power—and dragons countered it with our own—Fire Mountain could spin back into the suns that spawned it. It couldna deal with the pressure of so many layers of stability under attack at the same time."

Jonathan felt his eyes widen. "Are you certain? Aren't there lesser things that might happen first?"

Keene shrugged, and his scales clanked together. "Depends how much power is expended. We've always kept a tight rein on Fire Mountain. Its ability to sustain life hangs by a thread, so we've never had leeway to run experiments."

"I suppose Earth could return to its sun as well," Jonathan ventured.

"Not likely. All the non-magical life forms have a dampening effect. Nay, Earth's end will be much less dramatic, more of a gradual retreat."

"You do realize Earth will die if you shut the gateway between it and Fire Mountain." Jonathan didn't pose it as a question.

"What happens to humankind is of little concern to dragons."

So the dragons know. And they don't care, but then why would they?

Jonathan ran probability models much the same way he would've in game design. Not having a display in front of him was an impediment, but not a huge one. He'd created so many types of games, his brain was almost as quick as computer-simulated modeling.

"Hang on," Keene cautioned. "We're nearly there. Wouldn't do to have ye break your neck falling off my back."

"Thanks for the warning," Jonathan called with far more cheer than he felt. What could he say to reach the dragons? Creatures older than him by thousands of years. Creatures who saw humankind as the merest blip on a cosmic radar screen.

Why was he here? Was that his task? To avert the dragons from taking their magic ball and going home? Tarika knew, but she hadn't told him. Britta must know by now too, but she hadn't hastened to his side. Either she wasn't worried about him, or her dragon forbade interference. Or maybe she was on her way, but limited by the time shaft where travel took far longer.

"Looks as if Lachlan's here." The dragon blew smoke straight ahead.

The dragon's words cut into Jonathan's thoughts, and he narrowed his eyes to a tight focus. Lachlan was indeed there, with Maggie still cradled in his arms. If she'd regained consciousness at some point, she'd slipped away again.

An enormous gold dragon stood nose to nose with Lachlan, and even from Jonathan's vantage point, the sound of raised voices reached him, carried by the hot, dry wind.

Keene touched down, and Jonathan vaulted lightly from his back. The gold dragon stopped yelling at Lachlan long enough to shoot a poisonous look Keene's way. "More trash? What were ye thinking, Keene? If ye found human debris, ye should've sent him packing. Not brought him into our verra midst."

"He carries Tarika's mark and her instruction to allow him congress with our council." Keene pushed to his full eight-foot height. "Ye may feel comfortable ignoring edicts from our First Born, but I'm much younger than you. More likely to follow orders."

"What about my orders?" the gold snarled. "Which were to not allow anyone entrance to Fire Mountain?"

"Tarika's wishes outplay yours," Keene snarled back.

Jonathan shielded his thoughts. He'd never said a word about Tarika forcing the council's hand to allow him in. He bounded to Lachlan and laid a hand on Maggie's pale forehead. "Jesus!" he blurted. "She's ice cold. How could she be this cold here?"

Before Lachlan could answer, the gold dragon blasted Keene with fire. "Leave. Ye've done enough damage for one day."

Without a backward glance, the black dragon took to the skies.

"What can I do?" Jonathan asked Lachlan.

The dragon shifter trained haggard green eyes on him. "There's naught anyone can do unless the Guardian relents and allows a willing dragon to bond with Maggie. The Harpy stole her soul."

"Can't we hunt it down and get it back?"

Lachlan shook his head. "We killed it. Remember? Not just killed it, scattered its bits through several universes."

The implications arrowed home, and Jonathan swallowed hard. "Why didn't you say something? All of us targeted it. Hell, you stabbed it too."

"I dinna know." Lachlan's shoulders sagged, and he turned toward the gold dragon, the one he'd named Guardian. "Please. I'll do anything ye ask. Hunt for treasure to line your hoards for a hundred years."

"My answer is final." The Guardian clanked his dual rows of teeth together. "I suggest all three of you," he focused on Jonathan, his eyes dripping menace as they spun, "find your way home." The air around him hissed and bubbled. Jonathan blinked hard. If he didn't know better, he'd have believed the dragon melted into nothingness.

He stared at empty air where the dragon had stood. "What do we do now?"

"I have no fucking idea." Lachlan kissed Maggie's forehead, crooning to her in Gaelic. "None at all."

"We'll figure it out. Together." Kheladin bugled from where he exploded through the dead, dry air of Fire Mountain.

"Bondmate." Lachlan's head snapped up.

"Aye. We killed all but two of the Harpies, so Tarika released me." Kheladin thumped to the ground and breathed steam over Maggie. "Is she any worse?"

"Nay. Nor is she better."

"Did ye plead her case?" Scales clanked together as Kheladin moved closer still.

"You just missed it," Jonathan muttered. "Some gold dragon told us to go to hell."

"Was it the Guardian?" Kheladin eyed Lachlan.

"Aye."

"Who's the Guardian, and why does he hold so much power?" Jonathan demanded.

"'Twould take too long to explain," Lachlan said, his voice thin, pained. "I guessed wrong when we came here, and I doona believe she'll survive a journey to my second choice."

"Which was?" Kheladin prodded.

"Where else? The Celts. They hold the keys to immortality magic. Mayhap they could recreate a soul for her."

"There's got to be another way." Jonathan sucked breath past his clenched teeth. "If the Morrigan's any bellwether, you can't trust those fuckers."

CHAPTER 15

$\mathcal{A}$rianrhod barely had time to exit her traveling portal and crouch into a fighting stance when violence erupted all around her and Angus. Witches were still materializing from their own gateways. "Guard them as best ye can," she called to Angus. "Let's at least get them out here where they can help fight."

Angus ground his teeth together. "If the witches are cooked alive before they leave their gateways, I'll blame himself for the rest of my days."

Arianrhod created one protective canopy after the next. Angus caught on fast, and did the same. She paused long enough for a quick scan of the skies. Where were the fucking dragons? They could really use a spot of aerial support.

As if in response to her thoughts, dragons appeared with fire shooting from their mouths, but not the ones on their side. Five of them in multiple colors dropped from the skies, closing fast. When she absorbed what they faced, it took all her years as a warrior not to cut and run. Gryphons dive-bombed them, their eagle beaks snapping hungrily, and their lion hindquarters tucked under to not impede flight. All three Furies flew with them, howling their glee.

The air crackled with static electricity, as magic zoomed from all directions. Try as she might, Arianrhod couldn't locate her brother or Andraste—or any Celts for that fact. Except the Crow, clinging to a clifftop with her talons. Wings spread to their fullest black glory, she cawed loudly, exhorting her odd mix of troops forward. Four more rogue dragons ranged wide. Two on the ground and two in the air. She didn't see mages with them and presumed they were caught up in the bond that only allowed one physical form.

"Damn it! Come out and fight like men," she screamed, knowing full well no one would hear her over the din of cries, shrieks and roars. When she found out who the dark mages were, she'd crush them, just like she'd crushed Rhukon and Connor.

Just like we crushed Rhukon...

She took a quick tally of her magic. The only way to deal with dragon shifters was to break the bond they held with their dragons. Once the bond lay in ruins, neither man nor dragon was immortal. She ground her jaws together until her teeth ached. She could take them out, but only one at a time, which would alert not only the others but the Morrigan. No doubt the Crow would move heaven and earth to keep her immortal duos in the field.

"All the witches are safely out." Angus edged to her side. "They won't stay safe for long, I fear, but at least they're forming lines and blending power. Not all the dragons are bonded."

"How do ye know?" she demanded.

"How else?" A bloodthirsty grin stretched his lips back from his teeth. "The witches and I killed three of them."

A long, feral bugle drew her eyes skyward. Tarika and Eletea flew into the din, fire and magic geysering around them. Magics collided making an ominous booming sound, and Arianrhod shuttered her ears.

"Britta's riding Tarika, but where's Jonathan? Lachlan and Maggie are missing too. And Kheladin." Angus shaded his eyes with a hand as he scanned the sky.

Furies flew at them, their red eyes blazing with hatred. White skirts fluttered around them, but they were naked from the waist up. Coal dark snakes where hair should've been streamed backward, coiling, spitting, hissing, caught in the slipstream. Each Fury raised a torch with fire that burned straight up in defiance of the laws of physics.

Angus raised both hands and shouted a command in what sounded like ancient Gaelic. It was so long since she'd heard it spoken, it surprised her. He tossed more words after the first batch, wearing his power like a banner that spilled from him as he curried magic, drawing it from the earth he stood upon. Surprise bloomed on the Furies' faces, transforming them from menacing to something manageable. Arianrhod didn't wait for the bitches to recover, she charged them with magic of her own, cursing them back to where they'd come from.

Angus's words shifted to song. Blood spurted from fifty wounds, a hundred, as the Furies nailed him with barbs, but he didn't waver, and his skin healed as quickly as it ruptured.

"Ye have no congress here!" Arianrhod shook her fists at the three atrocities. "We havena sinned."

"She says different." One of the Furies pointed a long-nailed finger at the Morrigan.

"Taste my blood." Angus swiped a hand across his torso. His top was shredded and he extended bloody fingers toward the nearest Fury. "You'll discover my innocence."

Arianrhod held her breath as one of the snakes coiled forward, its tongue zooming out like a starving tiger intent on prey. Myth held the snakes carried deadly poison, but since Angus offered himself, the Fury couldn't unleash its venom.

The snake coiled back into place in the Fury's macabre hair, hissing long and low. Red eyes widened in surprise. "Ye spoke true." She shifted her unsettling gaze to Arianrhod. "Mayhap 'tis you who are the guilty party."

"Or them." Another Fury tossed a hand skyward where Eletea, Britta, and Tarika fought Gryphons.

"Perhaps 'tis them." The other Fury pointed at the witches, who'd formed groups to take on four of the dragons.

"None of us would be here if it werena for the Morrigan." Ariarhod held her ground. "She doesna care for aught but sowing chaos."

"Withdraw your power!" one of the Furies commanded Angus, who'd begun his chanting again.

"Only if you withdraw yours," he countered. Most of his wounds had closed, and blood no longer ran down his sides.

"Done." The Furies formed a tight, aerial circle, talking among themselves.

"I dinna know ye could heal yourself," Arianrhod said.

"Neither did I. At least not this fast." A wry grin twisted his face into a grimace. "They're leaving. I had no idea they hosted snakes. Are they related to Medusa?"

"Aye, related, but only in the most distant sense." She watched the Furies shimmer into motes of nothingness and considered what to do next. "At least we're making progress. If we get rid of the dragon shifters, the Morrigan will leave."

"How do you know that?" Angus narrowed his eyes and scanned the battlefield.

"Educated guess." She followed the line of his gaze. A few witches lay in the dirt, but most of them were still on their feet. Still no sign of Lachlan, Maggie, and Kheladin—or Jonathan. The quicker they could get this buttoned up, the better.

"I thought we wanted to capture the Morrigan and deliver her to Fire Mountain."

"Another reason to wipe out the dragon shifters. Tarika and Eletea seem to have the Gryphons on the defensive. They're not as brave as legends paint them. If they doona like the odds, they'll leave."

Angus sifted blood-stained fingers through his hair. "Aren't dragon shifters immortal?"

She eyed him. "Aye, but I can break their bond."

"Really?" His amber eyes gleamed with interest. "Map it for me. Probably better if we knock out two at a time. Maybe the others will take the hint and go."

"I really want to know who the mages are." She shouted to make herself heard.

"They'll never show themselves. They know you can chase them through time," he shouted back. Piteous screams rose around them, and he ducked to avoid a flaming Gryphon as it plummeted to the ground, spewing foul-smelling smoke.

The air grew even thicker with smoke, cinders, and the metallic reek of blood. Where the hell was Jonathan? Worry grew as time passed, and he didn't show up. She started to share the bond-severing spell with Angus, then stopped. What she planned required fire, lots of it, and his strengths were earth and water.

"Mine might work better." He'd clearly been inside her head. "What about this?"

Images shot through her head. At first she couldn't sort them, then they rocked her with brilliant cohesion. "Aye! Do it. I'll do the same. Ye're right about it being more effective. I'll take the green dragon."

"And I'll target the larger red. On my count of three. One, two…"

Arianrhod laced earth and water before blending fire into her working. Power ran hot through her, and she threw her usual stops wide open. The green dragon's mouth flew open in outrage. Its frantic bugling quickly shifted to a higher note as terror rippled through it.

A man took form next to the dragon. Fright rolled off him in waves, and his brown eyes went wide, with the whites showing all around. Dark, greasy hair fell to his naked shoulders.

Recognition flared. "Count Trenton," Arianrhod sneered. "When did ye join the dark side?"

"Never mind that." Angus deployed power so potent light formed a glowing nimbus around his hands, and another man, this one very blond with Arctic-blue eyes, took shape next to the red dragon. "You likely know this one too. I say we kill them, quick and clean."

She wasn't inclined to argue. Much as she wanted to slap sense into Trenton and the other man, who she actually didn't recognize, she'd lived long enough to understand her outrage wouldn't change a thing. A lethal, focused beam of death left her fingertips and arrowed straight into Trenton's chest. The man mewled, high notes of agony mingled with something that might've been regret, before he crumpled to the ground.

The green dragon stared at its erstwhile mate for long moments, and then spread its wings.

"Not so fast." Tarika landed in front of the green dragon with a thump that shook the ground.

The blond man took off at a dead run. Why wasn't he using magic? And then Arianrhod thought she knew. He'd been bonded to his dragon so long, it would take time for him to sort where its power left off and his own began.

"Stand back!" Angus barked. A poisonously sweet song flowed from his lips, filling the air with compulsion. Even Arianrhod found herself turning toward Angus, drawn by the Siren-esque timbre of his music.

The blond flapped like a reluctant marionette suspended from someone else's strings. Jets of white-heat shot from Angus' fingertips, leaving red flowers where they augured into the dragon shifter's body. Blood pulsed skyward from a ruptured artery. Before he could crumple to the ground, Gryphons converged on him and began eating him alive amid his squeals of agony.

The Gryphon pack snarled and snapped over him until one of them roared an invitation and bounded to Trenton.

"Thank fucking Christ that one's already dead." Angus rolled his eyes. "Two of them screeching like Banshees might be a bit much."

Tarika still faced off across from the green, and Eletea planted herself in front of the newly mage-less red.

Arianrhod shifted her gaze to the Morrigan. Still perched on the same rock, she'd folded her wings behind her body. The witches had redoubled their efforts to keep the remaining two dragon shifters corralled. Rather than defensive magic, their spells tethered the dragons, keeping them earthbound. The other two dragons wanted to leave. Nothing was worth losing the bond to their mages—the one conferring immortality. Clearly, they had no idea the mages were draining their magic.

I can fix that.

Arianrhod leapt lightly over rocks and settled near the dragons, a black and another red. "Your mages plot to drain your power. In truth, they've been draining it for years. Ye'd do well to return to Fire Mountain and shuck the bond."

The black writhed. "It's all I can do to keep my mage from breaking free. Filthy craven. He wants to run."

Tarika angled her head atop her long neck. "Doona let him free." She inhaled wetly. When she exhaled a golden net dropped over the green dragon. It struggled, but the power-imbued threads just drew tighter.

"Neat trick," Arianrhod muttered. "Need to learn that one."

"Why'd you do that?" the green demanded. "I demand to return to Fire Mountain with the others. If they get to go home, I should too."

"Denied." Tarika skinned her scaled lips away from her teeth. "Your soul is poisoned. Ye'll never darken Fire Mountain's gates again."

"It's my mage's fault," the dragon insisted. "I never would've—"

"Silence!" Eletea thundered. "You shame our kind with your groveling."

Tarika lumbered to where Arianrhod stood. Mauvreen joined them. "Get over here," Tarika called to the larger red dragon who stood in front of Eletea. Its shoulders drooped and its tail dragged over the uneven ground.

"Yes, First Born. I hear and obey," it said in a hoarse, croaky voice that rustled like dead leaves.

Tarika eyed the three dragons—two reds and a black. "I will open a portal to Fire Mountain. You will walk through it and turn yourselves over to our council to determine your punishment."

"The hell I will." The black spat fire Tarika's way.

"I didn't say that," the dragon protested. "It was my mage. Bastard. Get him out of me."

Tarika nodded sharply to Angus. "Ye heard my dragon. If ye'd be so kind."

"Who gets to kill him once he's out?" Angus raised one dark brow.

"Me." Tarika bared her double rows of teeth. "For denigrating the bond to one of my dragons."

Power flashed from Angus. The red-haired shifter was no sooner in his own skin before Tarika fried him with fire. The roasted meat smell of singed flesh rose into the smoky air, joining other noxious scents of death and destruction, just before Gryphons converged to finish him off.

Tarika ripped a portal into existence and sent the three dragons scuttling through it before she scanned the skies, bugling. "Five other dragons were here. Where are they?"

"The witches and I killed three," Angus said. "Likely the other two left."

"Killed?" Tarika bugled louder. "Killed means they werena bonded. How could this be?" She twirled to face the Morrigan, who stared defiantly. "Ye corrupted my dragons." She shot fire at the Crow, but the flames rolled off her shiny, black feathers.

The Morrigan clacked her beak together. "Clever of you to figure that out," she screeched.

Tarika flew at her, but a phalanx of Gryphons blocked her way. The dragon blasted them with blue-white heat.

Mauvreen bent her head close to Arianrhod. "Could you come, please? Two witches lay near death. They're beyond my ability to heal."

"Of course. Lead the way." She tore her gaze from Tarika and loped after the witch. "Were they your only casualties?" she called.

Mauvreen shook her head. "No. We lost half a dozen." She fell to her knees next to an older dark-haired man. His eyes were shut, and sweat sheened his brow.

Arianrhod knelt and laid her hands on the witch, assessing his injuries. "Gored by Gryphon claws?"

Mauvreen nodded. "Do what you can."

"'Tisn't the claws as much as the poison they carry." She sent power spinning through the places she touched the fallen witch. A ragged boom back near the dead dark mages told her the kinetics Tarika opened to ship her dragons home had shut.

She grappled with the witch's spirit. It was trying to leave, to escape the dying body. "Stay," she suggested. "I can fix this, but only if you stay."

The man's hazel eyes flickered open, registering her, before they dropped shut again. Arianrhod patched and spun, weaving magic into the witch's broken places.

"He's stronger," Mauvreen murmured from her place on the man's other side.

"Aye. He'll live to fight another day."

"Our healers can take this one from here." Mauvreen pushed to her feet and called a woman to tend to things. "Let's see if we have as good a luck with Sara."

Arianrhod patted the man's hands and thanked his spirit for having faith and believing in her. On her feet, she followed Mauvreen to another prone form. A glance at the woman's face made her hurry.

"She's gone." Mauvreen folded the woman's hands atop one another. Her short, blonde hair was cropped close to her head. She was young, probably not more than thirty, though it was hard to tell with witches.

Arianrhod crouched and laid a hand on either side of the woman's head, probing, analyzing. Her heart wasn't beating, but her spirit remained, not nearly as anxious as the man's to desert its body. "There is one way." She narrowed her eyes and met Mauvreen's troubled amber gaze.

"It's dicey magic, or you wouldn't sound like that. What's the risk for Sara?"

"She might go mad. My only choice is the immortality spell. It'll work, since her spirit lingers."

"Or she might die," Mauvreen muttered. "Mmph. Not relevant, since she's already dead."

"Hurry," Arianrhod urged. "If I'm to do this, I must start now."

"Ask her spirit." Mauvreen raised eyes lined with exhaustion. "I know you can talk to them, since I heard you do it with Micah."

Arianrhod nodded. *"Sara."* She sent her voice into the woman's soul. *"You've heard us. What do you want?"*

"Frightened. Cold."

"Do you want my magic to bring you back?"

"Will I lose my mind?" Her spirit voice grew dimmer, wispy.

"Maybe. I don't know."

Sara's spirit was silent for so long, Arianrhod feared it had left, yet when she felt for it, it pulsed faintly. *"Ye must decide,"* she said at last. *"Time is running out."*

"Let me go. At least this death is clean. Immortality would be a bitch if I went mad."

Arianrhod felt the wrenching pull when Sara bolted upward, heading for a light only she could see. Tears flooded her eyes at the young witch's bravery.

Mauvreen was weeping softly. "Not many would've had the courage to refuse," she said between snuffling sobs.

"Aye, not many at all." Arianrhod gently closed Sara's eyes and rocked back on her heels before getting to her feet.

A quick scan told her today's battle was over. Even the Gryphons had left, but not before they stripped all three dragon mage carcasses to nothing but bones. When she looked for the Morrigan, she wasn't at all surprised to find the rock she'd perched on empty.

Damn! Not that she expected the Battle Crow to stick around to face defeat. It wasn't her style.

Angus made his way to her. Dirt smudged his face, and his hands were still bloody. He wrapped an arm around her. "More will follow, but not today."

"Do ye know what happened to Jonathan? Lachlan, Kheladin, and Maggie are missing too."

He squeezed his eyes hard shut for a fast moment, and her heart skipped a beat. She twisted from under his arm and twirled to face him. "Tell me. Now."

"They faced Harpies as they flew here. One stole Maggie's soul. Lachlan took her to Fire Mountain—"

"Och aye." She waved an impatient hand. "To seek a dragon to share its soul through the shifter bond. But what of Jonathan? Where is our son?"

"He's gone to Fire Mountain too. Tarika figured out why Cathbad told you not to abort him all those years back. She marked him and sent him through the dragons' paths. You didn't ask after Kheladin, but he joined Lachlan."

Arianrhod fell back a pace. Marked by a First Born? Traveling through dragon-crafted kinetics? She chanted furiously, ordering a time shaft to appear, even if here wasn't a normal place for one.

Angus took her arm. "Tarika says you can't follow, that this is Jonathan's task."

"'Tis why Britta's still here, isna it?"

He nodded, his expression solemn. "Our son is a man. He'll figure this out. He's strong and capable."

Arianrhod loosed her spell. Her throat closed with emotion until breathing became a struggle, and she fought against an inane desire to throw herself into Angus's arms and sob.

Later.

She summoned different magic until it shimmered around her like an incandescent tide.

"Where are we going?" He stood tall.

She stared at him. Like her he was filthy, streaked with dirt, gore, and guts, but light shone from the depths of his eyes. Until he asked, she'd been about to go alone. "To Ceridwen to ask for help."

"Good idea. While we're there, shall we have a word with Gwydion and Andraste? Not sure about you, but I really want to know why they freed the Crow."

CHAPTER 16

*J*onathan placed a hand on Maggie, weaving a tendril of magic into the power Lachlan was using to hold life in her body. Rather than the multi-hued human spirits he was used to, he ran up against an opaque, gray wall. "That gray place. Is it hiding her essence?"

Lachlan shook his head sadly. "Nay, 'tis what's there in its stead. If I withdraw my magic, she'll truly be lost. Neither living nor dead —forever."

Kheladin straightened, careful not to jostle Maggie. "Did ye ask Eletea to bond with Maggie afore ye left?"

Lachlan's eyes widened. A cavalcade of emotion from embarrassment to shame to hope rippled across his face. "Och aye, and I'm a prime fool. A dragon—a good dragon, not one tempted by charlatans—was right there, and I ran the other way."

Kheladin sent a blast of fire skyward, followed by three more in quick succession. The air thickened with the stink of dragon magic, ozone mixed with sulfur, and the Guardian stepped through a fire-tinged gateway.

"How dare ye summon me—" he began, and then his whirling golden gaze fell on Kheladin. "Och, 'tis you." He folded his forelegs across his scaled chest. "Ye're on shaky ground too. I doona march to your song."

"Thank you for heeding my call." Kheladin bowed low, showing deference.

"What do ye want?" The Guardian hurried on without waiting for an answer. "If 'tis to plead for your dragon shifter's mate, doona bother."

Kheladin squared his shoulders and met the Guardian's gaze head on. "What I ask is small. Mark them."

"Whatever for?"

"I would take them with me through the dragons' paths, but I'm neither old enough nor powerful enough for our gateways to recognize a sign from me."

The Guardian uncrossed his forelegs and lumbered to where Lachlan stood, holding Maggie. He bent and dropped a clawed hand on her forehead. "How could ye have been so stupid as to allow a Harpy access to your mate?" he shrilled at Lachlan.

"Do ye not think I've asked myself the same question over and over since it happened?" Lachlan shot out a hand and gripped one of the dragon's talons. "Mark us, and we'll be gone from here."

The Guardian wrenched his talon from Lachlan's grasp. "What of you?" he asked Kheladin. "Ye were here with Tarika, and then both of you left. All dragons are to return to Fire Mountain by order of our council, yet ye left with one of our First Born."

"Nay. She left with me."

The Guardian raised one scaled golden brow. "If I grant your request, Lachlan and his mate willna require your presence in the traveling pathways, so ye'll remain here. Correct?"

"No deals." Lachlan cut in before Kheladin could answer. "Ye must offer your magic freely, or I fear 'twill carry unpleasant side effects."

"If I do this thing," The Guardian thumped Lachlan's chest, "ye must promise ye'll never use the dragons' paths again. Just this once, and then never again." He shifted his attention to Kheladin. "I want your vow too that ye'll never open a gateway for your bondmate after this one time. Before ye agree, there's something else. If we opt to close Fire Mountain, ye must give me your word ye'll return to your own kind."

"I hear and agree, Guardian." Kheladin bowed again, as stiff and formal as his words.

"I agree to your terms as well," Lachlan said. "And I offer my heartfelt thanks for your assistance and for allowing me the honor of one of your dragons as my bondmate all these years."

"Save those pretty words." The Guardian flashed forward and dragged a razor-sharp talon down both sides of Lachlan's face. When he was done, he made a similar mark across Maggie's forehead. Blood welled, then flowed. Lachlan's bright red, while Maggie's held a bluish tinge.

Kheladin didn't waste any time. He blasted the air with fire and a spell that made Jonathan's ears ring and set his teeth on edge. A gateway formed, and the dragon herded Lachlan and Maggie into it.

The whole thing was over so fast, Jonathan wasn't certain what he'd witnessed. There'd been a gateway, but all evidence of it was gone. The Guardian took on a shimmery aspect.

"Wait!" Jonathan raced toward the gold dragon. "Don't leave."

The dragon's outline firmed, but not by much. "Ye overreach yourself." His words sounded garbled, as if he spoke from the bottom of a well.

"Where can I find your council? I must speak with them."

The Guardian took shape again, annoyance flaring from his golden eyes. "We dinna request your appearance in our midst. I took care of Lachlan's problem. Ye must leave too. Since ye carry Tarika's sigil, ye doona need me for aught."

Here it is. What do I say?

Before anything came out of his mouth, the Guardian was truly gone. Vanished as if he'd never been there.

"Shit!" Jonathan picked up a nearby rock and heaved it at one of the many red dirt cliffs nearby. The land was bumpy where he stood, reminiscent of the knolls and barrows in Scotland and Ireland. Keene had brought him here, and this is where he'd found Lachlan. Presumably, the dragons' council chambers weren't far distant. No buildings marred the landscape, which meant whatever he sought had to be underground.

It made sense, but it would take hours, days, to search each of the lumps and cliffs ranged around him. Easy to lose his bearings too and waste time examining the same ground twice. He scanned the red dirt and pocketed white pebbles. They held enough contrast to show up from a distance. Next he found half a dozen flat red rocks. He built a cairn where he stood to mark a center point and searched in concentric rings, working outward.

Time dripped past, and he collected many more flat rocks and pebbles. Once he determined a mound wasn't the right one, he shaped the red dirt into a conical pattern and put a flat rock atop it, followed by three white stones. The pattern was different enough from anything that occurred naturally, it was easy to see which barrows he'd inspected—and which ones remained.

Thirst became a constant, nagging companion. He looked around more than once, thinking he should drop what he was doing in favor of hunting down water. There had to be some here. The twin suns clung to the horizon for an obscenely long time, blasting him with heat. He had a feeling it wouldn't be much cooler after they disappeared, but at least a third sun hadn't shown up to mock him.

He sank to a large, flat boulder atop a rise and surveyed his work. He'd moved a good quarter mile from where he began. Surely Keene wouldn't have dropped him off quite so far from his goal.

"I'm not thinking, at least not clearly," he muttered through parched lips. "They shielded the place with magic, and I've been hunting for something physical."

Feeling like the worst kind of fool, he plodded back to where he'd begun, grateful as hell he'd had the presence of mind to mark his launch point. He sat with his back against a barrow and splayed his hands in the hot earth by his sides to link to this world. Once he was certain he had a connection, he opened his magic.

At first nothing happened, but he waited, patient this time. If he couldn't find the opening he sought, he'd have no choice but to return to a world he knew, if only to find water. He dialed up his magic and sunk his hands deeper into the dirt. Heat scored his palms, but he ignored it.

Maybe it was the boost to his power, maybe the intensified connection to Fire Mountain, but one of the barrows ahead of him sparkled and took on an incandescent aspect, showing him an entrance.

Keeping his eyes dead on his target, Jonathan pushed to his feet and walked the fifty feet to where the barrow beckoned. Nothing shifted, so he walked through. Breath caught in his throat. A large cave was lined with various sized mineral chunks, reflecting light from an unknown source. Teal, violet, pinks, and greens flickered in a kaleidoscopic display. Beautiful. He'd never seen anything to rival it.

Even better, the distant sound of water splashing into something drew him like a magnet, and he loped toward the noise. If he'd ever smelled water before, he wasn't aware of it, but he smelled it now. Cool, damp, dense. He rounded a corner and threw himself onto his belly in front of a rocky pool, sucking down water in huge gulps. In between drinking, he dragged his hands through the water and sluiced it over his head. It dripped down his neck, doing combat with his overheated body.

Refreshed, he pushed to a sit. Puddles formed around him, but he didn't pay attention. The heat of this world would dry him as soon as he stepped outside the cave system.

Speaking of which, the odd light that illuminated the minerals he'd admired was still with him. It wasn't his magic, so where was it coming from?

Not important. I have to find the dragons.

What then? What do I say? Why am I here?

He began to rise, but sank back down. He needed a game plan, even a primitive one, before walking into a gaggle of thousand-year-old creatures. If he couldn't come up with something convincing to say, he'd be dead in the water before he began.

Strategy. I have to develop a strategy. Pretend this is a game. I found the dragons' cave. They're on the edge of sealing their world off forever. What would make them think twice?

His thoughts trailed back to a place they'd been earlier. What if shutting Fire Mountain would have negative consequences for the dragons?

Cathbad. I need Cathbad. If Tarika knew enough to send me here, maybe he's dreamed the same thing.

Jonathan's next thought flattened him. If Cathbad could dream it, then he could too. Maybe he didn't need the whole fire and blood ritual he'd been mapping out to get to the Druidic seer. Perhaps just a descent into sleep would do it. Cathbad had mentioned linking to him in dreams.

Was it safe to call a trance state?

Did the dragons know he was here?

It didn't seem likely, or they'd have rousted him out long since. What were they doing that demanded so much attention, they wouldn't notice an intruder?

Jonathan grinned. He hoped to hell they were arguing so vehemently, they'd never come to consensus about pulling Fire Mountain out of circulation.

He got to his feet and made his way to the crystal chamber he'd found just behind the cave's entrance. Confident he could draw earth magic through the crystals to shield his presence, he settled into a corner and chanted to summon oblivion. He'd be helpless for a span of time, but he didn't have much choice.

Darkness wasn't as quick to come as he would've liked. A corner of his brain clung stubbornly to awareness until he clipped the strands holding him on this plane. The descent into an inky void left him disoriented. Where was the tunnel and the light? For that matter, where was Cathbad?

"I'm here." The Seer's voice filled the darkness, lapping against Jonathan in waves.

"It's not the same." His words filled him with shame. "Sorry I said that. I didn't mean it."

"Of course ye did. No matter. What would ye ask?"

Surprise sluiced through him. This was like visiting an oracle. And why not? "What will happen to the dragons if they shutter Fire Mountain permanently?"

"They'll weaken and die out."

"I need details. Something they'll believe."

Muted chuckling tickled the edges of his hearing. "Ye cut to the heart of things. I'm proud to claim you as kin."

"You didn't answer me. I don't know how much time I have."

"Ye wouldna have had any were dragonkind not so lost in quarrelling."

"At least I was right about one thing."

"Doona let it go to your head." More chuckling. "What ye seek is this. There was a time when dragons could've kept Fire Mountain separate. That time has passed. When they opened their gateways and allowed congress in and out of their world, their magic scattered far and wide. Some of Fire Mountain can be found in every world. Those parts will wither and die if the dragons shutter their world."

Jonathan turned the information over, working on what it meant. "I'm not seeing how it impacts the dragons. I need something to convince them they'll be cooking their own goose if they move forward."

"Aye, lad. They'll understand far better than you. Imagine power as millions of strands, each with a beginning and an end, and a connection to at least one other strand—likely more. If a strand of magic on another world dies, that death will run through to the tail end of the strand, even if Fire Mountain is severed from all other worlds. Because the dragons willna have the ability to link to fresh magic to repair the damage, the mystery keeping their world alive will gradually ebb.

"Ye found one of only two water sources on Fire Mountain. They're magical founts, and 'twould be the first things to go."

"Thank you." Jonathan reached for power to sever his casting.

"Hold!" Cathbad's voice boomed around him. Not gentle lapping this time, more like a thrashing to get his attention. "That's far from all. Many worlds, Earth among them, stand at a nexus. Their configuration isna stable anymore. If the dragons withdraw their magic, 'twill provide impetus to push all the worlds into wide-ranging chaos that will eventually spawn the birth of a new age."

"Like what I saw when Britta and I visited the future." He recalled starving, grubby humans living in caves at the barest edges of survival.

"Exactly. But here's the important part. That new age willna contain dragons. They require magic, and there willna be sufficient to support them—no matter which side of Fire Mountain's barrier they live on."

Understanding rocked Jonathan. This was the Morrigan's master plan. To spin every world so deep into chaos, she'd have carcasses to pick off until the end of time. And to vanquish the dragons along with it.

"Good. Ye understand. Now, go convince the dragons. They willna wish to listen to you, but ye must find a way to hold their attention."

Jonathan tried to form words of thanks, but the dark capsule ejected him so fast it squeezed all the air from his lungs. He rejoined his body with a disquieting *thump* in the protected corner of the crystal cave where he'd left it. So he'd been soul-walking after all, when all he'd meant to do was dream his kinsman.

A cautious scan confirmed no dragons had come or gone in the moments he'd lain there helpless. He got to his feet. He'd needed a strategy, and now he had one. What if the dragons didn't listen? What if they kicked his ass out without so much as a hearing?

I can't worry about that. I have to get this train heading down the tracks.

He trotted deeper into the cave system, passing the pool on his way. He worried about not finding the council chamber, but the primary tunnel was impossible not to follow, as it wound ever deeper into the earth. The temperature, which had cooled from outside, began to rise again. He'd been so dehydrated before finding the pool, he'd stopped sweating, but dampness sheened his forehead and sides again.

The noise of voices reached him, and he stopped, thinking maybe he could glean something more to help his cause. He listened to the rise and fall of an old form of Gaelic for long moments, but all the dragons were doing was debating which of several spells would be best to close themselves off from the other worlds.

He needed to hurry.

The glow illuminating the cave's upper levels intensified, as he came around a corner and into an immense cavern, by far the largest he'd seen. The same multi-colored crystals were back in spades, and their brilliance made him shield his eyes. Dragons filled the space. All colors and sizes. Well over a hundred of them faced away from him, their attention riveted on a golden dragon twice the size of the Guardian.

A smaller gold flanked the leader on each side. One raised its snout, scenting the air and turned milk-white eyes on Jonathan. "We have a visitor." Its voice rustled like wheat sheaves in a staunch wind. The other flanking dragon trained its gaze on Jonathan too, displaying the same milky corneas.

Blind. They're blind.

They must be the Seers Keene mentioned.

The central dragon growled and shot flames at Jonathan. He jumped out of their path, but not before cinders singed his pants. "Get out!" the leader roared. "Out. Ye have no place among us."

Fear congealed his blood. Every instinct he had urged him to run, to leave while he could, and then he sensed dragon magic fueling his terror. It eddied about him like restless water. They were trying to push him out. At least they started with bullying. They were more than capable of killing him and being done with it.

He gathered the tattered edges of his courage. If every man had a life's task, and this one was his, he didn't feel very prepared. "Please." He pushed to his full height, which was pathetic surrounded by dragons. "Hear me out. You can always kick me out later. And I'll go willingly, but not before you've heard what I have to say."

"Why should we listen to him?" A dragon hissed.

"Why?" Others echoed. "He's nothing but a wretched human."

"Nay, not human." A black detached himself from one of the corners. Keene. "He's Arianrhod's son and carries Cathbad's blood as well."

"Cathbad?" One of the blind dragons at the front of the cave leaned forward, sounding intrigued.

"Aye, we would hear Cathbad's get," the other blind dragon seconded.

Jonathan filled his lungs. At least he'd get one chance to sway them. Whatever he said, he'd have to make it convincing. Make them believe him down to their dragon bones.

CHAPTER 17

*L*achlan gasped and gagged before he gave up and stopped struggling to breathe. It wasn't going to happen until the dragons' traveling pathways spit them out. He pulled Maggie's face against his chest, burying it inside his leather vest. Maybe there'd be a bit of air for her. The dead weight of her in his arms pulled at his heart, but the gentle rise and fall of her chest convinced him hope remained.

"Where are we going?" he asked Kheladin.

"Back to where we left everyone. It's as promising a place as any to track Eletea from."

"Why aren't you short of breath?"

Kheladin made a rumbling noise in the airless space. "Because these portals were made for those like me."

Lachlan didn't agree with his dragon's choice of destination. Either the battle would be long since over—and everyone would've left—or Kheladin would dump them back into the thick of things. Neither option was particularly good, but Lachlan didn't have breath to argue. At least if the battle was still going on, Eletea would be there.

Eletea.

Lachlan cursed himself for the worst kind of fool. Why hadn't he even considered the copper-colored dragon? When the answer came, he felt even worse. She was small, young, inexperienced. He'd never even considered her as an option, and he owed her a heaping share of humility for his hubris, especially since he'd have to explain why he left.

And why he'd returned.

"I wasna small, but I was young and untried," Kheladin said with a wry undernote, having clearly helped himself to their shared thoughts.

"That was different," Lachlan panted.

"Nay, not so much," the dragon replied. "Men look for strength first. I had that—in spades. So ye disregarded what others might've considered impediments."

"Never mind the philosophy. How much longer?" Lachlan rubbed at a tightness over the center of his breastbone. If he didn't get air damned soon, the magic he was funneling into Maggie to keep her from drifting even farther away would fade, and her along with it.

"Soon."

Lachlan held on. Maggie stirred weakly in his arms, and her forehead creased with what looked like discomfort. She may not be conscious, but the lack of air affected her too. He cradled her head closer to his chest.

"We'll be out soon," Kheladin said. "Ready yourself to fight."

Lachlan stared at the comatose woman in his arms. "We'll need somewhere safe for Maggie—if there's still fighting."

"Give her to me." Kheladin bent and extended his forelegs.

Lachlan was loathe to let go, but he recognized the dragon's wisdom. Kheladin could protect her better than him because the dragon's power didn't flow through his taloned forelegs. He kissed Maggie's forehead and told her he loved her in Gaelic, that he'd always love her, that she was his heart, his life. Somewhere in his litany, he realized he could breathe better. It wasn't perfect, but his lungs weren't on fire anymore.

He handed Maggie to his dragon and prepared himself for combat.

"For a moment there, I dinna believe ye'd let go of her." Kheladin twisted and laid Maggie across his back, binding her with fiery cords he fashioned from his breath.

"I dinna want to. What happened to her was my fault. I should've checked afore we destroyed the Harpy, but 'tis been so long since I fought them, I wasna at the top of my game."

"Save your recriminations. Look sharp."

A grinding, wrenching noise obliterated Kheladin's words, and the gateway split open. Lachlan bounded out, hands outstretched, power blazing from them. Kheladin's energy pulsed behind him, and fire shooting from the dragon's mouth scorched his back.

He spun in a full circle, spewing power blindly, wanting to smoke out anything that might be a threat to the helpless woman bound to Kheladin's back.

Truth sank in.

The battle was over. No one remained. He sheathed his defensive magic and deployed a simpler scan to determine if anything on the battlefield lived. Beyond forest animals come to feast on scraps, he didn't find a thing.

What next?

"Where do ye think they've gone?" Kheladin asked.

"'Tis unlikely they all went to the same place." Lachlan screwed his face into a mask of concentration. "Question is, where would Eletea have gone? She likely dinna return to Inverness, Fort William, or any of the other cities the witches call home."

"She wouldna have gone to the Celtic Council, either," Kheladin said. "I suspect Arianrhod may have gone there to rile her kinfolk into taking a more aggressive stance against the Morrigan."

Lachlan ran possibilities through his mind, knowing Kheladin hovered at the edge of their shared consciousness. "If ye think of something," he raised his gaze to the dragon, "doona stand on ceremony. Sing out."

Kheladin narrowed his scaled eyelids. "Eletea's cave is verra near here. I sense her hoard."

"Ye feel gold and gemstones?"

The dragon shrugged. "I miss my own treasure. 'Tis still beneath where your castle used to stand in Inverness. Why would it surprise you that I sense another dragon's hideaway?"

"Do ye believe she retreated to her cave? Even after all that happened here?"

"'Tis her home," the dragon said simply. "We'd be foolish not to at least look afore we throw ourselves on Ceridwen's mercy."

Not necessarily Ceridwen, but the Celtic Council was Lachlan's next idea too. Gwydion and Arawn had helped him in the past, and he still had a hard time believing they'd thrown their lot in with the Crow. Besides, Ceridwen could scry most anything with her cauldron.

"Lead out," Lachlan said. "I could determine where her cave is, but since ye already know, I'll follow you."

"Get on my back. We'll fly. 'Twill be faster."

Worried about disturbing Maggie, Lachlan climbed Kheladin's scaled hide until he perched next to her inert form. He worked as fast as he could to clip the magical strands holding her in place on the dragon's back. Once she was free, he gathered her against him and straddled Kheladin. A hasty trip inside her mind reassured him she hadn't sunk farther into the pit clamoring to claim her.

Leathery, copper wings spread on both sides of him, and Kheladin rose into the air, but not very high. After less than a quarter mile, he circled to land, bringing them out in a secluded glade with a fast running creek that turned into a waterfall as it tumbled off a nearby cliff.

Lachlan summoned magic to soften his descent to the ground and walked with Maggie in his arms to the opening of a cave. He sent a spurt of power to see if Eletea was inside.

"Aye!" He spun to face Kheladin. "Ye were right. I'd hug you if my arms weren't full."

"For Dewi's sake, what the fuck do you want?" Eletea stood framed in the doorway of her home. "It's a goddamned mess inside, and I was clearing up."

"Would ye like some help?" Kheladin focused his spinning green gaze on her.

"Pfft." Breath hissed between her teeth. "Right. Like I want another dragon's claws mucking through my hoard."

"I would never steal from you." Kheladin sounded injured.

Eletea shrugged. "Maybe not, but it's one less thing for me to worry about." She crossed her forelegs over her chest. "What do you want? Why are you here? Arianrhod and Angus went to Inverness to the Celts, along with Britta and Tarika. The witches went home, and I think Jonathan is in Fire Mountain. No one knows what's become of the Crow or her ragtag army—the ones we didn't kill, that is." A smug smile spread over Eletea's face.

"Aye, we've just come from Fire Mountain and spoken with Jonathan there," Lachlan said.

"So." Eletea continued to stare at them. "What are you doing here?"

Lachlan admired the dragon's directness, so he sucked in a tattered breath and met like with like. Eletea wasn't one to dance around a subject, and he wouldn't insult her by feinting from the sidelines.

"A Harpy stole Maggie's soul." He shifted the burden in his arms and uncovered her face. "The first thing I thought of was taking her to Fire Mountain. If I could've found a dragon—"

"—to bond with her and share its soul, you'd get your mate back," Eletea cut in, her voice heavy with something Lachlan couldn't identify. "Because the Dragon Council is debating closing off Fire Mountain forever, they sent you packing. Then you recalled another perfectly good dragon you hadn't considered, and here you are."

She dusted her taloned palms together. "Is that about right?"

Heat traveled up Lachlan's chest across his cheeks and over the top of his head. "Close enough," he mumbled. "I've cursed myself for being an ass. It's not that ye were my second choice…" He was digging himself deeper and knew it, so he shut up.

"Oh, I get it." Eletea nodded. "I wasn't second choice. I wasn't even in the running—until your back was against the wall."

"Chastise me all ye wish." Lachlan met the dragon's whirling eyes with his gaze. "I'm not proud of making a stupid mistake that may well have cost my mate her only chance at life. Nor am I making excuses for it."

"What's your next stop if I say no?" Eletea's words held a flat quality that felt like a knife blade entering his heart.

A new thought came to him. "Mayhap her grandmother, though I'm not certain quite how I'd accomplish that. 'Twould mean a trip to the Americas, where I truly have no knowledge of where anything is."

"Does the witch hold knowledge of how to fix Maggie?"

Lachlan's breath hitched. He had no idea, but the answer was likely no. He looked away from the dragon's unsettling gaze. "The Celts have some kind of immortality spell," he mumbled. "Perhaps they'd be a safer bet, and certainly closer."

"Aye, but that casting comes with barbs." Kheladin, who'd been silent since Eletea intimated he might steal from her, finally spoke.

Lachlan looked at Eletea again and took a chance. "Ye're at least considering this, or ye'd have told us to leave."

"Smart man. Aye, I'm considering it, but there are many problems. Mages study long and hard to become dragon shifters. Your mate's only knowledge of the shifter magic comes from what she knows of you and Kheladin. She's unconscious." Eletea flicked a talon Maggie's way.

"What if she wakes and decides she has no interest in being bonded to a dragon forever. What then? Or worse." Eletea forged ahead without waiting for him to answer. "She feels stuck with the bond, since it's the only thing keeping her alive, and is sullen, resentful."

"I'm certain she wouldna be either of those—"

"What do you think?" Eletea shifted her attention to Kheladin.

"Why would ye care about an opinion from some scoundrel who'd steal your treasure?" Kheladin blinked slowly.

Eletea tossed her forelegs in the air. "Fine. Sorry. I misspoke. Mostly I wanted you to leave, so I was rude on purpose." She stopped to take a breath and blew out a fiery plume. "I want your opinion because you're a dragon and you know her. If I do this thing, and it ends badly with the bond severed and Maggie dead, everyone will blame me for not trying harder to make it work."

Lachlan winced at truth in the dragon's assessment. Was his request as selfish as it was starting to look? He glanced at Kheladin, but the dragon wasn't in a hurry to answer.

When he finally opened his jaws, he said, "I canna give you assurances. Maggie is a good woman with an open heart, but she has a fiercely independent streak. I have no idea how she'd feel bound to a dragon she didn't have a hand in choosing."

"I figured as much, just from the little I've seen of her." Eletea nodded.

"We'll go to Ceridwen," Lachlan said. "If she refuses the immortality spell, will ye..." He couldn't get the words out.

"Aye, dragon shifter." Eletea smiled for the first time since they arrived. "I will risk myself if I'm the only avenue left to you. Now hurry, her life force dims with each passing moment."

"Thank you for your compassion." Lachlan fought mounting desperation, but Eletea had been more than decent, plus she'd brought up considerations that hadn't occurred to him.

"Don't mention it dragon shifter." She frowned. "You do understand if the Dragon Council gets its way, all of us—me, Kheladin, Tarika, and other dragons here and on other worlds—will be ordered to return. Whether or not we heed the call remains to be seen."

"What will ye do?" Lachlan asked.

She shrugged. "I haven't made up my mind yet."

"Thank you." Kheladin inclined his head. "I hope I get the opportunity to know you better."

"The feeling's mutual, dragon." Eletea puffed steam his way.

"I'll take us," Kheladin announced and summoned power to whisk them to Inverlochy Castle.

"Do ye want us on your back?" Lachlan asked.

"Nay. Just stand close."

Dragon magic zinged around Lachlan. If he inhaled deeply, it smelled like the sulfurous fumes and hot, dry air of Fire Mountain.

The green of the Highlands gave way to the whitewashed stone passageways of Inverlochy Castle. Kheladin knew enough not to drop them on the roadway in front of the castle. The spell dissipated, and Lachlan started up a nearby staircase. He'd been here when the castle was still standing and recalled its layout. Plus he and Kheladin had come out here after being shanghaied to the Middle Ages by Rhukon.

Lachlan swallowed a grim smile. He'd spent so much time here of late, it was beginning to feel like a second home. Two long flights up, he loped to the end of the hall and summoned power to open the enormous double wooden door with its runic carvings.

Raised voices met his ears as soon as the door thudded against its stops, and he stomped into the room with Kheladin right behind him. One good thing about these old castles was they were built to accommodate creatures Kheladin's size.

"Ye dinna request permission to enter." Ceridwen walked from behind her cauldron to face him.

He bowed as best he could with Maggie in his arms. "I'm requesting it now."

"Ye wish a boon, or ye'd not be here," the goddess of the world went on. "State your request."

Before he could get the words out, Britta stepped from the shadows behind Ceridwen. "His mate lost her soul to a Harpy. He went to Fire Mountain to seek a dragon to share its soul, but the Dragon Council must not have agreed." She walked briskly to where Lachlan stood and placed her hands on Maggie's head. Britta's eyes widened and she spun to face Ceridwen. "She's been marked by the Guardian. Lachlan too. Until Tarika marked Jonathan so he could use the dragons' pathways, such a thing was unheard of."

"We needed to travel quickly," Lachlan explained. "Please. Ceridwen, goddess of everything living, I've come to beg the immortality spell to save my mate's life."

Ceridwen stalked across the room. Floor length dark hair shot with silver swirled around her in a breeze that only touched her. She laid a long-fingered hand across Maggie's forehead, covering the Guardian's mark and shut her eyes for a moment.

When she opened them, she directed her dark gaze at Lachlan. "Margaret Melissa Hibbins would be beyond even my skill had the Guardian not marked her."

"Does that mean ye'll help her?" The spear of hope shooting through him was almost painful.

"She could go mad. She might die. Knowing that do ye freely solicit my aid?"

Lachlan swallowed hard. Once. Again. The price was steep, yet there was no choice. "Aye, I freely ask this boon."

"You all heard him." Ceridwen raised her voice.

"Aye, we heard," echoed through the cavernous room.

"Give her to me." Ceridwen held out her arms.

Lachlan wanted to protest, to say he'd hold onto his love to soften the blow of the powerful magic soon to come.

Maybe because he hesitated, Ceridwen said. "I doona need to explain myself to you, but I must take her to my cauldron. It amplifies my power."

"Can I come with you?" Lachlan thought he knew the answer but asked anyway.

"Nay. Do this thing or no, dragon shifter. I'll not offer a second time."

Lachlan shifted Maggie into Ceridwen's arms. The place where she'd lain against his body grew cold, and he stifled a shudder. What had he done? If she were to die, wouldn't it be better to lose her in his arms?

Kheladin stumped to his side. "Ye must hold faith. Your doubts might be the thing to unhinge Ceridwen's working."

"Your dragon speaks true." Britta gripped his arm. "When there are no good choices, trust the one ye picked."

Lachlan leaned against his dragon, but only for a split second. Thank Christ for Kheladin. He always saw to the marrow of things. Lachlan cleared his mind of everything but Maggie rising from the pallet Ceridwen laid her on. Not just getting up under her own power, but opening her clear blue eyes and recognizing everyone.

Angus and Arianrhod made their way to his side, followed by Tarika, who joined Kheladin, conversing quietly in the dragons' tongue.

Lachlan tried to thank them for being there, for their silent support, but stumbled over the words.

"No need to say anything." Angus clapped his shoulder. "We understand."

The area around the cauldron took on a glistening hue and turned opaque. Try as he might, Lachlan couldn't peer through it. He focused power, but couldn't break through the circle of heady magic pulsing around Maggie and Ceridwen, with the cauldron as its epicenter. When he tried using his third eye, his effort boomeranged back at him, a sharp slap across his face that opened the cuts the Guardian had made. They stung like mad, and blood dripped down his face.

Arianrhod tapped his cheek to get his attention and shook her head. "'Tisn't wise to send your magic into unknown situations."

Shame warred with guilt. He knew that. It wasn't as if he were a green mage, newly hatched, who'd just opened his first grimoire. "'Tis hard," he said through gritted teeth. "I want to help her."

"Och aye, laddie, 'tis far more than that." Arianrhod's voice was gentle. "Ye canna imagine your life without her."

He didn't reply because he couldn't. He was afraid if he opened his mouth, he'd howl with grief and pain. Bad enough to have stretched his magic where it didn't belong. He wouldn't compound it by making a disgrace of himself before Kheladin and the others.

The mist around Maggie and Ceridwen thinned. Lachlan sprang forward, intent on seeing if Ceridwen's magic had worked, but Arianrhod clamped a hand around his upper arm. "Wait. Ceridwen will tell you when she's done."

The goddess's clear voice rose in a multi-tonal burst of sound, obliterating the earlier silence. She spoke Gaelic, exhorting Maggie to rise. The gray-white vapor dissipated, drifting upward until Lachlan saw Ceridwen, crouched next to the thin pallet where she'd laid Maggie. Power formed a glowing nimbus around both women until it gradually leeched back into Ceridwen.

"Rise, lass," she urged again in Gaelic. "Rise and be whole."

Maggie twitched where she lay. The twitch turned into a convulsion as she pushed to a sit and then to her feet where she swayed unsteadily. Her blonde hair, long since loosed from its braids, formed a curtain that hung to her waist, obscuring her face.

Lachlan couldn't stand it. He sent a tendril of magic skittering forward, meaning to soothe, to bring her into his arms. Arianrhod still held him back, but no one restrained Maggie. She could come to him. He pressed harder with power, strengthening his suggestion for her to turn and see him.

In one uneven motion, she dipped her head forward and tossed her hair back from her face. The eyes that stared at him were still blue, but they held a flat, dead aspect. "Who are you?" Maggie turned in a full circle. "Who the hell are all of you and why the fuck am I here?"

He yanked free of Arianrhod and started for Maggie, his hands outstretched. She was confused, hurt. She'd get past this; he'd see to it.

"Stop right there!" She drew her lips back from her teeth into a snarl, and the blue of her eyes shaded to whirling silver.

Lachlan fell back a pace. Horror sent cold through him in icy waves until he feared he'd never be warm again. Silver eyes. Would she sprout wings next to join the Harpy sisterhood? Or would Ceridwen do away with her before that could happen?

His shoulders sagged. He had his answer. She was alive, but her mind was gone. Worse, the Harpy had traded some of its essence when it took her soul. No wonder Maggie didn't recognize any of them. Not able to face her or any of the Celts or dragons, he turned to leave. Walking was easier than magic, and right now he needed easy or he'd never get out of the Celts' hall with his dignity intact. As it was, Ceridwen's dark gaze brimmed with pity. He stared straight ahead, so he wouldn't have to look at any of the rest of them.

"What are ye doing?" Kheladin demanded. "Surely ye're not giving up this easily."

"She's gone from me. From everyone." Lachlan struggled for words. "Madness was one of the risks. I accepted it on her behalf, and look what I've done. Beyond that, I discounted risk of Harpy contamination—" He balled his hands into fists so hard his muscles ached. "By all the gods, however will I live with myself?"

"Where are you going?" Angus asked.

Lachlan didn't turn around. "To find the Morrigan. Mayhap I canna kill her, but I can make her sorry she was ever born."

Kheladin bugled, a long, mournful sound that stopped Lachlan just this side of the double doors at the end of the room. He turned slowly. "Give me a moment," he told his dragon. "I'll let ye know when I'm ready to leave."

CHAPTER 18

Jonathan cleared his throat and waited for the muted hum of dragon conversation to die down. He'd run enough meetings to understand silence was one way to command attention. If it worked with humans, why should dragons be any different?

"Speak," one of the blind dragons commanded.

"Aye," the other echoed. "Be quick about it."

Jonathan felt both dragons push for entry into his mind. He funneled magic into a barrier, but it wouldn't keep them out—not for long. They nipped from both sides with ability so ancient he could only guess at its roots.

Were they First Born too?

"Thank you for allowing me to address you," he began.

"That courtesy could evaporate in an instant." The huge gold dragon peered at Jonathan through narrowed eyes. "Get on with it. We were in the midst of important business when ye showed up uninvited."

Jonathan spread his hands in front of him. "Let's begin with something we all agree on. The Morrigan stands at the root of our current problems."

"Why do ye say that?" One of the Seers asked.

"I would know as well," the other cut in. "Your words ring with conviction."

"What I want to know," the Guardian lumbered from the shadowy rear of the cavern, "is why ye dinna leave when I commanded you to follow Lachlan and his mate."

Jonathan girded himself and wrapped his next words in a spell. They were part true, part not, and he didn't want the dragons to accuse him of lying and kick him out before he'd said what he needed to.

He faced the Guardian and bowed. "Apologies for not following your instructions. I feared I didn't have enough power to summon a time portal. I was weary, and using magic isn't all that familiar to me yet. I stumbled across the outer cavern in this cave system and drank some water before I laid down to rest.

"While I slept, Cathbad came to me in the dream world. The information I gleaned from him was shocking, I couldn't leave without making certain you had every single piece of data to inform your decision-making."

"Heartening ye care so deeply for dragons." Sarcasm trod beneath the Guardian's words.

"Ssht." One of the Seers directed a thin stream of fire at the Guardian. "Let us hear the lad out afore we ridicule him."

"I'll be brief." Jonathan hurried on before the dragons could begin to argue about the merits of allowing him to remain. "I was with Lachlan and Britta when we traveled to the future to rescue Tarika and Kheladin. I saw one possible future where humans were reduced to living in caves, struggling against famine and disease."

"What does that have to do with us?" A red dragon stepped forward.

"Cathbad says that's the future we'll have if you shut Fire Mountain off from the other worlds. It works for the Morrigan, since it provides chaos for her to suck energy from forever."

"I still doona understand what starving humans have to do with us," the red persisted. "We'll be here in Fire Mountain, just like we've always been."

"Magic is a self-perpetuating system." Jonathan widened his stance and squared his shoulders as he scanned the cavern. Whirling eyes stared back at him. "Once long ago, before you mingled dragon magic with worlds beyond this one, you could've shuttered yourselves in Fire Mountain and lived out millennia undisturbed."

He stopped to take a breath. "So many dragons have lived elsewhere for so long, dragon magic is interwoven into the magical threads of all the worlds. If you close Fire Mountain off from them, it will sever your connection to a surprising amount of your power, and the mystery that maintains the First World for dragons will gradually dim. Water will be the first problem, but others will follow in rapid succession."

"I would hear Cathbad's exact prophecy," one of the Seers demanded. "Not your words, but his."

"All right." Jonathan shut his eyes and dug into his memory. "Here is what he said as closely as I can reconstruct it.

"Imagine power as millions of strands, each with a beginning and an end, and a connection to at least one other strand—likely more. If a strand of magic on another world dies, that death will run through to the tail end of the strand, even if Fire Mountain is severed from all other worlds. Because the dragons won't have the ability to link to fresh magic to repair the damage, the mystery keeping their world alive will gradually ebb.

"Many worlds, Earth among them, stand at a nexus. Their configuration isn't stable anymore. If dragons withdraw their magic, it will push all the worlds into chaos deep enough to spawn the birth of a new age.

"That new age won't contain dragons. They require magic, and there won't be sufficient to support them—no matter which side of Fire Mountain's barrier they live on."

Jonathan opened his eyes and drew back. The glowing light emanating from the dragons had increased tenfold, making him squint against the brightness. A rustling susurrus grew as the dragons muttered among themselves. Fire and smoke thickened the air.

"Stop!" the lead dragon thundered. He turned whirling golden eyes with dark centers on Jonathan. "Is that all Cathbad said? Did we hear everything?"

Jonathan nodded. "Yes. As close as I can remember, that was his prediction, er prophecy."

"I was in his head when he relayed Cathbad's divination," one of the Seers said. "He speaks true."

The leader nodded, his scales rattling against each other. "Ye may leave now."

Jonathan recognized a dismissal, but he didn't want to leave. Not yet. "How will I know your decision?"

"Dragon affairs are not human affairs," one of the Seers said and shrugged. Its milky gaze bored into Jonathan. "Yet, ye'll know our decision at some point since ye're mated to Britta, and she's bonded to one of our First Born."

"Our original mistake was leaving Fire Mountain in the first place," a dragon called from off to one side.

"Aye, had we not done so…"

Heated conversations broke out all around him, and Jonathan hoped that perhaps he could withdraw to a quiet corner and wait out the storm. Fascinated by how the dragons dredged through their individual power to form a decision they could all live with, he edged toward the doorway he'd come through, intent on taking refuge in shadows. Maybe he'd get away with it, and no one would notice him. Minutes slid by, followed by more. The level of smoke, steam, and fire in the cavern escalated until he couldn't see the front of the room anymore. If he couldn't see them—

One of the Seers caught up to him near the entrance to the council chamber. "Ye must leave. There isna a choice in the matter. I would have your word ye will find your way outside and thence back to Earth."

"I thought that maybe... I mean, I hoped..." Jonathan stammered as he hunted for the magic bullet that would allow him to remain.

"Aye. While I'm grateful ye saw fit to talk with us, some practices were never meant for mortals to witness."

"I'm not mortal."

"Aye, but neither are ye a dragon. Thank Cathbad for me when next ye see him, but now ye must be gone."

"I could retreat to the outer cavern, make myself unobtrusive. You might need me. I can channel Cathbad—"

"We have more than enough information." The dragon bent and gripped Jonathan's shoulder so firmly, its talons cut into his flesh. "Leave. If I find you here, gratitude or no, I'll kill you. If it turns out you're immortal, I'll see ye're imprisoned in Fire Mountain forever. Do I make myself clear?"

"Very. I understand."

"Will ye leave? Or are ye planning to defy me?"

"The others. The Celts and Lachlan and Britta and the witches. They'll all want to know what the dragons decided."

The dragon kicked his head back and laughed until steam bubbled through his double rows of teeth. "How can ye imagine they willna know? If we close Fire Mountain, the call will go out to all dragons to return. Nay." The dragon clamped Jonathan's shoulder hard enough, he feared permanent damage from loss of circulation. "Ye want to remain for you, for your own curiosity. 'Tisn't a good enough reason."

"Busted." Jonathan stifled a grin.

"I'm not familiar with the term, but I can intuit its meaning well enough." The dragon let go. Sensation flooded back into Jonathan's arm with a pins and needles prickling that almost made him cry out.

"Thank you for making the others listen to me." Jonathan turned to begin the trudge toward the cave's entrance.

"One dragon canna force another to do anything. Farewell young seer. Your role in the current drama is far from done. Even if we doona disturb Fire Mountain's attachment to the other worlds, much remains for you to accomplish. None of it will be easy, or without cost to you and those you love."

Jonathan twisted back to face the retreating dragon. "Could you say more about that?"

The dragon stopped but didn't turn around. "I could, but I'm not going to."

"Please. I need all the information I can lay my hands on."

The Seer hesitated. "Aye, but most of what ye need isna mine to share. Mayhap one small thing, though. I dare you—challenge you—to keep moving forward no matter what. Ye'll be tempted to give up, but ye canna do so. 'Twill take more than dragons—and more than men—to overturn the Morrigan, particularly now that she's allied herself with the Infernal deities. We must work in concert, or we willna prevail. 'Twas why I invited your knowledge—once I realized who ye were." In a whoosh of magic-tinged air that reeked of sulfur, he was gone.

Jonathan stared at the spot of suddenly empty air, trying not to breathe too deep, since the chemical smell burned his nose and lungs. The dragon had called him "seer." What exactly did that mean? Surely he wasn't in the same ballpark as Cathbad or Angus. And he'd thrown down a gauntlet.

A challenge.

It's like meeting a key player in a game, but one whose message is shrouded.

Jonathan walked slowly away from the heat and din of the dragon's council cavern, his head bent in thought. He'd done what he could to avert the Fire Mountain crisis. What was left? Wincing at the naiveté of his question, he rounded turn after turn as he climbed upward. The temperature dropped, and his sweat-damp clothes felt suddenly chilly where they were plastered against his skin.

He stopped for water at the spring. Surely the dragons wouldn't begrudge him another drink to speed him on his journey. When he came to the crystal cave at the cavern system's entrance, he looked longingly at the corner where he'd curled up to reach Cathbad. A retreat to the dream world held an undeniable pull, but wasn't wise.

He emerged into the velvet darkness of a warm night. The sky was shot with millions of stars arranged in constellations he'd never seen before. Could he summon a time shaft anywhere on this world?

Won't know until I try.

If he wasn't successful, could he risk returning to the squabbling dragons to request assistance? His forehead burned, stinging where Tarika marked him, and he slapped his palm to the spot, making the discomfort worse. Could he chance using the dragons' pathways? He wasn't familiar with their magic, but they were a hell of a lot faster. Tarika had summoned the one he'd used to get to Fire Mountain. He'd have to figure out how to get one to open, then how to program it to leave him off where he needed.

"While I'm thinking this to death, I could've called a time shaft and been done with it," he muttered.

Since Tarika's mark continued to pulse, he decided he had to at least try the dragon pathways. Maybe it was a sign, and ignoring it would create some cosmic imbalance. He reached for the reservoir where his power lived, grateful to find it mostly intact. Whatever he'd burned through in the dream world and the dragons' cavern had replenished itself.

He touched two fingers to Tarika's mark and chanted experimentally. Nothing. He tried a different incantation. Still nothing.

Tarika. He visualized her shiny red scales and whirling golden eyes. The air directly in front of him split open. Jonathan grinned. Maybe because it was her mark, all he had to do was call up an image of her, and he'd end up wherever she was. In this instance, that would work fine. He could think of lots of times when it wouldn't, but maybe by then, he'd have more information.

He made a mental note to ask Tarika how to manipulate the dragons' pathways and walked through. This time he was ready for the abrupt lack of oxygen. It didn't make it any easier to cope with, only less shocking when his starved lungs grappled for purchase and didn't find anything to ease their discomfort.

Maybe I'm not supposed to travel this way—unless it's an emergency.

Too late now.

He hung on, feeling like a thinly stretched thread. Was this trip taking longer than the last one? What if the thing never spit him out? Would he die or enter some sort of stasis, like hibernation, but without oxygen. Some insects did that, and he recalled reading about a species of fish that lived so deep it had specialized eyes to focus light beams hundreds of feet below the surface.

His mind was wandering. Maybe he needed to visualize Tarika again to anchor the pathway—remind it he hadn't signed up for the forever plan. His thoughts felt thick, sluggish. The effort it took before Tarika formed behind his closed lids rattled him. His head spun, and remaining upright became a challenge.

What would happen if he laid down? Was there even a way for him to do that? Far as he could tell, he stood on two foot-sized platforms that moved with the undulations of the pathway. How the fuck did this thing accommodate dragons? Did they get a bigger platform?

From each according to his ability. To each according to his need.

"Aw shit. When I start quoting Karl Marx, I'm in big trouble."

The deep blackness around him shaded to gray. Hoping against hope it meant his journey was coming to an end, he cupped his hands in front of his face to capture what air molecules he could and took an experimental breath.

Yes! Goddammit, yes! I'm going to get out of here.

The air wasn't thick enough yet, but at least there was some. He inhaled hungrily, imagining fewer spaces between the particles, funneling a bit of magic to concentrate the mix into his lungs.

A wall split with an ear-rending screech. He didn't hesitate, bounding out of the prison that might've become his crypt. He didn't even care where he was. He could regroup and figure it out later. So what if the time shaft took longer. At least it held nodes to see where he was, and it had air, wonderful, life-supporting air.

"No more dragons' pathways," he mumbled, sucking huge slugs of air without bothering to look around him. Once his lungs stopped screaming, he'd figure everything else out. He bent over, hands resting on his flexed knees, gulping air like a landed fish as his head gradually quit spinning.

Don't be such a ninny. I'm alive, right? I had a task. I did it, and if the dragon Seer is to be believed, my job is far from over.

He straightened and looked around him. From the looks of things, he was in an old castle, one where virtually all the wall hangings, carpets, and sculptures had been stripped long since. He gathered a few tendrils of power and sent them spinning outward to orient himself.

The answers weren't surprising. He was in Inverlochy Castle, where the Celts hung out. Tarika was here. He sensed her energy above him, which was why the pathways spit him out here.

Noise alerted him and he looked upward to see Lachlan stumbling blindly down a steep staircase set into a sidewall. It lacked any sort of handrail and his feet came perilously close to the edge.

"Lachlan! Have a care. You can't die, but you could get damned banged up."

The dragon shifter slowed and raised eyes straight out of *Village of the Damned* to meet Jonathan's gaze.

"Shit!" Jonathan sprinted forward and met Lachlan one landing up. "What happened to Maggie? Did Eletea turn you down?"

The dragon shifter swiped a hand down his face, distorting his features. Raw pain gushed from him in waves that hurt Jonathan's soul. "'Tis a long story," Lachlan said. "Mayhap one not worth the telling."

"All stories are worth telling," Jonathan insisted. "Is she dead?"

"Would that she were." Lachlan slumped against the stone wall and raked his hands through his tawny hair. Lines creased his forehead and radiated from around his eyes like wagon spokes.

"Tell me. It won't make it any worse. Maybe I'll think of something you missed." Jonathan shifted from foot to foot, keeping his body between Lachlan and the twenty foot drop to the stone floor below.

"Eletea thought of many reasons not to bond with Maggie." A bitter note sat beneath Lachlan's words. "Turns out the dragon was smarter than me. She didn't turn us down, but urged me to exhaust every option afore returning."

"And?" Jonathan prodded.

"Ceridwen raised Maggie using the immortality spell, but the Harpy that stole her soul left some of herself behind."

Disbelief rooted Jonathan in place. "Maggie's turned into a Harpy?"

Lachlan ground his teeth together in a dissonant grating that made Jonathan want to shake him, order him to get hold of himself. "Nay, she… She's lost her mind. She doesna know any of us, and her eyes are spinning like silver pinwheels."

Jonathan searched through what little he knew about possession and magic. "Can't Ceridwen do something? Or Arianrhod? She's here, I feel her. Maybe Cathbad knows a counterspell…" The hopelessness that dragged Lachlan's face into a morass of bitter acceptance stopped the flow of words.

"Why are you here and not upstairs with her?" Jonathan ventured after Lachlan looked away, sunk so deep in misery it was hard to know whether to hug him or slap him.

The dragon shifter did look at him then. Shame joined the cavalcade of pain, misery, resignation, and guilt. "Because I'm a craven. I couldna bear to look upon her, so I fled." He swallowed audibly. "Even my dragon refused to follow me. Och, but I'm a sorry excuse for a man."

"Yes, well, you can have the pity party later." Jonathan kept his tone as non-judgmental as he could, but didn't do a very good job.

"Let's go back upstairs. There's lots of different magic here. One of us will come up with something. Say, is Mauvreen here?"

"Nay."

"Did anyone think to call Mary Elma?"

Lachlan shook his head. He turned and drove a fist into the stones, followed by the other one. His bones made a hollow, cracking noise as he drove them into the unyielding surface. Blood blossomed, dripping from his hands.

That did it. Jonathan drew back his open hand and slapped Lachlan across the face. "Stop it! Pull yourself together. You're not in your right mind."

Lachlan turned on him then, lips skinned back from his teeth until he looked like a creature out of one of Jonathan's games. "Ye'd lay hands on me? Puny, Druid seer. I'll teach you." He swung, but it went wide.

An idea took root before Lachlan could regroup. "You have to catch me before you can hit me." Jonathan bounded up the stairs and followed Celtic energy to huge double wooden doors. Lachlan pounded behind him, and Jonathan timed it just right. He flung the door open at the exact moment for Lachlan to burst through it.

Britta huddled next to Arianrhod and Angus, strategizing what to do. Maggie might not have recognized Lachlan, but she turned into a screaming harridan when he bolted from the room. Ceridwen bound her, and she hung over the cauldron, suspended by magic, alternating between babbling and hurling epithets at all of them.

"Jonathan's back!" Tarika lifted her head and lumbered toward the door just before it slammed against its stops, and Lachlan careened through with Jonathan at his heels.

Kheladin was next to Lachlan so fast, his copper scales blurred to near invisibility. Magic boomed, a loud popping noise, and Lachlan rocked back on the balls of his feet. It took Britta a moment to understand the dragon had joined Lachlan in his body. Murky, green eyes sharpened and cleared, just before Lachlan collapsed in a nearby chair.

"Och and can this get any worse? I've shamed myself, humiliated my dragon..."

"Shut up!" Kheladin seized Lachlan's vocal chords for his own use "Maggie got much worse after ye left. Revenge is understandable, but first we'll do our damnedest to figure out what happened to her. Mayhap we can fix whatever it is. She holds dragon magic from me—as do you."

"Agreed," Lachlan said thickly and got his feet under him again. "Thank Christ one of us still has their wits about them."

"Doona mention it," Kheladin said as their shared body bolted for where Maggie thrashed, kicking the air.

Britta raced to where Jonathan stood near the door and flung her arms around him. "Gods, I'm glad you're back."

"We all are." Tarika breathed steam over them. "What happened in Fire Mountain? Did ye talk with the council? What'd they decide?"

Jonathan buried his face in Britta's hair, and she stroked his neck, glorying in the feel of him back in her arms. Tarika shoved her hot snout between them. "Enough. Ye can play at making younglings later. Much later."

Britta let go, and Jonathan straightened. He sketched out what happened at Fire Mountain in just a few sentences, ending with, "...I have no idea the outcome, but I did the best I could."

"Ye say the Seers helped?" Tarika skewered him with her gaze.

"Yes. If it weren't for them, I'm not at all certain the big guy who seems to be the leader would've let me say a word."

Tarika's jaws opened in half a smile. "It bodes well. I canna recall when the council has ever gone against our Seers."

"Do they always come to the same conclusion?" Jonathan asked.

"Aye," Tarika answered. "I believe they do, but not without lengthy haggling over outcomes."

Britta shifted her focus to the front of the room where Lachlan stood just out of reach of Maggie's kicking feet. Rainbow-hued magic flowed from him and Kheladin, but if anything, it just made Maggie shriek louder.

"Let's see if we can help." Tarika started for the cauldron. Britta darted after her, moving fast to keep up. She kept an arm linked to one of Jonathan's, and he trotted by her side.

Arianrhod made her way to where they stood, with Angus

right behind her. Her forehead was drawn into harsh lines, and her mouth was screwed into an expression that looked as if it could kill. "May the Morrigan be damned forever and a day," she blurted.

"Aye, that bitch is drunk on her own power. I still canna believe she allied herself with atrocities outside our Pantheon," Ceridwen said, her tone fierce.

Britta's head snapped up. Ceridwen had vanished after calling power to bind Maggie. When had she returned?

The goddess of the world eyed her with cool amusement. "'Tis my chamber, and my cauldron."

"Since ye control so much," Arianrhod stepped within inches of Ceridwen, "how about if ye fix yon witch?" She jerked her chin at Maggie. "She's an innocent, targeted by one of our own."

A flash of black-tinged light illuminated the still-open doorway, and the Morrigan sashayed through a ring of flame that had to be illusion. "I heard my name!" The Crow's beak snapped audibly. "Ye're fighting over me. Och, but I feel the love. Go ahead, fight harder. Do more. Tear one another to bloody bits. Doona let me stop you."

"How dare you show up here?" Ceridwen stalked toward the Crow. Fury poured from her, making the air crackle.

"Why, sister." The Crow cocked her head to one side. "These are my halls as well as yours. Tch. Tch. I'd hoped for a warmer welcome."

A crone with black hair that reached her feet and swept behind her followed in the Morrigan's wake. She stood in the doorway, surveying the great hall through ice blue eyes. Soft ivory robes fell about her, sashed in deep blue with golden embroidery of the moon and stars.

Arianrhod's eyes widened, and something akin to hope flared from her.

"What?" Britta laid a hand on her arm.

"Ye'll find out soon enough." Arianrhod moved briskly toward the newcomer, stopping just long enough in front of the Morrigan to hiss, "This time, sister, ye've made a mistake. A big one."

"Whatever do ye mean?" The Crow sneered just before she shimmered into one of her many human forms. A woman with red hair in an elaborate up-do and glittering green eyes watched them, her translucent gown falling about her, as she pushed her shoulders back to better display a lush pair of breasts.

Lachlan raced from the front of the room, clearly intent on engaging the Morrigan in combat. His face was drawn into a scowl, and he roared his grief and outrage as he hurtled toward her.

Close, closer.

Britta girded herself for the explosion when they collided, but Lachlan bounced hard off an invisible barrier and almost ended up on his ass. His form took on an insubstantial aspect just before Kheladin emerged. The dragon shot fire, but it spread across whatever curtain the Morrigan had erected and didn't penetrate it.

"Fuck! May the goddess damn ye to hell for once and for all." Lachlan pounded the air with a fist. He and Kheladin stared at the Morrigan, who licked blood red lips.

She made come along motions with both long-nailed hands. "Come on, boys. I'm always up for some fun. It's only magic. Surely a mage—and a dragon—can find your way through." She tossed back her head and laughed. "Better hurry, though. I might just disappear on you."

"Think again." Ceridwen had worked her way around the Morrigan during her exchange with Lachlan, and she extended her hands. Light flared from her fingertips. It turned to snakes that wound around the Morrigan, not touching her, but covering her alchemical barrier with their writhing bodies.

Something flashed from the Morrigan's eyes—fear mingled with outrage. "Ye canna bind me."

"Really?" Ceridwen quirked a dark brow. "Try me. I believe I just did."

~

ARIANRHOD CLOSED the distance between herself and the crone in the doorway. Stopping a respectful distance away, she inclined her head. "Hecate. Welcome to my halls."

"Thank you. I'd call you sister, but you're not. Not really."

"Aye, but I am. We're both virgin goddesses who control the moon." Arianrhod moved closer. "Why are ye here?"

Hecate shrugged. "The Morrigan's been gathering us to her. Many years have passed—centuries—since I've had aught to do, so I took her up on her offer. Modern men no longer believe in us, so we wander. I roamed Hades's halls so long they grew stale. When an opportunity arose to leave—"

"I get it," Arianrhod broke in. "Ye'd welcome a task to remind you of your power, and I have one for you." Hecate turned her gaze away, but Arianrhod kept talking. "Ye oversee the magical arts. Witches consider you their goddess."

Hecate bristled. "It's because I *am* their goddess. Never mind painfully few recall my existence."

Arianrhod took Hecate's arm and spun her so she faced Maggie. "That woman is not just a witch, she's Mary Elma Hibbins's granddaughter. She was set upon by Harpies at the Morrigan's behest, and they stole her soul. Ceridwen called her back, but she's been poisoned by Harpy essence, and her mind isna her own. Ye must return her to us."

"Mary Elma Hibbins?" Hecate echoed.

"Aye, the same."

"She's one of the few who kept shrines to me, even after men no longer believed in deities."

Sensing an in, Arianrhod tugged hard on Hecate's arm. "Come. Let's examine her—and this problem. Surely there's power in blended magic: yours and mine."

"Have you tried to set the thing aright?" Hecate followed Arianrhod's lead, and they moved across the room.

"Aye and nay. Ceridwen drew her back from the Shadowlands, but she's mad, poisoned by Harpy fragments. When we couldna control her, Ceridwen bound her with magic."

"Did you seek the Harpy who has her soul? 'Tis by far the simplest solution."

Arianrhod shook her head. "Not possible. We destroyed the thing and, 'tis scattered far and wide."

"Mmph. I see." Hecate narrowed her eyes as she sent a magical probe toward Maggie, still suspended over the cauldron.

"If Ceridwen could've cured the problem, she would have." Arianrhod drew to a halt on the far side of the cauldron.

Maggie stretched her arms toward them, her hands curled into claws. "Bitches. Cut me down. This is an outrage." She shut her eyes and tossed her head back on a neck corded with tension, howling like a caged animal.

Hecate bit on her lower lip and frowned. "You say the Morrigan is responsible for this?"

"Aye. She loosed Harpies on us. Gryphons too. And stood on a nearby precipice overseeing the carnage."

Hecate's shoulders slumped. "What manor of deceit is this? To have her turn on her own kind. The world must truly be on the verge of ending."

Arianrhod nodded tiredly. "Aye, 'tis another problem. Shall we try to fix this one first?"

Half a smile crossed Hecate's ageless face. "I appreciate a challenge, but the cauldron mutes my power. We must move either it or her."

It made sense the cauldron would detect a different strain of power and protect itself. Arianrhod glanced at Maggie. What would happen if Ceridwen loosed her? "Easier to move the cauldron," she muttered and began to chant. The magical iron pot would follow Ceridwen, since it was bound to her. The goddess of the world could always move it back—or to another universe—if she chose.

Arianrhod hesitated for a beat, watching the iron pot. Maybe the power that kept Maggie tethered in place depended on it.

Guess I'll find out soon enough.

With a wrenching grunt, the pot's contents bubbled high and splashed over before it rose a few inches and skidded closer to Ceridwen, who stood with upraised arms next to the Morrigan.

Maggie continued to thrash against her bonds. Thank the goddess moving the cauldron hadn't altered the binding. One less problem to deal with. "What do ye think?" Arianrhod faced Hecate.

"I sense Harpy contamination, just as you said. We must drive it out before we can do aught else."

Lachlan slewed to a halt next to them with Kheladin in tow. "Who are you?" He grabbed Hecate's arm. "That's my mate hanging there. Ye willna harm her."

"Give me a little credit," Arianrhod sputtered. "I'd not ask for help from just anyone."

Hecate tossed back her head and laughed. "A witch mated to a dragon shifter. Priceless. That alone was worth leaving Hades's halls." She pushed an open palm Lachlan's way. "Stand back, mage. We can use your dragon, though."

Kheladin moved in front of Lachlan. "Anything. She carries my mating bite."

Hecate stalked around Maggie. Power flared from her, analytical, probing. She made her way back to Arianrhod. "'Tis risky, but we'll employ dragon's fire to drive what's left of the Harpy out. The madness may well leave at the same time."

"I could kill her," Kheladin protested. "I must sear her essence, burn it to nothingness. The Harpy's taint runs deep."

"We havena got a choice," Lachlan said. "She canna live as she is, crazed and bound by magic."

Hecate moved next to Kheladin and gestured Arianrhod to the dragon's other side. "Our task...sister, is to contain and funnel dragon's breath—the magical part, not the actual fire—so it targets the contamination."

"I canna see exactly where the Harpy left residue." Worry sluiced through Arianrhod. She refocused her third eye, but the broad swathes of darkness only got murkier. If they wiped out everything that looked black to her, Maggie would be reduced to a pile of cinders.

"I can, mayhap because Harpies share a link with my Pantheon. Join your magic to mine, and we'll begin."

"Tell me when you need my magic," Kheladin rumbled.

"Now!" Hecate shrieked and spread her arms. Power pulsed from her in waves that rocked Arianrhod, reminding her just how powerful the Greek deities were. Fire burst from the dragon. Hecate wove it into shining cords that dove into Maggie's body from multiple angles, front and back.

Her body arched like a bow, and she screamed, drumming her heels against the cords binding her. Black-tinged blood flowed from the places the cords entered her body and dripped onto the floor, where it emitted noxious smoke.

Hecate bent and ran her fingertips through the blood. Raising her hands to her mouth, she sucked hungrily. The glowing nimbus around her brightened, fed by whatever she did to neutralize the Harpy's taint. "More dragon's breath!" she commanded and absorbed the dragon's gift, forming additional castings, this time in the shape of small darts that bombarded Maggie.

"Please." Lachlan said, his voice laced with anguish. "Ye're hurting her."

"Nay." Hecate spared a glance his way. "We're saving her. Believe, mage. Turn your power to belief. Call to her through your mental bond. Call her back from the Shadowlands, from darkness."

Arianrhod felt like a lightning rod channeling dragon power, Lachlan's desperation, and Hecate's smoothly orchestrated flow. The die was cast. No going back now. They'd either save Maggie, or kill her.

No middle ground.

Maggie's yelps weakened. She sagged against Ceridwen's

enchantment, and the magic-imbued cords disintegrated, dropping her onto the floor. She moaned, a pitiful sound that tugged at Arianrhod. What had they done? She redirected a pulse of power, relieved beyond reckoning that Maggie still lived. Hope flared. Cerwiden's cords wouldn't have released her if something hadn't shifted.

The question was what.

Lachlan launched himself to his knees by Maggie's side and gathered her against him, crooning in Gaelic. She turned in his embrace and wrapped her arms around him.

Hecate reeled in her power. It disappeared into her body as she called it home. She patted Kheladin's flank. "Thank you. I think we did it."

"I love her too." The dragon's voice was strained. "Lending my fire was a difficult choice. Had I been the instrument of her death, 'twould have been hard to live with." He blew soothing steam over Lachlan and Maggie, adding a Gaelic chant to Lachlan's.

Arianrhod knew more than a little about hard choices. "Hold a moment," she said to Hecate. "I would speak with you, but there's something I must do first." She knelt next to Maggie and Lachlan and placed a hand on Maggie's head, pushing into her.

Arianrhod probed, going deeper when her initial examination yielded nothing amiss. Soon she exhaled noisily. The Harpy was well and truly gone. She glanced up to see Lachlan staring at her.

Hope danced behind his eyes, shading them to emerald. "Aye, she'll recover. Thank you." A small smile played over his haggard features and dark-circled eyes. "I dinna let myself believe she'd be whole again—until I held her in my arms."

Arianrhod moved her hand from Maggie to pat one of Lachlan's. "I'm grateful too, not the least of which is I doona have to tell Mary Elma we lost her blood kin." She let a rueful grin form. "I wasna quite certain how to attack that thorny issue."

Lachlan shook his head. "'Tis bad luck to speak of something unfortunate that dinna happen."

She placed a hand on his shoulder and levered herself to her feet. A glance at the far end of the room yielded nothing but an opaque whiteness. Was the Morrigan still thwarted by Ceridwen's magical pythons?

"What did you wish to speak of?" Hecate's harsh voice interrupted her thoughts.

"Unless ye're in a grand rush to return to Hades's halls, there are covens here, and in the States, who'd appreciate knowing ye're still among us."

"You jest. They haven't had any interest in me for at least the last two centuries, except for Mary Elma and a few very old witches who recall when I walked among them."

Arianrhod took her arm. "We could change that."

Angus threaded his way through bunches of Celts to where they stood. "Thank you very much." He inclined his head at Hecate. "You saved one of my friends."

"You're most welcome." She smiled warmly and held out a hand. "Who are you?"

Arianrhod's stomach tightened. Here it was. Time to confess to another virgin goddess. Would Hecate turn her discerning dark gaze on her and consign her to Hell for duplicity?

Some trade.

She's out, and I'd be stuck.

She felt Angus's eyes on her, waiting. He understood well enough, even if he hadn't agreed with her choices. Done with lying about the most important thing in the world to her, she squared her shoulders. "He's my mate."

Hecate's eyes widened, and then bursts of musical laughter rushed from her throat. When she could talk again, she sputtered. "Damn my eyes, but you're a gutsy one. I never could square how I'd face the others, so I kept my dalliances brief and private and—"

Ceridwen's howl of outrage rocked the chamber. The cauldron skated back to its normal place, settling with a metallic *clunk*.

Another screech kicked Arianrhod into motion, and she bolted across the room to where she'd left Ceridwen, the Morrigan, and the snakes.

Pythons crawled across the floor, winding into intricate patterns. The place the Morrigan had been imprisoned was nothing more than empty air. Sulfur and ozone invaded her nostrils, and Arianrhod clamped one hand over her nose, waving fumes aside with the other.

"What the bloody fuck?" She turned on Ceridwen. "How'd ye manage to lose her?"

"Do ye really want an answer to that?" The goddess of the world dropped her head into her hands for a long moment before she looked back up. "I'm not sure how she did it, but the Morrigan's power exceeds mine."

Hecate twisted her face into a sneer and spat on the floor. "That one! She drains power from everything she touches. Until I worked to salvage the witch, I didn't realize I was far stronger away from the Crow than when I stood near her."

"That doesna make me feel any better." Ceridwen grunted her dismay. "It means she drew from me as I stood near, holding my spell in place. Once she had enough, she broke through."

Jonathan sprinted into their midst, followed by Britta. "None of that matters. The problem will be getting her back."

"She wouldna have shown up here, were she not certain of her egress," Arianrhod muttered.

Hecate looked from Jonathan to Arianrhod and Angus. "Incredible! He's your son." She narrowed her eyes. "The Druid seer is mixed in this too. Tell me. Everything. We'll figure out a way to trap the Crow."

"Once she's trapped, we'll move her to Fire Mountain." Tarika came forward. "I was preparing a transport spell when she slipped her bonds."

"At least that explains why she left. She must've guessed your intent." Ceridwen balled her hands into fists. "Mayhap my time draws to a close, but I'd hoped for something better than being bested by that sorry excuse for a Celt."

"Nay." Hecate stood tall. "Our time begins anew." She shot a meaningful glance at Arianrhod. "Show me where those witches are. Once we harness their magic, we'll be unstoppable."

$\mathscr{J}$onathan made his way through the spells surrounding Mauvreen's house, noting they hadn't been disturbed by dark forces. Good thing. He couldn't remember the last time he'd slept or eaten, and he was tired. Britta and Tarika trailed behind him. For once, the dragon didn't insist on taking the lead. Maggie's near brush with annihilation had unnerved everyone.

Arianrhod, Angus, and Hecate should arrive soon, or maybe they were already here since everyone left at the same time.

Lachlan had taken Maggie to her flat outside Inverness to give her space to recover. They'd catch up with everyone at Mauvreen's tomorrow. The only way Kheladin would've fit in Maggie's place was if he melded with Lachlan. Rather than do that, he'd been muttering about a quick trip to Fire Mountain to check in with the Dragon Council—after he stopped by Eletea's to catch her up.

Keeping track of everyone was a job, not necessarily his, but Jonathan was used to arranging game pieces, so tired or not, he picked up the banner.

"Hope Mauvreen's here," Britta murmured and followed Jonathan through the door. "Did ye try to reach her?"

He shook his head, and then realized Britta might not be watching him. "If she isn't now, she will be soon."

"Find me something to eat," Tarika called after them. "Preferably something raw."

"Inconvenient she canna hunt here," Britta said.

"I'm sure Mauvreen has something in her freezer." Jonathan started across the broad entry hall, heading for the kitchen. He looked over a shoulder to make certain Britta was following him.

She winced. "When Tarika said raw, she meant fresh."

Mauvreen hurried down a steep flight of stairs, rubbing sleep from her eyes. "Maggie. Is she... Did anything change? I've been holding off on alerting Mary Elma until I had something more definitive to tell her." Worry lined her words like an unwelcome guest, one who refused to leave.

Jonathan switched courses and hugged the woman who'd been like a mother to him. "She's fine. If I'd been thinking, I'd have used telepathy to let you know."

"Which dragon did she bond with?" Mauvreen shook hair out of her face. "How's she feeling about becoming a dragon shifter?"

"We found another way," Britta cut in. "A better one. From the looks of things, we're the first ones here. Hecate will be arriving soon, along with Angus and Arianrhod."

"Hecate as in the Greek goddess of magical arts?" Mauvreen's voice shrilled, crackling with surprise.

"Aye, the same." Britta twitched her mouth into half a smile.

Mauvreen disentangled herself from Jonathan, her eyes much wider than usual. "Hecate saved Maggie?" At Jonathan's nod, a broad grin split her face. "Damn! That's fucking fantastic. Come into the kitchen. I'll brew us up some tea leaves, and you can fill me in on everything I missed."

They talked over tea and butter scones—after trotting pounds of raw, frozen meat to Tarika, where the dragon lolled on lush grass in the front yard.

"Did she grumble much about it being frozen?" Britta asked. "I dinna hear aught since I was rooting in the freezer, handing things out to you."

Mauvreen snorted. "Nope. She was too busy thawing the meat with dragon fire. It didn't stay frozen long. Hope it's enough. She cleaned out my freezer."

"If it's not, I'll make a trip to the market," Jonathan said.

"Bold of the Morrigan to show up in Inverlochy Castle," Mauvreen noted and poured herself more tea.

"Not surprising, though." Britta knit her brows together. "She would still see herself as a Celt."

Jonathan picked up her line of thought. "This isn't the first time her kin have reviled her. She thrives on chaos and dissent, so she pushes the envelope to force them to hate her. She probably thinks things will blow over this time too."

"Why not? They always have before." A staunch knock at the door brought Mauvreen to her feet.

"Sit." Jonathan motioned her back down. "It's Angus and Arianrhod, with Hecate. I'll let them in." It still felt strange to have his mother and father not just together, but back in his life. A whole lot weirder than chatting it up with a Greek goddess and dragons.

It's the gaming. I'm used to supernatural elements. Just not ones related to me.

He pulled the door open. "Welcome! We're in the kitchen. Come on. What took you so long?"

"We detoured past my house." Arianrhod pointed to the bow and quiver of arrows slung across her back. "I missed these."

"Since she had the means, we, um, borrowed a sheep for Tarika, knowing she'd be here and likely hungry." Angus's amber eyes sparkled with mischief.

Jonathan made a sound between a grunt and a snort. "Dragons are always hungry, but I'm sure you made her happy. Hope you got away without the shepherd spotting you."

"Indeed they did." Hecate spoke up. "I made certain no one would notice."

Jonathan pushed open the swinging door to the kitchen. Mauvreen stood next to the table. When she saw Hecate, she bowed so low her curls touched the floor. "Goddess." She straightened. "You honor my home."

A warm smile softened Hecate's austere features. "The pleasure is mine, witch." She plucked a warm scone off a plate and took an appreciative bite. "The dragon's not the only one hungry. Is there aught else?"

"How about if we order out from that restaurant down the street?" Jonathan asked. "It's easier than cooking."

"Order out?" Hecate frowned.

"Means someone else cooks it, and we go get it," Britta explained.

"If it's not made here in your kitchen, how can you assure yourself it isn't poisoned?"

"I wondered the same thing," Britta assured her. "'Tis just the air and water here that aren't particularly healthy, yet it canna be helped."

Hecate sniffed delicately, sampling. "Humph. Not my imagination then. How could anyone be so stupid and shortsighted to allow air and water to become polluted? When I walked the Earth regularly..."

GOOD-NATURED BANTER FLOWED around the table, along with pots of tea and sandwiches from a nearby bistro. Jonathan wanted to move forward, strategize, but he understood they needed a respite before getting down to business again. He built breaks into his games, where players could breathe a bit before the next catastrophe struck. One of these times, sooner rather than later, they'd face the Morrigan for a decisive battle. They had to do it right, or they'd be in a world of hurt—no matter what the Dragon Council decided.

He yawned, and then again. A glance at the clock told him it was closing on midnight. "Lachlan, Maggie, and Kheladin will be here tomorrow morning. Eletea too, probably. Maybe we could all get some rest."

"Mary Elma's also arriving." Mauvreen smiled knowingly. "I called her with the good news about Maggie after we fed the dragon. She should be here midday with several of her coven. I took the liberty of inviting local witches too. Most are well recovered from the battle." She paused to take a breath. "Every witch I reached wanted to be here right now. It was all I could do to keep them from flooding my house tonight. Between you," she gazed meaningfully at Hecate, "and Tarika, I couldn't keep them away for long, no matter how hard I tried."

Hecate clapped her hands together. "Excellent news on all fronts! I haven't seen Mary Elma in a very long time."

"She said the same about you." Mauvreen's smile broadened. "It's the most animated I've seen her in centuries."

"We're going to bed." Jonathan got up and extended a hand to Britta. "I'll be in my old room, Mauvreen."

"Arianrhod and I will be in mine." Angus winked broadly and stood.

"Ye'll need to show me where it is." Arianrhod got to her feet, leaning into him.

"Guess that just leaves us." Hecate planted her palms on the table and flowed to her feet. "If it's all the same to everyone, I'll visit with the dragon. She's one of the First Born, and I'm certain we share common memories."

"She'd love that," Britta said warmly. "I'm in the same position as Arianrhod," she told Jonathan. "I could likely figure out which room ye use by tracking your energy, but—"

He tucked her hand beneath his arm. "I'll show you. Would you like a bath before bed?"

Her golden eyes twinkled. "Certainly, if ye're in it. Is this like your home where hot water comes out of the wall?"

"Hurry!" Angus grabbed Arianrhod's hand and tugged. "They'll use up all the hot water."

She followed him, laughing. "We can always fall back on the old fashioned way to heat it. Ye know, via magic."

Jonathan made his way to one of the rear staircases, smiling to himself. To him, *old fashioned* meant heating water on the back of a stove and carrying it to a tub. Aside from his trance states, Angus had downplayed the magic running through him, only using it to muffle Jonathan's persistent questions about his mother.

He muted a snort. His life took a definite turn toward the mystical when Britta entered it.

"What's so funny?" She followed him up two narrow flights of stairs to the top floor and his room tucked beneath the eaves of the old stone manse.

"Nothing, really. I was thinking about Da and magic and hot water."

"There's an intriguing combination. Did he not use magic for everyday tasks?"

"No. He decided I needed a normal childhood, and normal children can't cast spells. It was only after I hit my teens, he taught me to manage my power. He didn't have much choice. Not really. Things were getting away from me, and the local school district was worried I was mentally ill."

"Aye, there's always been a link betwixt power and madness."

"So there has. Easy to talk about it now, less so when I was fifteen and truly worried I was losing my mind. Nothing quite like staring at something and having your thoughts come true. Good ones and bad." He took a measured breath. He'd never admitted that before. Not to anyone.

"Och, but I bet 'twas handy to tumble the lassies into your bed."

"I'll never tell." A soft laugh bubbled past his lips.

She linked her arm through his as they walked to the far end of the hall spanning the third floor.

"It's not fancy, but here we are." Jonathan twisted the knob and opened the door to his room. Untouched since his last overnight visit years ago, it reminded him of all the good parts of his childhood. A double bed was pushed under dormer windows. His old desktop computer still sat atop a battered walnut computer hutch. The room was lined with raw cedar and always smelled wonderful.

Her gaze swept the neat space. "It feels like you," she said at last. "I like it."

"It's one part of my life that was always the same," he blurted. "No matter how far Da sank into trance, this was always here, waiting for me. All I had to do was link to Mauvreen, and she came for me or paid for my passage to get here."

Britta moved in front of him and wrapped him in her arms. He hugged her back, though he tottered with weariness. Her strong hands kneaded his back and neck, soothing, pulling him into the special world they made for each other. Suddenly desperate for the taste of her, he cupped her neck in a hand and angled her head so he could close his mouth over hers.

The kiss began at a thousand percent and took off from there. It felt like years had passed since his mother interrupted their lovemaking in his Inverness flat, and they hadn't had any privacy since. She opened her mouth beneath his, and he plumbed the sweet depths of her mouth. She tasted of herbal tea, laced with scotch whiskey, and she tugged at his clothing, running her hands beneath his top, skin against skin.

Breath hitched in his throat, and his cock developed a life of its own where it lay trapped between their bodies. He wanted her, ached for her. To hell with a bath. They could clean up later.

She tore her mouth from his. "Aye, love. I came to the same conclusion." Reaching between them, she undid his trousers, catching them before they pooled around his feet, and pushed him into a clumsy, backward walk until his knees hit the side of the bed. He sat abruptly, pulling her down with him in a tangle of clothing and her long hair.

He kissed her again, breathless with wanting her. She levered a hand between them again and curved it around his erect cock. He felt his ridged flesh jerk in her hand and wanted nothing beyond sinking into the heat of her body, but clothing intruded. So much clothing. She wore breeches, and lace-up boots.

He moved his mouth from hers and on down the line of her neck and throat. The leather lacings of her top yielded to his fumbling, and he pushed it aside to expose a breast that he promptly took into his mouth, sucking hard on her pebbled nipple. She groaned and moved one of his legs between hers so she could thrust against him.

Wanting to feel what she felt, to sense her arousal on an intimate level, he joined his mind to hers and was swept into the heat of a climax as it ripped through her body. He jammed a hand between her legs to intensify her peak and ride it through with her until it ebbed. She cried out in Gaelic, followed by his name over and over again as she dug her nails into his back. Kissing his way down her stomach, he undid the laces of her pants then moved farther down to undo her boots and pull them off.

Finally. Skin. Acres of it.

He tugged her pants down her legs, followed by her silken smallclothes. The heady scent of her filled him with need so sharp and poignant, it was all he could do to hold back from plunging into her.

She tugged on his shoulders, clearly urging him back up her body, but he resisted. So long as he was close, he dipped his head and fastened his mouth over her swollen nubbin. She bucked against him, moaning, and he slid two fingers inside her, feeling her muscles clamp around them.

His cock was perilously close to release where it lay beneath him, but he couldn't stop his hips from moving of their own accord. Sensitive skin rubbed against the covers of the bed they hadn't taken the time to turn down. He wouldn't last ten strokes after he got inside. Better if she came once more this way.

He sucked hard on her clit and worked his fingers deeper inside. His mind linkage told him how close she was and exactly what she needed. He licked harder, faster, and when she buried her hands in his hair, holding his head so she could thrust against him, he upped the ante still further.

A high, shrill scream and a kaleidoscope of color bursting in her mind told him she was there. Her pussy convulsed around his fingers, and he held on for the ride. Long moments passed before her body quieted, and he licked his way up her belly and breasts until his cock seated at the entrance to her vault.

She raised her legs until they hooked around him, gripping his hips, and pulled him into her until he touched bottom. Heat blasted him and he rode herd on the climax simmering beneath the surface. Britta opened her thickly lashed golden eyes, and love blazed in their depths. Lifting her hips, she jammed her pubic bone against his, and then withdrew.

He got his hands beneath her butt, holding on tight, and drove himself into her. Lost in her eyes, lost in her body, lost in the wonder of the woman in his arms, he lost track of where she stopped and he began. His cock swelled, then swelled even more. Semen raced along the channels in the base of his balls. Still he held back. He wanted this perfect. They'd do this together.

He felt the slow climb of her arousal, felt it heat to boiling and ignite. When the first spasms of her climax gripped him, he loosed his own orgasm. Semen spurted from him in blasts of ecstasy that rocked him until his vision blurred at the edges.

Panting, gasping, he used magic to concentrate the oxygen molecules like he had in the dragons' pathways. Britta dropped her legs from his shoulders and pulled him down atop her. She wrapped her arms around him, murmuring endearments.

When he came back into himself enough to form words, he moved away so he could look at her, drink in her beauty. The classic lines of her face, her red-gold curls, and her dragon's eyes. "Did you always have golden eyes, just like Tarika's?"

"Aye, at least I think so." She smiled indulgently. "That was amazing. I love you to distraction."

"Aye." He aped her brogue. "I love you so much it scares me, lassie. So much, 'tis all I can think about."

"Apparently," she said dryly. "Ye promised me a bath."

"I never said when we'd take it," he countered.

She squirmed beneath him, her body still impaled by his cock. "Where's the tub? I'll draw water for us."

"Through that door." He jerked his chin toward the far side of the room. "Even if Angus and Arianrhod took baths, the water's had plenty long to recover."

She quirked a red-gold brow. "How do ye know they dinna do exactly what we did?"

He rolled his eyes and pulled out of her body to lie on his side, head supported by an upraised hand, watching her. "I don't."

"What aren't ye saying?" She swung her legs over the side of the bed and padded toward the bathroom door.

"Let me help." He made his way to her, unwilling to disclose that the thought of his parents as lost in sex as he and Britta had just been skirted into the *too much information* category.

She knelt next to the tub, testing the water with her hands. "What happens next?"

"Good question. We get some rest. Tomorrow we craft a battle plan and go balls out to catch the Morrigan, so the dragons can move her to Fire Mountain."

"What if the dragons close their world? Ye doona know the outcome of your intercession."

He scrunched his face into a frown, thinking, but didn't come up with anything. If the dragons moved forward and closed Fire Mountain anyway, the next logical stop was the Celts, yet he didn't hold much faith in their ability—or interest—in corralling the Morrigan for eternity.

"Have you asked Tarika if she has a Plan B?"

"Nay, but I'll do that while the tub fills." Britta walked back into the bedroom and pried open a window, calling for Tarika.

"Why not use telepathy?"

She tossed him a smile. "Because I dinna have to. She's right here. Never squander power. I have a feeling we'll need every bit we have afore this is over."

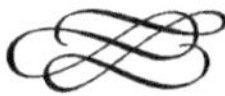

$\mathcal{L}$ ight spilled through Maggie's bedroom window illuminating her drawn face. Lachlan held her tight against him. He'd watched over her through the hours since they arrived, grateful her spirit didn't slip its bonds again. The effects of possession were hard to predict. Though he hated to wake her, they had to get moving.

"*Mo croi*, my heart, my love." He brushed his lips across her ear.

She stirred against him, and her lips formed a soft smile just before she opened her eyes. Seeing those eyes, clear and blue without a taint of madness, warmed him. Damn, they'd had a close call.

"What time is it?"

"Nearly midday. Past time for us to be up and gone. I let ye sleep as long as I dared." He smoothed tumbled blonde hair back from her high forehead. "How do ye feel?"

"Surprisingly good, considering everything." Tears sheened her eyes. "Thank you for not giving up on me. I was still in there—along with the Harpy—but she had me so hogtied beneath her darkness, I couldn't do a thing." A shudder wracked her frame, and she clutched him tighter. "It was horrible. Feeling parts of me gutter like a candle and wondering when they'd flicker out entirely."

He stroked her bare shoulders and kneaded the tension out of her neck. "Och aye, but I had a few bad moments when all I could think to do was chase after the Morrigan. 'Twas Jonathan who brought me to my senses—and herded me back into the Celts' council chamber. After that, Kheladin crashed into me. He loves you too."

She blinked her tears aside. "I understand. Truly I do. You were convinced I was gone and wanted to avenge me."

"Aye, but revenge would always have been an option. Ye should've been my first priority." He hugged her hard. "'Tisn't a mistake I'm likely to make again."

"Hopefully because I won't be stupid enough to allow another abomination access to me." She shook her head and moved out of his embrace, dangling her feet over the side of the bed. "I could've warded myself, but the Harpies shocked me, bombarded me with images of gloom and doom, until I couldn't think of anything else." She shuddered. "It was like the shadow world come to life. Everything I've ever feared—"

He moved to her side and turned her head to he could kiss her forehead. "Aye, 'tis how they operate. First they steal hope. Then they steal souls."

She leaned into him before getting to her feet. "I'm going to take a quick shower, and then we're out of here."

"Mind if I join you?" He raised a questioning brow.

"Love it, but we can't dawdle."

He grinned. "We made love last night, before I insisted on getting some food into you."

"After too, if I recall right. Maybe we can control ourselves for however long it takes to get clean."

"'Tis a worthy goal. I'll get the water going."

Half an hour later they emerged from her flat. At least they both had something clean to change into. He needed more modern clothing, but there'd never been time to do more than buy a shirt here and a pair of pants there. In truth, he missed his tartan—and the assortment of blades he used to hang off his body.

Her car made that odd, chirping noise it did when she unlocked it remotely—like a bird with something stuck in its throat—and he slid into the passenger seat. He needed so many things. Identification so he could get a license to drive, for example. Maybe if they ever got past their problems with the Morrigan, he and Maggie could settle down and raise a few bairns. His life would be much easier if they retreated to an earlier time where he still owned a manor house…

"Penny for your thoughts." She eased the car onto the roadway, heading for Mauvreen's. They could've used magic to travel, but it wasn't a very long drive, only about sixty miles.

He reached across the center divider and twined one of her locks around his fingers. "Many things, lass. Where we'll live once we get to the other side of this. Children."

Her cheeks developed a delicate rosy tint. "Kids, huh? What if I want to go back to work?"

He frowned. "I can take care of you. Ye willna have to work. Ever."

"What if I want to?"

"Ye mean as a healer?"

She spared him a glance before refocusing on the road. "I'm a psychiatrist. You knew that when you met me, even if you weren't quite certain what it meant. Anyway." She made a small, shrugging motion. "Things have been nuts ever since you crawled out of Kheladin's cave—"

"I dinna crawl. I walked."

"Manner of speaking. What's important is I haven't had time to do anything but fight for my life since then. Who knows how I'll feel about work if the dust ever settles."

He lowered his hand to grip her shoulder. "We'll work it out as it happens."

"Sort of the same conclusion I came to." She lapsed into silence, and he leaned against the passenger seat, content to lay a hand on her thigh across the center divider.

~

"Here we are." She swung the wheel to snug the car against the side of the road. "Wonder who all will be here?"

"I'd bet on your grandmother. If she heard what happened to you, she'll be frantic to lay eyes on you and assure herself ye're all right."

"Hecate's quite a draw, absent what happened to me. Aw shit!" She slapped her palm against her forehead before dragging the keys out of the ignition and pushing her door open.

"What?" He got out and hurried around to help her, but she was already standing.

"Grannie won't be the only one here." She smiled brightly. "You might get lucky and meet Aunt Chloe."

He sifted through his memory. "Och, the one on the telephone that night we borrowed power from Castle Balloch."

"The same." Maggie started for the illusory white-washed cottage, and they made their way through the layers of spells that hid Mauvreen's house from the neighbors. "I still remember my first trip here. I got trapped in Mauvreen's enchantment and ended up bawling like an idiot."

Lachlan took in the enormous stone manse that formed before them. "For one not used to magic—" he began diplomatically.

"Only reason she wasn't *used to magic*," a strident voice stopped him cold, "is because she's so stubborn."

"Guess I take after you, Chloe." Maggie walked through the last of the illusion and into her aunt's embrace. The older woman's bright red hair fell straight to her waist, contrasting with Maggie's blonde curls. She was tall, but had ample curves covered by a black robe affair, painted with runic symbols. When she turned her gaze Lachlan's way, a pair of silvery eyes examined him minutely.

He stood tall, determined not to flinch from her stare, battling confusion. After trading barbs, the women hugged each other. What manner of custom dictated such behavior?

"Get in here." Another harsh female voice instructed. "You're at least an hour later than I'd have liked." At least this voice was familiar.

Lachlan glanced up to see Mary Elma standing on the top step. Her long black hair was shot with silver and had been dragged into a braid that hung down her back. Intense dark eyes regarded him. She was razor thin and dressed in black from head to toe, a long sleeved shirt covering dark pants. He inclined his head. "Nice to see you again, mother-in-law."

"The pleasure's mine." Her tone warmed fractionally. "Now get in here. We have a goddess in our midst, and it won't do to keep her waiting."

Maggie moved away from Chloe and started up the steps. Lachlan would've followed, but Chloe grabbed his arm and spun him to face her. "Nice to meet you in the flesh, dragon shifter. I expect you to take better care of my niece from now on."

He winced. "My heartfelt apologies. No one suffered more than me—"

"Can it." She made a dismissive gesture with one hand and vaulted up the stairs, leaving him standing with his mouth open.

"Lachlan. It's okay. Her bark's worse than her bite," Maggie called from the porch, where she stood hugging Mary Elma.

"Don't bank on it, dragon shifter." Chloe's voice echoed from inside the house.

Shutting his mouth with a snap, he took the steps three at a time and followed Maggie and her grandmother inside. The house buzzed with activity. At least fifty witches milled through the large, open downstairs. From the looks of things, he and Maggie were the last to arrive, which made at least some sense because Britta and Arianrhod had slept here, along with their mates.

Mauvreen caught up with them, her eyes gleaming with anticipation. "Grab a plate from the kitchen, and then meet us in the great room."

"You look happy," Maggie noted.

"I am. There hasn't been such a resurgence of witchiness in a long time. I'm delighted Hecate showed herself to us. Gives us renewed belief in ourselves."

"'Twasn't her doing. 'Twas the Morrigan's." Lachlan tried to keep a sour note out of his voice.

Mauvreen pierced him with her amber gaze. "Does it matter? I'll take the goddess's providence, no matter who the messenger is."

He tamped back a grin. "Thank you for the reminder. Couldna agree more."

A few moments later, they made their way to Mauvreen's living room, plates laden with fruit and pastries. Maggie carried their food, and he balanced two cups of coffee, trying to keep the liquid from slopping onto the polished floorboards.

He'd no sooner settled onto a thick, Oriental rug embossed with cauldrons and magical staffs when Kheladin's voice blasted into his head. *"Eletea and I are almost there. Tarika says decisions are imminent. Wait for us."*

Hecate raised her hands, and every conversation in the room ceased abruptly. Her dark gaze settled on Lachlan. "Was that your dragon?"

He rose to his feet and bowed. "Aye, goddess."

"Dragons are part of this discussion too. I spent an instructive night with Tarika." Hecate walked to a window and undid the latch, winding it open.

A red-scaled snout appeared. "Perfect height," Tarika declared. "Here come Kheladin and Eletea now. She's too short to reach the window, but—"

"I'll manage," the small copper dragon cut in, amid the sound of flapping wings.

Hecate strolled back to the floor-to-ceiling stone fireplace and turned to face the assemblage. "The basic plan is to find the Morrigan, restrain her, and keep her that way. The first part will be easy, the second two less so. Her alliances compound our task, and they're troubling. When she showed up in Hell, I was so delighted to have a way out, I didn't question her motives."

"What do we face beyond Harpies and Gryphons? More specifically, who left Hell with you?" Tarika asked. "Ye told me last night, but the others need to hear too."

"Tantalus, Ixion, and the Furies." Hecate shook her mane of hair back. "Circe and Medea left as well, but they answer to me. I'm wondering which Celts may have taken the Crow's side, but I'm most concerned with where we hunt her down and how we hold onto her."

Arianrhod cleared her throat. "I would speak."

"Please do."

"The Morrigan is actually a triple goddess. Our safest plan is to force her to split into Badb, Macha, and Anann. Neither alone has sufficient power to escape us." She drew her brows together. "She split when we found her in the future—after I suggested she help us round up rogue dragon shifters and their dragons."

"But one of the verra oldest tales warns when the Morrigan splits into her three forms, destruction follows," Britta protested.

Arianrhod showed her a mouthful of teeth. "Aye, 'tis her own destruction that tale refers to. Verra few realize that."

Hecate narrowed her eyes. "I assume the Crow holds that prime piece of information rather close to the vest." At Arianrhod's nod, she continued. "We need to make her believe she'll save herself by splitting."

"Aye, that's the long and short of it," Arianrhod concurred. "Not just save herself, but that there's killing to be done, destruction to be sown, and three can do it better than one."

"Oh ho!" A knowing expression made Hecate look like the ancient creature she was. "We present her with a task, tell her we've rethought her role, and we need her facility for destruction."

"I like it." Kheladin stuck his snout through the window next to Tarika's. "All we need to do is track her down."

"I know how to do that." Jonathan rose from where he'd been seated next to Britta. A muscle danced in his jaw. "She'll come to me, and that particular draw has nothing to do with destruction."

"Nay!" Britta stood in a single, fluid motion and stalked to Jonathan's side. "I'm not in agreement with ye offering yourself as bait. I say we return to Arianrhod's suggestion. Create a battle and dangle it afore her like a shiny bauble."

"My idea is more logical," he argued. "And much easier than manufacturing a war out of thin air. She marked me with her beak that first night we met, tasted my blood. She's wanted me ever since." Breath hissed from between his teeth. "Actually, she started out wanting Da, but I'll do now that she knows me. Same blood and all."

"Do you offer this of your own free will?" Hecate asked, skewering him with her unrelenting gaze.

"Nay!" Britta grabbed his arm.

"Sorry, love." He faced Hecate. "Yes, I do."

A knife materialized in her fingers. "Give me your left hand." When he did, she made a quick, deep bite at the base of his thumb and raised it to her mouth. The touch of her tongue sealed the wound as if it had never been there."

"What did you do to my mate?" Britta hissed.

"Made certain we can locate him." Hecate shifted her penetrating gaze to Britta. "We're on the same side, dragon shifter. Never forget that. In years past, I'd have made you suffer for having the audacity to doubt me."

Color stained Britta's cheeks, and she curtsied stiffly. "Apologies, goddess."

She didn't offer excuses for her behavior, and Lachlan quietly lauded her for that. Britta understood she and Tarika couldn't be with Jonathan for his plan to have any chance of success, and it probably ate at her. He wondered if he'd be as strong if Maggie offered herself as a lure.

"We have much to do before we set that part of things in motion." Hecate gazed around the room. "I need time with the witches. One of you, likely Arianrhod, must figure out if any Celts stand against us." She swiveled to face the dragons. "Do any of you know if the Dragon Council came to a decision?"

"Not yet." Kheladin blew steam and smoke ahead of his words. "I was just there, and they're still closeted."

"Did ye disturb them?" Tarika asked and turned her whirling gaze his way.

"Nay. Even if I'd had the temerity to walk in, they would've paid scant attention to me. I'm quite low in their pecking order."

"Wise," Tarika burbled through steam. "By now, more than a few must be frustrated as hell. It's never good to provide a target when they're irritated."

Hecate clapped her hands together smartly. "The rest of you make certain your power is in top notch shape. We'll meet back here before the sun sets to finalize our plans. Witches gather close. This is exciting. It will be just like the old times."

Lachlan collected their dishes and rose. He gave Maggie a quick kiss. "I'll be outside with Kheladin."

"We'll be outside with Tarika." Britta latched a firm hand through Jonathan's arm.

"Not that I'm likely to have any visitors, but I'm out here too," Eletea called.

Angus grinned and wrested a cup from Arianrhod. "I'll finish drinking this. Best of luck dredging information out of your brother."

"Och aye, that one." Arianrhod made a dismissive gesture. "I'll need all the assistance I can get."

"I'll spend the time you're gone with Eletea." Angus gave her a quick hug and walked toward the front door.

Lachlan smiled to himself. The young dragon was brash and headstrong, but she held fresh, pure energy. "See you outside," he called and headed for the kitchen to leave his armload of dishes in the sink.

∼

JONATHAN LOLLED IN THE GRASS, leaning against Tarika with Britta next to him. They'd had words about his offer to lure the Morrigan, but the dragon settled Britta's ire—more or less.

Lachlan sat across from them, leaning against Kheladin, who'd told them about his journey to Fire Mountain.

Angus and Eletea stood off to one side, deep in conversation.

The plan they came up with was simple. Eletea would return home, and Jonathan would go with her, ostensibly to help her clear the remaining debris from when Angus and Arianrhod cast a sleeping spell to snare the Morrigan. Eletea would leave, and Jonathan would try calling for the Crow.

Whether she'd show or not was anyone's guess, but if she did, he'd have to woo her, make her believe he was interested. That he'd thought about nothing but her offer since she came upon him behind his flat. Because she'd used magic to ensorcel him, she just might believe his words. The next part was tricky. He'd mention being captivated when she split into three and hint he'd love to have it off with her and her sisters.

Suggestions got raunchy after that. Interestingly, Lachlan and Kheladin came up with the best scenarios to tempt the Crow. Creative combinations of his cock, fingers, and mouth to make all three come.

"When will all of you show up?" Jonathan demanded. "She smells so bad, I'll have a hard time disguising my revulsion."

"Was that a problem when she nabbed you behind your home?" Tarika asked.

He recalled his near to bursting cock and had the grace to feel ashamed. "Um, no. It's odd, the disgust was there, but floating in a distant corner of my mind. A really distant corner where I looked past it. In truth, it cost a great deal to break loose from her spell. I was grateful I had enough magic." He swallowed hard, not looking at Britta as he aimed for honesty. "If I'd waited even a few minutes longer, I'd have been lost."

"No wonder she's able to lure men to her bed," Britta muttered sourly.

"We'll show up," Lachlan answered Jonathan, "once she's split into three."

"I'm far from clear on how you'll be close enough, without her realizing she's sitting in the jaws of a trap about to spring shut."

"Ye'll have to be so captivating, ye hold all her attention." Lachlan winked lewdly.

"She's not stupid," Jonathan muttered. "She'll find the timing suspicious, since it falls on the heels of her visit to the Celts. Plus Hecate's no longer with her. Surely she knows about her affinity for witches—or rather witch kinship with her."

"If ye're having second thoughts," Britta said, "'tis fine by me. I dinna care much for this from the moment the words rolled from your mouth."

"No second thoughts." He gripped her hand. "I like to have my I's dotted and my T's crossed. I'd also like an out if things aren't going well. What if she wants to fuck first, before she splits into three? Do I tell her it's all or nothing?"

"Ye could, but she may well snare you in another spell, and that would be that," Kheladin said.

"I've got it." Lachlan snapped his fingers. "Tell her ye've thought of nothing but her, and ye wish to get to know her better. Dragons are on the edge of closing Fire Mountain. Tarika will rejoin her kin, leaving Britta dragonless. Ye fear she'll sink into a deep depression… Doona go further than that on the topic, but ask her advice. She's arrogant enough to believe ye wish the benefit of her knowledge."

He creased his forehead, clearly thinking, before he started talking again. "If the Morrigan launches herself at you, hang back, be coy, diffident. Make her drag what ye really want out of you."

Jonathan nodded slowly. A game of wits and strategy held a certain appeal. "I believe I can pull that off."

"I doona like it at all," Britta said dourly. "What if she doesna give a bloody good fuck about what ye wish and simply drops a net around you to get your pants off?"

"Then I guess I'm screwed until the cavalry shows up."

"Not the right answer." Britta bolted to her feet and stood over him, hands on her hips.

Tarika bathed her with steam. "Ye must let him follow the path the goddess put inside his head. Trust he'll do what he has to. Believe his ploy will work."

"Och aye, I can do all those things, but it doesna mean I have to like it."

"I've been listening with half an ear from over here," Angus said and walked to where they sat. "If the Morrigan wants kink, I say we give it to her." He met Jonathan's gaze. "What say we approach her as a team? Three of them. Two of us." He let a lazy, bawdy expression ramble across his face. "Could get interesting fast."

"I'm not feeling very confident—about any of this." Jonathan got to his feet and extended a hand to Angus. "I could kiss your feet. It's a deal."

Angus grasped his hand. "Foot kissing could factor in. I'm sure between the two of us, we can come up with some really creative angles."

CHAPTER 22

Jonathan flew to Eletea's cave on her back with her grumbling the whole way. "I feel bad enough about this," he finally said. "You're making it worse."

"Sorry. Sorry. I hate having anyone ride me. Always have. It's not you. Don't take it personally. Plus once I drop you off, I still have to go back for Angus. I could've taken both of you at once, but it would have been much worse for me." She circled to land. "Now remember," she adjured. "Shroud yourself with magic until I get back with your da."

"Don't worry. Last thing I want is a premature confrontation by myself." He ducked into her cave to wait out the few minutes until her return, cloaking himself in spells. He settled on a flat rock and took the time to make sure he wasn't missing anything critical. Arianrhod had returned with two pieces of good news. None of the other Celts admitted to an alliance with the Crow. To hear Gwydion and Andraste tell it, they'd responded to the Crow's distress call, thinking she was trapped inadvertently. Once freed, she promised to return to the Celts' hall under her own steam.

"It's a good thing to remember," he muttered. "The Morrigan tells part of the truth. She did return, but not alone and not immediately." The important thing was if the Morrigan once had allies among the Celts, they were distancing themselves from her.

The witches had left, taking Arianrhod, Britta, and Lachlan with them, along with Tarika and Kheladin. He wished he knew more about what they planned, but Mary Elma and Maggie convinced him the less he knew the better. He'd be in a delicate situation where the Morrigan could easily pluck key information right out of his head.

The thought chilled him, and he tightened the layers of spells around him before stopping himself. He needed to face the Morrigan as unshielded as possible, which meant taking what he truly couldn't share and either erasing it or burying it so deep no one could find it.

Dragon wings beating the air brought him to his feet just in time to greet Angus as he strolled into the cave. "Ready?" He eyed his dreamer of a father—who had far more mettle than he ever expected—and wondered how this would unfold.

"Not really." Angus grinned. "Never fear, we'll make this work. Eletea's gone. I suppose she hatched something up with the other dragons, but she wouldn't tell me what."

"Same reason the witches kept their mouths shut. It occurred to me this might not be the best place since you and Arianrhod trapped the Crow here, but that can't be helped."

"You're a lot like me." Angus cast a sidelong glance his way. "You overthink things. I've found it's not useful."

"Probably so. Ready?"

"Never readier." Angus turned and walked out into a relatively decent day. A weak sun shone, and fluffy clouds didn't threaten rain. He fell into the roles they'd agreed on. "Whew! What a big job that was."

"Glad it's over," Jonathan made his way to a nearby tumble of boulders. "Not easy clearing all that mess without disturbing Eletea's stash."

"We did disturb it. It's why she left in a huff." Angus settled on a large, flat stone and patted the one next to it. "Have a seat. She'll be back eventually. In the meantime, tell me more about the Morrigan dropping by your flat." He lowered his voice. "There was a time she and I almost got together—and I've never forgotten it."

Heat rose to Jonathan's face. At least he didn't have to fake that part. "That one is hard to forget. Maybe it's her magic, but she got me hotter than I've been in a long time. It took everything I had to drag myself away."

"It's just the two of us—no women to overhear." Angus lowered his voice conspiratorially. "Why'd you leave?"

Jonathan shrugged. It wasn't difficult to feign being uncomfortable. "Britta was waiting for me, and I was afraid she'd find out."

"Funny. I was in almost the exact same position. Your mother actually sent me off with the Morrigan to glean information." He rolled his eyes. "She suggested I seduce her, but not. You know?"

"Pretty hard to stop once she nails you with one of those human bodies of hers. She sure picks some lush ones." Jonathan licked his lips. "Too bad she's not around now. No one's expecting us anywhere."

"Aye, no one would ever know." Angus shaded his eyes and scanned the sky.

Jonathan felt power flow from his father in waves and wove his in with it. Minutes clicked by, but nothing happened. "Maybe wishing on a star isn't enough," he murmured.

"Well, we don't have a way to locate her. Wonder if maybe she left some feathers in the cave."

"Great idea. If we had something of hers, it'd be easier to find her. Now that we've started talking about her, I hate to not be able to finish things. She's been a hot number in my fantasies for way too long." He followed Angus, but before he got back to the dragon's cave something shifted in the air and he came to a halt.

Angus must've felt it too, because he turned. "Aye, lassie. That's it," he crooned. "Come to us. We're waiting for you."

Jonathan spun in time to see the Crow burst through a rent in the ether. She flapped her way to a landing a few feet away, regarding them out of beady, avian eyes. "What's up, boys?"

Angus smiled warmly. "You're here. It's almost too much to believe our good fortune."

"Aye, good fortune is it?" The Morrigan didn't move, nor did she shift into one of her human guises. "Neither of you were interested in me afore."

"That's not true," Jonathan protested and adopted a hangdog expression. "I was worried Britta would find out."

"I told you she wouldna." The Crow tilted her head toward Angus. "I recall our time near Rhukon's the day I was a white dragon."

"As do I." Angus glanced away, the perfect combination of bashful suitor and uncomfortable man. "Any chance you could find that form again? The medieval maiden with long, dark hair."

"I want the blonde in the low-cut suit," Jonathan protested.

The Morrigan's beak parted in a smile. "I can do you one better. Would ye appreciate a redhead in the mix?"

Angus' eyes widened. "Three of you. I'd heard rumors you could do that." He turned to Jonathan. "What do you say, son? Three of them. Two of us. The possibilities are enticing."

"More than enticing. Pretty fucking hot. Let's do this." He rubbed his hands together in anticipation.

A sharp blast of lust blanketed him, and his cock jumped to attention. Had the magic come from the Crow or from his father? Jonathan licked his lips. Full steam ahead. They were in the thick of things now. He cupped his erection through his pants.

He tugged his jacket off and yanked his shirt over his head, dropping his clothing over a handy rock. His nipples hardened into points of hunger. When he glanced at his father, he'd stripped to the waist too. Angus sauntered toward the crow, the front of his trousers tented with an erection of his own. He beckoned with one hand before curving fingers around his ridged flesh.

"Hurry up and shift or you'll be late for the party." Jonathan rubbed himself because he couldn't stand not to.

"A token first. Ye'll excuse me if I'm slow to believe both of you had a change of heart."

"Anything." Angus said, his voice thick with lust.

"Get those lovely cocks out. Let me watch you come. Then we'll have a spot of fun."

Keeping his gaze glued on the Crow, Jonathan unfastened his pants enough to draw his cock out. He widened his stance to keep his trousers on his hips and stroked himself from base to tip. The crow's form shimmered, becoming insubstantial. He closed his eyes and images of firm, bouncing breasts and pussies glistening with moisture filled his mind. He cupped his balls with one hand and worked his rigid flesh, willing himself to come.

The Morrigan was inside his mind, likely inside Angus's too, so he kept visions of Britta at bay. Instead, he borrowed a well-used image, one he'd jacked off to countless times before Britta entered his life. The game avatar cooed as she wrapped her mouth around his shaft, enclosing him with heat. Her long hair fell across his belly, and she breathed lust into him.

A familiar tightening in his balls told him a climax wasn't far away. The Crow urged him on. The avatar sucked harder. Semen burst from him in lazy gouts. He opened his eyes, panting, and gazed at the Crow. "There. Now I want the blonde."

"Aye, and I want the medieval maid," Angus said from somewhere behind him. "We did our part. It's your turn now."

The Morrigan cawed laughter. "So it is. Loved the energy. It made my day." She spread her wings and took to the air.

Jonathan stuffed himself back inside his pants. Still struggling for breath, he called after her. "Wait! You can't leave. We had a deal."

The Crow altered her flight path and turned, gazing down at him and Angus. "Ye truly wish me to return."

Jonathan draped his words in compulsion. "I've never wanted

anything quite so much. That was just a warmup. I felt you in my head. Now get back here."

"The die is cast," Angus said. "We can't tell our women what we just did. At least make our sin worthwhile." He righted his trousers too, gazing at the crow with palpable longing.

Jesus, he's a good actor.

Jonathan watched the Crow, silently urging her to return. His cock, which hadn't subsided, stiffened still more. Running on instinct, he drew it out and began stroking his erect flesh again.

The Morrigan landed in a flurry of black feathers. Magic turned the air around her incandescent, and the smell of flowers blended with carrion. When the air cleared, three naked women stood, identical but for hair color. All were tall with full breasts and curved hips.

"We are here," they announced in unison.

"And you're perfect. Just perfect." Angus waded into the midst of them and grabbed the brunette around her waist just before he lowered his mouth to suckle one of her breasts.

Anything less than total enthusiasm would give them away. Thank God, his cock was still cooperating. Jonathan forced a broad grin and beckoned to the blonde. "You're mine."

"Who will fuck me?" the redhead asked in the same monotone the three had spoken in.

Angus lifted his mouth from the dark haired woman's breast. "We'll work it out."

The blonde barreled into Jonathan, naked breasts pressed against his chest. She moaned and plastered her mouth over his. Afraid to do anything to clue the Morrigan she was vulnerable, he kissed the caricature in his arms, pretending she was something he'd designed for a game. He kept his mind blank of anything but lust.

The blonde reached between them, capturing his dick as she moaned into his mouth. Another set of hands grabbed his ass. "I want him," the redhead announced. "First."

He tore his mouth form the blonde's and twisted in her embrace. "I can handle both of you, darling." He sent an image of fucking one while the other sat on his face into both their minds.

"Maybe later," the redhead said. "For now, I want you to myself."

"Not going to happen." The blonde drew her lips into a snarl.

"Fighting doesn't turn me on." He glanced from one woman to the other. "If you both want me, play nice."

A quick glance Angus's way showed his father wrapped in the brunette's arms, kissing her. "Let's join them." He jerked his chin. "Make it a real party. I've designed some computer sex games. Love to try out some of the ideas."

He was buying time and hoped to hell they wouldn't see through him. Where was everyone? They could show up anytime and it wouldn't be too soon. He felt dirty, like all the soap in the world couldn't clean the taint from him.

The blonde drew back and frowned. Jonathan wiped his mind fast. "Games, sweetheart." He slapped her butt. "I'm a gaming kind of guy."

As if Angus read his mind, he moved away from the brunette and ferried her toward Jonathan and the other two parts of the Morrigan. "Amazing, simply fantastic." He punched Jonathan's arm. "If we'd known, just think of the adventures we could've had."

"Doesn't matter." Jonathan sent a disingenuous smile his father's way. "We're having them now."

The brunette narrowed her eyes, and all three women said, "You're stalling," in discordant unison.

"We want to enjoy you. What's the rush?" Angus's eyes glittered with promise, and Jonathan developed a new appreciation for his father. The man had guts and the ability to lie without missing a beat.

Jonathan wrapped an arm around the two women on either side of him, tweaking nipples and rubbing silky skin. Angus caught his eye and winked. Was it a sign? Had he forgotten something?

Without a shred of warning, the sky disintegrated, showering them with dragon fire. Lachlan rode Kheladin, and Britta sat atop Tarika. His war whoops and her cries of outrage filled Jonathan's ears. For the barest moment, he quivered with relief, and then he tightened his hold on both women, dropping magical cords around them. Cords the dragons reinforced with their power.

Angus did the same with the brunette. "Got this one." He dragged dragon's fire into his casting.

Eletea joined the fray, pelting the three parts of the Morrigan with still more fire. The redhead's hair ignited, but it smoked and went out.

Jonathan felt the blonde and redhead doing their damnedest to draw together. Two could probably pull in the third. He couldn't let it happen. "Britta! Tarika!"

"That's right," the blonde sneered. "Call women to save you. Pathetic!"

"If I'm so pathetic, how come you fell for our ruse?" He sneered back.

Tarika hit the ground near him so hard it vibrated. Britta leapt from her back and joined him. "I'll get this one."

"Nay." Lachlan strode into the fight. "She's mine. I'll dismember all three parts for what she did to Maggie."

"Doona argue," Tarika cried. "Make certain the three parts canna rejoin one another."

"Take this one to Fire Mountain." Angus dragged the brunette, kicking against invisible bonds, to Tarika's feet. "Best way to make certain she can't recapture her power is to get rid of her in parts."

"Excellent idea." Tarika shot flames mingled with dragonspeak, and the air split into a pathway Jonathan remembered all too well.

"Hurry back," Britta called to her dragon. "Here. Take some of our shared power to speed you on your way." A blue-white flash jumped from her to Tarika.

"I'll make certain this one gets to Fire Mountain." Eletea closed her jaws around the blonde, lifting her easily.

"I'll get you for this!" the three said as one. "All of you."

"For now, I'd shut up if I were you." Eletea switched to mind speech. *"If you don't, I'll bite clean through you."*

"Be back verra soon." Tarika motioned Eletea into the pathway and bounded in after her.

"I'll take the third," Kheladin said and followed his words with action. Once he jumped through, the seam in the sky closed as if it had never existed.

Jonathan stared at the empty place in the sky. "Jesus, I'm glad that's over." He did up his trousers and plucked his clothing off the rock he'd left it on. Tugging his shirt on, he slipped his jacket over it.

Angus started for his shirt, but stopped cold. "Goddammit!" He punched the air with a fist.

Jonathan spiraled power around him. "Not over," he shouted just before dark mages in the form of dragons converged on them, followed by Gryphons. No Harpies this time. Not yet, anyway. And no Furies.

"A little consolation prize she left us," Angus yelled and pelted the nearest mage with magic. It didn't make a dent since the thing was immortal.

"Was that even the Morrigan?" Britta asked. "Convenient all this crap was waiting in the wings to attack us as soon as the dragons left."

"Aye, 'twas the Morrigan. I'd know the feel of her anywhere," Lachlan said. "She's arrogant, and she misjudged. She assumed she'd be stronger than us, craftier. Too bad for her, she was wrong."

Jonathan scanned the field. The four of them faced over a hundred, but more fell creatures dropped out of rents in the sky by the moment. Lousy odds. Even worse, since many of them couldn't die, all they'd do would be exhaust each other.

Maybe they should leave while they still could.

"Where are the witches and Arianrhod? Britta, Lachlan, you were with them."

"I doona know," Britta answered. "Last we saw them, they were giving Ceridwen hell for not marshaling troops to help. Tarika sensed when the Morrigan split into three, and we hastened here."

Angus shoved telepathic magic so strong it rocked Jonathan, as he summoned reinforcements.

"Ye called?" Andraste, goddess of victory, stepped from a portal, resplendent in dove-colored leathers, blonde curls flying behind her. She rubbed her hands together in anticipation. "I was on my way when I heard you. 'Twas rumored there'd be a battle here. They're few and far between these days, so I try not to miss them." She surveyed the field. "Excellent! Love the odds." Power circled her like a golden cyclone before she whipped it into a Gryphon. It howled its misery before it exploded into grisly bits of bone and bloody flesh. Another Gryphon fell on it and began feasting.

Jonathan grinned. If he ever went back to work, he vowed to design an avatar just like Andraste. Everyone would want one. It'd sell a million copies.

Magic exploded around him, the air thick with the scents of cut grass and growing things he associated with witchcraft, but more than that a bittersweet undernote told him Celts were part of the groups emerging from glowing gateways. They joined hundreds of witches—and Hecate—and plowed into the enemy.

For the first time since he'd performed for the Morrigan, hope flared within him that they just might win this battle.

"Jonathan! Help me!"

The sound of Britta's voice dragged him back to the increasingly crowded moorlands in front of Eletea's cave. A Gryphon had attached itself to her back. She grappled with it, but couldn't get a firm enough hold to detach the thing.

Fury threatened to choke him. He hadn't come this far to see the woman who meant more than life itself injured. Careful to focus the flow of his power, he skewered the Gryphon, pounding it with lethal magic until it let go. As soon as it lay in the dirt, he hit it hard enough, it burst into green flames.

Blood poured down Britta's back from deep gouges. He expected them to begin to knit back together, but something was wrong. They expanded until her exposed back looked like raw hamburger.

Jonathan pulled her into his arms. "Why aren't you healing yourself? Tell me how to help you."

"Tarika," she said weakly. "Need Tarika back." Blood bubbled from the corners of Britta's mouth. "Agreed. We agreed she'd take some of my magic to hasten her journey to Fire Mountain."

Her eyes dropped shut, and she sagged against him. Healing magic had never been anything he knew shit about. "Mauvreen!" The raw anguish in his voice shocked him. No way she could hear over the screeches, whoops, cries, and howls rising above the field. He switched to telepathy, and eased Britta to the earth. It was his strong suit, and he pulled power from it, funneling it into her body and hoping to hell it would keep her alive until Mauvreen showed up.

A strong hand on his upper arm forced him out of the pit his thoughts had become. Dirt streaked Mauvreen's face, and she pushed hair out of her eyes with begrimed fingers. "Give her to me."

He handed Britta gently to the woman he trusted more than anyone else.

She placed her hands on either side of Britta's head, but not for long.

The look in her eyes clutched at Jonathan's heart. "She's not dying," he stammered. "She can't die. We have to save her."

"Not we. You. You're the one Tarika marked. You're who can use the dragons' pathways. She needs her dragon. It's the only way to pull her through this. You've got to get to Fire Mountain. Now."

"Dragons' pathways? Shit! It's a hard journey. Really brutal. She might not survive."

Mauvreen bit her lower lip so hard blood welled. "She won't survive here, either. Get going."

He was chanting before his feet found purchase, and he stood upright. The ether split before him, and he reached for Britta, feeling like he was choking, drowning.

"Do you want me to come too?" Mauvreen's eyes clouded with pain. "I'm not sure the dragons' paths will admit me, but I'm willing to try."

"No. I've got this." Clasping Britta firmly against his chest, he walked forward and said the words to shut them into the dragons' pathways. The one place he swore he'd never go again.

CHAPTER 23

onathan draped his jacket over Britta's head, hopefully trapping enough air that hypoxia wouldn't kill her before the pathways spit them out. His lungs began to burn almost immediately, maybe because he anticipated the pain.

Reaching deep, he linked to Britta's essence, her life force, gratified it still pulsed within her. Were the Gryphon's claws imbued with poison? Was there something beyond blood loss to combat here? He did what he could, marshaling magic to search for taint. It was hard. No air to breathe. Even standing was a struggle, but he had to hang on. If he collapsed, Britta would die too, and he would not, could not, allow it.

If he hadn't been lost in musings about game design, fucking game design of all things, he'd have noticed she needed help before she called him. Knowing her, calling out was a last ditch effort. She'd have tried everything she could before she caved and summoned him.

"My fault," he moaned. "This is my fault." Then he got hold of himself. He'd dunned Lachlan for the same thing. At least he understood now—at a deeply personal level that made him writhe

265

with discomfort—what drove the dragon shifter so deep into the pit of doom he lost his ability to reason.

"Hurry up." He yelled at the pathway. If it was anything like the time shaft, it might get pissed off and hustle them to where it could jettison them. He stared straight ahead, willing the unremitting darkness to develop the gray edges that meant they were almost there.

Yes!

At first he feared it was wishful thinking, imagination, but it was getting lighter, and there was slightly more air. Not enough to keep his lungs from seizing, but more than there'd been a few moments before. The pathway split with a rending sound he felt in the pit of his stomach, just before it chucked him onto the red, dry sand of Fire Mountain. He did his best to cushion Britta, but one of her arms hit the ground anyway, and she cried out from the depths of unconsciousness.

A caldera was too damned close, and he scooted them back from its edge. Britta's wrist fell at a wrong angle. Probably broken. Damn! Could this day get any worse?

"Tarika!" He raised his voice loud as he could make it, screaming for the dragon.

One winged toward him, closing the distance alarmingly fast, but it wasn't red. Before the black dragon landed, Jonathan directed a stream of words at it. "Tarika. You must take us to where she is. Fast. This woman is—"

"I know well enough who she is," the dragon broke in. "And I know you too. If ye werena so far gone, ye'd have recognized me from your last trip here. Get on my back. Tarika's with the council, along with Kheladin and Eletea—and the three parts of the Morrigan."

Jonathan gathered his waning power and landed between Keene's shoulder blades. "Sorry for not recognizing you and greeting you by name," he said, knowing better than to offer excuses to a dragon.

"Forgiven." Keene took to the skies. "Good work with the Morrigan. Tarika told us all about how you and Angus tricked her. Naturally, the Morrigan denied the whole thing."

Jonathan smoothed hair back from Britta's face. She was the color of old ivory, and sweat beaded her brow. If anyone could save her, Tarika could. "Hold on, love," he murmured. "Hold on. We're nearly there."

He wasn't sure if she could hear him, but he kept feeding her reassurances. Keene said something, but Jonathan hadn't been paying attention. "What was that? I'm sorry, my mind's not all here."

"Ye'll get a chance to confront the Morrigan once more."

His stomach tightened into coiled knots. Standing face to face with her was near the bottom of his list. "Britta may not have that kind of time. Besides—"

Frantic bugling he'd recognize anywhere cut off his words. When he raised his gaze from Britta to the skies, he saw Tarika cutting her way through the air toward them. "Put her down," the red dragon shrieked at Keene. "Here."

"But we're almost to the council," Keene protested.

"She'll be dead by then."

Fear closed a thorny fist around Jonathan's heart. He examined the threads of power he'd woven through Britta, and the truth in the dragon's words slapped him hard. Why hadn't he noticed?

Because I didn't want to see.

Keene hit the ground so hard it rattled Jonathan's teeth. A blast of magic moved him to the ground in front of Tarika. "Give her to me." She bent, holding out her forelegs.

He didn't want to let go, but the dragon had ripped him from Keene's back. He had no doubt she could tear Britta from his arms, and he didn't want to jostle her any more than necessary. He withdrew his magic and placed Britta tenderly in Tarika's forelegs.

"Ye may not wish to watch," Tarika cautioned. "If ye do, ye must not interfere, no matter how much ye may want to."

Words stuck in the thick place in his throat, so he just nodded.

Keene lumbered to his side and hunkered to lay a foreleg on his shoulder. He felt power from the black dragon flow into him, steadying him. *"What ye're about to witness is one of the mysteries of dragon shifter magic,"* Keene said into his mind. *"Ye must never speak of it, not even to another dragon shifter."*

Tarika chanted low in the dragons' tongue. Her forked reptilian tongue snaked out, painting runic symbols in bright red on Britta's pale face. With a high, keening cry, Tarika blasted Britta with red-gold flames. Fire enveloped her, and she writhed in the dragon's grip.

Jonathan would have rocketed forward, done his damnedest to jerk Britta from the dragon's talons, but Keene held him back, claws digging deep into his shoulder. "Let me go!" Jonathan shouted. "Let me go to her."

"Tarika loves her. Trust she treads the only path left to them."

The smell of burning hair and flesh stung Jonathan's nostrils. Keene moved behind him and added a second foreleg to hold him in place. A tower of flame rose high, enveloping Britta and Tarika.

Jonathan looked away. No matter what Keene said, he couldn't believe Tarika wasn't finishing Britta off. Giving her a heroine's ending befitting the Celtic and Norse deities, who sent their champions off on burning pyres with weapons stacked around them. Time slid past, and the pyre burned higher. Smoke plumed and billowed, some from Tarika, some from Keene.

Jonathan choked on it, but he couldn't breathe anyway around the obstruction blocking his throat. He'd heeded Mauvreen, but what if she was wrong? She didn't know much about the dragon shifter bond. He'd have fallen to his knees, but for Keene holding tight to both shoulders. Hot dampness ran down his chest, the dragon's claws drawing blood.

"Open your eyes," Tarika thundered.

Jonathan started. Until the dragon spoke, he hadn't realized he'd closed them to block out the sight of his beloved disintegrating into cinders. Britta stood before him. A buck naked

Britta without a lock of hair anywhere. She met his gaze out of golden eyes brimming with compassion. "I would have spared you seeing that, but Tarika told me there wasna time to argue you into leaving."

"Jesus! You're alive. Truly? I thought—" Words didn't matter. Keene let him go and he closed the distance between him and Britta, pulling her into a tight embrace. He stroked her silky smooth skin and cradled the back of her head, kissing her thoroughly. She hugged him back, sobbing softly in his arms.

Jonathan straightened and turned until he found Tarika. "Forgive me." He bowed low. "I never should've doubted you."

"Accepted." Her voice was rough, choked with emotion of her own. "For my part, I never should've borrowed against our bond to speed my journey with the Morrigan. Britta suggested it, but agreeing to her offer was pure selfishness on my part, since I dinna wish to spend an extra moment in the Morrigan's presence." Her scales clattered discordantly as she shrugged. "How was I to know the council would hold me afore them while they grilled the Crow's three manifestations?"

Jonathan still had his arms around Britta. "May I take her home?"

"Not yet." Keene exchanged a glance with Tarika.

"Come with me," Tarika said. "The Seers wish further audience with you, and someone else would like to lay eyes on you as well."

Britta disentangled herself from Jonathan. "It's unlikely, but would any of the dragons happen to have something in their hoards I could clothe myself with? They won't mind that I'm naked, but I do. I promise to return the items as soon as possible."

Keene dipped his head. "Aye, I have an item or two of Arianrhod's."

"I willna breathe a word of their origins." Tarika shut one scaled eyelid in a parody of a wink. "Meet us in the entry cave with whatever ye have."

Keene leapt into the skies, his wings beating so fast they blurred.

Jonathan still couldn't believe Britta stood before him pulsing with life. "Were the Gryphon's claws poisoned?"

"'Tis more complicated than that," Tarika said. "Dragon magic created Gryphons, so they hold an affinity for anything dragon-linked."

"That was why I couldn't fight the goddamned thing off," Britta cut in. "I did what I usually would to oust a foe, and I couldn't figure out why it dinna work."

"Aye, between me borrowing against my dragon link to you, and the Gryphon taking the rest, ye were laid raw to it siphoning your power to feed the dragon part of its nature."

"Good to have an explanation." Britta sputtered. "One more thing to watch out for if I ever face them again."

Jonathan draped an arm around her, reveling in the feel of her, still amazed she'd survived. "Let's get this council thing over with, so we can get out of here."

Britta leaned into him. "I'm sorry about my hair—"

He covered her mouth with a hand. "If that's the worst injury we sustain from today, we're golden. It's not your hair I fell in love with."

"Do ye wish to walk the last half mile?" Tarika asked.

Adrenaline still surged through his blood. "I'd like that." He turned to Britta. "Are you feeling up to it?"

"Och, and I could run there. Tarika blasted me with dragon essence."

"Are ye complaining?" the dragon asked archly.

"Of course not. Thank you for saving my life." She raised a foot, flexing it. "A side benefit appears to be that the dirt doesna burn my feet."

"No thanks needed, since the problem was of my own making." The dragon grimaced. "If it's all the same to the two of you, I'll fly."

Jonathan watched her take wing. "Are you sure you don't want me to carry you?" he asked Britta.

"Let me at least begin under my own steam. I'm certain I'll be fine."

He threaded an arm around her waist and herded them toward the mound holding the council chamber. "Do you understand what Tarika did to save you?"

Britta nodded. "For the most past, aye. She stripped me down to bedrock, and rebuilt me, layering dragon magic in with my essence. 'Tis similar to what happened when we first bonded, but much more intense. Dragons doona like to share that much of themselves, even with their bonded mages."

Jonathan thought about it, and the ramifications. "I'm guessing the dragons decided against shuttering Fire Mountain. If that ball was still in play, Tarika might've been more hesitant about what she did, and she all but dragged us off Keene's back, she was so anxious to begin working on you."

"Possibly true, but she's always been a force unto herself." Britta hesitated. "Ye used the dragons' pathways to bring me here."

"Aye. The time shaft would've taken too long. I can't take full credit. Mauvreen assessed—and correctly—that you didn't have much time. She reminded me of my ability to use the pathways and—"

"Ye hated it in there," she broke in.

"How'd you know that? It's true, but I never told you."

"I saw it in your mind when ye last returned, yet ye braved them again for me." Britta stopped walking long enough to throw her arms around him. "I love you."

He grinned crookedly. "I love you too. Wouldn't have it any other way. And I'd make the same choice again. We're here."

"So we are." She moved through the entrance into the cave. "I still canna believe my feet aren't burnt to a crisp, but they feel fine. Och, look! Keene beat us here."

Jonathan followed her inside. She stood over a small pile of clothing, sorting, before she snugged leather breeches up her legs, followed by a dove-colored leather top. A multicolor woolen cape came next. "Wonder why she left all these clothes here?" Britta murmured.

"Either the dragon hid them from her because he wanted something with her scent, or she thought she'd be back. Ready?"

"Aye. Not that I want to see the Morrigan again, but the dragons wouldna have requested your presence if they dinna need something important."

Jonathan made his way down into the bowels of the mountainside. The temperature gradually warmed, and sweat formed on his forehead and slicked his sides. Next to him, Britta removed the woolen cloak and slung it over an arm. The din of dragon voices hit him before they rounded the last corner.

He entered the chamber with Britta by his side. The Morrigan, back in crow form, stood in the front of the room, flanked by the blind Seers. The large, golden leader stood behind her, holding a plaited cord around her neck with one taloned foreleg. The cable pulsed with blue white light.

The Morrigan's gaze fell on him, and she jerked against her bonds, screeching. "Ye tricked me. Bastard. Ye'll roast in the fires of Hell for your treachery. Ceridwen willna let this outrage stand. She'll come for me."

Jonathan glanced around. "I don't see her here, but I'll make certain she knows you begged for her intercession."

"'Tisn't necessary. She'll come. I know she will."

"Silence." The dragon jerked hard on the cable, and the Morrigan teetered, struggling to remain on her feet.

Jonathan looked around for Kheladin and Eletea, not finding them.

"Their task was complete, and they chose to leave." The dragon leader had clearly been in Jonathan's mind. "The Crow drains anyone who spends overmuch time in her presence."

"I resent that," the Morrigan cawed, earning another sharp snap on her tether.

A figure detached itself from darker places along the sides of the council chamber. Cathbad strode to where Jonathan stood and placed his hands on his shoulders. "I dreamed this. Ye're here, so 'twas a true sending."

"Good to see you, sir." Jonathan raised his hands and placed them on Cathbad's upper arms.

The Druidic seer rocked forward and kissed his forehead. "I see ye've met my old friends." He glanced pointedly at the blind dragons. "They would speak with you." He let go of Jonathan and moved aside. Britta dropped behind Jonathan, joining Cathbad.

"Come forward." Tarika and Keene instructed with one voice from spots near the front of the chamber.

Jonathan squared his shoulders. Whatever was coming was big. He felt it in his bones. In the pit of his stomach. What would they ask of him? Would he be up to the task? He clamped his jaws together and started the journey across the cavern. Weariness dogged him, but there wasn't time for it. He'd thought his task was done after he presented arguments for the dragons to keep Fire Mountain attached to the rest of the worlds, but apparently there was more. He came to a stop a few feet in front of the tableau of dragons and the Morrigan, well out of reach of her snapping beak, and waited.

The blind dragons, Seers for their race, stepped toward him. "We took your counsel under advisement," one said.

"Aye," the other continued, "and we willna be closing Fire Mountain, based on Cathbad's prophecies, which we found to be true."

"We are in your debt," the first dragon said. "Yet your duty is far from complete, now ye've shown yourself to us."

Cathbad materialized by his side. "When I allowed the Celts to take Angus into modern time and hold him there, 'twas because I knew he'd fall in love and make a child. Ye were foreseen. 'Tis both a blessing and an obligation."

"What would you have me do?" Jonathan looked from Cathbad to the dragon Seers.

"Ye will be the link," one of the dragon Seers replied. "Ye'll connect Fire Mountain, Earth, and all the other worlds as well."

"I'll assist, of course," Cathbad said. "Angus too, once he knows."

Jonathan frowned. "Help me out here. What exactly does this link do?" What he really wanted to know was if any possibility still existed of him and Britta having anything approximating a normal life.

"Are ye refusing?" One of the dragon Seers stepped closer.

"Not at all." Jonathan spread his hands in front of him. "But before I jump in with both feet, I want to know what I'm signing up for."

The dragon's eyes whirled faster. "A dragon would figure that out as he went along."

Jonathan narrowed his eyes. "I'm not a dragon, but you already know that. If you don't like how I do things, then maybe you should assign this link role to one of your own."

Cathbad elbowed him in the side, but Jonathan didn't back down. He'd be damned if he'd blindly agree to something he didn't fully understand.

The Seers retreated to their leader, and the three spoke quietly in their own tongue. Jonathan wondered if Cathbad knew what they were saying, but he didn't ask.

"Still time to back out, sonny," the Morrigan hissed, earning her a sharp snap on her tether. "If I were you, I'd run like hell."

"Get her out of here," the leader growled.

"With pleasure." Keene beckoned to another black and grabbed an end of the cord. The air around them bubbled and hissed with dragons' fire. When the smoke and steam cleared, they were gone.

Jonathan breathed easier. Even tethered where she couldn't reach him, something about the Crow was unsettling, poisonous. He turned his attention to the Seers, curious what they wanted from him—and apprehensive too.

One turned and bathed him with steam. "Your task is to ensure dragon magic continues unimpeded."

"How?" the word burst from him despite his intention to remain silent while he gathered information.

"However ye see fit," the Seer replied and gestured toward Cathbad.

"There are many things I doona know," Cathbad told him. "But I'll try." He stepped in front of Jonathan and captured his gaze with somber eyes. "Ye've joined with me in the dream world, so ye know that part. The dragons believe—as do I—your role is to ensure dragon magic continues to flow through this world and others. Ye'll need to check for it and report places it's blocked or weak."

"How many worlds are there?"

"Many, but ye can accomplish much of this through the dream world. Not all of it, though. Ye'll need to be gone from time to time. Nothing takes the place of seeing something for yourself."

Jonathan thought about Angus's trance states when he was growing up. "Does this mean I'll be like Da? Forever gone from the world and those who love me?"

Cathbad shook his head. "Nay. If we split the task among us, it shouldna tax any one man beyond reason."

"Ye missed a key element," one of the Seers told Cathbad.

"What might that be?" Jonathan furled his brows.

Cathbad stood straighter. "Ye must come to Fire Mountain frequently to access the dream world from here."

"Fine. Why?"

"The pathway to that world is cleaner from here and your seeing more accurate."

"If that's true, why aren't you here?" Jonathan asked.

Cathbad smiled. "Because I refused. The visions are more accurate from dragon perspective, but less so from other worlds and races. I convinced the dragons I could do more good from the time bubble I carved out for myself." He stopped to take a measured breath. "That's your other choice. Ye could remain with me, yet I thought ye'd prefer to stay in the world ye're familiar with, at least some of the time."

Jonathan could've hugged the old man with the ageless face. He faced the dragon Seers. "I accept. It'll take me a while to get the hang of things, but I'm sure I can set up a computer program to facilitate making certain I don't miss anything."

Tarika made her way to where he stood and stroked a talon down the side of his face. "Ye've done well. Take my bondmate home. I'll find you there."

"Home to my house?" The question sounded lame to him, but after today, he didn't want any more misunderstandings or communication glitches.

The dragon stopped, clearly thinking about his question. "I misspoke. Take her to Mauvreen's. At least there's a place there for dragons."

He nodded and then said, "What about the fighting? Britta and I left in the thick of things. Shouldn't we all return there to make certain they don't need our help?"

Cathbad stepped closer. "The battle is done." A knowing smile spread over his face. "Hecate is one tough combatant. Betwixt her, Andraste, Gwydion—magician warrior that he is—and Ceridwen, the outcome was never in doubt."

One of the blind Seers raised its snout, scenting the air. "The rest of the renegade dragons mated to dark mages are on their way back here. Never doubt we shall treat with them accordingly."

Jonathan could figure out what that meant. The dragons would break the bond and kill the dark mages. Once that was done, they'd decide each dragon's fate on an individual basis. He wanted to ask about losses on their side, but he'd find out soon enough. In the meantime, he sent up a silent prayer to the goddess that all the witches had made it through unscathed.

He pressed his lips together. One last thing remained. "Mauvreen's it is. Before I leave, though, we need to get a few things out on the table." He stood tall and faced the dragon Seers. "This assignment you've tasked me with, it's a two-way street."

"Explain." One of the Seers gestured with a foreleg.

"Since I've never done this before, I need to be free to ask for help. And for feedback along the way about how I'm doing. If things aren't going well—on either side—I want to know about it at the beginning, not after things have gone to hell, and it takes me twice the effort it would've at the front end to fix things."

"Fair enough," the Seer answered.

"Will you join me in the dream world?" Jonathan asked, curious how things would work.

"Betimes," the other Seer replied.

Other questions crowded on the heels of that one, but it was enough for today. He wanted to get Britta home, reassure himself she truly was recovered.

"Good choice." Cathbad spoke into his mind.

"We'll pay you a visit," he told his kinsman. "Sooner rather than later."

Cathbad cracked a rare smile. "I'll welcome you anytime. Bring that father of yours along too. Once I finally got to spend some time with him, I grew quite fond of the fellow."

Jonathan made his way across the chamber to the accompaniment of dragon chatter. Britta extended a hand and he clasped it, moving them toward the warren of tunnels leading to the surface.

His heart was so full, he feared it would crack and spill onto the packed earthen floor of the cave. He could have it all. Britta. A life to call his own. A key role in monitoring magic that held the world together.

He stopped at the spring and bent to drink, holding water in his cupped hands for Britta too. "I was afraid they'd ask for more than I could give," he told her.

Britta looked up with water running down her chin. "Dragons are canny about not doing that." Tiny lines creased the corners of her eyes as she offered him a warm smile. "Take us home."

He stood and walked the few feet to the cave's entrance by her side. "Okay by you if we summon a time shaft?"

"More than okay." Her eyes warmed to burnished copper. "A few more months together, and ye'll have me talking like a modern woman."

"Arianrhod hung onto her archaic speech. I'm sure you can too, if you want to and put your mind to it." He swept her into a hug, and she clung to him as he chanted up a time shaft to return them to Earth.

CHAPTER 24

"We're almost back." Jonathan spoke gently, but Britta bolted awake. She'd fallen asleep slumped against him almost as soon as the time travel shaft encased them. "Sorry, love. Didn't mean to startle you."

She wriggled out of his grasp and rubbed sleep from her eyes. "I canna believe I dinna waken. Not even once."

He spoke a few words, and the shaft's vibrations slowed. "I admit I checked in on you a few times. The repair work going on inside your body is fascinating."

"How so?" The shaft rocked to a halt. A rift spread up one wall, and she got unsteadily to her feet.

He stood and wove an arm around her, guiding her into the dawn of a new day. "Dragon essence is growing, rather like targeted radiation."

She shook herself and ran her hands down her body, smoothing Arianrhod's borrowed clothing into place. "Ye'll have to say more. I doona understand."

"I still see injured places inside you from where the Gryphon latched onto your dragon power and siphoned it. Whatever magic Tarika added is seeking out those spots and fixing them. The net

279

effect is you have something that looks like golden latticework spreading inside you." He hesitated before adding. "It's very beautiful, and mesmerizing. During my last visit—for want of a better word—I had a hell of a time tearing myself away."

She narrowed her eyes, and he felt her turn her energy inward, taking stock. "Aye, I see what ye mean. I'm feeling quite well though. Refreshed. Fit." She glanced around them before zeroing her gaze back onto him. "Ye look like hell."

He muffled a snort of amusement. "Thanks. One of us needed to stay awake. It's not a short journey back from Fire Mountain."

"Och, thank you for watching over me." She angled toward him and brushed a kiss across his lips. "Mauvreen's is that way. Shall we?"

He didn't answer, just linked an arm through hers and started walking. Anxiety gnawed at him. What would they find at Mauvreen's? How many of his friends had died picking up the banner for a war that truly wasn't theirs to fight?

"But it was," Britta said.

It took a moment before he understood she'd been inside his mind. "How so?"

"If Earth magic fades, witches would lose their power as well." She tossed her head. "Actually, 'twas all of our concern. Every single living creature on Earth, with or without magic. If it wasna so, ye'd never have acceded to spending what will amount to untold years trundling back and forth to Fire Mountain."

He stopped walking and planted a kiss on her forehead. "You're wise as well as beautiful."

Britta laughed. "Not so beautiful as all that." She patted her bald head before turning toward Mauvreen's house. A frown creased her face. "The energy holds a different feel."

Jonathan pushed his power outward, sensing, analyzing. "Different, yes, but not bad. Not like when we had to blast through it."

Britta clasped her hands together. "It took me a bit, but I

recognize the spell now. Hecate blended an enchantment with Mauvreen's. None of us are used to the feel of Greek power." She extended a hand and barked a command, but the barrier didn't yield.

"Mauvreen!" Jonathan raised his mind voice. *"Let us in."*

The air crackled and zinged around them, developing an azure tint as a whirling passage formed. "Sweet! Wonder if Hecate can teach us to create something similar for wherever we end up living. After you." He gestured Britta ahead of him into the spinning channel that smelled of the sea and growing things.

"Why would we need to barricade ourselves behind aught? The Morrigan's imprisoned in Fire Mountain."

The spinning intensified, pulling at him in all directions before it faded. Britta's question was reasonable, but after what they just lived through, he'd be damned if he'd ever be caught flat-footed again, like the afternoon the Morrigan accosted him behind his house.

It took a few moments before the air cleared. Kheladin and Eletea lounged in the yard, chomping on the dead, bloody ruins of what might've been goats. Kheladin raised his whirling gaze from his meal. "The others said to send you inside." He swiped a foreleg across his mouth. "When will Tarika join us?"

"Right now." Her form blasted through the opaque, blue-white shield surrounding Mauvreen's house. With a few wing flaps, she settled on the ground several feet away. "Is there more where that came from?" She tilted her snout at the carcasses.

"Aye." Kheladin nodded. He stood straighter to the accompaniment of clanking scales. "First Born, what of the dragons we sent to Fire Mountain? Two were my friends."

Tarika twisted her head to glance at Britta and Jonathan. "Run along. This conversation is for dragons only."

Jonathan started up the stairs with an arm around Britta's waist. He knew Tarika well enough to understand when it was pointless to argue. He wanted to know the Dragon Council's decision about the rogue dragons too, but maybe he'd dream it—or the Seers would tell him next time he showed up in Fire Mountain.

He twisted the knob to open the oaken door with its curved top and runic carvings. The hum of voices told him everyone was gathered in the large front room. "Come on."

"Och aye, best to get this next part over with. Loss isna easy to deal with—ever."

Understanding rocked him. "The era you came from was nothing but battles."

She cracked a wry smile. "I wouldna go quite that far describing it, but aye, many a young man lost his life."

They reached the arched entry into the great room. His assessment was correct, the room was stuffed to the gills with witches and Celts. A table off to their right groaned under the weight of food and assorted drinks. He was guiding Britta that way when Mauvreen worked her way clear of the mass of bodies.

Relief cut deep into her face when she saw Britta, and she rushed toward them, sweeping her into a fervent hug. "Thank fucking Christ you're okay. When I sent you off with Jonathan, you were half a step from death's door."

"Chalk it up to one determined dragon—and a man who loved her beyond wisdom or reason," Jonathan murmured.

Mauvreen let go of Britta and hugged him. "What about one bitchy witch who insisted you take the dragons' pathways to speed your way to Fire Mountain?"

"Yeah." He grinned. "Her too." His smile faded. "Cathbad told us the battle was over and we won. What was the cost?"

Mauvreen's smile dimmed as well, replaced by a resolute expression with her lips set in a thin line. "Six witches, three from Mary Elma's group and three from ours." He opened his mouth, ready to ask the hard questions and find out who'd died, but she saved him the trouble. "The only one you knew well was Caty, and it was a quick, clean end. She didn't suffer."

Jonathan pictured the tall, broad-shouldered woman with long black hair and green eyes. She and her witches patched him up after his first skirmish with the Morrigan. "It's a significant loss." He faced Mauvreen, "She was strong magically and an inspirational leader for her coven."

"Hecate sang her to the other side." Mauvreen wiped away tears. "I'll miss her too."

"Thank Christ the Morrigan can't ever do anything like this again," he muttered.

Hecate emerged from the throng and raked her sharp gaze over him from head to toe before shifting to Britta. "I heard my name. Good to see both of you back here." She favored Britta with a raised brow. "I'm quite fond of your dragon, and I see there's even more of her inside you than there was before."

The goddess shifted her focus to Mauvreen. "Everyone is accounted for. We can begin."

"Begin what?" Jonathan asked, but Mauvreen waved him to silence. He covered the short distance to the food table and poured several fingers of scotch into two paper cups. Britta took one from him, and he took a stiff jolt from his. The liquor burned his mouth and throat, but at least the dragged-out feeling in his head eased a little, replaced by a pleasant buzzing sensation.

He hoped whatever they were beginning wouldn't take too long. He lusted after his upstairs haven and hours of uninterrupted sleep, with Britta lying next to him.

"Over there." Britta pointed. "Angus and Arianrhod and Lachlan and Maggie are sitting on the floor with her grandmother and a bunch of other witches I doona recognize. They beckoned us."

Jonathan followed her, stumbling with weariness. He was afraid if he sat down, he'd nod off. Remaining awake in the time shaft had been a struggle, but he needed to watch over Britta, and fear for her kept him conscious. Dragons didn't seem to require much sleep. Maybe they'd be willing to share some of their secrets—now that he was working for them.

He smothered a snort. His mind was wandering, and he needed

to pay attention. Something told him whatever Hecate and Mauvreen had in mind was important, and he didn't want to miss anything. He settled into a cross-legged sit between Britta and Maggie. The witch leaned into Lachlan, seated on her other side, and he kept a protective arm curved around his mate.

"We did a good thing today." Hecate's unmistakable harsh rasp reached every corner of the room, despite her not raising her voice. All side conversations quieted, and he felt the attention in the room shift to the goddess.

Hecate swept the room with eyes that missed nothing. "Indeed, we did a good thing, yet don't make the mistake of believing our task is over. A few of you questioned the heightened warding about this house. You'd do well to copy my example. The Morrigan is caged in Fire Mountain, but she did much damage before we corralled her—"

"Apologies, goddess." Ceridwen stepped into view. "We dinna fully understand, or we'd have employed staunch measures years ago. We meant no—"

"Save your energy." Hecate spoke over her. "I don't need apologies. You're well aware of the destruction created by your lackluster efforts to contain her."

Color stained Ceridwen's cheeks, and Jonathan looked away, not wanting to witness her shame. The Celts had learned a lot from this. He hoped the lessons would stick.

"Moving on from here." Hecate picked up the thread of her earlier words. "The Crow released Tantalus and Ixion. They still range free, as do the Furies, Circe, and Medea. I hold little concern about those last three, but Tantalus and Ixion could create problems." She stopped to take a breath. "I asked Hades for help, but he doesn't want any of the lot back—except me—and I told him I wasn't interested."

Andraste and Gwydion flanked Ceridwen. "I, for one, am grateful the battle isna over." Andraste sifted her hands through her blonde curls.

"Make that two." Gwydion grinned. "I'd miss the din of combat if it flickered and died out."

Angus muttered something from behind Jonathan that sounded like, "Bully for you," and Jonathan bit back a grin.

Andraste settled her hands on her hips. "Do ye have a plan?" she asked Hecate. "If ye do, count me in. If ye doona, I'll help craft one."

"I'll second that," Gwydion said.

Dressed in black as always, Arawn stepped from the shadows— or maybe he'd hidden his presence with illusion. His long black hair was unbound, and his face screwed into a frown. "Ye may borrow my army of shades. They grow restless and would welcome a bit of adventure."

Voices raised throughout the room, shouting variations of assent, peppered with offers of help.

"Tarika and I will do whatever is necessary," Britta called.

"As will Kheladin and I," Lachlan added. "Eletea too, unless I miss my guess."

"You don't." The copper dragon's voice drifted through an open window.

Jonathan opened his mouth, but nothing emerged. His face heated as shame came to blows with defensiveness, but in truth he preferred his skirmishes in the virtual world.

"Ye have a role," Britta spoke into his mind. *"And a key one at that. Ye dinna cut your teeth on the battlefield, and there isna any shame in your antipathy for battle."*

Love for the woman next to him welled so deep, it threatened to choke him. Rather than seeing him as a wimp, a loser, she made excuses for his fears. He pushed to his feet and squared his shoulders, facing the roomful of witches, mages, and gods. He was seriously outclassed, but if they didn't want to hear what he had to say, they could tell him to shut up.

He tried to develop a quick script, but in the end he said to hell with it and let his heart dictate his words. He had to wait for a break in the many conversations flowing around him. When one came, he jumped on it. "May I speak, goddess?" he asked Hecate.

She slitted her eyes at him. "Yes. Make it succinct."

"Thank you. I'll try. I have many things to apologize for, but that's not why I want a few minutes of your time. We lost friends yesterday including Caty, a witch I knew and respected. She never had much use for me because until very recently, I gave my magic short shrift. I wasn't interested in having a goddess for a mother, and Da's magic scared the crap out of me."

He sucked in a ragged breath. No stopping now. He was in it until he either finished, or they muffled him. "Da's magic required soul walking. I saw what it looked like up close and personal when I was just a kid, and Da looked dead to me. I'd ask Mauvreen or one of his other watchers, and they'd do their damnedest to reassure me, but I swore I'd never grow up to be like him—and yet here I am."

"You're speaking in riddles." Hecate's voice held sharp edges. "Don't make me work over hard to understand you."

"What I'm trying to say," he met her unsettling, timeless gaze, "is no one can escape their destiny. Now that I know what mine is, I won't run from it, no matter how uncomfortable I am with being a seer—for anyone, let alone dragons."

Her eyes widened. "Damn my eyes, so that task has fallen to you —in conjunction with their blind duo, no doubt. I knew someone would have to do it, yet I was certain it would be either Cathbad or Angus." She drew her brows together. "Cathbad's been filling that role until now. What changed?"

Jonathan didn't hear his father get up, but Angus materialized by his side, exuding solidness and a comforting warmth. He laid a quick hand across Jonathan's lower arm and announced, "Aye, Cathbad has worked in conjunction with dragonkind, but he understood he was only a placeholder, until Jonathan owned his power. In the future, it's a task the three of us plan to share." He hesitated, perhaps for effect, before adding. "Don't mistake things, though. Jonathan is the primary holder of that particular responsibility."

His father's deep voice was welcome, and he turned to him. "Cathbad said as much, but you don't have to—"

"I want to," Angus said firmly. "The least I can do is share my knowledge of the dream world with my son. I've waited a long time for this opportunity."

"Surely ye dreamed it." Ceridwen seemed to have recovered from her earlier embarrassment.

"That's the problem," Angus said. "I dream many iterations of the future, but I'm never certain which will come to pass until it does." He met Jonathan's gaze. "You weren't done, and I interrupted."

Jonathan searched his soul. He'd thought he was close to done, yet Angus saw more clearly than he did. He reached a hand to Britta, and she scrambled to her feet and took her place next to him. "This woman and I are mated through dragon shifter ritual, but we're going to have a wedding too."

Britta stiffened next to him. "Have ye spoken with Tarika? She gave you her mating bite. Ye doona wish to offend her."

He smiled, willing Britta to see the depth of the feelings he had for her. "You didn't let me finish. We've had enough pain and darkness for a while. I'd like to propose a triple wedding—and an enormous party. What do you think?"

"If we're part of the triple," Maggie spoke up, "I'm all for it."

"But I already married you," Ceridwen protested.

"Who's to say we canna say our vows twice?" Lachlan demanded.

The edges of Ceridwen's mouth twitched into a small smile. "No one, dragon shifter. Mayhap, ye could get me to officiate—again."

"Grand idea, son!" Angus clapped him on the back. "Arianrhod thinks so too." He twisted to look at her. "Don't you?"

When Jonathan glanced at his mother, she looked as close to flustered as he'd ever seen her.

"Well?" Angus prodded, mischief sparking from his amber eyes.

Arianrhod got to her feet and made her way to Angus's side,

weaving an arm around him. "A lifetime of hiding will take a bit to overcome, but I'm up for it. More than up for it, actually."

"This doesn't excuse us from dealing with the Infernal deities running amok," Hecate cautioned.

"Of course not." Jonathan caught her eye. "I didn't propose it as a diversionary tactic." He let go of Britta and spread his hands in front of him. "It's no secret I build games, but they're more than games. They mirror life. They're mostly how I used my magic up until recently." He paused, gathering his thoughts. "I understand—by God, I even accept—we're still under fire, but it doesn't mean we have to stop living. If we can't blend sweet with sad, hope with despair, we'll lose our perspective. Our humanity."

He breathed in deeply and released it. "I'll give you everything I've got—on both sides. If there's destruction to be sown, I'll do my damnedest. If the dragons hold me for months scrying for them, I'll do my best there too. But don't tell me I can't enjoy my life or my love."

He grasped Britta's hand again. "When any of us give up on happiness and replace all the cheerful places with concepts like duty and obligation, we're being cowards. It's easy to hide behind obligations, substitute them for living a full life, but if we do that we lose an important part of ourselves along the way."

He took another breath and realized he truly was done. He could keep talking, but he'd hit the high points. Some more than once. He turned to Britta and gathered her against him.

"I love you so much," she murmured into his ear.

Words wouldn't come, so he just hung on, willing her to feel the love surging through him as he stroked her back and neck and rained kisses down her face.

The room erupted in whoops, cheers, and whistles, but he didn't care. Everything that mattered to him was right here. Home, hearth, family. He'd never thought he'd have any of them, yet now he had them all.

EPILOGUE

The Morrigan drove her beak into the fire surrounding her. She'd done it hundreds of times. Maybe thousands or even millions by now, with the same results. Fire raced up her face, singeing her black feathers and making her brain feel like it was frying.

Damn!

At first, she'd truly believed Ceridwen would rescue her, but the goddess of the world never materialized. Even prisoners were allowed visitors. Had the goddess shown up in Fire Mountain, only to be turned away by the dragons?

That had to be it.

Och. Mayhap not.

Ceridwen's distaste for dragonkind wasn't particularly secret. For her to travel to Fire Mountain for anything might be pushing things.

The Morrigan withdrew to the exact center of her prison cell. Fire blazed in a circle around her. Fire that never dimmed. She was amazed she still had any feathers. Or any eyesight. The heat was horrendous. So was the brightness. Shutting both inner and outer eyelids didn't block a tenth of the light streaming from the ever-present flames.

No food.

No water.

Since she was immortal, it didn't matter. She'd live no matter what they did to her. When it became clear no one was coming to rescue her, she tried various ways to end her life. Walking into the flames was the most obvious, but other than charring the tips of her feathers, fire didn't hurt her. She also couldn't walk far enough to pass the barrier around her. Once she'd walked for what felt like days, only to be snapped back into the center of her prison as if she'd been attached to a giant elastic band.

She'd held her breath until she passed out, but consciousness had a nasty way of returning. Every goddamned time.

How long had she been here? She had no way to mark the passage of time. Her magic was intact, but it wasn't strong enough to transport her out of the bottom of whatever caldera the dragons had tossed her into. The thought of remaining here forever was enough to drive her mad, but that wouldn't kill her, either.

She forced a shift to one of her human forms. The crone. It made the heat much less bearable, but it gave her hands to drag through the red sand floor of her cell. Falling to her knees, she grappled with handfuls of dirt until her nails broke and blood streaked down her arms.

At least it was something to do. That was the worst of this. Total, utter boredom. No one to talk with. Nowhere she could meddle.

"I'm not thinking," she muttered. "I'm reacting. Surely there's a way out of this. There has to be."

She let the crow form take her again and balanced on one foot, thinking hard.

Time passed. She had no idea how much until an idea finally took shape in her avian brain. Dragons were a curious lot, particularly the young ones. She focused her magic into a kaleidoscopic funnel and set it to pulse at odd times.

Would her magic penetrate the barrier around her? She couldn't get out, but slivers of her magic might. At the very least, she had a task. Something to do beyond railing at her fate and sticking her beak in dragon's fire.

The Crow waited. Sometimes patiently. Sometimes not.

After what felt like forever, a small voice pushed into her head. *"Who are you?"*

It was such a shock, the Morrigan was certain she was hallucinating. She waited, intensifying her bursts of multihued magic, and willed the voice to return.

Please, she prayed to Danu, to Ceridwen. Please, help me find my way back to you. I promise I'll alter my ways. I've learned my lesson. Just please doona leave me here forever. To her horror, her throat thickened with unshed tears. Birds couldn't cry, so she shifted to a human who could, choking on bitter tears.

More time passed. Much more time before she heard the voice again. *"Are you real?"*

Ready this time, the Morrigan infused warmth, love into her mind voice. *"Aye, verra real."*

"Where are you? I've tried to find you, but I can't. I only see your magic."

The Morrigan took a shaky breath, realized she was still human, and reached for her bird form since it freed up power. She spun a tale—truth mixed with lies—she'd had eons to create and crossed her talons the dragon would believe her.

"I once ruled worlds, but I made mistakes. Big ones. I hurt those I love. More details doona matter. What does is I'm verra sorry and wish to be reunited with the other Celtic Gods."

A rapid intake of breath. *"You're a god?"*

The Morrigan smothered a satisfied smile. *"Aye, and I'll grant ye whatever ye wish."*

"Really?"

"Truly." Och aye, and the dragon must be extremely young. Did it hold enough power to spring her from her prison?

"I'll tell Mother." The young dragon sounded excited. *"She can fix anything."*

"Nay. Wait." But the dragon was gone.

Frustration mingled with fury pushed the Morrigan back into the flames. She walked through them, wishing for death. For anything other than what her existence had turned into.

Something caught her in a web and slung her back to the center of her fiery cell. She landed in the sand with a *splat*, not bothering to pick herself up. For what?

The air shimmered oddly and the two blind dragon Seers took shape. More fire streamed from their mouths. "Ye corrupt our younglings," one pronounced.

The Morrigan pushed wearily to her feet. "I could give a fuck less about your younglings," she sneered. "I just want out of here."

One Seer turned to the other. Something passed between them, but she couldn't decipher it. The Seer who'd spoken narrowed his milk-white eyes. "We've come to offer you…something different."

She straightened. "Anything would be better than this."

"Doona count on it," the other Seer muttered.

"Quiet." The first Seer countered. "Ye've been naught but trouble since we agreed to sequester you."

The Morrigan sucked in a tightly held breath, waiting for what would come next.

"Aye." The other Seer nodded agreement. "Hades agreed to spell us. Ye'll spend half a year with him and half a year with us."

Excitement raced through her like a live thing. She could escape from Hades. She was certain of it. He was powerful, but his attention to detail was sloppy. Careful to not give anything away, she lowered her beak. "If 'tis all the same to you, I'd prefer to remain here."

"Ye lost that choice when ye reached beyond the barrier, hunting for an innocent to free you. Thank Dewi, she had the good sense to alert her mother to your plotting."

"'Tis truly sorry I am—" the Morrigan began, pleased her faux humility was working.

"Shut up. We're both heartily sick of you."

The Morrigan hung her head. How would they transport her? Would there be a chance to escape that way?

Both Seers began to chant. In the blink of an eye, the fiery walls of her prison on Fire Mountain shifted. She was still surrounded by fire, but everything else changed. Vile, knowing laughter pounded against her. When she peered through the flames, Gryphons, Harpies, and her old allies, the Furies, ringed around the thin curtain of fire.

She squared her shoulders and faced them. "'Tis glad I am to see old friends."

"Save it," one of the Furies barked.

"You lied to us," another cut in.

"For that, you'll be punished," the third echoed.

Gryphons and Harpies blasted through fire and converged on her. The Morrigan focused her power to fight them off, but more attacked until they surrounded her. A Harpy shrieked. A Gryphon roared.

The pack closed on her, biting, chewing, tearing. It didn't matter how much magic she shoved their way, more showed up.

Realization slapped her, hard, hot, and bitter. There were worse things than her cozy cell on Fire Mountain. Here she'd be eaten again and again and again, never dying, her flesh resurrecting itself for further torture.

"Good job, girls." Hades's booming voice floated from somewhere. "It's a big job, but you get a break in six months when she goes back to the dragons."

"Please," the Morrigan shrieked. "Have pity."

"Why?" Hades countered. "You never held any—for anything or anyone. Enjoy the fruits you've sown."

You're reached the end of the Dragon Lore Series
Thanks so much for reading through to the end.
Please take a moment and leave a review.
You might enjoy my other dragon-based series, Earth Reclaimed.
I'm including the first part of it below as a sample.

ABOUT THE AUTHOR

Ann Gimpel is a USA Today bestselling author. A lifelong aficionado of the unusual, she began writing speculative fiction a few years ago. Since then her short fiction has appeared in a number of webzines and anthologies. Her longer books run the gamut from urban fantasy to paranormal romance. Once upon a time, she nurtured clients, now she nurtures dark, gritty fantasy stories that push hard against reality. When she's not writing, she's in the backcountry getting down and dirty with her camera. She's published over 70 books to date, with several more planned for 2019 and beyond. A husband, grown children, grandchildren and three wolf hybrids round out her family.

Keep up with her at:
>   http://www.anngimpel.com
>   http://anngimpel.blogspot.com
>   Twitter: @AnnGimpel
>   http://www.facebook.com/anngimpel.author

If you enjoyed what you read, get in line for special offers and pre-release special reads. Sign up for Ann's newsletter on her website or her blog.

Resilient, kickass, and determined, Aislinn's walled herself off from anything that might make her feel again. Until a wolf picks her for a bondmate, and a Celtic god rises out of legend to claim her for his own.

Aislinn Lenear lost her anthropologist father high in the Bolivian Andes. Her mother, crazy with grief that muted her magic, was marched into a radioactive vortex by dark creatures. Three years later, stripped of every illusion that ever comforted her, twenty-two-year-old Aislinn is one resilient, kickass woman with a *take no prisoners* attitude. In a world turned upside down, where virtually nothing familiar is left, she's conscripted to fight the dark gods responsible for her father's death. Battling evil on her own terms, Aislinn walls herself off from anything that might make her feel again in this compelling dystopian urban fantasy.

Fionn MacCumhaill, Celtic god of wisdom, protection, and divination has been laying low since the dark gods stormed Earth. He and his fellow Celts decided to wait them out. Three years is nothing compared to their long lives. On a clear winter day, Aislinn walks into his life and suddenly all bets are off. Awed by her courage, he stakes his claim to her and to an Earth he's willing to fight for.

Aislinn's not so easily convinced. Fionn's one gorgeous man, but she has a world to save. Emotional entanglements will only get in her way. Letting a wolf into her life was hard. Letting love in may well prove impossible.

Books in the Earth Reclaimed Series:
Earth's Requiem
Earth's Blood
Earth's Hope

EARTH'S REQUIEM, FIRST PROLOGUE

*S*alt Lake City, Utah

Aislinn tried to stop it, but the vision that had dogged her for over a year played in her head. She squeezed her eyes shut tight. Mental images crowded behind her closed lids, as vivid as if they'd happened yesterday. She raked her hands through her hair and pulled hard, but the movie chronicling the beginning of her own personal hell didn't even slow down. She whimpered as the humid darkness of a South American night closed about her...

Her mother screamed in Gaelic, "Deifir, Deifir," and then shoved Aislinn again. She tried to hurry like her mother wanted, but it was all too much to take in. Stumbling down the steep Bolivian mountainside in the dark, she ignored tears and snot streaking her face. Her legs shook. Nausea clenched her gut. Her mother was crying too, in between cursing the gods and herself. Aislinn knew enough Gaelic to understand her mother had tried to talk her father out of going to the ancient Inca prayer site, but Jacob hadn't listened.

A vision of her father's twisted body lying dead a thousand feet above them tore at Aislinn. Just a few hours ago, her life had been normal. Now her mother had turned into a grief-crazed harridan. Her beloved father, a gentle giant of a man, was dead. Killed by those horrors that had crawled out of the ground. Perfect, golden-skinned men with long, silky hair and luminous eyes, apparently summoned through the ancient rite linked to the shrine. Thinking about it was like trying to shove her hand into a flame, her pain too unbearable to examine closely.

Aislinn was afraid to turn around. Tara had already slapped her once. Another spate of Gaelic galvanized her tired legs into motion. Her mother was clearly terrified the monsters would come after them, but Aislinn didn't think they'd bother. At least a hundred adoring half-naked worshipers remained at the shrine high on the mountain. Once Tara had herded her into the shadows, her last glimpse of the crowd revealed one of the lethal exotic creatures turning a woman so he could penetrate her. Even in Aislinn's near-paralyzed state, the sexual heat was so compelling, it took all her self-discipline not to race to his side and insist he take her instead. After all, she was younger, prettier. It didn't matter at all that he'd just killed her father.

...Aislinn shook her head so hard, it felt like her brains rattled from side to side in her skull. Despite the time that had passed since her father's murder, she still fell into these damned trance states, where the horror happened all over again. Tears leaked from her eyes. She slammed a fist down on a corner of her desk, glorying in the diversion pain created. Crying was pointless. It wouldn't change anything. Self-pity was an indulgence she couldn't afford.

Pull it together. The weak die.

Even though she wasn't sure why life felt so precious—after all, she'd lost nearly everything—Aislinn wanted to live. Would do anything to hang onto the vital thread that maintained her on Earth.

A bitter laugh bubbled up. What a transition: from Aislinn Lenear, college student, to Aislinn Lenear, fledgling magic wielder. A second race of alien beings, Lemurians, had stormed Earth on the heels of that hideous night in Bolivia, selecting certain humans because they had magical ability and sending everyone else to their deaths.

It was a process. It took time to kill people, but huge sections of Salt Lake City sat empty. Skyscraper towers downtown and rows of vacant buildings mocked a life that was no more. In her travels to nearby places before the gasoline ran out, Aislinn had found them about the same as Salt Lake.

Jacob's death had been a harbinger of impending chaos—the barest beginning. The world she'd known had imploded shockingly fast. It killed Aislinn to admit it—she kept hoping for a miracle to intercede—but her mother was certifiable. Tara may as well have died right along with her husband. She hadn't left the house once since they'd returned a year before. Her long, red hair was filthy and matted. She barely ate. When she wasn't curled into a fetal position, she drew odd runes on the kitchen floor and muttered in Gaelic about Celtic gods and dragons. It was only a matter of time before the Lemurians culled her. Tara had magic, but she was worthless in her current state.

The sound of the kitchen door rattling against its stops startled Aislinn. On her feet in a flash, she took the stairs two at a time and burst into the kitchen. A Lemurian had one of its preternaturally long-fingered hands curved around Tara's emaciated arm. He crooned to her in his language—an incomprehensible mix of clicks and clacks. Tara's wild, golden eyes glazed over. She stopped trying to pull away and got to her feet, leaning against the seven-foot tall creature with long, shiny blond hair, as if she couldn't stand on her own.

"No!" Aislinn hurled herself at the Lemurian. "Leave her alone."

"Stop!" His odd alien gaze met hers. "It is time," the Lemurian said in flawless English, "for both you and her. You must join the fighting and learn about your magic. Your mother is of no use to anyone."

"But she has magic." Aislinn hated the pleading in her voice. Hated it.

Be strong. I can't show him how scared I am.

Something flickered behind the Lemurian's expression. It might have been disgust—or pity. He turned away and led Tara Lenear out of the house.

Aislinn growled low in her throat and launched herself at the Lemurian's back. Gathering her clumsy magic into a primitive arc, she focused it on her enemy. Her tongue stuttered over an incantation. Before she could finish it, something smacked her in the chest so hard she flew through the air, hit the kitchen wall, and then slumped to the floor. Wind knocked out of her, spots dancing before her eyes, she struggled to her feet. By the time she stumbled to the kitchen door, both the Lemurian and her mother had vanished.

An unholy shriek split the air, followed by another. Aislinn clapped a hand over her mouth to seal the sound inside and clutched the doorsill. Pain clawed at her belly. Her vision became a red haze. The fucking Lemurian had taken her mother. The last human connection she had. And they expected her to fight for them? Ha! It would be a cold day in Hell. She let go of the doorframe and balled her hands into fists so hard her nails drew blood.

Standing still was killing her, so she walked into blindingly bright sunlight. She didn't care what happened next. It didn't matter anymore. A muted explosion rocked the ground. She staggered. When she turned, she wasn't surprised to see her house crack in multiple places and settle. Not totally destroyed, but close enough.

Guess they want to make sure I don't have anywhere to go back to.

Her heart shattered into jagged pieces that poked her from the inside. She bit her lip so hard it ached. When that didn't make a dent in her anguish, she pinched herself, dug her nails into her flesh until she bled from dozens of places. Fingers slick with her own blood, she forced herself into a ragged jog. Maybe if she put some distance between herself and the wreckage of her life, the pain sluicing through her would abate.

As she ran, a phrase filled her mind. The same sentence, over and over in time to her heartbeat. *I will never care for anyone ever again. I will never care for anyone ever again.* After a time, the words etched into her soul.

EARTH'S REQUIEM, SECOND PROLOGUE

*E*ly, Nevada
Two Years Later

Rune paced from the kitchen to the living room and back again, hackles at half mast and tail twitching behind him. Marta, his bondmate and the woman who'd rescued him from a trap when he was just a wolf pup, was resting. At least he hoped she was. Something between a whine and a growl slipped past his clenched jaws.

Damn her, anyway.

Didn't she understand she'd been targeted by the dark gods? Ever since she took to spying on the Lemurians in Taltos, their underground city, things turned to rat shit. Something hideous happened on her last trip. He wasn't certain quite what because he wasn't with her, and she refused to tell him. Many moonrises had passed, and she was only just now beginning to talk and think normally.

Rune paused to stare out a large window. The front yard was absolutely silent. So was the road fronting Marta's house, but then it would be since most of the humans were dead, and gasoline to make their cars run had long since run out.

He shook his fur out and came to a decision. Should he tell Marta now or wait until she woke?

She solved the problem for him. The sound of her footsteps made him spin to face the door into the living room. She was dressed to go out and had shoes on. Not a good sign.

"There you are." She favored him with a maternal smile, the one that made him want to bite her. She may have rescued him when he was too young to care for himself, but that was long ago.

"Here I am," he agreed and trained his amber eyes on the woman who meant everything to him.

"I'm leaving for a while—"

Rune's decision roared out of him. "Not without me, you're not. Never again. Look what happened last time."

"Be reasonable." She smiled again, and Rune felt magic prowl beneath her words.

He slapped up power of his own. "Reasonable has nothing to do with it. Last time they nearly killed you. I wasn't certain until yesterday you'd get enough of your memories back to be yourself."

"Neither was I." Her smile developed grim edges. She sank to the thick Oriental carpet and held out her arms.

Rune stayed where he was. "All the more reason to take me with you. You can merge your senses with mine. Together we're stronger. It's why we chose the Hunter bond."

"Aw, Rune." Sadness etched lines around her eyes and into her forehead. "You don't understand. None of us will get out of this alive, but we have to fight until we can't fight anymore. If we don't, it's like turning Earth over to those bastards, and I won't do that." She slapped the floor with the flat of her hand. "I won't."

"Neither will I." He gazed cooly at her. "Where are we going?"

"I can't take you with me. It's too dangerous."

"If you don't take me, you're not going, either." The wolf stood his ground, but it was shaky. She could order him, and he'd have to obey. It was how the Hunter bond worked.

Marta looked away, studying her hands. Her long coppery hair was in its usual tight braid, and she was dressed in loose-fitting black trousers and a black jacket, with stout lace-up boots. She was tall, almost as tall as the Lemurians, and she sat with her legs splayed in front of her.

Rune kept his gaze glued to her, willing her to capitulate. He was fully prepared to take her on in combat to keep her in the house, if she refused his company. "I'm not being stubborn," he said. "I need to be with you for me, not just for you. How do you think I'll feel if you don't return? How can I live with myself if you die in a place where I wasn't there to help you?"

"I could die anyway." She did look at him then, her clear green eyes filled with something he didn't have a name for.

"So could I, but if we're together at least we'll know we did everything we could for each other."

Marta nodded once. "All right. I don't have enough energy to argue with you. We're going to one of the mining camps to the west of us. Some humans are still alive, and they need my medical skill."

"How do you know anyone's alive?" he countered.

She shrugged. "Call it a hunch. I dream things sometimes, and this came to me not long ago. We'll do a travel jump. It's not far. If the place is deserted, I'll bring us right back." The same, sad smile returned. "With luck, we'll be home in time for supper."

"Ready when you are."

She got to her feet. "Are you going to come closer than that? I already said I'd take you, Rune. Bondmates don't lie to each other."

Shame filled him because she'd nailed his reticence. He didn't trust that she wouldn't trick him. He made his way to her side and felt her magic as she opened a portal for them to travel to the place she'd seen in her dream.

They rolled out into high, arid desert, and the remains of a mining camp sprawled about them, buildings falling into disrepair. Bullet holes riddled tin roofs and corrugated siding. Rune sent his senses spinning outward.

Nothing lived anywhere near here.

"Curious," Marta murmured. "I was so sure."

Rune's hackles hit full alert, standing on end the length of his back. "We must leave," he snarled. "It has to be a trap."

Before Marta could reply, another gateway opened a little way away. Bal'ta poured out. Marta flung magic at the disgusting creatures, minions of the dark, but she barely made a dent. They stood between five and six feet tall, with barrel chests, and their bodies were coated in greasy-looking brown hair. Thicker hair hung from their scalps and grew in clumps from armpits and groins. Ropy muscles bulged under their hairy skin. Orange eyes gleamed, and their foreheads sloped backward.

Rune had faced them before. At least they didn't have magic of their own beyond a shared intelligence. The flood had slowed, and he gathered himself for action. He and Marta could take them. They'd faced worse odds. Apparently she agreed, and he felt her merge her consciousness with his.

"I'll take this side," Rune growled and thrust himself into the thick of things, avoiding the cudgels and maces they used in battle. Rune knew to stay out of the line of Marta's magic. He sliced into one neck after another until he was coated in blood. The air was thick with the coppery stench of it. For some reason, Bal'ta avoided him. Something about his animal energy burned them, and he took full advantage of their hesitation.

He glanced at Marta from time to time, grateful beyond thought she was still on her feet. In addition to magic, she held a knife in one hand. A knife dripping blood. Dead bodies piled around both of them.

Rune danced to one side to avoid a cudgel aimed for him skull. He sent out a call for forest wolves, but none came to their aid. Maybe there weren't any living here—or maybe they didn't see the point in taking a stand in someone else's battle.

No matter. He and Marta were winning. Only a few Bal'ta remained. He'd begun to work his way back to his bondmate, when another gateway opened, this one black and edged with flames. A man sashayed through. Rune stopped cold, staring in disbelief. The remaining Bal'ta faded away from that gaping maw; in moments they'd summoned another portal and left.

Rune focused on the newcomer. It had to be one of the dark gods. No one else held that level of deadly beauty. Long dark hair streamed behind him, and he trained his shrewd dark eyes on Marta. She squared her shoulders and stared back.

"Kill him," Rune urged.

"I can't," she ground out. "Much as I'd love to."

The dark god tossed his shapely head back and laughed; the sound was disturbing, discordant. "Your bondmate is wise," he told the wolf. "She's clever not to get too close."

"Which one is he?" Rune demanded.

"You may as well ask me, since I'm right here." Dark eyes crinkled in chilly humor, and he mock bowed. "My name is Tokhots. I'm also known as the trickster." Dark robes fluttered around him, sashed in gray.

While Tokhots had been talking, Marta sidled farther from Rune and severed her connection with him. Worried, he tried to determine just what she was up to. If she planned an attack, he didn't want to be in the way and ruin things. Nor did he plan to leave her to the mercy of the dark god. Maybe if he kept Tokhots chatting…

"What do you mean by trickster? It's not a term I'm familiar with."

Tokhots did a funny little side step. "I play tricks. I'm funny. I'm a hell of a nice guy. If you got to know me, you'd—"

A ball of fire immolated one side of his robes. Tokhots' pleasant expression shattered, and he batted at the flames—and at jolts of power Marta hurled his way. Rune wanted to launch himself at the dark god, but Marta's power kept him rooted in place.

Finally giving up on extinguishing the flames, Tokhots shucked his robe, revealing golden-hued skin beneath. "Bitch!" he spat and raced to Marta so fast he beat Rune, who was also headed that way at breakneck speed.

"Don't bite him," Marta shrieked. "His blood is deadly poison."

Rune aborted a leap in midair and crashed to the rocky ground. He'd been about to close his jaws around Tokhots' neck.

The dark god held a writhing Marta in his grip. "You can't hurt me either," he taunted. "One drop of my blood and you'll be deader than the shades that roam the countryside."

"What do you want with me?" Marta gave a mighty heave.

Rune thought she might free herself, but Tokhots tightened his hold. "You've become an inconvenience. I sent the Bal'ta as a diversion until I could get here."

"What happens next?" Marta's voice was steady, but Rune sensed her fear, and it filled him with fury. He worked his way closer to the pair, not moving very fast.

"That's for me to know." Tokhots laughed again.

Caution departed. Rune judged the distance and leapt. So what if he died? At least Marta would go free. The air around him thickened, holding him suspended above the ground. Darkness dropped over him like a curtain until he couldn't see. He thrashed against the magic holding him and plummeted to earth, landing hard on jagged rocks. Ignoring pain, he vaulted toward where Marta had been, still running blind in unnatural darkness.

She wasn't there. Neither was the dark god.

He still couldn't see, but he could smell and hear. He employed both senses, ears pricked forward and nose snuffling so hard it began to bleed.

Nothing.

Marta's scent was strongest right where he stood.

Rune threw his head back and howled his desolation to the skies. He'd failed. The dark god had his bondmate, and he had no way to go after them.

By the time the darkness receded, his throat was raw with grief.

He called for other animals, birds, even insects, to tell him what they'd seen. If they knew anything, but no one answered.

Despondent, guilt-stricken, Rune put one paw ahead of another. No point in staying with the dead Bal'ta. Tokhots would never bring Marta back here.

The dark god had taken his bondmate on a oneway trip. Rune knew, as clearly as he knew anything, she'd never run by his side again. She was still alive, but her life force ebbed through their Hunter bond.

Soon she'd be no more, and it was his fault. If he'd been quicker, hadn't hesitated…

He shook his head hard and broke into a run.

EARTH'S REQUIEM, CHAPTER ONE

Aislinn pulled her cap down more firmly on her head. Snow stung where it got into her eyes and froze the exposed parts of her face. Thin, cold air seared her lungs when she made the mistake of breathing too deeply. She'd taken refuge in a spindly stand of leafless aspens, but they didn't cut the wind at all. "Where's Travis?" she fumed, scanning the unending white of a high altitude plain that used to be part of Colorado. Or maybe this place had been in eastern Utah. It didn't really matter anymore.

Something unnatural flickered at the corner of her eye and she tensed. Standing still bought trouble with a capitol T. She swiveled her head to maximize her peripheral vision. *Damn! No, double damn.* Half-frozen muscles in her face ached when she tightened her jaw.

Bal'ta—a bunch of them—fanned out a couple hundred yards behind her, closing the distance eerily fast. One of many atrocities serving the dark gods that had crawled out of the ground that night in Bolivia, they appeared as shadowy spots against the fading day. Places where edges shimmered and merged into a menacing blackness. If she looked too hard at the center of those dark places, they drew her like a lodestone. Aislinn tore her gaze away.

Not that Bal'ta—bad as they were—were responsible for the

wholesale destruction of modern life. No, their masters—the ones who'd brought dark magic to Earth in the first place—held that dubious honor. Aislinn shook her head sharply, trying to decide what to do. She was supposed to meet Travis here. Those were her orders. He had something to give her. Typical of the way the Lemurians ran things, no one knew very much about anything. It was safer that way if you got captured.

She hadn't meant to cave and work for them, but in the end, she'd had little choice. It was sign on with the Lemurians—Old Ones—to cultivate her magic and fight the dark, or be marched into the same radioactive vortex that had killed her mother.

Her original plan had been to wait for Travis until an hour past full dark, but the Bal'ta changed all that. Waiting even one more minute was a gamble she wasn't willing to risk. Aislinn took a deep breath. Chanting softly in Gaelic, her mother's language, she called up the light spell that would wrap her in brilliance and allow her to escape—maybe. It was the best strategy she could deploy on short notice. Light was anathema to Bal'ta and their ilk. So many of the loathsome creatures were hot on her heels, she didn't have any other choice.

She squared her shoulders. All spells drained her. This was one of the worst—a purely Lemurian working translated into Gaelic because human tongues couldn't handle the Old Ones' language. She pulled her attention from her spell for the time it took to glance about, and her heart sped up. Even the few seconds it took to determine flight was essential had attracted at least ten more of the bastards. They surrounded her. Well, almost.

She shouted the word to kindle her spell. Even in Gaelic, with its preponderance of harsh consonants, the magic felt awkward on her tongue. Heart thudding double time against her ribs, she hoped she'd gotten the inflection right. Moments passed. Nothing happened. Aislinn tried again. Still nothing. Desperate, she readied her magic for a fight she was certain she'd lose and summoned the light spell one last time. Flickers formed. Stuttering into brilliance, they pushed against the Bal'tas' darkness.

Yesssss. Muting down triumph surging through her—no time for it—she gathered the threads of her working, draped luminescence about herself, and loped toward the west. Bal'ta scattered, closing behind her. She noted with satisfaction that they stayed well away from her light. She'd always assumed it burned them in some way.

Travis was on his own. She couldn't even warn him that he was walking into a trap. Maybe he already had. Which would explain why he hadn't shown up. Worry tugged at her. She ignored it. Anything less than absolute concentration, and she'd fall prey to his fate—whatever that had been.

Vile hissing sounded behind her. Long-nailed hands reached for her, followed by shrieks when one of them came into contact with her magic. She snuck a peek over one shoulder to see how close they truly were. One problem with all that light was it illuminated the nasty things. Their backward sloping foreheads leant them a dimwitted look, but they were skilled warriors, worthy adversaries who'd wiped out more than one of her comrades. Their insect-like ability to work as a group using telepathic powers scared her more than anything. Though she threw her Mage senses wide open, she was damned if she could tap into their wavelength to disrupt it.

Chest aching, breath coming in short, raspy pants, she ran like she'd never run before. If she let go of anything—her light shield or her speed—they'd be on her, and it would be all over. Dead just past her twenty-second birthday. *That* thought pushed her legs to pump faster. She gulped air, willing everything to hold together long enough.

Minutes ticked by. Maybe as much as half an hour passed. She was tiring. It was hard to run and maintain magic. Could she risk teleportation? Sort of a *beam me up, Scotty,* trick. Nope, she wasn't close enough to her destination yet. Something cold as an ice cave closed around her upper arm. Her flesh stung before feeling left it. She snapped her head to that side and noted her light cloak had failed in that spot. Frantic to loosen the creature's grip, she pulled a dirk from her belt and stabbed at the thing holding her. Smoke rose when she dug her iron knife into it.

The stench of burning flesh stung her nostrils, and the disgusting ape-man drew back, hurling imprecations in its guttural language. She snaked her gaze through the gloom of the fading day, as she assessed how many of the enemy chased her. Aislinn swallowed hard around a painfully dry throat. There had to be a hundred. Why were they targeting her? Had they intercepted Travis and his orders? Damn the Lemurians anyway. She'd never wanted to fight for them.

I've got to get out of here.

Though it went against the grain—mostly because she was pretty certain it wouldn't work, and you weren't supposed to cast magic willy nilly—she pictured her home, mixed magic from earth and fire, and begged the Old Ones to see her delivered safely. Once she set the spell in motion, there'd be no going back. If she didn't end up where she planned, she'd be taken to task, maybe even stripped of her powers, depending on how pissed off the Lemurians were.

Aislinn didn't have any illusions left. Her world had crumbled three years ago. She'd wasted months railing against God, or the fates, or whoever was responsible for robbing her of her boyfriend and her parents and her life, goddammit, but nothing brought them back.

Then the Old Ones—Lemurians, she corrected herself—had slapped reason into her, forcing her to see the magic that kept her alive as a resource, not a curse. In the intervening time, she'd not only come to terms with that magic, but it had become a part of her. The only part she truly trusted. Without the magic that enhanced her senses, she'd be dead within hours.

Please... She struggled against clasping her hands together in an almost forgotten gesture of supplication. Juggling an image of her home while maintaining enough light to hold the Bal'ta at bay, she waited. Nothing happened. She was supposed to vanish, her molecules transported by proxy to where she wished to go. This was way more than the normal journey—or jump—spell, though. Because she needed to go much farther.

She poured more energy into the teleportation spell. The light around her flickered. Bal'ta dashed forward, jaws open, saliva dripping. She smelled the rotten crypt smell of them and cringed. If they got hold of her, they'd feed off her until she was nothing but an empty husk. Or worse, if one took a shine to her, she'd be raped in the bargain and forced to carry a mixed breed child. They'd kill her as soon as the thing was weaned. Maybe the brat, too, if its magic wasn't strong enough.

The most powerful of the enemy were actually blends of light and dark magic. When the abominations, six dark masters, had slithered out of holes between the worlds during a globally synchronized surge linked to the Harmonic Convergence, the first thing they'd done had been to capture human women and perform unspeakable experiments on progeny resulting from purloined eggs and alien sperm.

Aislinn sucked in a shaky breath. She did *not* want to be captured. Suicide was a far better alternative. She licked at the fake cap in the back of her mouth. It didn't budge. She shoved a filthy finger behind her front teeth and used an equally disgusting fingernail to pop the cap. She gripped the tiny capsule. Should she swallow it? Could she? Sweat beaded and trickled down her forehead, despite the chill afternoon air.

She'd just dropped the pill onto her tongue, trying to gin up enough saliva to make it go down, when the weightlessness associated with teleportation started in her feet like it always did. Gagging, she spat out the capsule and extended a hand to catch it, but it fell into the dirt. Aislinn knew better than to scrabble for the poison pill. If she survived, she could get another from the Old Ones. They didn't care how many humans died, despite pretending to befriend those with magic.

Her spell was shaky enough as it was. It needed more energy—lots more. Forgetting about the light spell, Aislinn put everything she had into escape. By the time she knew she was going to make it—apparently the Bal'ta didn't know they could take advantage of her vulnerability as she shimmered half in and half out of teleport mode—she was almost too tired to care.

She fell through star-spotted darkness for a long time. It could have been several lifetimes. Teleportation jaunts were different than her simple Point A to Point B jumps. When she'd traveled this way before, she'd asked how long it took, but the Old Ones never answered. Everyone she'd ever loved was dead—and the Old Ones lived forever—so she didn't have a reliable way to measure time. For all she knew, Travis might've lived through years of teleportation jumps. No one ever talked about anything personal. It was like an unwritten law. No going back. No one had a past. At least, not one they were willing to talk about.Voices eddied around her, speaking the Lemurian tongue with its clicks and clacks. She tried to talk with them, but they ignored her. On shorter, simpler journeys, her body stayed with her. She'd never known how her body caught up to her when she teletransported and was nothing but spirit. Astral energy suspended between time and space.

A disquieting thump rattled her bones. *Bones. I have bones again... That must mean...* Barely conscious of the walls of her home rising around her, Aislinn felt the fibers of her grandmother's Oriental rug against her face. She smelled cinnamon and lilac. Relief surged through her. Against hope and reason, the Old Ones had seen her home. Maybe they cared more than she thought—at least about her. Aislinn tried to pull herself across the carpet to the corner shrine so she could thank them properly, but her head spun. Darkness took her before she could do anything else....